Till Death
and
Beyond

Lyn C. Johanson

Copyright © 2013 by Lyn C. Johanson
Cover art © Renu Sharma | www.thedarkrayne.com

ISBN-13: 978-1505551310
ISBN-10: 1505551315

I would like to thank all my readers for spending their precious time walking the labyrinths of my mind. It's where this story was born, after all.

It is my first book so I'm beyond excited to start this journey with you.

Wishing you all the best,
Lyn C. Johanson

Prologue

When the day was night and the night was day, a witch was born in a raging thunder storm.

The earth trembled and shook, welcoming its destined fate ... hundreds of witches sang – salvation finally in their grasp.

The prophecy once foretold was alive in a form of true beauty, with only death on her mind.

The witch was supposed to be feared and worshipped, all living creatures to tremble at the sight of her – all men to fall on their knees by the will of her...

* * *

"She's the sweetest little thing in the world," Deron admitted to himself as he watched his nine-year-old daughter run through the garden calling, "Mummy ... Mummy."

Despite the darkness of her curls, they radiated light as they bounced up and down. Sunshine played on her face and her lips curved into a glowing smile. Mischief sparkled in her deep light-blue eyes, giving a glimpse of his daughter's true nature. Her expression turned even brighter as she stretched out her hands and proudly revealed an exotic purple flower.

"Amira, sweetie, where did you get that?" His wife examined the blossom in the child's small palm and narrowed her eyes.

Instantly Deron knew the answer—she hadn't found it. Once again their daughter was playing with magic, doing tricks even his beloved Eliana couldn't—a witch strong and talented, who had practiced her art for many years.

Amira's smile widened, but not a sound of explanation flew out.

"It doesn't belong here. Why don't you take it back?" Eliana suggested.

Surprisingly, the little one obeyed.

"I am scared, Deron," his wife confessed. The fear for their daughter's safety cast a shadow over her beautiful eyes.

He took her into his arms, trying to stay strong for her, to comfort her as best as he could. The truth was, he knew those fears all too well.

A few years ago, the Order of Venlordia had renewed their witch hunts. No longer were the friars satisfied with sermons, it seemed. No longer were they leading people to salvation with the help of prayers and faith. They had raised a sword in the name of a sacred cause—to eradicate the evil.

It was a ludicrous lie the Venlordians spread to justify their actions. Every few hundred years or so, they raised impious war against witches, be they good or evil. They didn't differentiate. Worse still, thousands of innocents suffered at their hands. And now the bloodshed was commencing all over again.

"You are safe here, you both are," Deron tried to reassure his wife. If he was certain of anything, it was this place; and the people of Trinton, who would protect their daughter no matter what. He relied on them, just as they relied on him and his family.

They all contributed. All did their share in keeping the town clean and free of marauding witch-hunters and the self-imposed law of the Venlordians. Something he wished he could relieve his whole country of.

Unfortunately their organization ran deep, deeper than any of them thought. Even his brother-in-law, the king himself, began to squirm uneasily in his throne. No wonder Eliana was afraid.

"Mummy, mummy." Amira's tearful voice shook Deron.

"What is it, sweetie?" her parents asked, almost in unison.

"Please, help her," she begged, "help her…"

Eliana immediately scanned the area looking for the "her" her daughter was so worried about—only there was no one around. Still, Amira kept crying. Pearls of pain were rushing down her pale cheeks. Her lips trembled.

Eliana cupped her daughter's jaw, searching for an answer—pain was all she could sense, but she couldn't fathom the origin of it. There was no wound to be seen, only cries of agony no child should suffer.

The shaking came next. Amira's small, limp body quivered in her father's arms and fresh sobs broke from within her, consuming her with the ferocity of a flood.

For a second there, it seemed as if their daughter was about to choke, but then a line around her mouth thinned and a sound, strangled and foreign, escaped her parted lips.

Amira screamed.

The sound shook Eliana so deeply, she gasped, trying to take a breath into her frozen lungs. Tears filled her eyes. She heard grief and she heard terror coming out of her daughter's throat—in someone else's voice.

"What's happening?" Deron demanded, carrying

their girl inside, straight to her soft little bed.

"I don't know." Eliana blinked the fog from her eyes, only to see Amira convulsing with pain. "I don't know."

A feeling of uselessness overwhelmed her. She was supposed to know these things, be able to make them go away, but the fact was she knew nothing about what was happening, and even less about what she should do.

A potion! She needed to make a potion, Eliana murmured under her breath, prepared to rush back to her room for the herbs. She wiped her tears with trembling fingers, pivoted, and almost smashed into Giles.

The elderly man gently righted her, and without so much as a word put something in her hands. Eliana looked at his offering for a moment, not comprehending what she was holding. Then she exhaled.

"Thank you," she hugged the butler fiercely, grateful beyond words. If only she knew what to use — Eliana's next thought made her hands tremble even more fiercely.

She didn't see Giles's concerned expression anymore, or any of the pale faces standing behind the man. Eliana focused her attention on Amira — a thrashing and moaning girl, whose hands fought an invisible foe.

Her daughter's face was twisted with pain, her eyes red from crying. She kept pleading for help for someone, but whoever it was lived in Amira's dreams alone.

Or nightmares, Eliana thought, picking a catnip plant from the vast collection of herbs she kept. She hesitated to choose a second herb, glanced at her husband's expectant gaze, and swallowed a new lump of trepidation.

What if she chose the wrong one? What if she harmed her little angel? Eliana had never felt so lost before.

"You can do it," Deron whispered, his belief in her giving her strength to make a selection.

Eliana nodded, mixed the herbs and began the chant. She forced her daughter to consume the potion, all the while desperately praying for a miracle. A prayer that was joined by a dozen more people as the entire mansion kept vigil on their little lady's sleep.

All the servants gathered in the hall, waiting. Some of them sat quietly. Some paced with their heads bowed, hands clenched in fists. Others simply watched the closed doors. But all of them hoped to hear those doors opening. Hoped to see black curls bouncing, and that sweet face laughing.

Sadly, none of that happened.

When Amira finally came out of her room she was just a shadow of the sweet girl they all knew and loved.

Chapter 1

"You are to be captured." A soft, feminine voice drifted from somewhere behind Amira.

She didn't turn around. Instead, she leaned on the windowsill and closed her eyes, for one fleeting moment trying to imagine herself alone, free. She failed. Some things were just not meant to be.

Still, she ignored the order, even knowing it would cost her. Every second she refused to acknowledge the goddess would be taken from her—in the form of blood, most likely. But no matter how many times she told herself to get on with the program, or how many times she found herself in a similar situation, everything inside her screamed that she was not ready to die.

She hadn't even tasted life yet. She'd been robbed of joy many years ago—her heart had been ripped out of her chest that fateful day. And in return, she'd been given memories one at a time of the lives she'd once lived. She'd been given more nightmares.

Why she even wanted normal life, drenched with feelings and sensations, she had no idea. Being numb to the world made it so much easier to go through what she was forced to endure. And yet she craved everything others took for granted.

"I will not repeat myself." A searing sensation meant to emphasize the words shot through Amira's back so suddenly, she barely managed to stifle a moan.

White-hot pain traveled down her body. Her fingers

dug into a wooden plank, preventing her from collapsing on the floor as she felt every scar, every wound she'd obtained throughout her existence being ripped open by way of a slow, cruel punishment.

Despite the excruciating agony, Amira knew her scars were perfectly healed — not a drop of blood was staining her expensive gown. Nope, she was not bleeding; Hope was simply using her ability to make Amira suffer by reliving past injuries and pains — and the goddess had plenty to choose from.

In return, Amira's own power seethed, desperate to be freed. Desperate to taste fear, pain and misery. To gorge on it.

"One day..." she muttered, everything inside her trembling with a craving to reciprocate. The urge was so strong, she barely managed to quash it.

She would lose, no doubt about it, but that didn't mean she would remain impotent for much longer. With every reincarnation, she came back stronger, more powerful. Amira yearned for the day she would be able to mete out some justice.

"Say that again." Hope's emotionless tone washed over her like iced water. The chill spread through her flesh, but the cold didn't bring the desired reprieve.

Amira shivered, despising her reaction. It was a weakness she couldn't afford. Standing up to them might have proven to be hazardous to her health, but bowing down seemed to be even more painful to her soul.

"I live to serve," Amira spoke through gritted teeth, every word dripping with sarcasm. She waited another minute for the pain to subside and only then, gathering all her strength, she turned around.

Her body felt stiff and sore, her movements constrained. In an effort to disguise it, she lingered, playing with her hair and checking her nails as if she had nothing better to do.

For the damned life of hers, Amira wouldn't have been able to explain what drove her to antagonize divine powers at every step. But antagonize them, she did.

When you had little to lose, she mused, fear ceased to be the driving force. On the contrary, she cherished and welcomed death's cold embrace. He was her own knight in shining armor, who brought peace in the midst of agony. Temporary as it was.

Traynan, her personal angel of death, had once asked her how she managed to stay sane. Amira had shrugged, having no real answer to give. But now, looking back, she realized maybe she hadn't. For sane women her age didn't wake at the break of dawn gasping for air and clutching sheets, unable to separate nightmares from reality—only to realize that the nightmares *were* their reality. They surely didn't use others for their own personal gain without any qualms of conscience; and they definitely didn't contemplate murdering a god. Let alone all of them.

But no matter how hard she tried, she couldn't prevent dark thoughts from creeping in, just like she couldn't stop ominous visions.

Sometimes, Amira could swear it felt like insects crawling under her skin, devouring both her body and soul, until neither belonged to her.

Not once had she thwarted such visions. Not once had she succeeded in coming out of it alive. All because she consistently failed to fulfill a prophecy written eons ago. A prophecy that defined her very existence, and yet, she knew nothing about.

Amira was stuck in a vicious, never-ending cycle.

She was desperate. But a fool she was not. She knew Hope would never help her.

A blinding flare of light exploded all around,

forcing Amira to shield her eyes. But she didn't bow. She didn't land on her knees in awe of the powers she faced.

That ship had sailed hundreds of years ago. Now all she wanted to do was yawn. She quelled the urge by concentrating on her nails again.

A few moments later, the goddess got it through her thick skull that such theatrics were lost on her, and instead of a glowing apparition, a tall, beautiful redhead appeared.

Garbed in a white, long one-shoulder gown, with porcelain skin and ruby-red hair pulled up in an intricate twist, she looked demure and innocent. Fragile — to an untrained eye.

Amira saw behind the fake façade, right into the merciless soul of hers.

"You live to defy us," Hope accused her, emerald eyes flashing.

Not true! She'd done the obedient dog routine a couple of times. The memories were painful enough to even consider bringing it up. Instead, she tried to concentrate on her present. But did it really matter whether she was stoned to death, drowned, decapitated or stabbed? The outcome would be the same as always.

"Who's it to be this time?" she asked, knowing the answer would not change much. She wasn't even curious. It was either a Venlordian with a righteous smirk on his face, or some sweaty fat witch-hunter fancying himself doing a favor for this world. The thought would have made her shudder, except for the fact she no longer felt fear. Maybe she should be grateful for the hollowness inside her after all.

Hope moved around her bedchamber — which resembled a greenhouse — with an ethereal grace Amira could have admired if she hadn't hated the goddess so much. Plucking off a purple blossom, Hope looked at it with such intensity, the emeralds in her eyes turned to silver, and one by one the petals fell to the wooden floor, forming a small pile of blackened charcoal.

"You know," she said "You might find a way if you opened up once in a while."

Rii-iight—Amira would have laughed if she knew how. She'd tried that already. People either didn't believe her, thought her crazy, or ran scared. None of these actually helped, only created a shitload of problems.

"You're one to talk." She lifted her hand, palm up, and waited till every last piece of the flower landed on her skin.

Such a useless death, Amira sighed, and brushed her other hand over the ashes. Slowly, a new life was born. Large and purple, it bloomed right there in Amira's hands, filling her palm with beautiful, feather-soft petals.

She looked at her creation—an exact copy of the flower so carelessly destroyed, right down to the three yellow spots. And yet, it was not the same. Amira didn't have the ability to raise the dead. The first was lost forever, and this one…

"You should know better." Hope moved closer, and the little thing withered, becoming nothing more than dust.

The goddesses never liked being disobeyed. Even in the smallest of ways. And to Hell with innocent life. Collateral damage—never their concern.

You're one to talk—Amira threw the same phrase back at herself.

She blew out a breath, sending the dust flying—the irony of all of it not lost on her. How many lives was she responsible for destroying in her attempts to survive? She should be guilt-ridden; and yet, the heart she possessed was as cold as the one Hope carried inside her divine ribcage.

There was no love lost between Amira and humans. Too many memories of painful deaths had rubbed off on her, but this flower ... It was ridiculous. Just a small plant. And yet, it didn't sit well with her.

Maybe because she saw her own existence in it.

"You are not to reveal your true identity, or the extent of your powers," Hope began naming conditions she would be required to follow, or else ... meaning whoever was to capture her didn't have the power to do so. Not that anyone had — unless she was stripped of her magic, of course.

"Should I lift my skirt too?" she almost yelled. Amira may have been prepared to do a lot of what she was ordered to, but she also had limits.

"Don't care." The goddess waved her hand elegantly, dismissing her outburst, and again, Amira found herself on the verge of unleashing her pent-up powers.

It was ridiculous. Playing with potions and blood sacrifices had never been her thing. She was not a practitioner like Eliana, or any other witch on the face of the earth. Magic was in her veins, and it demanded constant release.

"Ride to the woods and you'll meet both your hope and your doom. Be sure to make the right decision," the goddess added, already vanishing in mid-air, as if her ludicrous wishes should be obeyed without a question. "Oh, and take Natalie with you."

Why Natalie? What did her cousin have to do with this? Amira wanted to yell. She was so sick and tired of being used and ordered around. So sick of being a pawn in their twisted game, she was this close to snapping.

Once, just once, she wanted to feel what it would be like to be more than someone's means to an end. Maybe then living wouldn't be that pointless.

She gathered herself, knowing orders were orders, even if all she wanted to do was shove them someplace far and deep. She walked to her closet, determined to find something less sumptuous than her golden empire waist gown. Only then, standing in front of a huge mirror, did she notice she wasn't wearing it any more. Instead, she was in some cheap, azure-blue muslin monstrosity, two sizes too big and full of patches.

Her hair was down, tied in a simple braid. She looked like a homeless person *sans* the dirt. Oh, but she had no doubt she would be as clean as a chimney-sweep by the same time tomorrow — if she managed to survive, that was.

This was disturbing. Not the appearance — she didn't give a damn about that — but the fact that she had failed to notice when her garments had changed.

Now's not the time to think about it, Amira reminded herself, and after taking a deep breath, opened the door.

It wasn't hard to evade maids, but nabbing Natalie proved to be time-consuming.

First, Amira had to wait till her cousins arrived, and then, true to his fashion, Ciaran didn't let his twin out of his sight for even a second. That one had over-protectiveness etched right down to the marrow of his bones.

Amira understood his motives, but a shadow she didn't need.

"Is she coming down any time this century?" Ciaran's annoyed voice interrupted her thoughts. "Or is she already down and on her way to those damned woods?"

Not yet, Amira mouthed. Ciaran's mistrust didn't surprise her. After all, it was well-earned.

She waited for him to get restless and watched, hidden in her corner, as he ordered Natalie and the youngest, Logan, to stay put, while he rushed upstairs taking two steps at a time. No doubt ready to break down her door.

This was her opportunity. The ten-second window she had to make do with.

Don't disappoint me, she silently willed the blonde witch to defy her brother's orders.

"Well, you can do whatever you want, but I'm not going to stand here like an idiot just because our brother has a stick up his—"

"Nat!" Logan exclaimed, but like so many times before, Natalie marched out without a backward glance, not caring that she was courting her twin's wrath.

Silly girl, Amira sighed, even if her running away was what she'd hoped for.

"And where do you think you're going?" she asked as she caught up with Natalie just outside the stables.

"Amira!" Natalie stumbled, taken aback by her sudden appearance. "What … what are you wearing?"

Amira rolled her eyes heavenwards. "Not the expensive silks any vagrant would love to get his hands on, that's for sure!"

She looked Natalie up and down, again wondering what the hell she was thinking. Just because Ciaran was annoying as Hell, didn't mean he was wrong. In Natalie's case, at least.

"I … I …," she mumbled, lost for words, "please don't tell Ciaran. I just wanted…" her trembling voice trailed off and Amira immediately realized Natalie's desire.

"Freedom," she uttered, knowing both of them wanted the same. "Come with me, then." She'd give her an adventure and a lesson all wrapped in one.

The girl needed to understand that running away had nothing to do with freedom. Amira ran constantly; and yet, she was never free.

Natalie followed her without a protest, mounted her

mare, and took off as if Dazlog himself was in pursuit. She threw back her head and laughed. Pins were flying all around, her long golden hair escaping its imprisonment strand by strand, while she kept laughing, enjoying the moment. At least until she noticed their destination.

Her laughter died. Even the smile disappeared from her face.

"I don't think this is such a good idea," Natalie shook her head, inadvertently slowing the pace of her mare.

"It's safer here than in a town," Amira assured her. All true. Venlordians, just like witch-hunters rarely ventured into this forest, while every town except Trinton had stakes ready for the burning.

Somewhat comforted by her words, Natalie followed, but her reluctance was still evident in the way she flinched at the smallest sound, nervous of every quivering shadow.

The further they rode, the stiffer her cousin's posture became. Amira caught her glancing up more and more often, as if searching for the light through the murky dense branches. Or maybe even praying.

This cringing every two seconds was getting on her nerves; and to top it all, Amira sensed Ciaran and Logan swiftly closing on them.

Not good, she sighed, and drew reins.

Amira petted her horse's mane and placed both hands over the creature's eyes—the energy sizzled as it exploded from her fingers. The air vibrated with magic. It was a simple command for their horses to halt.

Amira didn't need Ciaran here.

She had a date with destiny, and time was running short.

Chapter 2

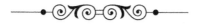

"Are you crazy?" Natalie shrieked, pulling the shawl on her shoulders tighter, as if she was the one naked and exposed to the world.

Probably, Amira decided, jumping into the water.

Thanks to the little trick she had performed, her cousins would arrive too late. Which reminded her how precious time was. Before she was captured, she wanted one last taste of freedom.

Amira swam around for a few minutes, not caring about anything, and when it became obvious peace and quiet wasn't meant for her, she said, "you should try sometimes."

"I beg your pardon?" Natalie sounded horrified, "if this is how you think you'll teach me, then I ... I ..." her words trailed off, and Amira couldn't help but arch her brows, daring the young woman to utter another ultimatum.

"Still not undressing," her cousin muttered and turned around.

Amira sighed at the reminder of how little her latest family knew her. Dancing under the moonlight in her birth costume—yeah right! It was right there next to painting her body in animal blood and seducing some poor sap on the forest floor. Even in her previous lives, when she'd been required to perform all those things to unleash her powers, she'd refused. And now, all she had to do was form an image of what she wanted in her mind.

There were risks, of course. Serious magic tended to separate mind and body, forcing them to walk in different worlds. The threat of losing oneself was great. Something all the witches were susceptible to, whenever they tried something they could not handle.

For Amira the risks were even greater since she didn't use spells, potions, or sacred marks. Her magic came from within, not from learning dozens of incantations and mixing herbs.

Truth be told, she hated making potions, especially since some ingredients were disgusting and acquiring them involved killing.

She'd seen plenty of death in her time—had no use for more. She preferred channeling her energy.

"Can we go home now?" Natalie's trembling voice interrupted her thoughts.

Stop scaring her, Amira told herself, not even considering the request. She would not be going home anytime soon; and Natalie—well, since she was already here, she could learn something useful for once.

Slowly, she rose from the water, all of her nerve endings tingling in awareness. Strange, she thought, brushing the sensation away, when she didn't detect anything threatening about it. On the contrary, it felt nice, as if someone was caressing her.

Amira glanced around, confirming that they were alone, stepped into the dress, and with Natalie's help buttoned it up.

"Sit," she told the other woman, and quickly followed her.

Once they were seated on a patch of grassy ground, Amira untwined her loose, wet ribbon, and placed it on the ground between them.

"Give me your hands." She stretched hers out, and waited for Natalie to close the circle. "Now concentrate on it and make it fly."

Natalie closed her eyes. Her brows knitted in an attempt to concentrate, but the ribbon didn't move an inch.

"I am trying, but it's not working," said Natalie, sounding as frustrated as she looked.

"Try harder," Amira ordered.

After a few more minutes and a dozen attempts, Natalie still sat, eyes closed, arms stretched, her face furrowed with despair. Finally she lifted her long lashes, revealing an agonized look from beneath them.

"It's useless."

"Are you saying I'm wasting my time with you?" Amira gave her a warning glance. "You just need to master how to control energy." She squeezed Natalie's hands. "Do you feel that?"

Natalie gasped. "It's so strong."

Amira squeezed even harder, enveloping her in an uncouth power which coursed through her veins whenever she took it inside of her.

"It's not all mine," Amira explained. It was everything around them. Water, earth, trees, air … The world was full of vigor, full of life. Sometimes she couldn't understand how people didn't see it, didn't feel it. How could they have forgotten?

It was the reason why witches used herbs, animal parts, even water. It all gave life-force, helped to create a miracle. Dead things, however, could never match live ones, full of power, full of energy she could use to her own advantage. Neither potions nor incantations could ever touch it. The true magic lay everywhere; one just had to know how to tap into it.

"Let me show you." Amira touched the ribbon with her fingers and it began levitating.

"Don't look at the ribbon," she said, "only at the energy flowing through it".

She clenched her arms behind her back, purposely showing she didn't need to touch to command it. She simply needed to embrace the life force all around. Feel the magic in the veins of world.

"One ought not to see or touch, one ought to feel," she finished, feeling cold steel pressed to her throat.

"Feel that, witch," came a low, deep male voice from behind her.

The ribbon fell on soft ground.

Natalie screamed.

Chapter 3

Amira slowly turned her head towards the cold steel, and Natalie's scream faded into the background. The forest became eerily quiet.

She lifted her chin to meet her enemy, letting her gaze travel from the muscular arm holding the weapon to his broad shoulders, calmly absorbing the width of them.

Despite the danger she faced, Amira wasn't nervous or scared. With cold determination she continued taking in details about her captor and possible killer, her eyes immediately noticing an amulet underneath his leather coat. It looked like…

"Yes, the amulet of Arushna. So don't you try anything, witch." His voice sent unexpected chills down her spine, and it had nothing to do with the powerful charm all Venlordians carried for protection.

A potent hatred washed over her like a wave of pure, unadulterated fire, scorching everything in its wake. It was tearing something inside her asunder, and suddenly, she felt a desperate need to see the face of the man who had made her heart ache in unexpected anticipation.

Utterly taken aback by the strange emotion, she let her eyes climb higher, experiencing a new one— regret—as she was forced to squint against the brightness of the sun. Amira blinked, and decided to take matters into her own hands.

It wasn't enough for her to know that his dark eyes were burning into her. She stood up.

Her gaze focused on the harsh planes of his face and the cadence of her heart gained momentum. The winds rose responding to her inner turmoil, stirring his thick black hair—he frowned at the sudden change of the weather and pinned her with his stare.

Their gazes locked, and Amira had to literally bite her tongue to stop herself from gasping as the last chains that had held her emotions snapped. She found herself fighting for every breath, hands trembling, legs in desperate need for support—all because she knew she had met her destiny, and it wasn't smiling upon her.

She felt dizzy. Felt emotion after emotion being awakened from deep slumber.

She tried to breathe slowly, focusing on the air her lungs craved, yet didn't seem to accept. Her thoughts, however, kept going back to the one question she had no answer to: was he the one to bring a long-foreseen death, or the one she had to help? Was he her lifeboat, or a sinker?

The look of those dark eyes, the stiffness of his body, didn't offer much hope. Neither did her attempt to read him. All Amira's concentrating on the sable of his eyes accomplished was a new wave of dizziness taking over her. She didn't give up. It wasn't in her. She delved deeper, swallowing this anxiety; but instead of knowing everything about him, she got carried someplace afar, and returned immediately with her senses shaken.

She couldn't remember a human who had proved to be such a challenge. Thoughts, feelings—she was able to read everyone like an open book. Everyone but him, apparently. Hatred, anger and bits of emotion she suspected to be pain was all she could get from him.

If she could touch him, she thought—her hands

already moving toward her goal to amplify her power—but she caught herself before her fingers reached his face. A muscle ticking in his jaw was all the warning she needed. She had to seem as harmless as possible. An ordinary witch not capable of laying him low even with a potion in her hands. A plan with a flaw the size of the Vortex of Shyau, Amira realized, once she was finally able to take her raging emotions under control and hear a silent sob from her frightened cousin.

What was she thinking of, taking Natalie here? Guilt stabbed Amira's heart. She knew it would be dangerous, and yet she had chosen to expose the young woman to danger she was not equipped to handle.

Herself, that was what she was thinking of. With that last thought her guilt intensified. And now, because of her selfishness, Amira had no other way but to expose the extent of her own witchcraft, disobey the goddess, earning punishment and probably risking her life. But of course, that was exactly what Hope wanted in the first place, wasn't it?

She should have known it was a trap.

"Run," Amira's voice rang in a thousand tones, shaking Natalie out of her staggering fear.

"There will be none of that," the man warned, before her cousin could even take a step.

"Natalie!" Amira chose not to pay any heed to him. If he plunged his sword, the vicious cycle would claim her again, and as collateral damage Natalie would be left in mortal danger. But if she disarmed him...

Damn it, Amira wanted to scream. Using her powers would not save her—it never had. Sometimes she wondered what was the use of having them in the first place. It brought her nothing but despair.

"Turn around and walk away," she said, with a calm she didn't feel. Amira made her decision. It was her fate. Hers alone. Natalie played no part in it.

21

Still, her cousin hesitated.

"He won't harm me," Amira bluffed. "Go. Now."

"Just wait a minute!" Raven found himself struggling against a strong urge to lay down his weapon. His grip on the sword tightened until his knuckles turned white, but the hypnotic effect her voice had on him refused to dissipate.

"She is not going anywhere," he said, slowly emphasizing every word, trying his best to contain the fury boiling inside.

He had plans. He couldn't risk destroying everything he had fought for in a stupid moment of hatred. But feeling the tendrils of her witchcraft wrap around his throat wasn't helping.

Worse again, he could not look at her and not remember the image of her stepping out of the water. She'd been a magnificent sight. Still was. She stood tall and beautiful. He even found her courageous, and the thought made a lump of bile rise in his throat.

Witches were nothing but filthy monsters. He despised witches. Had dreamed of seeing one particular hag choking with fear for years. He didn't expect to be affected by a witch's deep bright-blue gaze, devoid of malice, threat, or fear.

Raven could not shake off the feeling that those piercing eyes could see right through him. Unfold his darkest secrets, unleash his damnedest monsters.

Which was a threat in itself, was it not?

"Yes, she is going," the witch's strong voice brought his wandering thoughts back and Raven barely contained an urge to curse her. Or maybe he should curse himself. It was his own fault he couldn't concentrate. At least he wasn't so blind as not to see her fingers inching toward the crying witch.

Raven immediately stretched out his free hand, but when he tried to grab Natalie, it smashed into something.

He shook his hand, clenched and unclenched his fingers to ascertain his bones weren't broken. But it hurt like hell. Felt as if he'd punched a wall.

Slowly, he reached for it again and managed to find a barrier. An invisible wall was standing between him and the escaping witch.

"Remove it," he told his captive, turning the handle of the sword.

The blade nicked her skin. She gulped, but didn't cower. The only answer he got was her eyes narrowing.

You need her alive, he told himself. Alive!

He didn't believe in hurting just for the sake of it, so after one last glance toward silken robes disappearing into the woods, Raven dropped his sword.

His witch didn't move an inch. She kept standing still, strong and unshaken, but when he grabbed her hands, he felt them trembling.

Their gazes met again, and he saw the exact moment of realization dawning on her. She lifted her chin higher and pressed her lips tighter, as if daring him to say something. Well, she could wait an eternity for all he cared. He finally had a witch and his plan was in motion—ridiculous challenges had no place in it. And he would've recognized a challenge in her stance from miles away, but those eyes … those eyes dared him to do his worst and promised to survive. They promised to…

Raven shook his head, confused at what he'd seen only a moment ago. Or maybe felt. He couldn't remember.

Snap out of it! he commanded himself, and tied the knot swiftly, securing her hands behind her back. It was safer that way. For both of them. For she wouldn't be able to work another spell. And he wouldn't be tempted to cut her black heart out. More than he was tempted right now, at least.

"Leave her alone," a loud command interrupted him, about the same time as his witch gasped "Logan…"

Raven pivoted, only to witness someone coming at him like a wooden ram destined for collision. He waited patiently, and in the last moment possible turned his body sideways, causing the man to lose balance on impact and go down with a hard thud.

Raven's boot was on his throat the next instant, applying just enough pressure to scare him off.

"Stop it!" the witch yelled, jamming her own shoulder into his side in a futile attempt to move him. Futile—yes, for he didn't follow anyone's orders, much less some witch's; but that voice of hers made him want to, which only enraged him further. And … shit…

"You are a child," he exclaimed when he finally got a better look at the one on the ground.

Fair-haired, green-eyed and only around sixteen, the boy struggled to breathe, but was far from capitulating.

Raven removed his foot instantly, but rather than scrambling farther away, the boy came right back at him. With a dagger.

"I'm not a child," the kid snarled through gritted teeth, going straight for Raven's throat, "I'm a man!"

"I have no doubt you are." Raven rolled his eyes heavenward, disarming the kid with a few well-executed maneuvers. Only when the weapon was safely tucked under his belt did he allow himself a slow perusal of the witch—not that he needed any reminders of how she looked—and added, "Who wouldn't be?"

She possessed this ethereal beauty one would never

forget, even when she was red with anger, her eyes hurling daggers at him.

"Now, if you are done…" he began, ready to finish this spectacle; and ended having to evade another attack.

"Are you stupid?" he couldn't help but ask, throwing the kid on the ground one more time. It wasn't that easy to catch Raven off guard. He had years of practice behind him, years of fighting, and this one … would be lucky to last another month with his penchant for saving witches in distress. The Venlordians would make sure of it.

He took the dagger he'd acquired moments ago from under his belt, but before he could explain some truths to the kid the witch jumped in front of him, covering her unlikely savior with her body.

"Don't…" she breathed, "don't hurt him."

"No!" the kid underneath her protested, trying to get up. He wasn't allowed to move one inch or utter another word. She touched him, and the boy slumped to the ground. Unconscious.

"He is harmless. Now leave him be!"

Logan was harmless, all right. Something he couldn't say about the other one. Even with her hands tied up, she looked ready to commit murder. The air was cracking with power barely leashed; he could sense it.

Her murderous stare embodied the sheer definition of the witch, exactly what he would have expected; and yet, for the life of him, Raven couldn't fathom who the hell she was.

Chapter 4

Hours filled with nothing but an occasional chirping bird passed agonizingly slowly as Raven was forced to travel on foot, dragging a very skittish horse who still refused to carry him, and a witch who refused to look at him. Better silence than a tantrum, Raven decided. Besides, if he never saw those eyes of hers again, it would be too damned soon.

The fear and courage he'd glimpsed there touched him so profoundly, he didn't even know what to think or how to react. He felt amazed and angry at the same time. For a moment Raven forgot what she was, seeing simply a woman—a beautiful woman—protecting another. A woman he came across while stepping out of the shadows and into the clearing.

He'd been mesmerized by her long, graceful hands coming out of the water and disappearing under it. He could still see her nearing the bank and standing up. The water flowed just above her breasts creating a tantalizing vision. There was nothing for his eyes to feast upon, and yet too much for his starving imagination to withstand.

Something as innocent as a single dark lock, plastered to her sun-kissed skin and disappearing under the surface, became the most sensual thing he'd ever seen.

He remembered trying not to imagine the ends of her hair brushing against her rigid nipples, shaming

himself to turn around before she saw him spying like
some sort of a pervert; yet, he'd been unable to pry his
eyes away. And the image of her lithe, wet body was
branded on his mind forever.

Clothed and silent, she walked near him, angry
even; her moves, however, lacked none of the grace and
determination he'd seen earlier. In his mind's eye Raven
saw every detail as the memory surfaced before him.

The air shifted around the woman, shadows
swirled, but before Raven could question his sanity, or
his eyesight, she turned and laid her eyes on him.

He felt breathless looking into those large, blue,
bottomless oceans a man could easily drown in. She had
high cheekbones, a dainty nose and lips—a pure rosy
temptation. But it was her gaze that beckoned him the
most. It glanced straight at him, touched him, and at the
same time looked through and beyond. As if he wasn't
even there.

Raven couldn't understand how she failed to notice
him, especially standing so close, but he felt her gaze
like a physical touch and it raised something inside him.
Something undeniably strong, and yet, utterly
unfamiliar.

He shook his head in an effort to clear his thoughts.
Unfortunately, everything remained hazy. Except for
the woman with extraordinary eyes.

A witch, he all but chanted, desperate to regain
control. He'd seen the proof with his own eyes. He
could not desire a witch!

Raven ground his teeth in hellish frustration. He
could not desire a disgusting, wanton creature whose
only purpose in life was to gain more power and
command over all; no matter the consequences for
everyone else.

They seduced, they killed, and all for the greed to
obtain more power. Lied, stole, tortured. Animals or

human, it didn't matter. Raven had seen too many victims of their cruelty. Too many scars. He didn't know which were more bloodthirsty: Venlordians, who murdered so many innocents just for the possibility of killing a witch, or witches, who used anyone in their path any way they wanted.

Mercy was not in their vocabulary. Compassion was something they exploited, not exhibited. And risking their lives in order to save another was unheard of. Yet, she seemed sincerely concerned about the boy. Which baffled Raven. Selfless, witches were definitely not.

This had to be some trick. Or there had to be a reason behind her sacrifice.

Of course! the realization dawned on him. Everyone knew that a witch's powers grew with every man she lay with, but only few were privy to one little detail—if the male, a witch used to draw her power from, was to die suddenly, before she broke the bond, she would not only lose what she had gained from him, but much more. And the younger, the better. Innocence, after all, gave few extra benefits.

That's why she tried to defend Logan. She was protecting herself, Raven deduced, disgusted by her. Who knew how many slaves she kept.

To be this powerful…

The last witch he encountered had seven cages in her lair. Five of those occupied. And she came nowhere close to the one walking beside him.

It had taken him one look at the tortured souls, and the witch's fate had been sealed. Even the fact that he desperately needed a witch hadn't saved her. Thank the gods he had caught this one without the cages around.

"What did you do to him?" Raven asked, suddenly wondering if he had done the right thing by leaving the boy. Maybe he needed to go back and make sure she reversed whatever spell she'd put on Logan.

The witch glanced at him, her eyes burning. "Who says I did anything? Maybe you banged his head on a rock?"

"Yes, and I was born yesterday." Raven stared her down.

"It explains why you have no manners," she shot back, "or is threatening women with sharp weapons, tying them up and dragging them heaven knows where something you've been taught your whole life?"

"But you forget one thing," Raven answered, intrigued by her against his own better judgment, "you are not a woman."

"Let me guess," she said without missing a beat, "I'm a filthy monstrous whore who breaks marriages, preys on innocent children, and curses your fields and animals to wither and die, right?"

Raven couldn't help but stop in his tracks. The way she said all those things...

There was no misplaced, misguided rightful indignation, no anger, not even self-pity. It was as if it truly didn't bother her.

"And you are fine with what people think of you?"

"People see what they want to see. I may be an angel, but if they paint me as a demon..." she shrugged, "am I to cry now? Life is short. And I refuse to spend what little time I have wallowing in self-pity."

"No, of course not, you'll spend it ripping the hearts from their chests. Angel."

She sighed, for one second almost belying her words about not caring what people thought of her, but then she lifted her chin higher and uttered, "having control over someone else's life is so-oo exciting, isn't it?"

"What did you do to Logan?" Raven refused to rise to the bait.

"Saved him from you." Her words were so sharp,

he barely refrained from checking his chest for the wounds.

"What did you do to him?" The line of his mouth tightened and his voice grew harsher.

"Made him sleep."

"For how long?"

"Not long," she admitted. "I believe Ciaran woke him up already."

"Ciaran?" His eyes widened. "Never mind." He really had no wish to know all her lovers by name. "Just keep those hands away from me."

She narrowed her eyes, "and you'll keep yours to yourself?"

That was the plan, even if something lit up inside him every time she glanced his way.

"Besides," she added, "that amulet of yours would protect you from any nasty, wicked witch."

Despite the seriousness of the situation, Raven was forced to suppress a smile. How could he be intrigued and disgusted by her at the same time? There was just no logic in it.

She had to be working some spell. That had to be it. He refused to believe he could be attracted to a monster—no matter how lovely she appeared on the surface. The amulet he carried protected him from a lot, but there was always a way around it.

He looked at her and realized his mistake the moment he found himself drowning in those blue oceans of hers again. They seemed stormier than ever. Darker and more intense.

Raven had to fight the pull he felt. He had to force himself to take a step back. He took a deep breath, and glanced up.

The sun was already setting, leaving them with no other option but to camp outside.

Raven looked around, deciding it was as good a

place as any. He tied the witch to the nearest tree, and went to gather wood for the fire.

"Am I supposed to just sit here?" she asked, and he could swear he heard a note of irritation in her voice.

"Unless you can wiggle your nose and make a fire, yes," he shot back without even looking.

After a moment of silence, Raven pivoted and found her staring at him, her brows lifted. He had a funny feeling she might just set a fire. Under him! Instead, she dismissed him and concentrated on his horse.

Plotting a way to steal it? — the thought crossed his mind. Well, good luck with that. Lightning didn't let strangers sit on his back, or sometimes even touch him without Raven's help. Which, it turned out, she didn't require.

His witch bowed her head, slightly touching Lightning's frontlet, and in return the horse bowed his.

Could she command animals? he wondered with uneasiness settling inside.

What exactly was the extent of her powers? And why did it seem as though her magic didn't require potions?

"Sit down," he told her, thinking it best to keep her and Lightning apart.

Reluctantly, Amira obeyed.

She sat down on a fallen tree and watched him work, the image of him making her forget everything, except his presence. It baffled her more than anything. He was a handsome man, true — which should have not mattered to her at all — and yet she found herself examining him as a woman would. Not as a captive looking for a vulnerability to exploit.

His rugged chin showed determination; his

masculine body, power; his graceful movements, capability; but his dark midnight eyes revealed pain. The combination was perilous, and given his burning hatred, even more dangerous to her. Yet, with a heart full of anger and loathing, he was not the brutal, atrocious animal she would have guessed.

What was he going to do with her? Kill her? He'd threatened to, but he hadn't tried. Not really. He didn't even try to touch her.

Usually killing, or violating and then killing were the only options available for a witch. It could only be a matter of time — but still, why did he hesitate? Why did she see something more in him than just a villain?

Amira followed him with her gaze as he piled branches, his leather coat placed on the grass. His shirt sleeves were tucked up. And suddenly, she had a flash about those hands wrapped around her body in a possessive embrace, about his fingers caressing her naked skin. And from what she could see, she was more than willing.

Her spine stiffened at the unexpected vision, and she found herself breathless and shaking. She would have rubbed at the goose bumps on her flesh, except her hands were tied.

Amira gritted her teeth, torn between lust and irritation. She was this close to turning him into a tadpole, she had to clench her fists, jabbing her nails into her palms, hard, to keep herself from doing something stupid.

"What?" her captor snapped, as if sensing the change in her. He turned, and the moment their gazes met, Amira felt a wave of heat crash over her.

What? The same question rang inside her mind.

Amazed and confused, Amira barely managed not to drop her jaw. Impossible. No one except gods, demons and her, could communicate this way.

Definitely not mortals. And yet, the evidence was staring her right in the eyes.

Amira cleared her voice "I … I was just wondering about your …" think of something! "your … sword," she finally stuttered.

Her mind was in turmoil over the discovery. It was also plagued by visions of their passionate encounter. Stringing a coherent sentence together was a challenge.

At least she hadn't lied. She was thinking about his sword—just not the one he had in his scabbard.

"And what about it?"

"Well…"

Amira turned her head, no longer able to look him in the eyes. Her visions vanished but instead of relief, she got a full dose of frustration.

"A dagger I could understand, but a sword?" she said at last, proud of her level tone. "Pistols are much more efficient, aren't they?" Though truth be told, she knew exactly why the sword.

Pistols weren't that efficient when dealing with witches. Most of them had shields strong enough to protect them from a speeding bullet, yet were powerless against the blade.

If anyone asked her, she would have preferred a bullet to the stab wound, especially since a huge part of why no Venlordian carried a gun was the satisfaction of twisting the blade and watching them die writhing in pain.

Amira almost shuddered as a memory from far away surfaced in her mind.

Most importantly, while burning meant purification of the evil soul, even if Venlordians believed every witch to be evil, chopping off her head meant reversing any spells she cast upon the executioner.

Was he cursed in some way? That would surely explain a lot.

She tried to piece the different parts. A sword ... a witch ... the hatred ... and more importantly, the hidden pain; it all led only to one thing...

"I find it rather fitting for beheading." His lips curved in a hollow smile.

"And yet, mine is still intact."

His glare darkened. "Don't tempt me."

"Oh, I wouldn't dream of it." *Liar*. Her nature was to push people till they seethed with emotions. So strong and so close to the surface, for a brief moment Amira could actually feel them.

Pathetic, but robbing a little from others was the only way for her to experience anything. With Raven, however, she had no idea where the edge lay. Or how close to lashing out he was. Dangerous. But when did she ever shy away from danger?

Raven went to tend his horse, spread the blankets, made a fire, and decided to eat the last scraps of bread and cheese he had left. It wasn't much. He hadn't expected to be stuck in this forest for the whole day — especially since the nearest village was about a day's journey from there. But, he had a witch and that's what really mattered.

Raven looked at her sitting there, and realized she must be hungry by now. He sure was. He gazed at his meager meal, wondering why he was even considering it. One day won't do her any harm; but then again, even the condemned were entitled to a last meal, were they not?

He stood up, went to her and cut the rope tying her to the tree.

"Come," he told her.

She glanced at him from under her lashes. "I don't

consider watching you eat that irresistible."

"Me neither" Raven smirked. "So how about you come eat. It's not poisoned."

He expected some clever retort, but she simply stood up, walked to the fire and, turning to the side to show her bound hands said, "I guess these are not coming off any time soon."

She was right. The ropes were staying just the way they were. Raven couldn't risk untying her. So he did the only thing he could — helped her sit down and stretched out his hand.

She ate silently, giving him enigmatic glances before every bite, and he found himself holding his breath. The image of her eating out of his hands was strangely erotic, and when her lips brushed his fingers, the last air rushed out of his lungs.

It didn't seem deliberate, but his body still stood to attention, reacting to every light touch. It was sheer torture to endure.

Raven tried to take a deep breath to restore even a semblance of self-control, but the flick of her tongue shattered it completely, and suddenly he wanted nothing more than for the earth to part and swallow him alive. At least he would've been spared from the images forming in his mind.

Raven blinked, attempting to clear his vision. Not understanding what was happening around them. *Was it some kind of a spell?* a sane part of his mind suggested. Or simply a trick of imagination, carried too far? Whatever it was, madness walked side by side with it.

Raven refused to be controlled that way. Especially by a witch. The fact that the bonfire felt like a puny flicker compared to the fire burning inside him was a sign for him to get a grip. No sane man would consider bedding a witch. It was suicidal.

Didn't matter how vulnerable and peaceful she

appeared, sitting quietly not a feet away. It was a blinding and deceptive beauty she exuded. One which could lull you into submission without you being any the wiser.

Raven wanted to believe he was smarter than that. Especially since he needed his head clear in order to help Dacian—his little brother who spent day after day in a dark room reliving the nightmare that had occurred years ago.

Raven couldn't stomach witnessing his grown brother having less perception of the world than a five year old. But mostly, he couldn't bear the guilt. Couldn't even contemplate the shame he would feel if Dacian should awaken and find out that instead of helping him, Raven had got caught in the witch's web.

Not if—when, Raven corrected himself. When he awoke. 'Cause no one, not even the gods, was going to stop Raven from bringing his little brother back. And especially not the creature with the most amazing eyes he had ever seen.

They seemed to glow as the reflection of the flames danced in her gaze. He gulped, and the world shifted out of focus. For a second his perception changed. He blinked again, and realized he'd fallen asleep.

Raven opened his eyes to the burned-out fireplace, crumpled blankets, and an empty place beside him.

The witch was nowhere to be seen.

Chapter 5

Amira loved the freedom of galloping with the wind. She knew it was only an illusion, but for a brief moment she could forget the goddesses and her uncertain future—yet she couldn't forget the man she had left behind. The image of him stayed with her no matter how fast the horse ran.

She had hoped to clear her mind and sort the mess in her head, but alas, she was close to their campsite already, and still nowhere close to answering the questions plaguing her. The only thing she knew was that she wasn't running away.

Suddenly, Lightning reared up and neighed. Amira patted the beast to calm him down. She didn't want the noise to break the spell she had put Raven under, not until she was ready. But the moment she jumped down and turned to the side, her gaze collided with his.

Amira swallowed the streak of curses that threatened to escape her mouth. She didn't know why her magic failed her, or what was so different about him that the simple sleeping spell couldn't hold him down, but with his midnight gaze focused on her, she had no hope of figuring it out.

Torn with indecision, she stood stone still, waiting. Her heart, however, raced faster than Lighting had just minutes ago. And when he closed the distance with long, angry strides, grabbing her arms and clutching them behind her back, she didn't fight. She faced his anger and watched it transform into confusion.

Lightning neighed again and brushed his side against her. Amira stumbled forward, smashing into her captor's chest. His grip loosened, and she realized he had taken her into his embrace.

For a second, neither of them moved. Neither of them even breathed, it seemed. And then, she lifted her eyes, to meet his, and swallowed again.

His mouth closed hard on hers. Not coaxing, but demanding her lips to part, to let him in. She did. Couldn't have stopped even if her life depended upon it.

The wave of heat rippled through her body, melting everything away, leaving them the only two beings on the face of earth. And even that was suddenly slipping from under her feet.

He took her mouth swiftly, exploring every inch of it with his tongue. Claiming, not asking; demanding, not requesting.

There was nothing soft or gentle about the kiss, and yet it was everything she craved at the moment. It was pure bliss and an absolute torture.

Amira could feel his heart pounding, and the rhythm of it was hypnotizing. She couldn't understand her reaction. She could only feel. Want. Need. It was as if everything that had been denied to her for so many years had rushed back to her. Her head was reeling.

She tried to wrap her arms around his neck, but she couldn't free them from their prison—and finally, a sliver of sanity broke through her lust-clouded mind.

He hated her. What was really the difference between this and some random member of the Order trying to force himself on her?

Her, she told herself. She did want him. But that was not enough. Lust was not enough.

Just because he didn't beat her into surrender didn't

actually mean she had a say in this. He took, and she ...
had never been as desperate as to barter her body for ...
she didn't even know for what.

Stop! She wanted to yell, but her voice wouldn't
obey.

Raven! Stop!

Raven froze at the sound of his name.

The reality of what he had done crushed down on
him. He released her instantly, as if her touch had
burned him, and backed away.

"Shit," he uttered.

Had he actually been that close to taking her? He
had lost his mind completely. All he remembered was
the overwhelming desire to possess her. Body and soul.
The need had been consuming. It still blazed inside him.

If she hadn't screamed his name, Raven would have
stepped over the cliff and fallen down. Straight into the
hands of the most dangerous demon in the guise of an
angel, waiting to rip him apart. And yet, she didn't seem
to be trying to do anything.

Bright eyes, which were riveted on him shone with
confusion. Her hands wrapped around herself, as if she
was cold. An awkward silence settled between them.

Why was she not trying to reach for him? Exploit
his weakness? His desire was obvious. He would be a
fool to disregard it. He only hoped that by accepting it,
he would become more aware of how to defend himself.
No witch he ever heard of had passed over the
opportunity to press an advantage. Unless it was a
tactical retreat.

Dear gods, but he was giving himself a headache.
Sorting through the chaos in his mind probably required
more brain cells than he had working right now.

If he was being honest with himself, only one part of his was functioning properly at the moment. Way lower down than the one he would've preferred.

Raven couldn't imagine what would have happened if she hadn't said his name. His ... wait a minute, Raven halted, "how do you know my name?"

She closed her eyes for a brief second, and murmured something he couldn't identify. Something that strangely resembled a curse. And not a magical one.

"I simply know."

"You simply…"

"Yes," she said, "sometimes."

"Sometimes", Raven repeated to himself. Now why did that make his skin crawl?

"Tell me your name," he said, and again got a strange pause.

"You know mine," he prompted. "What can I call you?"

"What difference does a name make when witch is all I am to you?" she countered his question with her own. A question he had no answer to, only the need.

"Surely you have a name."

"Hundreds," she said. "They don't define me, though."

Fine, this was not getting anywhere in any case. He needed to get going. They already had too many interruptions, and of course, there had to be one more.

Raven grabbed for the sword the instant he heard growling. Shoving the witch behind him, he tightened his grip, preparing for an attack, but the moment the huge silver wolf appeared she stepped forward and walked straight toward the beast.

"Are you deranged, woman? Do you wish yourself killed?"

"So I'm a woman now? And all it took was a kiss from ... you?" She shot him a glance.

Raven didn't appreciate the reminder. But before he could form any intelligent thought, she added, "He won't harm me."

As if to prove her point she reached for the wolf. To Raven's astonishment the beast relaxed his muscles and howled. He even sniffed the air around her and licked her hand.

She rived off a hem from her skirt, pulled out a few bristles from the wolf's mane, and put it on the torn fabric. The beast didn't even flinch. Then, something strange and unfathomable occurred. A bright light emerged from her palm and vanished as quickly as it appeared.

"What just happened?" he asked, shaken to the core. It was the most extraordinary thing he had witnessed in his life. Nothing he'd ever heard or seen could compare. It wasn't a spell, or a potion; she didn't draw any marks or murmur any incantations. She simply took a wisp of hair.

How strong was she?

"I called Shadow's pack," she said, still stroking the animal's fur.

"Rii-iight…" One wolf wasn't enough, apparently. What was she planning? To feed him to her wolves? "Come, we're leaving."

"Shadow was right," she retorted, "you are a lost soul."

Fabulous — Raven gritted his teeth, praying for patience. She was talking with a wolf about his soul. Now that was a concept.

Amira sighed. Nothing was going as it was supposed to. Her magic was almost worthless. She had already exposed herself too much and now, she had to deal with the wolf.

Normally, she would have been dead three times by now. All things considered, he was taking it better than she would have thought possible. Or maybe she was that valuable to him.

Raven had even stepped in harm's way, protecting her with his body. Was he even aware of what he had done, or was it simply a reflex on his part? Either way, for that brief second her future looked promising.

You are using too much magic, Shadow, the messenger from the gods, warned her.

And I suppose you coming here helped me, she snapped. *How am I to get out of this now?* she asked.

Running is still an option, he suggested. Running was always an option. The one she had chosen a few times in her past. Never again.

First, by running it was impossible to meet her destiny with dignity. And second, it still caught up with her. Always. Made it ten times worse. In the end, the cycle was bound to start over and she—to find herself in a similar morass she so desperately wanted to avoid.

Even with all the hatred Raven felt toward her, and all the frustration she carried, she didn't want anyone else. Figuring him out was the key to survival. And it had nothing to do with her unexpected desire, she told herself.

His closed mind didn't offer much comfort. All she could sense were fragments of his most intense and rampant emotions, except … except moments ago, when he'd been burning with desire so strong, she could still taste the heat. Yet, he had ceased at her behest.

Raven hadn't forced her. He had reacted as though he'd been disgusted by himself. That much she'd seen clearly. It too gave her hope and a bitter sense of hurt. For the first time in her life, Amira wanted not to feel again.

If she hadn't, she would never have been caught in a situation where his entire inner world was open to her, vulnerable, and she couldn't bring herself to violate him. Not to mention that her mind had actually been absent at that moment. Only her emotions had been alive.

Amira sighed again. She was in a deep, deep trouble.

Chapter 6

Raven expected problems with the beast—was prepared to fight if necessary—but to his amazement the wolf turned around and left them.

"You do understand you had more chances with him by your side," Raven pointed out, knowing he had to dig to the bottom of her strange behavior.

She stood still for a moment, and then simply shrugged. "I was afraid you would harm him. He's just a pup." But looking at her eyes he saw something along the lines of: *I could still call him, if you'd like.*

What kind of game was she playing? Raven couldn't shake the feeling that he was missing a crucial part to this puzzle.

"A pup?" he snorted. It was the biggest damned wolf he'd ever seen. "Do you know what I could do to you for trying to escape?"

She didn't answer him, but the way her hands clenched and her jaw set, he knew she was bracing herself for the worst, which succeeded in shaming him. Tears wouldn't have done it. But her silent courage…

Raven cursed.

So instead of tying her to the horse and letting her run, he tied her hands and lifted her to mount the horse in front of him. A huge mistake, Raven realized after a few moments of riding.

Holding her so close, breathing only the fragrance of her hair brought back the memories of their kiss—

something he wished to the gods he could forget.

He still couldn't believe he'd kissed her. And apparently his stupidity had no limits, because he wanted to taste her lips again.

Honey, he thought, she tasted like honey. But with a certain bite to it.

Oh dear gods, help me, he uttered under his breath. The irony of it didn't elude him. Being a person who rarely prayed, he sure had asked for a lot of divine help lately. Only who wouldn't have? Especially with such beauty nestled against his chest. His whole body was only too aware of her every delicious curve.

Raven urged his horse harder. He had to reach his home fast before the last shreds of his strength of will vanished and he did something he would regret for the rest of his life. Being a mindless slave to a witch was not on his agenda.

Just a day more, just a…

An eternity more. A full aeon seemed to pass before he spotted a village.

He circled the place, careful not to alert its residents to their presence, and halted after noticing a solitary roadhouse.

Raven jumped off his horse and after pulling her down, loosened the ties.

Something told him he would regret this, but what could he do? Exposing her as a witch was the last thing he needed. He had no desire to fight the whole village to keep her from the pyre.

Amira rubbed her wrists, slowly examined the area, and waited. It didn't take a genius to understand what would happen next. There were just a few options after all. Running, which she didn't consider at all. Being dragged to the village all tied up, which would result in a public execution. Or, the one she thought Raven should be contemplating right now, since public execution would defeat his whole purpose. He definitely had plans for her, and death was not on the menu—at least not yet.

"One wrong word or move from you," Raven's voice washed over her in a warning, "and public execution will be the least of your problems. Understood?"

"Don't worry, darling," Amira mouthed the last word deliberately slowly, "you've kind of grown on me. Besides, I wholeheartedly believe in one kidnapper at a time."

Did she actually say that? Amira wondered. She had lost her mind completely.

She managed to bite her tongue all the way to the room he'd paid for, but once in it, she took a piece of the roasted duck, and faced him.

"Evolyn?" she exclaimed, referring to the name he'd given to the innkeeper, "do I look like Evolyn to you?"

"You would have preferred me calling you witch?"

Amira considered his words as she chewed her next bite, swallowed it, and asked again, "but Evolyn?"

"And what's wrong with that name?" Raven placed his hands on his hips waiting for an answer.

His gaze was cold as ice. It should have given her the first hint to keep her mouth shut. Any wise person would have heeded the warning. Amira, she simply went with the flow, even if it was destined to crash straight into rocks.

"I have no doubt it belongs to someone very charming," she moved closer, "like your … uhm," she thought about it for a second, "your mother, or some childhood love, but with such a name you are bound to be burned," she finished, sensing his muscles turning to steel.

Oh, this time she had done it—the thought crossed her mind the same instant he closed on her and seized her.

Amira could tangibly feel menace radiating from his body; fury boiling inside, but still locked tight behind the unbreachable walls. And pain. The sharp, cutting your soul in half feeling was unmistakable and overwhelming.

She tilted her chin to meet his burning eyes and was immediately trapped by their locked gazes—his inner world slipping through the cracks of his cast-iron control.

"I am sorry about your sister," she uttered, unconsciously reacting to bits and pieces she got from him.

The glimpses weren't flashes of events like from every other person she got. She didn't see a single memory of his—simply knew small, unrelated facts. Things that mostly didn't help her.

Things such as what he ate a month ago, or that he never drank. For some reason dreaded returning home every single time. Buried his sister Evolyn.

Reacting on pure instinct, Amira closed her eyes, severing the connection between them, and with it, the flow of information. Her chest froze with the sudden revelation—the more intense Raven's emotions were, be they anger, pain, or lust, the less control he had over protecting his thoughts and memories from her. If she pressed harder, she knew she could widen the fissures in his armor. Yet her eyes remained closed.

It wasn't a matter of conscience. It wasn't! It couldn't be. Her past selves had never had any compunction against ripping a mind open if it was a necessity. Amira needed to know everything he'd buried inside. She had a strong suspicion that one of Raven's secrets would lead her to her destiny. To the prophesy. And still her eyes remained closed.

"What is it about you?" she whispered, cupping his face.

He stood in a trance-like state, showing no visible reaction, yet through her touch she experienced it all.

The pain was crippling. She felt every tear he'd shed kneeling on a freshly-dug grave. Every sob. She trembled, but she could do nothing to relieve him of it.

Maybe if he willingly let her in...

But he didn't. She was an intruder. And she wasn't a true empath who could heal such wounds without breaking into one's mind.

Amira released him, and moved to the bed. He had to find the way out of the nightmare she had inadvertently sent him to, all by himself.

Amira sighed. Her powers were a mess around him. And she—full of guilt.

* * *

Amira!, a voice she recognized as Hope's woke her up.

"What?" she yawned, rubbing her sleep-laden eyes. Blinked. And realized Hope wasn't in the room.

She sat up and glanced around. The sun was already rising, though the room still drowned in shadows. Her captor was seated in a chair, placed so as to block the doorway, sword in hand; ready to spring up at any moment, no doubt.

The small, hard chair seemed uncomfortable, and judging from the angle of his body he was definitely going to feel this night for the next few days. And yet, he'd left her in a bed.

The man kept surprising her.

Amira removed the covers, stood up, and only after she took a few steps did she notice that Raven wasn't sleeping. His eyes were half closed, but he was vigilant of everything going on around.

At least he had been, before Hope stopped time and left him frozen like a statue.

"You were warned," Hope said. "You can only blame yourself for what happens next."

A second later everything started spinning.

Amira grabbed for the corner of the bed, only to find no bed. She fell. Still, the spinning didn't cease. For a long minute Amira felt no floor beneath her feet, no furniture or walls to grab onto. And suddenly, her body hit the ground. Hard.

All the air rushed out of her lungs and it took her a moment to lift her head.

Amira cursed, seeing she was no longer in the room. Worse, she had no idea where she was. Or how to get back before Raven missed her again.

Teleportation wasn't in her skillset. At least not yet.

"Laugh all you want," she yelled, scrambling to her shaky feet, "but the day will come..." she swore to herself, finally finding a doorknob in the pitch-black jail she had been thrown into.

The door creaked, but opened enough to let her out. Amira didn't stop for a single moment. She ran.

As fast as her legs could carry her, she flew out of the abandoned barn straight to where she sensed Raven would be.

Her swift, large steps ate the ground as she furiously raced against time, determined to prevail. Failure wasn't an option. To her, failure equaled death.

Her breathing became shallow and rapid, barely taking in the air her stinging lungs needed. Her hands shook, beads of perspiration sprang up on her brow, but she didn't slow down.

Amira gave it everything she had. Barefoot, she ran through the forest, ignoring rough branches scraping her arms, and sharp stones digging into the soles of her feet every time she placed one on the forest floor. She never took her eyes away from her goal—a small village just beyond the trees.

As she jumped over the fallen log, her dress got caught between leafless, weathered branches, forcing her to a halt. With no finesse, Amira grabbed the hem and pulled, causing the fabric to tear. The second she was free and about to leap into another run, Amira found herself face to face with Raven. And he was furious.

She was caught. Dragged to the horse, tied up and thrown over the beast like a sack of grain. She didn't try explaining; it wasn't like she could defend herself, nor did he demand answers. He simply secured the knots and mounted the horse.

It was humiliating to be in such a position, forced to feel every gallop reverberating through her bones, every piece of dirt land on her face, and only the speeding hooves in her sight.

She had a feeling someone above was having a great time at her expense.

On that joyous note Amira heard distant voices greeting her captor, offering help. And then, silence. A silence so deep, she could swear it would be possible to hear butterfly landing a mile away.

Amira swallowed, knowing that even if her ears failed to detect malevolence, her skin prickled as dozens of eyes landed upon her.

"Could it be?" someone standing nearby asked.

"Yes, a witch." Raven said simply, "would you…"

Almost instantly she was grabbed by her waist and

pulled down.

Amira gritted her teeth at the rough handling, yet it was nothing compared to the images slamming into her of what the man would like to do to her.

She didn't know how she managed to stand her ground and not recoil.

It wasn't simply hatred that almost succeeded in frightening her — it was the pleasure she knew he would experience in choking the last breath out of her. It was the knowledge of his twisted and sick thoughts she was forced to digest, as she stared into the face almost as ugly as his soul.

The face may not have been his fault. Actually, Amira was certain the monstrous look was given to him by Venlordians.

Half of his face was burned with acid, the other half marked by a large, red and angry "S" standing out on his pale cheek. It singled him out as a condemned sinner. A male who had tried to hide or protect a witch.

The face may not have been his fault, but hatred toward real witches — because his wife was executed as one in front of him — was all of his own choosing.

"I'll show our hospitality to the guest, my lord," he said all too gleefully.

"Do so…" Raven was already turning from her, "…and Owen, I know how your fingers itch," he paused. "Don't."

Amira hoped it was a good sign, but when she saw what Owen was looking at, a shudder ran down her body.

The chains and the carved symbols that prevented witches from using their powers were daunting enough, yet that was nothing compared to the blood-drenched aura of the place.

Amira found herself fighting for breath as Owen dragged her and chained her to the wooden pole. Worse still, people started gathering around, and their emotions leapt at her. It made her feel nauseous.

And to think she had almost forgotten what it was like to be hated simply because of what she was. Almost. Nightmares from her past lives were never far away. Reminding her how dangerous crowds like these were.

"Burn the witch!" someone shouted. "She must pay."

There was a big murmur, a few seconds when the voices seemed incoherent — but then another suggestion rang out, "Gut her!"

"Stone her!" others yelled.

Shouts merged into an overwhelming cacophony, threatening to swallow her alive, to make her pay for all of her sins.

Of course, every natural and unnatural disaster in the world was her fault. It was her fault someone's wife was burned or daughter raped. Who else, if not a monster such as her, was responsible for all of it? After all, she was a perfect target.

Anything went with crowds like these. They were like vultures attacking the weak, imagining themselves strong just because of their number. But in a split second capable of turning against one of their own.

Well, she was not weak. And scavengers didn't intimidate her.

Amira bit back a groan when an apple hit her chest. She refused to show pain. She refused to cry or beg, or even gasp. She looked straight at her executioners, waiting for another blow that was certain to follow.

She witnessed the boy who threw the fruit disappear into the crowd, only to be replaced by more dangerous individuals. Rocks, not apples, were held in their hands, and despite Amira's resolve, she felt her heartbeat gaining momentum.

Was this it? Was the cycle to begin again? Had she failed this time too?

It was almost ridiculous that after so many deaths her heart still rolled down to the soles of her feet, but it did. Nevertheless, she didn't crumble. She was determined to meet her doom proudly standing.

Even if her knees began to wobble, she refused to let her bones liquefy into a puddle. She ordered herself to stand no matter what.

A rock the size of a fist flew an inch past her. Another one was ready.

Stand tall, she chanted, no matter what, just stand.

"Stop that!" a young girl shouted, stepping in front of the crowd, "You'll kill her."

"So?" someone asked.

"If I recall correctly, master Raven forbade such a thing."

"Mind your own beeswax, Nyssa," Owen threatened, "or I'll chain you next to her."

The blonde girl stood her ground. "So be it, I'll just go and tell the master of your plans."

Owen lowered his rock. He spat a few insults regarding the girl's foolishness, and stepped aside.

After the man left, some of the others began to leave as well. Those remaining simply watched her.

Nyssa waited a few more moments and then carefully approached.

"You are a real witch?" she whispered.

"I am."

"You don't look like one." she said in a curious voice while examining every inch of her.

"And how do witches look?" Amira inquired.

"They are old nasty hags with big noses and crooked teeth." Nyssa was picturing every child's nightmare. Little did she know about real witches, it seemed.

"Are you a maid here?" Amira asked, still not comprehending why there were so many people.

Nyssa burst out laughing. "No, not really. My mom and I asked for protection about eight years ago."

"It's a sanctuary?"

"Yes. People were calling my mom a witch, 'cause she knows herbs. Then the Venlordians came..." Nyssa's smile completely disappeared and she shivered.

"We got away," she finally whispered in a timid voice, as if trying to reassure herself.

Amira didn't ask to elaborate further. It was obvious. The Venlordians had harmed them. Was Nyssa...?

Amira probed her mind a bit and felt a huge wave of relief wash over her when she found out that the girl hadn't suffered at their hands. But her mother had. And the boy who threw the apple was the fruit of some friar's brutality.

"The others?" Amira tried changing the subject without actually changing it.

"We all shared the same fate; just some of them were not as lucky as we were."

It truly was a sanctuary, Amira thought, seeing the place and the guards all around with a new understanding. And if it wasn't for the chains binding her arms, she would probably admire the man. But despite this kindness, she had to wonder how many witches he had dragged and chained to this accursed stake. How many of them were stoned to death, or burned alive?

The blood-drenched auras didn't lie.

Chapter 7

Raven tightened his grip on the horse and ordered himself to move. He couldn't show mercy to a witch. Plans were finally set in motion, and he desperately needed them to bear results.

So why did it feel so wrong? Why couldn't his eyes let go of her, his body turn away from her?

He felt frozen to the same spot he handed her to Owen, unable to shake off a sensation he was setting something else in motion. Something dark and ugly. And for a moment there, he had to remind himself of all the reasons this was necessary.

Seeing her manhandled by the man he wouldn't normally trust his dog to made it even harder. But the moment, she'd been chained to that damned stake, brought memories so painful, his heart was cloven in half. Again.

Guilt and pain were his constant companions. Following him wherever he went. Reminding him of a tragedy he would have sold his soul to avert. Intensifying, and catching up with him every time he returned home. But now, the wounds weren't just stinging. They weren't simply rubbed in salt. They were ripped open and bathed in acid.

Raven hadn't even realized he'd taken two steps towards her the moment it appeared that people were about to disobey him and begin a public execution. He couldn't let that happen.

Alive she had to stay.

Luckily, Nyssa had been there to prevent a disaster. But it wasn't Nyssa, Raven observed.

His gaze was fixed upon a fearless creature, standing tall in such glory, she appeared more like a goddess than a murderous, abhorrent being.

With her hair flying loose in the wind, her chin and shoulders raised high, her eyes without a single trace of surrender, she was untouchable. Radiant.

For a moment she was the only innocent in this, and he, the bastard who had tossed her to the wolves. The moment the thought formed in his head, Raven winced. She was perfectly capable of taming any ferocious beast she wished. And he'd sworn on his mother's grave to save Dacian. Mercy was something he couldn't afford.

Finally, Raven turned his back to her.

He marched through the door and froze. He'd been so focused on what was going on outside, he forgot.

A shiver ran down his spine. Every hair on his nape prickled. Chills danced over his flesh. The echo from deep within his memory rose up again.

Despite the time gone by, he could still see the damned drama. Hear his mother's cries, feel the same impotence.

No more, he vowed. Soon the news of his captive would reach the ears of the witches and they would come. They had to come.

"Why on earth did you bring that poor girl here?" Martha inquired.

She was the housekeeper at his home, who had served his family for more than thirty years. She was the only one who knew him since childhood. Practically raised him. One of the few people to know about his brother, and care for him. The only person to berate Raven on his quest.

Raven looked at the old, grizzled woman. "I believe

you know the answer."

"That is what I am afraid of." She folded her arms over the chest and swayed her head. "Raven, my dear boy, you will only bring more suffering into this home."

She was mistaken. He would bring peace into this home, not suffering.

"How is Dacian?" he asked uneasily.

Martha lowered her faded brown eyes. "The same, I'm afraid."

"I will go to him," Raven said, turning for the stairs, "and later, I would like a word with you."

"Me too," she nodded, making it clear he was to hear her opinion about the consequences of his actions. Like he needed it! — his fingers tightened on the wooden rail. He really, really didn't. Not when everything inside him was already in turmoil. Worse still, the closer he got to the door, the faster his heart beat.

By the time Raven reached his goal, his heart was pounding like a sledgehammer against his ribcage. He wrapped his fingers around the knob, barely noticing the trembling in his hands, and twisted it, dreading the sight awaiting him behind those doors.

The not knowing what would greet him was killing Raven. Would his brother be lucid enough to recognize him, or would he be some pitiful, mindless creature? The same question crossed Raven's mind every single time he found himself in this spot.

He took a deep breath, and swallowing his anxiety, stepped in.

Dacian's chamber weltered in darkness. No oil lamp, not a single candle was visible. Huge windows stood covered by heavy, dark drapes protecting Dacian's curled-up body from the smallest ray of light.

Raven didn't bother looking for a candle — his brother didn't like light. It probably reminded him of the fire he'd been caught in. At least that was what half of the scars on Dacian's body attested to. Truth be told, Raven had no idea what his brother had gone through. And the knowledge brought new wave of guilt — something that invariably assaulted him the moment he entered this room.

Raven moved a wooden chair to the bed and positioned himself in front of his brother. For a few moments he just sat there looking into Dacian's sad and distant eyes.

Normally he would tell him about his travels, about things he'd seen and heard, about the people he'd encountered. But never about witches, or Venlordians, or even about his plans.

The first time Raven had killed a Venlordian, being barely fifteen, he'd felt blood on his hands for a week. He remembered telling his brother about it years later; seeking confirmation and support for the path he'd taken more than he dared to admit. Dacian's reaction, however, had been the opposite to what he'd expected.

Three men had to hold his brother, while he thrashed and screamed as Raven shoved medicine down his throat.

Raven hated such procedures. A far cry from a simple witch's touch.

He pinched the bridge of his nose in frustration.

Just great; now he yearned to have such a power; and partly not for his brother, but for himself. He hated seeing Dacian crazed. It was one of few things that still made his heart sore.

So from that day he never spoke about the gory part of his life. He only wished he could talk to Dacian, not just speak to him. Today however, words eluded him completely.

His thoughts constantly returned to that particular person chained in his yard.

"Soon, my brother," Raven whispered — a promise

he would move heaven and earth to keep.

He stayed with his brother a little longer, just sitting there, thinking about the day when the witches would come; and especially the one who called herself Ethely, he hoped. When he would chop off her head and take her pitiable life, Dacian would regain what was stolen from him.

Of course, Raven knew it wouldn't be that easy. She wouldn't stand meekly awaiting her fate. She might not even come.

Good thing having a witch opened up new possibilities. All he had to do now — was wait.

Chapter 8

Every time Raven came home time seemed to drag at a snail's pace, torturing him until the last moment he rode off, revenge the only mission in his mind. This time it simply froze.

He couldn't relax. He felt haunted.

The moment he closed his eyes, darkness swallowed him. His witch appeared.

Out of the shadows of the morning mist the dark angel glided on the back of a huge beast. Lightning pranced and neighed.

She looked tall and proud and fatally lovely. Like a conqueror come back for his soul.

She kicked free of her stirrups, swung her leg over the pommel, and jumped down.

It was like a memory of a dream. He could swear it was exactly what had happened the day before, but at the same time even the concept of her returning was ridiculous.

He had chalked it all up to her disastrous sense of direction, but now he had to wonder. It felt like his mind was full of holes whenever he thought about their time together.

Raven knew he needed answers, yet at the same time, he would have been glad if he could forget her for five seconds.

Her presence seemed to follow no matter how gloomy his thoughts turned. And the more he tried to clear his head, the brighter the image of her became; until he could swear she stood before him—so lovely, the shadows retreated.

Her eyes were glittering sapphires, her skin soft as silk as she reached for him and touched his face.

Raven swallowed hard; it was all he could do not to succumb to her gentle caress.

Her fingers sank deep into his hair, pulled him closer. Their lips were an inch apart, their breaths mixing, the taste of her already in his mouth. She didn't kiss him, though.

Come to me, a soft wind carried the words in. A whisper, sweet and hot, danced on his skin, leaving him powerless in her presence.

Her fingers caressed his tawny flesh, slowly pushing him over the edge. Pushing him to the point where both sanity and reason were no more. He no longer cared.

If he was in Zcuran, the hell-realm, it was the sweetest and most diabolical torture he'd ever experienced. And by the gods, he wanted more of it.

In an instant she was standing utterly nude, her shameless, brazen eyes full with welcome invitation. Raven bit his lip, trailing his gaze up and down her magnificent body, hardly believing the fantasy in front of his eyes. He felt his mouth go dry.

No longer able to fight his urges, he took her in his arms, thrusting his tongue deep into her mouth. Her lips parted in acceptance and surrender. Her soft moans tore away the last shred of his control.

He had to have her.

Nothing else existed, except the feeling of her soft skin as he ran his fingers over her body. Except the honeyed scent that filled his nostrils, intoxicating him like a drug. Nothing existed, except the need to pull her closer. To taste her ... forever.

A strange sound assaulted his ears, bringing him back from the land of fantasy.

Raven lifted his head to see Ethely standing just a few feet away. Laughing.

Her rough, dry voice ignited his disgust … with himself. Her cursed face mocked him.

His hands suddenly felt empty, his fingers curled into fists aching more for the loss of his dream angel than for the blood of the witch.

"You are a fool, always were, always will be," Ethely sneered.

Raven didn't hesitate for another second. He charged.

He grabbed her, but she disappeared into the night, leaving his clenched fists strangling the thinness of the air. He tried to search for her, all in vain. Only a rippling laughter came crushing down on him.

He cursed the blasted hag or maybe himself—he wasn't sure which—but he knew one thing—he was going mad. A few more days like that and he would join Dacian in his insanity.

Just as if to drive home the point, another sound reached him. This time, not the raspy voice of Ethely, but a melodious tone, an angelic sound reverberating someplace inside him.

Raven jerked his eyes open.

He was in his home, lying half-submerged in already cooled-down water. His chest heaved. His heart pounded.

He stroked his fingers through his hair, trying as he could to recover from a nightmare, yet the sensations lingered.

He felt cheated.

Raven brought his fist down into the tub, splashing water everywhere. It was futile. The way he felt made no sense, but…

For a moment he held what he'd desperately sought for years. He had his brother's life in his hands. For a moment it wasn't a dream.

He also held an angel and, despite everything, he could still feel her kiss. Every cell of his body craved for more. His mind longed for that one blissful, pain-free moment.

Raven took a deep breath, reminding himself it was his brother who mattered, not his own needs or wants. But when he heard singing in the same melodious voice, every desire he tried so hard to quench rose again.

* * *

How was this possible? Amira breathed heavily.

Damn him. The man was not supposed to … what? Remember it? Fight it? Turn it against her?

Yes, yes and most definitely yes, her mind screamed as she resumed singing. He was not even supposed to notice it.

Apart from the fact that it was troubling, terrifying, and unfathomable, it was also amazing. She could not remember the last man, except immortals of course, thousands of years ago, to be capable of control in the dream plane. And to think she'd thought it would be easy. Probably her fatigue talking there.

The unknown had made her uneasy. The possibility of a night spent chained to the damned pole, with only her torn dress to shelter her, had convinced her to try anything. She'd thought she couldn't worsen things. As if! Now she could only roll her eyes heavenward.

Minutes before, she'd been weighting her options quite differently. What was she supposed to do?, Amira had asked herself. Break the ties and turn any man who tried to hold her into a stinking mushroom? Not without the godly interference.

What she could do—had to do—was reach him. Somehow. Shake down his fences.

The answer was simple and easy. Something she had learned in one of her prior lives just for the fun of it. With Raven, she had a purpose, and a connection Amira was convinced she should not have. Yet, it was there. She had only to think about him and it seemed she was right beside him.

That should have been the danger sign, cautioning her to rethink. But had she listened?

She hadn't been just blind, she'd been tempted. Or maybe she'd been blind because she'd been tempted to see how his world looked like. Either way, she'd ignored everything, thinking he would not notice it. Wouldn't even remember. At worst, think of it as a dream, a figment of his imagination.

With that thought, she'd taken a deep breath, letting go of her shackles. One moment she'd been standing firmly on the ground, and the next, floating in the air, glancing down at herself—at the body chained.

Amira remembered closing her eyes, thinking of Raven and the next moment appearing in front of him—gazing at his powerful body half-submerged in water, drowsing in his bathtub.

She should have paid more attention to the state of his mind, instead of touching every inch of his mouthwatering body with her starving gaze. She could not help it, though. Droplets of water had glistened on his tanned skin, urging her to lick every one of them, taste the texture of his flesh.

Amira had trailed her eyes to the relaxed features of his face. His eyes had popped wide open then. He looked at her as if he could see. She'd ignored that warning as well, saying now or never; and had reached out, invading his still-unawakened consciousness.

Darkness had overwhelmed her, shadows assaulted her. Amira had fought them back, finding him one more time.

It was the most intense journey she had ever experienced. With him fighting at first. Losing eventually. But contrary to her hopes, his loss had not been her victory. She'd lost control and he'd gained power. He'd become the master, and she — the slave.

Even now she trembled at the memory of how they ended up standing naked, toe to toe, face to face.

Shake it off, the sane part of her had screamed, *break the connection, while you still can.*

Amira couldn't. Most importantly she wasn't sure she wanted to. She'd been his for the taking, and he most definitely had been doing just that.

She hadn't wanted to lose his hot embrace, his burning lips — mouth savoring her without remorse. It had felt heavenly. Yet, transformed into hell the moment he'd stopped.

His gaze had changed, body stiffened, and his sole focus had shifted to a witch standing a few feet away.

In a splash of a second, he'd let go of her, and Amira had found herself back in her chains. Singing.

She always sang when leaving her body. It was part of the transformation, part of the spell, if one could call it a spell. Her singing was her guide, her way back out of the darkness. This time, once back, she didn't cease. She kept singing, determined to succeed even if she had failed at first.

If she could unleash his inner feelings... If only she knew what she was up against...

Unfortunately this was not an empty forest, the one and only place she normally sang, but a place with dozens, maybe even hundreds of people. And her voice was affecting everyone around. If she didn't stop, she could kill someone.

But then, what did she care about people, who were willing to stone, gut, and burn her? It would serve them right, a part of her snorted. Only a small one. Apparently her conscience was not as dead as she'd thought.

Amira sighed.

It was hard and draining to separate such a big crowd from the influence of her song, but she managed; leaving Raven alone in his struggle.

After the next verse, Amira glanced toward the mansion, noticing a man's figure framed by the second-story window. He was garbed in nothing but a counterpane of sorts, his broad chest dripping wet.

Their eyes met, gazes tangled, her toes curled under the piercing stare. Hot, so hot.

Amira focused everything she had into the song, letting her voice travel through time and space. She allowed it to grow and reach everything it could; finally touching something deep inside him, something he had buried long ago.

It also made her realize that a part of her was still with him. With the sound of her voice they were together. He was still touching her, kissing her.

Raven was burning. The two lovers he saw in the sky were none but themselves, fresh from his dream. Except it was not a dream. She saw it too. He was certain.

The view left his mouth dry, his whole body throbbing, but her voice stirred something in his heart. For a second there Raven felt once again alive. Then, everything went dark.

They've been sucked into a world without light or

hope. An abyss of lost souls filled with screams of vengeance and wrath.

The darkness was blinding. All around thunder roared, echoing long after the last traces of it should have vanished; and only then lightning cracked the sky apart. Its long sharp talons scratched through the clouds, wringing tears of pain and sorrow from above.

It was a freakish storm Raven could not even begin to comprehend, and his witch was standing in the middle of it.

The blistering storm tore her apart, ripping her slim dress to shreds. She decisively stood her ground, singing more fiercely than before, ignoring the wind pulling her sable locks, ignoring the rain coursing down her body. Her eyes burned into him, and the only option left for him was to drown.

For a moment, even the storm retreated into the shadows when faced with a stare so fiery Raven felt dizzy, breathless. He could even see glimpses of his past playing in front of his eyes, which kicked him wide awake as nothing would.

"Magic," he uttered, his anger mounting. He could remember reading about witches capable of controlling weather, but it was said that about a dozen were required.

Here she stood, alone with a power ten times greater than normal, controlling the forces of nature; not to mention digging into his memories. Under the markings of the Zearr no less.

He cursed under his breath, and violently tugged at the curtains, almost ripping them down. He couldn't let her see him.

He couldn't let her see into him.

Contrary to what Raven believed, Amira was not controlling anything. Somehow she had managed to lose the upper hand in this game.

She was suffering.

Still, she refused to surrender. She kept her voice strong and bright. And when Raven disappeared from the window, breaking their locked gazes, everything went still.

Suddenly she understood. She couldn't control the storm, because it was not she who had raised it. It was him.

She got what she wished — his inner world.

She had tasted his passion, and it was only natural to experience his anger. And still, she had to wonder, what else was he hiding behind those locked doors of his? What else was making his eyes so guarded?

Chapter 9

Raven always thought of himself as a patient person, especially considering how many years he'd spent travelling, searching, or waiting for opportunities. But the hole his carpet was in danger of sporting belied Raven's conviction.

He was going demented. Walking the edges, so close to the point where he would lose it and choke the witch, just to hear silence once again. Consequences be damned.

With her incessant singing every waking hour for the past day, he felt trapped and haunted. Worst of all, her voice had gotten under his skin, and it was driving him crazy.

The only reprieve he had was when she was eating, something Raven was not able to do himself since Martha refused to even let him into the kitchen until he released the "poor girl from those damned shackles" as she so eloquently put it. But even if he had a king's feast laid out in front of him, Raven was certain he wouldn't be eating. He'd lost his appetite.

Massaging his temples, Raven groaned and resumed pacing. His head felt as if it was split in half. He was getting frequent nose bleeds. His whole body shook with rage, because he suspected it was witchcraft that was making him ill.

He could gag her, he supposed, but somehow just ended up wearing out the same circle on his carpet instead of leaving the room.

For Dacian, he was ready to sacrifice everyone and everything. Including himself.

Raven whipped the blood running down from his ear, trying his damnedest to ignore the pain which seemed to be accumulating, and an escalating urge to strangle her.

He had to remind himself every other minute that he needed that witch. Without her, he had no leverage. Nothing. Without her, his brother was doomed.

Without her ... he would be able to breathe.

Raven clenched his fists at the wayward thought, hating himself even more, because deep inside he knew he was close to begging for this singing to stop.

It wasn't just pain that assaulted him, but memories and feelings; and it all gnawed both his body and soul with such intensity, he knew he had only hours, maybe, till he dropped. No matter how steely his resolve.

* * *

Amira sat on the wooden dais, her eyes closed. Every muscle in her body was sore, and her head ached from protecting hundreds of people.

With every word she sang she had to fight exhaustion, but try as she might, she was weakening. The energy she sensed all around her no longer obeyed her. Worse still, she could not stop singing.

This was a punishment, she just knew it. She should never have played that trick on him.

The first time she used magic Raven had almost killed her; then he tied her up, threw her like a sack of grain over his horse. The moment she tried to mess with his mind, he gained control over her. And yet, she was still messing with magic.

Or maybe, for the first time in her existence, magic was messing with her.

Suddenly her arms fell down from their uncomfortable position, and she realized that someone had freed her from the chains. The smallest of hopes had blossomed inside her chest, and withered the moment she saw Owen standing behind her. Her throat closed off.

"Praise the gods!" he spat out, and began dragging her to a more secluded corner. "A beautiful voice you may have, but it's starting to give me a headache."

"Let me go!" she ordered, barely refraining from bursting something up inside his skull. Now that would give him a headache.

"You are in no position to demand anything, my sweet little whore."

Amira decided to focus on the word *little*. She suspected she was actually taller than the man, but who cared at this point. She simply tried not to think about the other word, the name he took such delight in calling her, so she wouldn't forget that using magic right now was too dangerous.

She could die. He would definitely die. Instead, she used all the appendages of her body, tired and aching as they were, to break free.

She dug her nails into his wrists. In response he cursed, and threw her down. A thousand stinging needles pierced her body as she slammed into the ground.

Amira scrambled to her feet, but the moment she got up, Owen grabbed her again and pushed her toward the building.

Disoriented and dizzy, she fought against his hold, but it only tightened. She was pressed between the wall and his body. She was trapped.

He smiled then and took her lips with his.

Amira recoiled. She pushed Owen as violently as she could, determined to free herself. She didn't care about the consequences anymore. If she was to die, so be it, but she was not going to let anyone rape her. Ever.

Her action, however, didn't even faze him. It didn't send him flying ten feet away as she had envisioned.

The scream of anger and frustration rose high in her throat.

She was powerless, damn it! The goddesses had taken her magic. Maybe just for a few minutes, since even gods could not bind the ancient power for long; but the few minutes it normally took her to regain her magic could seem like an eternity.

Amira was tired of their games and tests she had no wish to be a part of. Usually, when her powers were stripped, Venlordians would simply kill her. They never took time with her, never tried to take advantage of her state — at least not after the lifetime in which she became strong enough to defeat them.

Throughout the centuries they had hunted her, and yet never lingered before driving the knife into her heart. It was no coincidence. They knew. Had always known how dangerous she could become within a matter of seconds.

Owen was ignorant of all this. And as such, much more dangerous to her.

He ripped the front of her dress, fumbling in an attempt to grab her breast, and Amira bit his lip, determined not to let this happen. Magic or no magic.

She spat the piece out.

Owen growled, and a moment latter Amira felt a sharp pain as he struck her once, twice. She tasted blood — her own. Her head was ringing. She fell down and moaned.

The next thing she knew, Owen was on top of her,

holding her hands atop her head in a vice-like grip, parting her legs. She could not move. She could not kick, or scratch, or bite; she could only watch as he tried to unbutton his pants with one hand.

"No!" She tried to wriggle. "Stop that!"

"Soon you'll be begging me not to stop." He leered as he leaned over her.

"Get. Off. Me." She screamed, trying to summon her magic, which was still refusing to obey her.

She squirmed and squirmed frantically, trying to shake off his grip, but she was no match for him, probably not even on her best day.

"Stop wriggling, whore," Owen ordered.

Amira spat like an alley-cat—it was the only thing left for her. She could have begged, she supposed, but she knew he would not listen.

"I'll kill you," she vowed, "you rotten piece of—"

Amira got slapped again. At least he wasn't fumbling with his pants. If she had to call him all the vilest things in the world to stall him, even if it earned her a slap, it would be worth it.

"You—"

"Bastard!"

Owen flew through the air, landing ten feet away from her.

Her eyes widened. How could this be? She couldn't access her powers.

"Is that how you thank me, by taking what's mine?" Raven's voice finally reached her.

Amira sighed with relief, though inside she was still screaming. She was not his! Mentioning it, however, didn't seem prudent, especially since Owen was not pawing her anymore.

"If my lord wants a first go, its fine by me. I'll wait."

"Yes, you will." Her unlikely savior's voice was cold, no emotions showing, and it made her question his motives for interfering.

She tried to get up, but the world was spinning, and her legs didn't obey.

"Need help?" He reached for her, but she flinched at his touch.

How dare he be nice and gentle now? Was that a plan of his? She probably wasn't thinking straight, but a splitting headache could do that to a girl. What she needed was to be left alone. To lick her wounds.

"I can manage," Amira murmured. Her pride was still intact, and she was not going to let him see her begging. No matter how much all of this was her own doing. She may have pushed and probed and used too much magic, but she refused to feel guilty. Or ashamed.

"True to the last." Raven shook his head, refusing to listen to her.

Was he mocking her? Amira stepped forward, but her stiff legs stumbled. She fell. Straight into his embrace.

Her first instinct was to jump out of his grip, but then she saw his eyes. There was no mocking in them, only warmth, and despite everything, her body relaxed. Her hands curled around his neck, she cushioned her head on his shoulder, and the shivering stopped.

The strangest feeling overwhelmed her. She didn't care where he was going or what he was going to do with her; in that moment, she felt safe.

"Thank you," she whispered.

For Raven, her gratitude felt like a well-deserved rebuke. He should have known something like this could happen—and that meant he shouldered at least a part of the blame.

He was no saint. Never pretended to be. Raven

might not like what his life had come to be, but with time he had gotten used to the blood on his hands. He didn't shy away from killing monsters anymore. But this... It was one line he knew he would never cross. Nor would he let it happen in his own home.

Raven glanced down. She looked sleepy and peaceful, though the bruises on her cheeks and crusted blood on her lips betrayed her real condition. It was the first time he'd seen her afraid for herself. But instead of the satisfaction and pleasure he thought that would give him, he felt protectiveness. He even felt proud of her in a way he didn't understand. Her courage... She didn't crumble, or beg. She fought.

Slowly he passed the wooden stake, and without a second glance turned for the mansion where Martha was already waiting for him.

Raven ignored the stern look on her face, climbed to the second floor, and headed straight for his own room. Making a beeline for his bed.

He leaned in an attempt to lay her on it, but her hands were locked in a tight grip around his neck. An action that brought a poignant smile to his lips.

Everything was so messed up.

"It's alright," he breathed, "you can let go now."

Amira released her hold.

Despite her earlier resolution to fight to the death, she felt her mind drifting away. Her body felt so weak she could barely keep her eyes open. Figuring what was going to happen next was so beyond her, a part of her didn't even care.

Either way, reading Raven was next to impossible, and considering her spinning head ... she gasped as their gazes locked, and every last doubt she might have had died in mid-air. For the first time she didn't see hatred looking back at her, only concern and guilt.

"Out!" a sharp voice interrupted, severing the link between them.

Amira tried to gather the pieces of what was once called a dress and stand up, figuring it was her someone had a problem with; but could barely move. Instead, it was Raven who stood up.

"If you hadn't noticed, it is still my room, Martha." Amira looked around, her eyes instantly going to a beautiful blade hanging on the opposite wall.

"And you brought her here, because…?" The old woman kept her hands on her hips, staring Raven down.

"You would prefer me to take her to the stables?"

Martha eased a little. "Out," she repeated.

"I'm going, I'm going." Raven stepped towards the door. "I still have a small matter to attend to," then looking over his shoulder added, "give her something to wear."

Amira could only imagine how she must look. Her dress was torn and dirty, her hair—an unruly mess—and she was very grateful she could not see her face. The bruises hurt, though.

"Good heavens girl, just look at you," the woman approached, sat down and, gathering Amira's jaw in her palms, examined the beaten face. Her friendly brown eyes smiled sadly.

"I raised him better than this. To leave you to that criminal … I don't care that he's too old to be spanked," the woman said vehemently.

That, she would pay to witness, Amira yawned, her sore, exhausted body refusing to stay awake for another minute. She shifted in his bed, and closed her eyes.

The pain vanished.

Chapter 10

Amira awoke in the middle of the night, for a few moments struggling to remember where she was, or what she was doing in this room. It was definitely not hers. It was Raven's, she soon realized.

She also remembered how Martha had helped her bathe, brought dresses that looked fit to be worn by a queen rather than a maid, and then left her to rest.

Slowly, Amira climbed out of the bed. She donned a beautiful crystalline silk night dress, and, holding onto the ledges of the furniture, walked to the bookcase.

She drew out the first leather-covered book, only to read the words "Black Magic" on the dusty cover. She withdrew another, then another—they all looked the same. "Magic", "witchcraft", "witches"; all the covers had some mixture of these words. Several even sported all of them.

The man was obsessed. No wonder he kept a stake in his yard, a sword on his hip, and an amulet of Arushna on his chest.

And now a witch in his bedroom…

For what purpose? Amira wondered. If his sister had been murdered by Venlordians, it stood to reason he should be hunting them. And judging by the protection charm around his neck, he hadn't been sitting on his hands. There was no other way to obtain the amulet than by pulling it off the dead man.

Why did he even need it? The amulet of Arushna

didn't protect from sword wounds. Again, her thoughts went back to the witches and his hatred. What role did she play in all of this?

If he were simply hunting witches, she would have been dead by now. But every time he had an urge to strangle her, he refrained. Unless … unless it was not her head he needed. Amira remembered a witch from his dream.

So she was here to lure her out—finally pieces began to fall into place. Which led Amira to the next question: was she supposed to help him murder a witch, or was she to stop it?

The reflection of the moonlight on the surface of a steel blade caught her gaze and Amira bit her lip. She winced when her teeth scratched at the wound; her eyes however, didn't leave the sword. It appeared to be mocking her, baiting her to use the opportunity. An opportunity to die, she all but snorted.

Amira had no strength to lift it. Even if she had, for the life of her, she didn't know how to wield a blade this long. Swords had never been the weapons of her choice. But for a fleeting moment she allowed herself to entertain a fantasy of crossing the room, taking the sword into her hands and by some miracle managing to hold Raven at the sharp end of it. For what purpose?

Hers was a fight won not on a battle field. Gaining a secret was not the same as defeating a foe in combat. Except, she had no idea how to proceed. As the past events attested to, she couldn't force herself to rip his mind open; which left her with what?

Discarding the jumbled thoughts that threatened to gift her with another headache, Amira focused her attention on the bookshelves.

After a long and diligent search, she found a small, paper-covered book free of spells and enchantments. She rifled through the well-worn pages, her eyes still searching, until she recognized a poem she'd heard a very long time ago.

I walked through the night like a shadow,
I held no one close to my heart,
Until the day that you reached me
Until you banished the dark.

Amira had always loved those lines.

"No one will hear it." A familiar male voice reached her, and she nearly jumped out of her skin. She hadn't realized she'd spoken out loud.

Amira turned around to find Raven standing twenty feet away from her, leaning against the door with one of her quickly forgotten books in his hand.

His ivory shirt was open at the neck, exposing well-developed pectorals. Yet curiously, she didn't see the amulet. What she did notice was his neatly shaved jaw, and tousled ebony hair.

Amira had an imprudent urge to bury her fingers in his hair, but instead of obliterating the distance between them, she leaned against the window.

"It seems to me someone did hear it."

He said nothing, but the glimpse of sadness she caught in his eyes affected her more strongly than any words could have.

Her heartbeat sped up, and she was grateful for the support behind her back. With those mesmerizing midnight eyes burning into her, she felt weak in the legs.

"So did the Lord finally decide which it would be," she uttered, both tired of the unknown, and needing distance — despite the whole room between them.

"I beg your pardon?" Confusion stretched Raven's face taut.

"A sword through my heart, or ravishing me and

throwing me to the dogs, as Owen suggested?" Amira asked, hoping to unveil something, anything, about his intentions. "I am entitled to know my fate."

Raven placed the book back in its proper place, and smirked. "And which one would you prefer?"

Amira froze, uncertain of what she was getting into this time. The only clear thing was that she wouldn't get her answers.

"You mean to tell me I can choose?" She finally found her voice. Which was somewhat of a miracle, considering that his eyes were trained back on her.

"I wish to know if you would prefer death to my touch," he asked, closing distance between them.

Amira hoped he wouldn't notice how her legs were trembling. Trying to stand her ground, she tilted her chin higher, and refusing to surrender, met his bold gaze with hers.

"What am I supposed to say? I'd sooner die than surrender my virtue? According to you, I'm sure I have none."

"You don't?" he inquired, reaching for her.

"Some. Maybe." Her answer caused a raised eyebrow.

"So?"

"So, I don't want to die," she breathed deeply as his fingers trailed down her neck, "but I refuse to lie with a man who hates every little thing about me."

"A wise answer," he admitted, giving nothing more than a simple, gentle touch with the tips of his fingers. She felt it to the core of her essence though. Then leaning closer, only an inch from her lips, he whispered, "but not a choice."

Amira felt her traitorous nipples harden. His lips were co close, she shivered with anticipation. Yet the kiss was not coming.

"Then I guess my fate is in your hands," she

whispered back, biting her lip to stifle a moan from leaving her mouth. She ached so badly.

A few more moments and she would have begged for the thing she refused. Fortunately, Raven had more sense than she did. Not that she thought herself fortunate at the moment.

He stepped back, releasing her, and breaking the moment.

In a way, Amira realized, she had won a small victory; only instead of delight she felt loss. Her body was still aching for him and her heart wished he could see the real her, and not what he wanted to see.

Biting her lower lip even harder, she turned from him. Out of sight, out of mind. Or so she hoped.

"So what exactly did you come here for?" Her voice was no longer breathless—maybe irritated a bit—and Raven found himself studying her reflection.

Even bruised, she was a sight to behold. Especially standing near the window, wearing nothing but a gossamer silk gown that seemed almost see-through against the moon light.

"Despite Martha kicking me out, this is still my room," he said, reluctant to reveal the real reason he had waited for the whole house to drown in sleep before sneaking in.

He had felt ridiculous, creeping into his own room like a thief afraid to be caught because he wished to avoid a possible confrontation. Yet confrontation would have been welcome compared to what he'd encountered.

Those damned lines had shot through him like a jolt of lightning, forcing long-lost memories to resurface. For one second he could have sworn he'd been transported back to a time when both he and Dacian had wanted for nothing more than to escape their mother reading from her favorite book for the thousandth time. Yet the memory had vanished, leaving only the woman in front of him.

"And does Martha treat you like one of her subjects often?" Her question almost made him smile.

"Let's say I fell from her good grace by binding you," he confessed, focusing his attention on the chest of drawers.

"Well, I am sorry to hear about your discomfort," she retorted angrily. "Try sleeping while chained to that pole."

Raven stopped rummaging through the second drawer, and glanced over his shoulder. She had finally turned, and her narrowed eyes were throwing daggers at him. She exuded this power that felt as tangible as the handle of the drawer he held. It flowed, wave after wave. But despite her emotions appearing violative, the energy he sensed felt more like a caress than a slap.

"Try looking in your nightstand," she suggested.

Raven slowly walked to the other corner of the room and opened the first drawer. On top of the huddle of papers lay his amulet. He gaped. "How did you know?"

"I'll tell you my secrets if you'll tell me yours," she offered.

"Maybe some other time." He fastened the amulet around his neck, but before he could take a step toward the door, she moved closer.

"What about your bruised knuckles?"

"It's nothing." Raven tried to hide them and the knife wound across his hand, but it was already too late.

"I don't remember seeing it earlier," she arched her brow in a questioning frown, determination showing in every inch of her face. "What happened?"

"Nothing," he repeated. Nothing at all. His fist had simply decided to punch a wall the moment he'd left her battered body in his bed, and then merge with a very stiff skull.

Raven didn't know how he'd managed to control himself when he'd found Owen hurting her. Or how he'd managed to breathe the whole way to his bedroom with her curled in his arms. Maybe he hadn't breathed. For all he remembered now, was the rage he'd been choking on. As the result, he'd beaten the crap out of Owen and had told him to gather his things and leave.

Raven didn't want her to know any of it. He didn't want his witch to realize how much she affected him, but when she looked at the wound understanding lit in her eyes.

"A small matter?" she asked without smiling or gloating.

"The smallest."

She looked at him as if digesting the information, and then she reached for his arm, "Can I?"

"There's nothing you can do." He tried to dodge her touch, only to find his palm in hers.

"That only proves how little you know," came the reply, and glancing toward the bookcase she added, "despite all your books."

Raven was on the point of objecting, when a sudden warmth took all his words away. The feeling was stupefying, like a bolt of energy surging through his veins. Fever fully overwhelmed him. Scorching flames licked his hand.

He could not explain why, but worry was the last thought to cross his mind. Right then, all he was was curious.

"All done," she breathed unsteadily.

Raven looked at his arm — not a single scratch. Then at her — a pale, fatigued face came into his view. He noticed her riotous respiration, her trembling body, and had a feeling she was fighting a war to keep herself upright. He knew she would never admit it. So without a single word he swept her in his arms and carried to the bed.

"How… Why… You are white as a sheet," he finally said.

"I guess I didn't realize how weak I was for such a trick," she murmured in a sleep-laden voice.

"Rest now," he told her, rising from his bed.

Somehow he ended up in the empty corridors, wandering. His head was splitting from all the unanswered questions and feelings he had. The witch was right in saying he knew little. None of those books mentioned anything vaguely similar to what he had just experienced.

They all spoke of thousands of unimaginable ways to destroy body, mind, and even soul. But not a single one of them suggested the possibility of healing. He didn't think it was feasible until he saw it with his very eyes. "A trick," she'd said — a miracle more likely.

Why did she do it, if it cost her so heavily?

She was an enigma who chose love poems instead of the craft books. A prisoner who healed his wounds, and a temptation the like of which he'd never encountered before.

She was a witch he should not want to touch, yet craved every moment, even in full knowledge of what it could cost him. It was madness, the way she was conquering his mind. The more he knew her, the more he was intrigued. And even though he would never admit it, he admired her spirit and strength. Not many would've been able to stand their ground after everything that had happened.

Raven raked his hand through his hair, wishing he could understand her.

I'll tell you my secrets if you'll tell me yours, she'd said.

It meant opening his heart, releasing all the demons he fought so hard to keep at bay. Even worse, letting her in, allowing her to poke at the darkest corners of his soul. The bargain was not acceptable to him.

He'd lost too much to pretend. He'd sacrificed his life to the only person who mattered—his brother. He could not jeopardize Dacian's wellbeing.

It was Raven's fault Dacian was the way he was. Raven's fault Dacian was captured by a witch and tortured till his mind fractured. Every time he thought about his brother his heart bled with pain and guilt. That's why he needed to tie her to the stake again, to do whatever it was necessary for him to get to Ethely. The problem was—he couldn't.

Maybe it could still work, he figured. Her being in his bedroom...

People tended to blow stories out of proportion, after all, and by the following week it would definitely be the case of a young witch chained to his bed for the things he didn't even want to imagine. Or he would never be able to sleep again.

He just needed a few guards for her, since he couldn't watch her every moment. Neither did he want to. Too much of a distraction.

Tomorrow, he thought. Today she was going nowhere.

Chapter 11

"We need to send word to the Lord and Lady St. Clair," Giles suggested.

"No," Natalie interrupted him. "My uncle and aunt have enough on their minds right now. What we need is to find Amira."

"But we searched everywhere we could." Logan raised his grey-green eyes—a few shades darker than his sister's—and still no one could see his guilty expression from under shoulder-length blond hair. He barely looked directly at people anymore.

"Our inquiries are turning up new questions we can't answer," Ciaran said, pacing the length of the room, his thoughts darting erratically. The gaze from his dark brown eyes jumping from person to person.

"She is a witch, and by law…" he paused, cursing the damned law, the ignorant people, even the king, who became a puppet in the hands of the Order years ago. "We can't draw more attention, it would only seal her doom—that is if she is not already…"

"Stop that!" Natalie shouted. "She is not dead, she can't be."

"Then where is she?" Ciaran asked, barely managing to keep his wrath under control. Nothing was going the way he wanted. He couldn't find Amira the day she vanished, when there was less than a mile between them; and now, after three days of searching high and low, desperation was taking hold of him.

"I don't know," said Natalie, her eyes filling with tears for the hundredth time in the past few days. She quickly blinked them away.

"That's great!" Ciaran lifted his hands in frustration. "And who the hell knows?"

"Stop it!" This time it was Logan's voice that echoed inside the four walls of the study they were gathered in, succeeding in drawing everyone's attention.

"How do you think it makes me feel? I was the one who let him take her away. I was the helpless one! He overpowered me with such ease…" Logan's voice trailed off and he lowered his head again.

Damn, Ciaran almost kicked himself. Control your temper, he ordered. Logan was still too young for any of this. His brother didn't need the guilt for something that wasn't his fault.

"We need to gather our thoughts, not argue," Giles suggested, looked at his sister, and asked, "miss, could you tell us everything again? Maybe there was something we overlooked. A detail that seemed unimportant?"

Natalie retold her story with eyes closed, as if she was trying to relive it in order to remember the smallest detail. But at the end it wasn't helpful, and Ciaran felt frustration creeping up on him again.

"The description of the tall dark stranger with a black horse and a sword really helps us," Ciaran snorted, though he had to admit his brother couldn't offer much more. More importantly, what really mattered was an amulet of Arushna Natalie had mentioned. Which meant Amira was utterly helpless.

And if he was a Venlordian, she was far worse than doomed.

"I just know one thing," she insisted: "Amira is alive, I feel it, and…" Natalie's voice sharpened a tone, "you may think otherwise, Ciaran, but she can take care of herself—she has the power."

"And you are delusional," he whispered under his breath.

"One day you'll regret you weren't nicer to your sister," a familiar voice drifted into the conversation, catching him off guard.

Ciaran pivoted, fast on his heels, searching for the source of the sound, yet encountering nothing but an empty space.

He was about to demand for the person, creature, whoever it was, to show herself, when a translucent figure flickered inside the doorframe, revealing the face of a woman he had known since both of them were children.

He failed. Ciaran's fist landed on a huge, oak desk, the sound deafening to his own ears.

"Dear gods," Natalie covered her mouth with her palms. After a moment, sobs broke from deep inside her, spilling copious fresh tears onto her cheeks.

"She's dead," someone gasped.

"Don't cry." Amira took a step toward Natalie. "Despite the appearances, I am very much alive."

"Then where are you?" Ciaran demanded, still confused by what he was seeing.

Amira shook her head in a blatant refusal to answer.

"Where are you?" he repeated, gritting his teeth. He leaned on the desk, letting his hands support his weight, and stared her down, daring her to refuse again.

"Don't come after me," she said instead.

"You have got to be kidding me!" Ciaran violently pushed himself off the surface of the furniture and strode toward her with no real plan of what he was going to do.

"I've had it with your constant disappearances," he all but shoved his finger into her face. "You listen to me carefully—"

"Don't look for me," Amira continued as if she hadn't been interrupted. "Trust me, please," she added, and vanished, leaving him dumbstruck.

Ciaran ripped at his hair with his fingers, barely restraining himself from pulling out a tuft of it. If she thought he was going to sit and wait, she was sorely mistaken.

"We go after." Logan stated, not even pretending it could be a question.

"We go after." Ciaran nodded.

* * *

Amira inhaled deeply, keenly aware of a sluggish return into her battered, exhausted body. She exhaled and had to dig her nails in, to prevent herself from leaving with the gush of air. She swayed back, landing on a soft mattress, her arms and legs splayed across the bed.

Deadened with fatigue, Amira stared at the ceiling, watching vision after vision play against the smooth surface. She saw Ciaran heading to the stables in another attempt to find her. Saw him succeeding, instinctively knowing his rescue to be a disaster in disguise.

No need to panic, she assured herself. There was still time to prevent it. If she could muster enough energy.

She should never have spirit-walked in such a condition, especially since she knew her pleas would fall on deaf ears.

What had possessed her? Where was this need to ease the minds of people she barely knew coming from?

Amira was overwrought by feelings she found hard to comprehend. Or control. Feelings that compelled her to find her parents and ascertain their wellbeing.

She closed her eyes and separated herself from her body with such an ease, she froze for a moment to consider the risks.

The process had been too swift. As if her essence was ready to leave her body permanently. Yet the nagging presentiment she had was stronger than the fear. Her only regret was that she couldn't sing. She didn't want to alert people to what she was doing this early in the morning.

Amira reached with her senses as far as she could, grateful to the blood ties for keeping her on a straight path, and found them in a shady inn with her uncle Regan and cousin Pharell.

She neared them, keeping herself invisible. She was curious as to what could they be doing in such an unusual place.

"Why didn't you bring Amira?" Regan whispered, though his voice was anything but gentle.

"I am not about to jeopardize the life of my daughter," her father calmly said. "I would have thought you could understand that."

Such protectiveness, Amira almost rolled her eyes. Deron was a good man, but keeping her tucked away under lock and key was something Amira had never appreciated.

"I do understand," the king's voice interrupted her thought, "but wouldn't you wish for the same if you were in my shoes?"

Her father stood silently, in a way answering the question.

"I prepared as many potions as I could," Eliana said, taking Regan's hand to comfort him. "The amulets won't save them."

"We will get your wife and daughter back," her father added.

"So let's go," Pharell finally spoke, taking his eyes from the corridor for a second.

Amira could sense fear and anxiousness in him. The first one was only natural, but the second surprised her. Her cousin was always the silent and logical one. He thought things through a hundred times before acting on them. He didn't rush into anything. Ever. Impulsive, rash and anxious were simply not in his vocabulary. He was as calm as Ciaran was hotheaded, though she supposed his mother and sister being in danger changed many things.

Even the steady gaze she was so used to flickered with emotions she had never seen before. He was burning inside and out, his control on a very short leash.

Amira's heartbeat grew stronger, faster, and she realized that she wasn't in better shape than he was. She was on the verge of exposing herself—or even disappearing, she knew not which—because her emotions were getting the better of her.

Breathe, she ordered herself, knowing how tenuous her control was. If she let it slip, she wouldn't be able to help anyone, especially not her family.

Her family—the words rang in Amira's ears. An answer to the questions she had asked before. She'd had many families, yet she rarely let herself get attached. It wasn't worth it, Amira had always reasoned, yet these people managed to get under her skin somehow.

"We won't help them if we're caught," Eliana tried to sound calm, something Amira knew she didn't feel right now.

"We can't risk waiting any longer," Pharell almost yelled, his fingers clenching into fists. "My mother and sister are with those bastards. What do you think they are doing to them, aunt?" He all but spat his words, his blue eyes burning with rage.

Pharell left his spot by the door and began pacing

back and forth, his hip-length braid swishing like a whip through the air every time he made a hasty turn. He was on the edge. The smallest squeak, and in a second his hands were guaranteed to land on the handles of his two long slim blades that were crossed on his back.

"Pharell," Regan breathed in warning, "as long as we do what we're told, they are safe. Safe," he added one more time, as if to convince himself rather than his son.

Amira sighed. She could have freed them in a matter of hours. Not in this form though. Not when she could only affect their minds for a handful of moments. And considering the distance…

If only she were free.

What good were all these powers if she couldn't run from a place where no one was capable of holding her? Amira knew that the moment she escaped she would be signing her own death warrant. She would sooner be struck by lightning, or fall off the horse and break her neck than reach her destination. And what good would that do for any of them? No, she needed to work on Raven and hope the women survived till then. Hope *she* survived till then.

"I still have a few people I can trust," the king continued, "but we can't strike for another few days. There's a whole army of them down there right now. But according to my source they are planning to move. Most of them anyway. Something big must be happening for them to concentrate such forces. When they leave, we go in."

Amira stared at them as they analyzed the passages on the dungeon map, trying to find the safest escape route, when she heard stairs creaking, and she knew.

"They are approaching," Amira whispered a warning for her mother's ears alone, and moved to intercept the

danger.

If the king was caught conspiring against the Order, the whole royal family would be sentenced to death. She could not allow it.

But despite her determination, Amira felt her form flicker. She was too weak to generate a distraction that would last. A minute at most — even that seemed to demand a miracle.

She took a deep breath in and stretched out her hands, not even looking as her family ran the other way. Finally she could see the Venlordians. Damn. And double damn. There were ten of them.

She concentrated hard and entered their minds. All at the same time. They stopped. Shook their heads, confused at what was happening, not understanding the sudden emptiness around them.

Amira would have kept them immobile a bit longer, but the amulets were draining her, and the strongest of them was already starting to see walls around him.

She had to draw back. Instead, she inhaled one last time and sent another wave through them.

As soon as it left her, she stumbled, almost falling to the knees, her own mind dizzy. She had reached her limit, she knew it. She needed to return to her body as soon as possible. Only it was so far, and without the singing she was losing her path. There was nothing to guide her.

Bright Eyes... she heard a faint echo. *Bright Eyes, wake up...*

Amira opened her eyes, recognizing Martha's voice as the woman shook her shoulders. She was so grateful for her good timing, she didn't realize her powers were still unleashed. Martha's initiated contact had acted like a catalyst and, before she knew what had happened, a memory sprung up out of the hidden corner of the woman's mind.

"I won't let her take you," Martha whispered, trying to hide the boy.

Fear in dark eyes met her gaze.

Martha stumbled back and the connection was severed. The memory disappeared. The woman turned paler than a sheet, forcing Amira to use even more energy to reverse the damage she'd inadvertently caused. Energy she could hardly spare.

Her essence refused to merge completely with her physical body after the return. And now, she found herself on the verge of drifting away.

"You alright, child?" Pale brown eyes met Amira's.

"Yes," she reassured her, glad the little incident had gone undetected. "I was probably a bit more tired than I thought." The understatement of the century.

Amira still wanted to know what had happened to the boy from the vision, but the woman's mind had already been tampered with. By an amateur, no less. Given Martha's advanced age and Amira's state, she simply didn't dare. She wouldn't have dared, even if she wasn't so weak.

"Come, you need to eat." The woman was already standing up and waiting for her to get up, dress, and follow.

Well, the good news was—Amira's condition wasn't too obvious. The bad news—if she didn't find a way to unite her essence with her body once again, and soon, she wouldn't last long. Especially if she needed to use magic.

"Won't there be trouble?" Amira asked, not having the slightest wish to get up from such a fine bed. Wishing, however, was a luxury she rarely enjoyed.

"Don't be silly, child," Martha smiled, and handed her a gown. "What is the worst that could happen?"

"I could think of a few things," Amira replied, taking the garment. Slowly, she donned the light-blue gown, not sparing it a second glance. It could have been rags for all she cared. She was dressed, and that was enough.

Amira followed the woman out of the room and down the stairs, aware that she herself was being followed the whole time. She'd expected it. What she didn't expect, though, was a banquet prepared for her as if she were an honorable guest rather than a prisoner.

Amira ate quickly. She didn't feel she had the strength for another encounter. But the moment she stood up, she came face to face with Raven.

Their gazes collided. She gasped.

She saw confusion. Desire. She saw emotions waging a battle.

For a moment she lost herself in a myriad of sensations. Then suddenly the air around her changed. His gaze hardened.

"Take. It. Off." Raven mouthed silently. But the impact of those clipped, stern words was far stronger than if he'd been shouting.

There was no fire burning in his gaze anymore. Only cold, unyielding determination to rip every last ruffle off of her if she didn't comply immediately.

His order had nothing to do with him wanting to see her naked, and everything with the fact that in his mind she had just defiled this beautiful gown.

Why did Martha give it to her? A question formed in Amira's head the same instant she saw Raven turn his attention to the woman, who, despite his obvious anger, stood as relaxed as ever. Even with a small wry smile on her lips.

"You crossed the line," was all he said to her, before turning back to Amira.

"Was I not clear?" he asked, swallowing up the few feet that lay between them.

"Crystal clear," Amira uttered, more than willing to

give the garment back. It was not worth fighting over it.

"Lady Catherine would've loved to—" Martha began but was not able to finish her sentence.

"Don't you dare tell me what my mother would or would not have loved to give to a witch. Don't you fucking dare!" he yelled at her, his restraint breaking down completely.

Amira felt as if she were intruding. She truly wished she hadn't gotten up from her bed today. But before she could do anything, another voice entered into the mix.

"My lord, my lord!" Judy ran inside, as if she was being chased by an axe murderer.

"My lord!" The girl trembled like the last leaf in a cold autumn breeze, and everyone turned to the maid, the damned drama with the dress now forgotten.

"Take a deep breath in." Raven pulled a chair for the girl, and it amazed Amira that not a shadow of his anger seeped into his words. "Now, breathe out and tell me what happened."

Judy did as she was told, and after wiping off the tears, whispered, "Owen, my lord. He didn't leave."

Raven pinched the bridge of his nose, as if knowing the day was about to get even worse. "And?" he prompted.

"He murdered Nyssa," Judy confirmed his fears.

Chapter 12

Amira rushed after Raven, the three barely audible words Judy had uttered roaring like a thunder inside her head.

He murdered Nyssa.

She hastened her pace and almost bumped into Raven, as he came to a sudden halt.

Masses of people were gathered around. For Raven, the crowd separated at once, letting him pass. Amira, however, had to fight her way through the mob, reaching the middle of it just in time to hear the morbid news.

"I'm very sorry," Raven whispered, placing his hand on the shoulder of the weeping woman. She cowered and hugged the limp frame of a young girl tighter, closer to her heart.

"Why?" she creamed in anguish. "Why?"

It was a gruesome sight that Amira witnessed. Blood and sorrow, despair and bewilderment. She glanced at Raven, whose face was taut with anger and sadness. His eyes sharp in a way she'd never seen before. She studied Nyssa's pale skin and huge empty eyes, and gasped.

"There's still hope."

Amira's words weren't received kindly. Nyssa's mother lifted her head and grief turned into pure hatred.

"It's all because of you, witch!" She spat out the last word with such scorn, it sent shivers down Amira's spine.

"My Nyssa tried to help you. You killed her. You!" the woman yelled. "It should be you, not her! Not my baby!"

Amira tried to ignore her, concentrating on the angel of death. He was lulling Nyssa's body into an eternal slumber and calling her soul to follow him.

"No!" she yelled, in forlorn hopes of pushing the Grim Reaper away. For as long as the essence clung to its mortal vessel, Amira could change the outcome. In theory.

He didn't even blink. The angel continued his ministrations on his latest victim, Amira's voice obviously having no effect on him.

"Move!" she ordered, this time gazing at the people. The weaker ones obeyed; others didn't. Damn, but she was too weak herself.

What are you doing? Traynan's silky words almost strangled her. *I don't want to be forced to take you too.*

"What is the meaning of this?" Raven demanded, his eyes narrowing at her.

Amira ignored Tray's question, focusing on Raven. "Trust me, please," she breathed the phrase the second time that day, not even knowing why. Her cousin didn't listen, so what was the chance Raven would?

Still, she stretched her hands and made a pushing gesture. It seemed like she was trying to push a ton of bricks, but she succeeded in separating herself from the mob.

Her breaths became rapid, shallow. She kept her arm raised in their direction, afraid that if she lowered it, the barrier would unravel. She needed every last ounce of energy she could muster. Even then, Amira was not sure she would have enough.

As if to prove her point, people began shouting, banging on the shield. It felt more like banging on her head. Her legs wobbled and she felt her knees slamming into the ground.

What are you doing? Traynan's fingers stopped in his tracks and the numbness began to spread through her own flesh. *Don't do this!*

"Leave ... her ... alone." Amira's throat constricted from coldness.

"Who are you talking with?" Raven roared at her.

You won't save her...

Body shaking, she dug her fingers deep into the ground, trying to push herself up, take as much power as she could while still holding the shield. She needed energy. Needed to get up...

Stop this and you will still be able to save yourself ... please.

"Too late," she whispered, standing up. Maybe dying wouldn't be that bad if she did at least one good deed in her life.

"You ... won't ... take ... her..." she gritted her teeth, absorbing as much raw energy as her weakened body could allow. It was too raw. Too potent. Amira's whole body quaked from the pressure. She inhaled deeply and her knees gave out, sending her to the ground again. And still, she needed more.

"What the hell is going on?" Raven demanded for the tenth time.

Trust me, she'd said. No explanations. Nothing. He was taking an enormous leap of faith here. If normally he would have put an end to this whole spectacle the second it started, something in her eyes stopped him. There was such a raw determination, such power—he could swear he felt it tingling on his own skin. But what affected him the most was not the lack of malice in her eyes, but the sad resignation carved in the lines of her face.

He ignored the people shouting from the other side of the barrier she had obviously created. He ignored the pleas of Nyssa's mother, Mode, and touched his amulet. It was the only reason he stood on this side.

Raven sighed. Apparently he was jumping. May the gods have mercy on him.

"You have ten seconds to convince me," he told her.

It took only one. She brushed her fingers along his knuckles and he understood everything.

She exhaled and collapsed again. This time, Raven caught her. He cradled her, at a loss as to why her fingers were ice cold.

"How dangerous is this?"

"Like a walk in the park," she ... lied.

He remembered how easily she had created the shield the day they met, and witnessed the toll it took on her today. What about healing? Yesterday she almost fainted from healing a single scratch; today ... she was going to die.

"At least you will get your gown back," she scoffed as she tried to stand up.

Was that supposed to be funny or comforting? Raven could read the truth straight from her face, and it didn't scream confidence at all. It didn't even whisper. It merely stated plainly he would get the gown back. Soon. Strangely enough, it was not the gown he was thinking of at that moment.

"Can I help?"

"You want to help *me*?"

"I don't want Nyssa to die," Raven assured her.

She looked at him for a second, then nodded. "Put me near Nyssa, place one hand on the tree-trunk, and give me the other one."

"What am I to do?"

"You have to keep me grounded." The answer didn't explain anything to him. Grounded? How?

"I cannot absorb any more raw energy. You will need to filter it for me, and if the time comes you'll know … *when* the time comes," she rectified herself, placing one hand in his, the other on Nyssa. "But whatever you do, don't let go of me, unless you wish both of us dead," she said, and closed her eyes.

In an instant Raven felt warmth rippling through him, reminding him of the night she'd healed his fist. Only this time the energy was coming from the tree.

Wave after wave, the heat traveled through his skin and seeped under it. The heat raged and grew until it consumed him in scorching blazes. Until he yearned for nothing but to free himself from this insufferable inferno.

How can she stand it? Raven wondered, seeing the witch's serene expression. He could swear he was being burned alive.

He held on, suffering a relentless series of searing energy rushes, desperate for it to cease. Yet it didn't. It swirled and swirled, devouring every inch of him.

Something has gone terribly wrong, a voice inside him whispered. Except, Nyssa looked better and better with every moment, forcing Raven to doubt his senses.

Nyssa opened her eyes and took a deep breath in.

"Go," he told her, concentrating on a woman whose flesh was cold as ice. Lifeless. While he burned with a fever he could barely endure.

Raven reached for her cheek and trailed his finger along the edge of her jaw, fascinated and at the same time alarmed at the burning trace he left behind.

In a flash Raven perceived three things: she had healed Nyssa, exhausting her own energy; what she needed was at his disposal; and, she would die if he didn't find a way to pass it on to her.

Her sacrifice was hard for him to swallow. Unfathomable. But witch or not, no one deserved to die for helping another.

Raven placed his palm on her neck, waiting for it to do the trick. Her skin began to turn back to normal around his palm. The heat spread outwards. Yet she remained numb, her flesh frosty.

It wasn't enough.

He was losing her; the thought pierced his heart like a dagger.

Not knowing what else to do, he cupped the back of her neck and, angling her head, lowered his mouth onto hers.

He kissed her with an urgent desperation, sparing nothing but his soul; losing everything except his craving for more.

"Raven," she whispered after a few moments.

He reared back. Their eyes met, and he became transfixed by her earnest gaze.

"Am I turning into a frog?" she asked.

"Now that offends me."

"I was kissed by Owen, wasn't I?" She shuddered and an inexplicable desire to comfort her overwhelmed him.

"At least I have my lips intact." He tried to keep it light.

Her eyes lowered to his lips, but there was nothing light about her gaze. It was hot. Intense. It brought back the memory of the kiss.

"For a man who claims to hate me, you sure save me a lot." She sounded breathless.

"Are you complaining?"

"On the contrary," she assured him. "Though I would like to know why?"

"Maybe I still need you alive."

"Oh!" her lips curved in a perfect circle, "and I thought it was because you liked me. How utterly disappointing…"

He didn't hear the ending. Suddenly the repercussions of this whole debacle struck him like a rearing horse. People had seen her free, and there was no changing that, no way of stopping the gossip from spreading. Was his brother doomed?

"They will come, don't worry."

"What?" Raven tried to understand her words, but had a hard time focusing.

"Witches," she replied, wriggling out of his embrace, "they are coming."

How could she know it, he almost asked, but her stated conditions were clear. A secret for a secret. He felt as if she was doing this on purpose. Teasing him, letting him steal a quick glimpse of dessert, but leaving him with a bitter taste of overgenerously peppered broth. Well, no matter. He believed her on this matter — or maybe he just needed to believe — because the only other possibility was unacceptable.

"Where are you going?" he asked, finally releasing her.

"Why, to change, of course," she said seriously. "I believe you wanted the gown back."

"Keep it." He stood up and turned for the house as well. "It's yours."

She looked at him, gave the smallest of nods and disappeared inside the house, leaving him bewildered.

How did she do that? How did a simple gesture manage to affect him so? But then, he knew. Raven felt this connection he wouldn't have been able to express or explain from the moment he'd kissed her. He felt the truth in her voice, and gratitude in her heart. Still, a part of him couldn't help but wonder if this was not a spell.

Raven tightly grasped the amulet he carried around his neck, and wished to all the gods he could trust his senses. Because lately, he wasn't himself.

Was he so weak, Raven pondered, that the slightest touch could distract him from his goals? His will so frail that the smallest kiss could make him forget who he was?

The smallest. Indeed. Raven would have laughed, only there was nothing funny about it. Just as there was nothing small about the kiss.

Even now he was staring at the closed door, too absorbed in his own thoughts to notice the lack of sounds and people. This had to stop.

Daydreaming got you killed. Raven turned and marched toward the huts, looking for any sign of living. All he could find was locked doors and closed shutters.

He knocked on the first door. No answer. Tried for the next—still nothing. He was about to yell when Burt stepped out of a nearby house looking relieved, as if an immense burden had been lifted from his shoulders.

"My lord," the man exclaimed, "we thought she would most certainly kill you! When the fiery circle claimed you…"

"Fiery circle?" Raven asked, trying to make sense of the man's words. "Why did you barricade yourselves?"

"At first we couldn't get past the barrier, and when Nyssa ran to us, the circle of fire enfolded you." Burt touched his forehead. "It instantly expanded, exploding straight into us."

"So you ran." Raven finished Burt's thought. The man just looked to the floor, not able to look him in the eye, ashamed of himself.

"I am so—"

"Don't!" Raven interrupted his apology. "You did the right thing."

Who knew what would have happened if Burt, or

any other, had stayed. It was dangerous times they lived in, and by bringing a witch here he magnified the risks tenfold. He was confident he could keep himself safe, but what about the others? He could not guarantee anything at this point. Especially since he had mixed feelings about her.

And maybe because he had mixed feelings people had to be careful.

"Where is Owen?" he asked, changing the subject.

"Dead," the man informed him. "Was stabbed while trying to escape."

Raven rubbed his brow, thinking on how some days needed a do-over. At least no one would miss Owen. He had no family or friends. Maybe in Areth people wore cravats and fancied themselves as civilized beings, but here no one even blinked or asked questions when a man disappeared. Sometimes he thought the ones living in the capital didn't even know what the hell was going on. It was the only explanation he could give for the king's silence, and his reluctance to interfere while the Order operated as it pleased.

"We will take care of the body," Burt interrupted his thoughts.

Raven nodded. "One more thing…"

Burt stopped in his tracks.

"I would like to see Nyssa."

The man pivoted, gesturing with his hand toward the nearby hut. "Of course."

Raven lowered his head to enter the small wooden construction containing only one room and a closet-sized kitchen. The shabby cloths separating the sleeping corner were pulled apart to make more room. Still, people were crammed in the shack like an apple stuffing in the seasonal duck. And in the middle of the chattering throng lay a girl, squirming and protesting.

He immediately noticed Nyssa's desperate attempts

to get up, and the effort her mother put into keeping her tucked in bed. For a woman whose daughter had survived such an ordeal, she didn't look pleased—in fact, she looked more distressed than happy.

"Is she alright?"

"My lord," the girl's mother gasped, "we thought … I mean we saw … uh … she must rest—"

"I am fine," Nyssa raised her voice, interrupting her mother's incoherent prattling. "More than fine. I've never felt so good in my entire life."

"I am glad to hear it." And he was. Nyssa was a sweet, courageous girl he often imagined his sister would have been like. If she'd lived. Real pity her mother was such an angry, suspicious woman, who kept her children on the tightest of leashes.

Raven had offered help many times. After all, children deserved better than a leaking roof over their heads, rags for clothing, and rumbling stomachs, but their mother refused.

Mode was convinced he would demand payment for the kindness. And even though she'd never dared to say it to his face, Raven had heard enough arguments between her and Nyssa to know how scared the woman was.

Raven suspected she would have run away, if not for the fact that she was afraid of the world outside his property even more. And with good reason. She'd been victim once; he didn't want it to be repeated ever again. That's why he decided to leave them alone. The girl was alive and well, and it was the only thing that mattered.

"My lord!" Nyssa shouted, as he was turning for the door. "Could you thank Bright Eyes for me?"

Raven smiled. The name Martha had chosen for the witch had spread faster than he would have ever thought possible. "You could do it yourself—"

"No!" Mode objected.

"No?"

"I am sorry, my lord," the woman lowered her head, "it's just that I don't want that witch near my daughter." She glanced at Nyssa and brushed a golden lock from her face. "It's her fault my baby was almost killed."

Incredible. "That witch just saved your daughter's life, almost giving hers in return and you..." Raven paused. He quickly composed himself, taking a deep breath, and turned towards the door for a second time. "I will, Nyssa," he said without slowing down.

Finally outside and away from the dozens of peering eyes, Raven leaned against the wall and closed his eyes.

What the hell was happening to him? When Mode spoke of his witch in such a vicious tongue, something inside him snapped and he yelled. He was actually yelling at that woman in front of dozens of people.

For what? To defend a witch? The irony of it made him laugh. Only a sennight ago the notion would have been preposterous, but now...

Now, he was not certain of anything. And the strangest thing was — he was still feeling her, as though she was standing next to him; hearing her, just like on the day she spent chained to the wooden stake.

Raven grabbed for the wall, afraid to open his eyes, afraid to see that the world was not going mad — it was he who was beyond any hope.

Chapter 13

Amira lay on the bed of flowers, her eyes closed, heart still racing. She stretched out her hands, expecting to recuperate from what she had lost, but nothing was happening.

Raven had snatched her from Traynan's clutches, but her magic—that was another story. Her body shook from tension. She clenched her fingers into fists and took a deep breath.

Nothing.

As the last resort, she started singing, but all she could see was him. His midnight eyes made her heart beat even faster.

Amira ceased singing. Being so out of control and fantasizing was not wise.

Did she care about being wise, though? She had had lifetimes of it, and where had it led her? Now, she simply wanted to live. She wanted to forget about the shadows haunting her; death always walking in her wake. She shook off those thoughts just like she shook off the fantasy.

Wanting was dangerous. Wanting was painful. She should have learned that lesson by now.

Maybe goddesses hadn't stripped her powers and left her for dead this time, but who could really guarantee it wouldn't happen? It had happened to her more times than she could count. Another disappointment was something she didn't think she could survive.

Amira sighed. This was frustrating. The things she yearned and the things she was afraid of were so closely intertwined with each other, she was not sure where she should start.

"Either give me a sign or end this misery right now," she shouted. "Do you hear me?"

"Do you often talk to yourself?" Her eyes flared wide open. The voice was rich, silky, tantalizing, just like the creature himself. His green eyes were gleaming at her in amusement.

"Go away," she said, knowing *him* she could not command at all.

"Now, now, sweetie—" Dazlog's towering figure cast a huge shadow over her. "Is this how you welcome your friends?"

The man was a demon. Worse, a sweet-talker, who could seduce you to beg him to take your soul for an eternal torture, and then thank him afterwards.

His face appeared more angelic than ever. His lips curled into a lazy smile. His chiseled features beckoned to touch, to kiss, to caress all that tanned flesh.

There should be a ban on looking at him, Amira thought. All these muscles and ... nothing inside her ached for his touch. Since when was she immune to those green fires burning in his gaze?

"Friends?" she snorted, "when you have friends like that, who needs enemies?"

"But we could be." He sat near her, but she refused to acknowledge that she was tempted. He did have the answers she sought.

"Do you honestly think Ven or the others will help you?" he finally asked, referring to the Goddess of Vengeance, the queen among gods, the deity the Order worshiped and Amira's constant tormentor. "You must hate her just as much as I do."

"Must is a strong word," Amira said, expecting Ven to be listening to them.

"Admit it, you need my help. We could help each other."

"No." Any pact they made would only help him at the end. "I will prevail. By myself."

"Suit yourself," he waved his hand through the air, standing up, "but know this, you will come to me. And when you do—"

"I won't," she cut him off.

"See you later." Dazlog laughed and disappeared.

"Never," she retorted to the vanishing shadow.

Do you often talk to yourself? a question echoed in her head.

What was she going to do with this one? Amira wondered as the pair of dark eyes landed on her.

"My curse, apparently," she whispered, raising her head. "How is Nyssa?"

"Desperately trying to run from her nursemaids." Raven raked his fingers through his hair and lifted his head upwards as if he was avoiding her eyes. "She asked me to thank you."

The sentence was simple, though not easy. She imagined that by saying it, he was going against everything he believed in. The discomfort was written all over his face.

Step by step, though little ones they were, he was coming around. Oh sweet progress, her heart sang. It was precisely what she needed. And without any help from Dazlog.

"Why didn't she come herself," Amira paused "Oh, … I understand." She really didn't expect a crowd cheering, but to be afraid to approach her … she felt a pang of pain in her heart.

"Well, I can't blame them, can I?" she said sadly. "I am still the spawn of a demon and they are just innocent people." She deliberately forgot to mention stones and torches.

"Sometimes I'm afraid of myself, so why shouldn't they be?"

Raven sensed it wasn't really a question. He watched her take a deep breath and lay her head on the grass, realizing he'd never heard her laugh, or seen mirth in her beautiful eyes.

There hadn't been a single occasion for it, true, but all of a sudden Raven wanted to see her smile. For some inexplicable reason he wondered how would it transform her face. And before he could stop himself, he was on the ground, near her, his hand reaching.

His fingers found her bruised cheek and gently, so as not to cause more pain, caressed it, regretting his own part in all of this. If only he could…

The bruise faded.

"How is this possible?" he choked out, his eyes wide with wonder and confusion.

"Good question." She sat up and touched her healed face. "I have a better one: who are you?"

"What?"

"Like you said, this shouldn't be possible. For a human. And yet…" her explanation trailed off.

"I *am* human."

"I wasn't saying you weren't."

"So what are you saying?"

"I'm saying … thank you."

"You could do better by telling me how I did this." Raven needed to understand at least one thing. This day was getting weirder and weirder by the second, and he yearned for some solid ground he could stand on.

"You wished it."

"I also wished for this whole day to start again, but I don't see that happening any time soon," he said, watching her for the clues she was lying—or so he told himself.

"Only a rare few—even among gods and demons— can manipulate time. Compared to that, this was a simple channeling of energy. Although," she paused, with a speculative glint in her eye, "it isn't that simple. And you shouldn't have been able to do that, no matter what was inside you."

Raven signed, realizing that he might never understand this completely. It wouldn't have been the end of the world, except she seemed to have a better inkling of his desires than he had. And it disturbed him.

"Why didn't you heal yourself?" he wondered.

"I can't. I heal fast, but the energy I can take from around me is only for my magic."

It felt like she was sharing a secret, and yet she didn't seem so stupid as to expose her weaknesses when she had no idea of what he would do with them. Either she was exhausted and not thinking rationally, or she had a plan. Whichever it was, her ulterior motives paled in comparison to her nearness.

"Now you know how it feels," she finished, her expression serious and fixed.

"As if I haven't slept in two days?"

"It's temporal."

"And it was just a bruise. Why do it?" Raven inquired, still thinking about Nyssa.

"Let's just say I owed her," the witch answered without misunderstanding his question. "Besides, no one deserves such a fate."

In that, she was correct.

"But she is not a witch, she is not one of *you*." He insisted, trying to comprehend her. He was getting tired of never knowing where reality ended and fantasy began.

"And the difference is?"

"Never mind." He didn't want to go down that path. Too many memories.

"So if I understand correctly, healing someone means expending your life force; and what about taking life?"

"You mean killing?" Amira asked, only too aware where he was going with it.

Raven nodded.

"It means gaining strength," she replied without even blinking. She just watched his face, waiting for another storm to swallow her. "It is the only way I could heal myself."

She was stupid and she knew it, but somehow she couldn't help it. Words were flying out of her mouth and she was powerless to stop them.

"And have you…" he seemed hesitant to ask her the next question.

"Have I ever killed anyone?" she finished it for him. "It depends on which of my lifetimes you're referring to."

"There's more than one?"

Amira nodded, but she could see he didn't take her words seriously. Mortals, after all, only lived once.

"Well, I'm not talking with your past selves, am I?"

"Then I hate to disappoint you," Amira said, standing up, "but none."

"Who said anything about me being disappointed?" Slowly, he stood up as well. Their eyes met as if searching for each other, and she could swear she felt his gaze as if it were a caress.

Amira should have been used to this breathless

sensation she experienced every time they came close. Yet every time, it caught her by surprise.

"But the day is still young." She didn't try to conceal the fact. She wasn't some lily-white miss, afraid of dirtying her hands. She may not like it, but if it was necessary — it was necessary.

"I hear you," he told her; and the way he did it made Amira realize it was something they had in common.

The blood on his hands brought him no pleasure, yet for some reason he was willing to scar himself for life. It wasn't just blind revenge and survival. Amira knew he had lost his family, his sister — in a brutal way, most likely — but she still felt like she was missing a piece to this puzzle. A piece that became insignificant when faced with his searching gaze.

She felt like her bones could melt.

Amira licked her lips, her mouth suddenly becoming as dry as a savanna waiting for the rainy season. She didn't understand this reaction, especially when the topic was anything but light, yet she couldn't deny the heat spreading through her.

His midnight eyes had her desperate for his touch.

As if sensing the need in her, he reached for her face and gently, with the tips of his fingers, brushed a lock of hair from her cheek.

A touch so innocent shouldn't have sent myriad rippling pleasure waves through her, should it? It shouldn't have raised a tempest inside her. Yet she felt something far beyond a simple touch, or the warmth of his breath. She felt his heart beating, his soul whispering.

Impossible. Unbelievable. Undeniable.

Just looking into his eyes made everything around them cease to be. Leaving them alone, surrounded by the mist and their thoughts.

This is a spell, he exhaled roughly. *Can't be feeling…*

What? What could he be feeling? What? Every fiber of her being demanded to know.

Tell me it's a spell, he demanded instead.

Amira groaned, shaking off their locked gazes, and severing the connection between them. She focused on anything but him, and noticed the same two men who had followed her this morning. Amira frowned.

"Strapping young fellows you have there," she pointed out, "though I would suggest you look for someone more like Owen; their hearts are too pure for the job."

Raven looked at the pair of footmen, and signaled them to approach. "Jim and Willy are here for your protection. They will watch you in case—"

"In case someone takes a notion to chain me up?" she interrupted him, feeling anger rising inside.

Deep down she knew she wasn't being rational. She'd known about Jim and Willy, hadn't she? She also knew she'd revealed too much of her powers, and not a single reason why she wouldn't try to escape. Still, she hoped, against all hopes, that he wouldn't think of her as a murdering monster. Stupid, she was so stupid. And strangely … hurt.

Amira bit down on her lip to wait out the wave and not fall to temptation, but…

For my own protection. For my own protection. For my own protection.

It rang and rang in her head.

Weren't the guards around all the corners not enough? He had to appoint someone to follow her. Right, for her own protection! Was that why they wore amulets? This was a humiliation. What next? A demonstration down through the streets of Areth?

She glanced at Raven, and any remaining restraint vanished as if it had never existed. She wasn't without weapons, nor he without weaknesses. And Amira was angry and hurt enough to use them.

She was not about to bow down and take another humiliation. Never again, she promised.

Chapter 14

Raven scowled at the change so unexpected and sudden, every instinct he possessed went hunter-still. The transformation was stunning. One moment the witch was furious, her eyes promising a slow, excruciating punishment, and the next—pure wickedness sparkled in her gaze.

She tilted her head and brushed her ebony locks aside to expose a long, graceful neck she traced with her fingers. With a lingering caress, her hand went lower, almost to her breasts. Her feet carried her forward and before he knew it, she was standing an inch from him.

There was no escaping those eyes so fiery. They caught him, took him prisoner. A lump welled in his throat.

She sank her fingers into his hair and pressed her breasts against his chest.

Raven drew back, his eyes finding their way to her lips as if of their own volition. The slight pull of his body caused her nails to trail down the back of his head, sending sensation after tantalizing sensation through his skull and down his spine. Raven couldn't restrain a shiver.

Her infliction of torture didn't cease at that. She brushed her cheek against his, and breathed out. Heat enveloped him. Seeped into his flesh.

"What kind of game are you playing?" He tried to uncurl her fingers, but it proved to be harder than tearing wreathing bindweed apart, although she used no force, offered no resistance.

"Yours," she spoke against his lips and immediately wrenched herself away before the contact was made. Yet instead of leaving him be, her hands landed on his biceps. They caressed, slowly traveling upward to his shoulders, his neck. The moment her fingers reached his bare skin, flames ignited, leaving a trace of burning wherever her fingertips brushed.

Raven suppressed his urge to take her in his arms. To kiss her. A part of him yearning for nothing more than to let her do whatever she wished with him. Another part knowing this had to be a trick. Possibly a spell. Not real.

Fight it. It's only magic. Only magic, he repeated, ordering himself to take control. He couldn't. *Only magic.* He uttered silently.

"Not yet." Apparently not silently enough.

Raven felt a feather-light touch against his jaw. Her thumb went to his lower lip and he sucked in his breath.

"I am fire," she whispered. "I am stronger than desire."

She moved even closer, her lips all but touching his ear. "I am the flame within your cravings." Her voice, a soft, low-pitched enchantment, rippled through his veins. "Heat awaken, doom awaiting."

Raven almost fell to his knees. Something inside him was definitely awakening.

She let go of him. He wanted to beg for her touch. Beg? He was surely doomed.

If it was a torture before, this was now something words could not describe. Raven felt as if he was choking. As if phantom hands were digging inside his chest in an attempt to wrap their fingers around his heart in an ironclad fist.

He had an urge to rip his shirt open to ascertain that

there was no wound, no hole. Despite everything suggesting otherwise, it wasn't a dream he could wake up from, nor a fantasy he could banish to the darkest, smallest corner of his mind; it was real. Or as real as she wanted him to believe.

He couldn't even trust his amulet to help him. Worse still, a part of him didn't care. Not anymore. Not while he was transfixed by the luscious lips, by the tip of her tongue tracing their soft edges. He was helpless.

Ye gods! but he hated it. Deep down he knew what she was doing. Deep down the last shreds of his sanity screamed. A scream so silent, it faded away with every lustful thought surfacing in his mind. Deep down, he was dying.

He couldn't breathe. Could barely support his own weight. He couldn't stop his hands from shivering. Couldn't cease the craving.

Everything around was a blur. Except her. Nothing mattered. Except her.

Had to have her. Now.

His hands reached for her, but she evaded him.

Why? Why would she ignite such all-consuming flames within him, only then to refuse? Just to tantalize? What did she want from him?

"I want your apology, for starters," she whispered, and his heart leapt at the sound of her voice. Magical.

Damn. *Don't do this,* something inside him roared. He barely heard it.

She approached then. Her eyes never leaving his.

A single feather-light touch, and his body quivered. His shaft stiffened even more than before. It was almost painful. He craved for…

Surrender to me. Her eyes sparkled. Enchanted him. *And you will know the taste of me. You will know the passion you crave.* It seemed it was all he could hear, ringing inside his head. A sing-song voice he hated, yet yearned for. Feared, yet was fascinated with. He was going demented. Obviously.

He would have pulled his hair out, if it meant he could get rid of that voice stirring up everything inside him. He doubted it would help. It persisted. Probed him.

Surrender to me. Penetrated.

Or do you want me to touch you? Enticed him.

Kiss you? Pushed him to the edge.

Stroke you? Was there even a straw he could clutch on to?

Or maybe lick you?

Yes! Yes! Yes! Every fiber of his being screamed.

"No!" he didn't know where the strength came from. He didn't care. He needed more.

No, he needed her!

Damn. It was so confusing.

"And this is what a spell is like." She snapped her fingers, turned ostentatiously, and left him. Alone.

Only then did Raven let out a breath.

And this is what a spell is like, she'd said. The feeling was unmistakably different from what he carried inside. It wasn't any stronger; it wasn't even more consuming. It had, however, obliterated his free will, abandoning him to her mercy. The sweet, sumptuous desire the spell brought left nothing but an icky taste in its wake.

The feeling was so welcome and unwanted at the same time, he thought he might go insane. All because of a witch. He laughed bitterly, stroking his fingers through his hair.

Do you want me to stroke you? her voice echoed in his head. His shaft throbbed. Damn it. He didn't just want her to stoke him. He wanted her to take him in her mouth and suck him dry. He wanted her in every way imaginable and possible.

The spell was broken. Yet there was still no

reprieve. The flames burning his flesh showed no sign of abating. The whole scene kept replaying in his mind until he could swear her voice had been in his head. He couldn't remember her lips moving.

He needed to get to the bottom of it, but he was not sure he could trust his own head right now. Spending more time thinking about her was the last thing he needed. This was more than obsession. This was madness.

He had to distance himself from whatever enchantment she wielded. Meaning, he had to distance himself from her. Not spells. Not magic. Her.

Raven went to check on his brother, and found him nervously pacing the confines of his utterly trashed room. From the looks of it, there was nothing left to break, except for the bones.

Raven winced as Dacian rammed his fist into the wall. As expected, the wall didn't break. His brother's knuckles, however, began to bleed.

Dacian didn't even blink. He swung his fist again, succeeding in knocking the breath out of Raven when he tried to intercept the hit and was a fraction too slow.

Raven grabbed Dacian's hand before he could strike again, and held the injured fist between his palms till his brother's half-conscious gaze met his eyes.

Raven never knew how lucid Dacian's mind was behind his dark empty eyes. This time, when those eyes looked back, Raven saw tears welling. It was like another punch straight to his gut.

Dacian was the only one he had left. But it was in moments like this that desperation managed to creep up on him, shackling him in chains. And no matter how fiercely he fought, Raven couldn't get free.

"It's alright. Everything is going to be alright," he attempted to reassure his brother, his voice gentle and confident.

Raven couldn't let his inner monsters show themselves for even a fraction of a second. He couldn't betray the chaos eating him alive.

Raven wanted to hit something, but knowing that if he allowed even the smallest glimpse into his inner struggles, Dacian would lose it again, Raven buried his own sorrow and rage.

"Why don't we sit down," he suggested, slowly leading Dacian's battered body to his bed. He was afraid to stumble in the darkness. With every drawer pulled out of its place and thrown on the floor, sheets tossed aside, even Dacian's own clothes lying in their way, the room was a bloody maze he could barely navigate.

He carefully settled Dacian among the pillows, straightened the quilt and covered him. He grabbed a fallen chair and sat down himself.

"We need to look at your wound," Raven told him, but Dacian covered his knuckles with his other hand, hiding it from him.

"No one is going to hurt you," Raven promised, not once letting his eyes wander away.

He tore a piece of material off of his shirt and reached for his brother's arm. Dacian recoiled.

"I won't hurt you," he repeated. "I would never hurt you."

But he had. No wonder Dacian flinched from him. As fractured as his brother's mind was, it seemed it sometimes remembered the truth.

The moment passed as quickly as it came, and Dacian let him tend the wound. If only temporarily. He would wash and re-bandage it later. Once he was calmer. Once his eyes weren't dancing the wild mad-man dance. Once—

"Who is she?" Dacian suddenly grabbed Raven's arm, his voice even more impetuous than his glare.

Raven sighed. Even here, he couldn't escape her.

"I don't know," he confessed honestly, "I really don't know."

The woman was infuriating, and he found that refreshing. She was a witch he should hate, yet instead he burned for her. She was like no one he'd ever met. More beautiful than any goddess and not a drop of vanity in her eyes. Strong in her convictions. Relentlessly determined when she got something in her head.

She truly was someone who could stand her ground no matter what kind of monsters lunged for her. He hated to admit, but he admired her courage, even her boldness.

Raven covered his face with his palms. "What I am to do with her?"

There was no answer; the only sound he could hear was his heart pounding like a drum. Though maybe it was the only answer he *could* give himself. He knew he couldn't let her go, not yet. Not until the witches came. But her staying under his roof, in his bed, inflamed yet another problem.

Inflamed being the precise word, he thought.

Every time she got near him, he felt like a fool, incapable of controlling himself. And for the first time in his life, Raven began to doubt his beliefs.

Raven stood up and leaned toward the backrest of the chair. His mind was swirling with thoughts and questions. Too many questions. Too few answers.

"Leaving?" His brother's desperate voice brought him back to reality. Reality, where he had a duty and a goal. Where his fantasies were of no importance. Where his softening towards her was a weakness he simply could not afford.

"Never." Raven closed his eyes. "I'll always be with you, little brother." No matter what.

Chapter 15

Amira's furious steps didn't falter all the way to her room. Her room? His! She groaned and slammed the door with all of her strength, probably smashing it straight into a few noses. She exhaled, and just like that, her anger melted away. Yet the tremors raking her body didn't cease.

She closed her eyes, instantly understanding her mistake—when darkness enveloped her in its cold embrace, she found herself yearning for Raven's heat.

She remembered his searing gaze, the feel of his strength under her fingers. She remembered how his voice grew darker, hungrier in her mind. Amira doubted she would ever forget.

He'd been burning and yet he'd fought her. Raven had resisted the invisible chains trying to bind him. And now, she was the one who had to fight the same shackles.

Both love and lust spells bound the will but, if placed on someone who ignited similar reactions without the magic, they always backfired. When was she going to learn?

Amira had a hard time coping with her feelings ever since she'd looked into Raven's eyes for the very first time and found herself drowning in the sea of myriad emotions. It didn't justify her foolishness. Unfortunately, it explained it.

She'd been angry and humiliated. She'd wanted to

repay him. If a witch was all he saw, then a witch was what he would get, she had decided, and had uttered the spell so many of them used. Yet Amira was not like any of them—never could be.

If she had been, she would have had no other choice but to stifle her urge to teach him a lesson. Originally, the ritual required a kill. Lucky for her, all Amira had to do was utter the words.

Yes, she was so lucky! At finding trouble.

She swayed back and laid her head on the bed, frustration taking hold of her. She had recklessly uttered the spell. Was stuck with the consequences—and all for what? Raven's will hadn't been hers for a single moment. The man had the strongest self-control she'd ever encountered, causing her to curse the difficulties it raised, and yet admire him at the same time.

Was anything simple around here?

Just then a knock sounded at the door, and her heart leapt against her better judgement, expecting him, and plunged to the ground when she realized it wasn't. Why did it not listen to reason? Amira wanted to scream. This was not what she had imagined it would be like to *feel*. This was not what she had dreamed of for all these years.

Be careful what you wish for—people liked to say. Well, they didn't know the half of it, Amira thought.

"Come in," she called out, and watched as a snowy-haired woman stepped inside—and behind her, Amira's new watch-dogs.

"Shoo." Martha swiped her hand through the air, ordering the men to leave. They hesitated for a second, their gazes moving from her to the woman and back again before they obeyed.

"I will speak with that demon of a boy about them," Martha promised her once they were alone.

"There's no need," Amira assured her, knowing that

he wouldn't yield to the woman's wishes. The demon of a boy, as Martha called him, had his own agenda.

"Oh, there is a need, but it is not what I came here to say." She straightened, softening her expression. "Thank you."

Amira blinked.

"For saving Nyssa," she elaborated. "I heard it was a dreadful sight."

Heard? Her brows lifted at the word. Why would she … everything around Amira stilled and she closed her eyes to listen and watch with her senses. The threads of waning energy she encountered made her blood run cold with ice.

There was a curse placed on the woman, preventing her from stepping a foot outside of this house.

Amira doubted Martha had done anything to deserve it. The only problem was, curses were complicated. They always required some kind of sacrifice. Furthermore, she needed to know every single detail, but a guarded heart was rarely capable of supplying them.

Again, her thoughts meandered back to Raven.

Was he cursed? Was it the culprit of the haunted pain she sometimes witnessed in his eyes?

"Can't get him out of your mind now, can you?" Martha's question caused her thoughts to scatter.

Her eyes flared wide. Was it so obvious? Never once saw a person inside of her.

"Don't worry, he is just as confused as you are," the woman reassured her, when she continued to stare. Amira didn't know what to say to that.

"If you're feeling up to it, you should come down," Martha added. "You have a guest."

"A guest? Who?"

"You will have to see for yourself." Martha smiled, and turned to leave.

Honestly, Amira didn't know if she was up to it. Trusting her luck, it would probably be some disgruntled villager with an axe, or maybe a rope. Yet she gathered herself, and followed the woman.

She entered the dining room, prepared for the blow. Instead, she found a child nervously biting his nails.

He was around eight years old, and as black as a sweep, his tattered clothes barely covering his skinny frame. The boy lifted his deep-blue eyes, and Amira froze, recognizing him as the same boy who had thrown an apple at her, the same one who had wanted her dead.

"What is your name?" she asked, not sure if she should look into those eyes.

"Adam," the boy muttered, barely taking out his grubby nails from his mouth.

Now what? She wondered. She wasn't used to interacting with children.

"Was there something you needed?"

"I came because of me sis. Me mom didn't want me here, but I still came when she thought I fell asleep. But I couldn't sleep." His words flew out of his mouth so fast, it was hard keeping up with them. "... I wasn't allowed to go outside either, but I saw ... I saw Nyssa lying, like dead ... and then you came and she wasn't dead no more." Adam's eyes filled and the tears stopped his confession.

"Shh." Amira crouched in front of him and wiped the tears away. "It's alright. Everything is alright."

Adam nodded, rubbing his eyes with dirty fists. He inhaled a few times and she took his hands into hers to stop him from irritating those eyes further.

"She said you are a disgusting, hideous monster — but you are no such thing," he declared passionately. "You saved Nyssa, and you are beautiful!"

Amira had never felt the urge to smile as strongly as she did now. If only she knew how...

Her eyes drifted to the little hands she held, and the urge to smile vanished.

"Who did this to you?" she demanded, turning his hands slowly, noticing bruise after bruise underneath all that dirt. His whole body...

Dear gods, she inhaled. The scars ... she was going to kill someone!

"Who?" she repeated when she didn't get an answer.

Adam pulled his hands away and turned to leave.

"I'm sorry, I don't bite, I promise," Amira reassured him. She didn't want to scare the boy.

Adam laughed. It was an innocent childish chuckle she imagined people rarely heard. A shame, she thought. A child as young as he was should be happy and carefree for as long as was possible.

"You wanted to ask me something, didn't you?" Amira inquired, after a bit of mind-reading.

He nodded. "My pug broke a leg, and —"

"And you were wondering if I could heal him?" she finished it for him, also knowing that the dog didn't just break its leg. It was broken by Mode. On purpose. Only the why of it eluded her.

He nodded again. "How did you know?"

"I can read minds," she said. "Lead the way."

Adam's smile widened. Taking her hand, he dragged her towards his home, if one could call it such, and showed her the kennel.

She crouched over the animal, only too aware of the mob gathering around her to witness yet another show. She focused on the dog instead.

He whined, raising his head. The small, pathetic brown eyes that gazed at her were full of fear and pain.

"What is she doing?" someone murmured in the crowd.

Amira blocked the voices. She wasn't interested in

people cursing, railing, or whispering in fear.

"Don't be afraid," she said as she reached for the dog.

The instant her hand touched the dog's fur, Maddie's memories popped into her head—Mode's anger penetrated her senses, and Amira understood. The woman hated her own son for the way he was conceived, and constantly lashed out at him. This time, she punished him by injuring the dog he loved.

Amira released just enough energy to mend the bone. The dog happily yapped and jumped up. Adam gasped.

The next thing she knew was the boy's hands coming around her. Amira froze.

She felt lost and flustered. Warmth intruded on her heart. Chill gripped her spine. Chill?

Amira lifted her eyes to the woman staring down at her. Frost and ice. If there ever was a colder gaze, it would surely freeze her into a callous stone.

"Adam!" his mother's raised voice made the boy spring up, "come to me at once. And you, witch, stay away from my kids." She ordered.

Amira clenched her fists and stood up.

"Don't you think your behavior is a bit unwise, Mode?" the man standing nearby intervened, as if sensing the change in Amira.

"Asinine, I should say," a woman agreed. "Do you really want to test this … this girl?" she added after a pause. It was apparent they were afraid, and thus careful, if not respectful, around her.

"A girl?" Adam's mother yelled. "She is an abomination. Because of the likes of her, we decent folk can't live in peace!" She grabbed a cane from the ground.

"Mode," someone whispered, "I don't think the Lord will be happy—"

"Well of course he won't," Adam's mother interrupted the speaker, "don't you see he's already under that thing's spell? After all, spreading legs is one of their talents."

That did it. No one called her an abomination, a whore, and attempted to beat her with a cane, without consequences. Amira gritted her teeth, and without even touching Mode's body, lifted it a few feet above the ground.

The woman shrieked, flailed, waved with her stick—which appeared in Amira's hands a second later—and called for help. Amira glanced around, trailing her gaze from one person to another, encountering no resistance. People actually took a step back. Only Adam stood motionless, stupefied.

The child's big blue saucer-like eyes brought Amira back. She clenched her fist around the cane even harder, trying to regain control. Fear was the last thing she wanted to see in Adam's eyes.

She approached the woman, and with the tip of the stick touched her chest. "If I notice another mark on Adam's flesh, you will answer to me, understood?"

"Who are you to tell me how to raise my children?" The words came out as a timid squeak.

"Someone who will be very upset if even the smallest hair is to fall from his head. And you really don't want to make me upset."

Amira released her hold on the woman. And Mode crashed to the ground, sputtering insults.

"Oh, and I really think Adam could use a bath," Amira added, feeling the way she never thought she would feel again. Herself.

"Try to stop me now," she muttered, as lightning cracked the sky. Damn, but this felt good.

Chapter 16

"She did what?" Raven took the sword from the wall and threw it to Jim.

Jim caught it with his left hand, measured it in his palm and nodded. "I believe she made lightning strike the wooden pole."

Raven knew, just knew he heard it right the first time. Still, he had to ask. Again. Leave that woman to her own devices for a few hours and she would turn his whole world upside down. Leave her for a few days and it would cease to be his entirely.

He groaned, and focused his full attention on the wall in front of him, his eyes struggling to concentrate on the cold, stainless steel.

"How often do you practice?" he asked Jim, examining the sharp edges and carved handles in front of him.

"Not as often as I'd like to," the man admitted. "It's been a busy few months with all of the construction going on."

Raven knew that building proper homes was important, since his own couldn't contain everyone, but… "You need to find time."

They harbored a lot of so-called witches, and an attack was a definite possibility. Newly built homes wouldn't save them from the sharp blade of the Order. Only skills and weapons could do that.

Raven had provided them with the means, but he

couldn't force the dedication.

"I know," Jim agreed. "This is why we need these practices whenever you return home. A good kick in the butt sometimes goes a long way toward reminding us of the fact."

Raven laughed and picked a simple, long, double-edged sword. He lifted it. Changed hands and swiped it through the air, testing the sword's balance. He wasn't left-handed, but he'd learned to use both, knowing no skill could ever really be inutile. He lived by the sword since he was fourteen years old and trusted the thing he held in his hand more than a human at his back.

A sword could break, but it couldn't betray.

"Ready?" He faced Jim, nothing but a few pieces of damaged furniture between them.

"Yes." The man advanced, his long legs eating the space they reserved for indoor practices.

Raven felt the rush in his blood. He anticipated working himself until exhaustion claimed him, yearning for a dreamless sleep. Yet when their swords met and clanged, he found himself questioning Jim about his "guest's" activities.

Their swords separated, and met again. On and on they went, swinging lethal blows at one another, dueling until the sweat beaded over his opponent's skin and the answers came in a ragged breath.

"Maybe I'll tell you the rest after..." Jim panted, forcing Raven to notice how his blows became fiercer with each new tidbit he learned.

"Maybe you should concentrate more!" Raven sidestepped, throwing Jim off balance. Too easy. Oh, what he would give for a practice session with a worthy opponent.

"She conjured up a pony." The man moved, placing a chair between them.

Raven was about to ask how long he was going to

hide behind furniture when the meaning of Jim's statement sank in.

"A pony?" The sound of his amazement was quickly followed by a loud clang of their swords. "She conjured up a pony?" Why not, he almost snorted. She could probably conjure up a dragon. Why not a pony?

Raven ducked to avoid Jim's hit and seized the opportunity to bypass the chair. He turned, countered a clumsy strike with one of his own, and went into a full-frontal attack.

"It appeared regular horses were too large for the boy," the other man breathed shallowly, moving backwards.

"What else?" Raven swung his sword again.

"She helped during Lizzy's labor." Jim took another step.

"How exactly did she help?" Another swing. Another move.

Jim gasped, finally feeling the wall against his back. His grip on the sword loosened. Raven kicked. The sword flew from Jim's hand and landed loudly on the floor.

"Always observe your surroundings," he advised, pointing the tip of his own blade into the man's chest. "Leave yourself space. And never let anyone corner you unless you plan it that way. Understood?"

Jim nodded.

"Good." Raven withdrew his weapon. "So how did she help exactly?" he asked again, retrieving the fallen weapon.

"I'm not sure," Jim muttered. "I only heard women talking about how she put her palm on Lizzy's stomach. Something similar to Adam's dog."

Or Nyssa, Raven added the last one, to himself.

"I see," he said. Though actually he didn't. Not a bit. She wanted to render him demented apparently. It had to be it. Why else would she use magic every other second, doing things like frightening the hell out of Mode, transforming his sun-chamber into a freaking jungle, or conjuring up ponies—instead of trying to run away.

Her behavior was unfathomable. Something about her made him re-evaluate the whole picture, yet all he got from doing it was a splitting headache.

If only he didn't have to sit and wait... But going after the witches was futile. He'd already tried that. For about ten years. The one time he killed a witch aside, he hadn't found another until just recently. Until her.

Raven had to remind himself he would not be able to enter the Impenetrable Mountains. No man could. And leaving this place would most definitely guarantee his missing the witches and his chance, along with them.

He had to sit and wait. But damn it, if it wasn't killing him; stretching the limits of his patience, for sure. Mostly because of one rebellious beauty unleashing havoc under his roof and in his head.

Raven grabbed his shirt from the hook. He wasn't ready to finish the practice. Far from ready. Jim, on the other hand was. Frustrating. It was just frustrating—that's what it was.

He didn't even break a sweat. Oh, but it took one thought about her, one stray, wayward thought, and he was burning, his skin heating up.

Raven frowned, realizing where this kind of delusion could take him. Some place where every cell of the body craved, and yet his common sense was dead against going to. The place of pleasure? Probably. A place to forget all his troubles? Perhaps. A place of betrayal? Absolutely.

He didn't need it. Just like he didn't need daydreaming about her. It was dangerous. He could lose his head one day. How many times did he have to remind himself of that?

As if conjured by his thoughts, the woman walked into the room. There was nothing but confidence in her stride. And despite it all, Raven admired that about her.

She sat down in the only good chair and looked at him.

"We need to talk," she stated solemnly. "Could you please send the boys away?"

She glanced at Willy casually leaning against the wall, and then at the still-panting Jim. "Not that I don't like the company, but enough is enough."

Raven signaled them to leave, and without waiting for the door to be closed behind the men, turned his full attention to the woman.

"So, I am all yours," somehow just slipped out.

Bright Eyes narrowed her eyes, as if to say *really?* but held her tongue. For a second.

"I'd say you've been avoiding me." She lifted her hand and her fingers began playing with one of her bobbing locks. "Now why is that?"

Raven ignored her question. "You are not here to make demands. I think I am being more than reasonable—"

"Yes, you are the epitome of reason," she interrupted him with a snort.

"Just by not tying you up again, I risk a lot—you do understand?"

She looked at him with one of her soul-searching gazes, and softened. "If you worry about the witches, don't. I guarantee you they will come."

"How do you know?" He leaned forward, his hands settling on the backrest of the second chair.

"You really wish to know?" she asked, standing up and moving towards the wall.

She examined weapon after weapon, finally stopping in front a small dagger with a dragon's tail wreathing around the handle.

"Yes." His eyes never left her fingers as they gently stroked the steel. "No." He remembered her conditions. "I don't know," Raven answered truthfully.

She took the dagger from the wall, pretending to study it more closely. "You better decide which one."

Raven's brows arched slightly. He would have told her to be careful. She was treading on dangerous ground. Instead, he just swallowed hard. There was something sensuous about her with that dagger.

She toyed with it for a second and directed her gaze onto him once again. "Everything would be so much simpler if only you could trust in others."

"Meaning you?"

"Why not?" she shrugged.

"Why not?" he repeated the question with bewilderment in his voice. He could have stated hundreds of reasons, except suddenly he couldn't remember a single one of them.

"Do you think every human is worthy of death just because there are few bad seeds among them?" she asked.

"Of course not." He released the chair and leaned against the wall. Watching. Studying.

"But you do think every witch is worthy of death just because some of them committed crimes." It was not a question.

Still, he answered. "Not any more, apparently, or you would've been dead. Already."

When did he become so frank with her? When did he lie to her? He wondered.

"I thought you needed me." Was this desperation he was hearing now? Surely not.

"They are coming, you told me yourself." He believed her few days ago, but now, he sensed them coming. "Meaning I no longer need you."

"Then let me go," she sounded more demanding. Forthright. Her flaring eyes all but nailed him to the wall.

"And if I said no?"

Confusion darkened her face. She shook it off and began trailing the dagger edgeways on the table.

Back and forth. Back and forth. Slowly. Deliberately. Raven was only too aware of the dagger she so innocently wielded in her hands. The only thing missing was a mischievous smile curling her lips, but as always they were devoid of mirth. Her eyes, on the other hand, were sparkling.

"Then, we shall dance," she said lifting the blade, the tip pointing at him.

"Angel, you don't even know the steps," he protested.

She approached.

Raven met her in the middle, completely exposing his scarcely-buttoned chest. He felt the coldness of the steel against his feverish skin, and waited.

He was insane. He had to be insane. Yet he looked into her eyes, and stepped forward.

She stepped back.

He took another step, and watched her move again.

They continued this dance until she was trapped between the table and him, with nowhere to go, nothing to do but plunge the dagger straight into his heart.

Her grip loosened, and he wrapped his fingers around it to steady the sharp object.

"Do you want to hurt yourself?" he asked, switching the direction of the blade so the sharp end would rest between her breasts.

She gulped, but didn't take her eyes of him — her blue irises having hypnotic effect on him. The moment stretched, and he almost missed it when she turned her fist, and the dagger pressed into his chest again.

"Do you?" he whispered, his eyes never once going down.

"I want you—" she licked her lips, and he felt his shirt parting as one of the few buttons holding it together fell, nicked by the tip of the blade, "to kiss me."

Raven didn't know what shocked him the most, the plea or the demand, yet they both shot straight to his head, heart, and some other throbbing places.

"Do these tactics actually work?" he asked, his voice hoarse with desire.

"You tell me." She trailed the dagger up, parting his shirt at another button, and Raven realized he hadn't been this excited in ... forever. And to think all it took was a witch and a dagger to his throat.

He forced her armed hand behind her back, heard the sharp rattle as the blade met the floor, and leaned down.

"I don't believe you asked for words," he said just before capturing her lips.

Amira moaned and surrendered to the force of his need. It was a living, breathing flame inside her.

His desire was seductive. It cursed through her veins, feeding fire to her own needs. She freed her hand, and sank her fingers into his dark unruly hair.

The kiss intensified. Her nails dug into his skin, and then slowly trailed downward. She felt him shiver and groan, and a shuddering wave of anticipation washed over her. It seemed like a promise to take her deeper, to drown her in the ocean of desires.

As if she wasn't drowning already.

She poured every last ounce of her frustration, loneliness, and all the mixed feelings she'd been carrying, into their kiss. Into the wild dance of their tongues, which neither was willing to tame.

It was madness, and it stripped them both of the last shreds of sanity, yet she didn't care. Pleasure sizzled wherever he touched — her pulse a raging, wild thunder in her veins.

He tasted it, pressing his lips against her neck, and she bit her lip, aching for more. His fingers worked the laces of her gown, managing to loosen her so-stiffly laced bodice. And when she felt her breast in his palm, her nipple stiffening against his fingers, she almost exploded.

The raw, addictive sensation that swept through her was stronger than any magic she'd ever touched. It embraced her. Overwhelmed her.

Raven slid his hands down her back, down over her hips. He gripped her bottom and lifted her up to settle her on the ledge of the table. Her thighs fell apart, welcoming him between her legs. She wrapped them around his waist and arched her back.

His lips came down onto her exposed breasts.

Raven kissed her breasts slowly, his tongue grazing her nipples, and Amira squirmed with impatience. It was both ecstasy and torture — his touches so light, she ached for more.

As if sensing it, he took it into his mouth and sucked. Hard. She almost went crazy when he switched back to a gentle caress, his tongue circling her throbbing bud. And then, he used his teeth on her.

Amira gasped, but held on to him. She held on as his touches alternated from featherlike to nearly painful, yet the combination was so amazing, she felt herself teetering on the brink.

I want you, Angel.

Those words reverberated through her body in waves, until she felt intoxicated by them. Her every cell tingled with energy.

Amira lifted his head and put her lips on his. She couldn't take it anymore. Now more than ever, she needed to feel his flesh.

Her fingers went to his shirt, and without even breaking their kiss, he slipped it off as she brushed the material over his shoulders.

Her hands slid over his muscled chest. Her fingers stroked and caressed his tanned skin. Her wrapped legs drew him even closer until she felt the rock-hard mount pressing between her spread thighs. She rubbed herself against it.

She didn't even notice the mere scraps of material in between; all she felt was a wave of heat surging, rising higher every time they met. The pressure was accumulating.

I need you…

Raven groaned as she rubbed against him. Again. His hands were on her calves, moving higher, under the skirt.

"Ease your hold," he pleaded, his voice hoarse and low.

Amira surrendered to him, realizing his mind was fully accessible. It didn't matter. All she cared for at the moment was the passion they shared. Everything else could wait for another day. For another decade, she decided.

She moaned as she felt his fingers brush her inner thigh. Another wave of heat flooded her. It brought his desires, his emotions to the surface, uncovered his raging thoughts. It exposed his intentions. Every detail of what he wanted to do to her, every breath-taking image.

Amira opened her eyes. "Your thoughts almost make me blush," she whispered in an unsteady, low-pitched voice.

"You are not blushing," he managed between

kisses.

She looked into his smiling eyes and licked her lower lip, "I said almost."

Suddenly, his eyes widened, his jaw tensed. His fingers stopped an inch away from her nether curls.

Raven didn't know why, but he felt a sudden overwhelming impulse. His brain was forcing him to cease. His body screamed in protest, though.

He felt he had less than enough strength for it. Still, he uncurled her legs and stepped back, trying to create a distance. To quench this burning desire inside him.

Even looking at the confusion in her face was too much for him to deal with. Too painful. Too hard. Gods, but *he* was hard. And panting. He craved for her flesh more than he had craved for any other.

"I can't," he uttered, "we shouldn't."

Amira watched in devastation as he grabbed the shirt he had tossed down only minutes before and slipped it on. She slowly stood up, flicked the skirt down her long legs, and touched his hand.

"Raven," —she didn't recognize this husky whisper as her own— "what's wrong?"

What's wrong? He couldn't explain it. Couldn't put his finger on it. Yet even if it was only a dim echo compared with the roaring thunder in his body, he couldn't ignore it.

"What is your name?" he asked, raking his brain to understand the uneasiness he felt.

She stood still, the answer not coming.

"Just as I thought," Raven sighed, knowing he needed to get out of there.

* * *

The doors slammed closed, and Amira sank to her knees, both angry and distraught. She tried to take the calming breath in, but when she exhaled, every weapon hanging on all of the four walls fell down with a deafening clash.

What the hell was happening? Every time she met him, she swore she would be strong. And yet, every single time, she melted into a puddle.

She knew she'd come looking for him to discuss something important. If only she could remember. Images of his mouth and hands on her were all her racing mind was producing.

Amira shivered. For a moment all she wanted was to hug herself and wallow in her misery. She refused. She was not one to wallow. She needed to think. Unfortunately, her unabashed fantasies aside, her mind was utterly blank.

No, not utterly — her brow furrowed as she realized when and why he'd stopped kissing her.

It hadn't been the lack of desire. His body was hers. It was his mind that rebelled when she told him she knew his thoughts.

Amira doubted he recognized the reason. Not consciously at least. Otherwise there would have been questions. But he felt it. He instinctively protected his secrets.

Being with a witch, on her terms ... well, it invited trouble. Stupidity wasn't a strong enough word. A man who came into a witch's bed was risking enslavement far worse than any cage could impose. And there she was, exposing his inner thoughts, yet refusing to share her name.

It didn't inspire trust.

Except, he knew too much about witches. What if telling her name was crossing the line? Ah, who was she kidding, she'd crossed the line five minutes after they'd met. She had disobeyed almost every order the goddesses had given her. What difference would another make?

Amira understood where his actions had come from. Even if she was a bit shaky and angry at the rejection, she understood. It didn't mean, however, that her heart felt the same.

She knew he was changing. Would have been a fool to expect it to happen in a day. Her little escapade with the dagger was a true miracle which would've ended in a bloody mess only a week before. But even if it gave her hope, it did nothing to alleviate the hurt.

Her own damned fault, she breathed angrily, standing up. She shouldn't have mixed business with pleasure, yet she knew, given the chance, she wouldn't have stopped it. She also knew—she was not giving up. Not as long as she had breath in her lungs.

Chapter 17

With heavy steps, Raven descended the stairs, completely lost in his own thoughts. He walked without noticing a single person. The only thing imprinted on his mind was the image of her welcoming, sweet body.

The night had been a torment. An uncomfortable sofa he'd found in the sun-chamber — a torture device. Especially with her gatecrashing his dreams, and refusing to leave even after he'd woken up.

A part of him was desperate to claim his own bed, and the woman who slept there, yet he fought those cravings with every step he took.

He still wasn't sure what was real when it came to her, or what he could trust. He wasn't convinced he wouldn't regret it. But if it was worth anything, he did regret leaving her standing in the middle of that room with her lips swollen, her breasts glistening from his kisses. Her crystal eyes wide with questions.

Questions he really had no answer to.

How had he mired down into such a morass? He had no idea. He just knew deep in his gut it was not right. For either of them. Especially for his brother who endured suffering while he…

Raven broke the thread of his thoughts. His needs and desires were of the lowest priority. It was the way it had to be, and the way it should be.

He reached for the doorknob, only then noticing where his legs had brought him. And with that realization came an unbridled, foolish hope of seeing her standing with a dagger in her hand, inviting him to another dance.

Right! He snorted at his own stupidity as the empty room opened up for him. He reached for the carelessly discarded dagger — the same one she'd held yesterday — and threw it at the wooden door. The sharp tip of the blade sank into the surface.

He barely registered the piles of weapons everywhere. He grabbed another one, but as he was about to throw it, the door opened. She stepped in.

Her eyebrows shot up at the dagger sticking out, but she didn't comment on it. She simply closed the door — making him aware of how quickly the reasons why he shouldn't had vanished — and the air became heavier and charged with tension.

"We need to talk about Ryna," she said, her eyes giving nothing away, and it succeeded in raising his frustration. He had to grind his teeth to stop himself reaching for her, while she seemed entirely indifferent to him.

"Who?" he shook his head in perplexity.

"Robin and Lizzy's baby girl," she explained. "Have you seen where they live?" She didn't wait for an answer, but proceeded with her thought "So, I was thinking … maybe you could take Robin as a footman, since the two of them are doing nothing save hovering around me."

"I really don't need another footman, or any type of servant for that matter," he stated; "There are too many as it is and — "

"I don't care — " she cut him off, her gaze catching fire more intensively with every passing second. "They need a better shelter. They need a room such as Jim and Willy share, for example."

"Now may I finish?" he enquired. She narrowed her

eyes, but finally nodded.

"As I was saying, there are too many servants here as it is and," he purposely paused in the same place, "I was happy to give away the last empty room in the west wing yesterday."

If not for his brother, Raven would never return to this place. It was his property, but it wasn't his home. Hadn't been for a very long time. And while he mostly lived on a road, at least it served some good for others.

He'd never intended to make this house or the lands around it a shelter for so many. All he'd done was save a few people by offering a place to stay, and with time the number kept growing and growing.

"And no relocations required," he added. Except he was forced to sleep on sofas from now on.

"Oh! All right then. Now that this is settled… " She turned to leave. "I have other pressing matters of concern."

Raven shook his head at her statement. Some prisoner she was…

Maybe he should tell her she was free to go. It was not like he needed her. Hers was not the blood that could bring his brother back. Moreover, from the moment she'd saved Nyssa it was obvious she wasn't being tortured here. And as crazy as it sounded even to his own ears, he sensed the witches coming.

He opened his mouth, but the words got stuck in his throat.

"Just don't conjure up any snakes," he settled on requesting. He already had a jungle in his house. More of it was truly unnecessary.

"Can't promise you anything," she said. But instead of leaving immediately, she stopped in front of the door and pulled the dagger out.

She walked to him and handed him the weapon, handle first. And Raven understood — it was his move now. His decision.

* * *

Amira sat down on the grass and began singing. She was not taking the risk without her guiding melody again.

Her spirit separated from her body. She closed her eyes to see the path in front of her, took a deep breath in, and after a few seconds, found her parents.

They were approaching the dungeon used by the Order for torturing and keeping witches.

Such places were kept secret. Even from some of their own. No wonder it took months for her uncle Regan to confirm his wife's and daughter's whereabouts. Not even being the king helped — probably only made it worse.

Amira watched as Pharell and Regan bound, gagged and hid the two guards they had knocked out, while Deron stood watch. His eyes were going back and forth from the dusty road to Eliana and back to the road. Yet it was not the road where the danger lay.

Amira stepped inside the catacombs and hurried down the winding stairs, stopping only when she encountered two Venlordians stationed at the foot of the stairs.

Without the slightest compunction she ripped through the barriers of their minds and sent them away just in time to see four figures emerging with their swords drawn.

The narrow, tunnel-like space they abandoned as swiftly as possible was brilliantly designed to leave assailants at disadvantage. Broad enough for a single person and twisted in such a manner that the one who descended would be forced to fight with his left hand.

It wouldn't have presented any difficulty for Pharell. Amira had seen him wield his two slim blades he'd named *dao kanjis.* She knew he was more than proficient with both of his hands. The loud clangs of weapons meeting, however, would have been a dead giveaway.

Now, with the guards gone, they encountered no resistance and Amira could take a quick glance at their surroundings.

She heard the water slowly dripping down somewhere to her left, and only when her eyes adjusted sufficiently did she see damp, mossy rocks glistening under the torchlight. Torches were fixed on the right wall every fifty feet, illuminating a narrow rocky tunnel that seemed to have no end.

She wasn't endeared to the poor visibility, but the foreboding she carried bothered her even more. For the moment she could swear the walls were closing in and all the air, humid and foul as it was, leaving her lungs.

Amira shook the thought away just in time to see the four form a circle with Eliana in the middle. Her mother drew a witch's mark on the ground, sprinkled it with bits and pieces of something that looked like hair, and gave the small ritual dagger to Pharell. Her cousin cut his palm, letting blood drip on the mark, and returned the dagger to Eliana.

"From blood of blood and witch's pain," she cut her own hand, "guide us spirits, light our way."

The small ball of light formed out of the mixture of hair, Pharell's and Eliana's blood, and rushed forward, revealing the safe passage-way.

The four of them followed. Yet all too soon the ball of light started fading and died, forcing Eliana to repeat the ritual.

That was what Amira hated most about spells. They required blood and were still so temporary. Of course, in the tunnels one could easily get lost; a temporary guide was better than nothing.

She turned another corner, and froze in her tracks as a naked, limp body came into view. It hung from the ceiling by a set of chains, beaten and bruised so severely, it didn't look human anymore.

Eliana gasped at the gruesome sight, and then ceased breathing. Silence reigned.

They all stood, unable to move, their eyes going from one red welt to the other. Logic dictated it was a girl, probably young—but with half of the skin burned, and her hair brutally chopped off, it was hard to tell.

The image made Amira gag. She had seen death in many forms. Experienced it firsthand more often than she would have liked to, but this ... she shook with rage and fury at what the poor girl must have suffered. Was still suffering, Amira realized, as Pharell swung his blades, his aim true, bringing a quick, liberating death.

Amira closed her eyes for a brief second, opening them involuntarily as the head met the cold and dirty ground. She averted her gaze, and against her will was caught and held captive by the sight of her mother's face buried into her father's chest. Silent sobs were shaking Eliana's body while she held on to Deron as if her own life depended upon it.

Somehow Amira felt even colder in the presence of a loving, consoling embrace. She was used to standing alone, dying alone, simply being alone; she didn't hope for or expect otherwise. But right now, she could barely control her emotions, meaning she was an inch from revealing her presence or even worse, returning to her body.

Amira did her best to shake off her desires, pain, grief and horror, as she followed the others and their new guiding light again, but two images were stuck in her mind: the suffering of one witch, and the comforting embrace of the other. The first one she was desperately trying to avoid. The second, she could never really have.

Amira focused on the cells in front of her, scanning the areas behind the metal bars just as the others did. But as far as her eyes could see, the cages were empty. Of people anyway. For every last one was furnished with various devices such as hanging chains, or crosses with multiple restraints for ankles and wrists. Some of them were mounted on the walls, while others lay about three feet above the ground. Thankfully, at least every damned thing was empty.

Amira turned another corner, only to witness more cages. More chains. More crosses. Empty, thank goodness.

No, she realized, as she saw a shadow moving on her right side. She turned and came face to face with Sofie's haunted eyes. The exhaustion and dread there wrapped around Amira's heart like cold fingers, squeezing it until emotions threatened to choke her.

The girl ran to the darkest corner of the cell the moment she heard footsteps and curled into a ball.

The three seconds it took her family to find her seemed to last forever. Even for Amira. And she was not the one scared and curled up barefoot on the cold, damp, ground.

"Fia, oh gods," Regan whispered, with such tangible relief Amira felt it to the marrow of her bones.

"Daddy!" Sofie's ecstatic cry echoed down the corridor as she jumped from her curled position and ran toward her family. She shoved her hands through the iron bars and grabbed the front of her father's clothes.

"You came!" Her shaking fingers moved up to touch his whiskered chin. "You came."

"Shh, sweaty, not so loud," Regan breathed out, his own eyes moving frantically, searching for any indication his little girl was harmed. Examining her from the loose brown hair to the bare feet.

"Did they hurt you?" he asked, so afraid of the answer his own hands trembled as they clasped hers. "Did they—"

"No," Sofie shook her head, "they brought me food once a day and left me alone, but I was so afraid... " her un-shed tears glistened in her eyes, "I thought—"

"We'll get you out of here," her brother promised, already unlocking her prison with the key that could only have come from one of the Venlordians. And Amira couldn't help but wonder at the price. Venlordians were believers in their cause. They didn't sell out their own.

The moment Sofie's cell opened and Pharell took her into his embrace, Sofie let out a breath she'd been holding in, and hugged her brother back.

"Let's go," Deron finally spoke, his gaze locked on the corridor. "We need to find Milla and get out of here as fast as we can."

Amira agreed with her father. Something felt wrong. It felt ... too easy.

"Where's your mother?" Regan asked.

"There," Sofie pointed to the right, "I think."

"Stay behind with your aunt," Pharell directed her.

The five of them crossed another twenty feet and turned, finally finding the cage in which Queen Milla was being held. Again, Pharell unlocked the bars, but his mother didn't leave the cage. She stood at the opposite wall, barefoot just like Sofie, her long brown hair hanging loose, her gown dirty. She shook her head. "Leave, just leave me."

"My love," Regan rushed forward, leaving the others to stand in front of the door, "come."

"I can't," she whispered, "I am chained." Milla lifted the hem of her skirt, revealing a thick metal cuff around her ankle, and a chain linking it to the wall.

"I don't have a key for that!" Pharell said before his father even breathed a word.

"Damn it," Regan cursed, "we'll get you out ... somehow we'll get you—"

"No," she shook her head again. Her hands cupped his cheeks and tears ran down her face. "Leave me. Save Sofie."

"Milla—"

"Listen to me," she cried, "you have to go. They knew you would come." The last statement got everyone's attention. "Save my daughter. Leave ... please."

Damn! Now it was Amira who swore. She felt so impotent looking at the horror on her uncle's face. In this form she couldn't do anything about the chain. And breaking it with pistols and swords, if it was even possible, was a sure way to invite the enemy.

All she could do was watch as Regan took his wife's lips in such a heart-wrenching kiss Amira was sure she would have cried if she was able to. His every pore reeked of desperation and agony as he refused to let go of her. Even when the sound of footfalls reached their ears.

"Please," Milla begged.

"Deron, take my children and go," he told Amira's father, his eyes never leaving Milla's pleading ones. "Run!"

But before Deron could react, the Venlordians were already there. About a dozen of them. With their swords at the ready, they surrounded her family, leaving no way off escape.

"You didn't think it would be that easy to bribe one of us, did you, Your Majesty?" one of them laughed and engaged Pharell.

Amira didn't wait either. She breached the minds of two friars, forcing each to believe the other one was an enemy. It reduced the number of opponents, giving both Deron and Regan a better chance, yet Amira could see that the skills of the older men were rusty. Worse still, Eliana's potions immobilized for only a few seconds.

But despite being outnumbered four or five to one, they fought, flanking the women at the entrance to the cell, where Milla stood with her palms covering her mouth, as she watched her husband's desperate movements.

Amira was trying to help as much as she could, but the cacophony of swords clashing, men yelling, and bodies grunting with exertion belied her every effort to deceive them, allowing the Venlordians to get their bearings too fast. It was a losing battle and she knew it.

Even when Pharell killed one, his *dao kanjis* slicing the man's chest, and her father wounded another, they were still outnumbered and being relentlessly backed against the iron bars. Having less and less space to maneuver.

"Surrender, or you'll watch your women being burned alive," a Venlordian threatened, but they didn't cease fighting. There was nothing stopping the Venlordians from burning them alive, even if the men surrendered. Fighting was their only option.

Their backs now completely against the bars, they guarded the doors, where the women stood cuddled together, with their very lives. They blocked each and every attack, but how much longer they could manage to hold, Amira didn't know. They were already on the defensive, and tiring fast.

Amira gathered all the strength she could muster and touched every mind she was capable of, incapacitating them for few precious seconds.

"*Run!*" she shouted, knowing Regan would not leave his wife, but maybe the others could...

Pharell and Regan used their advantage, killing

three more, while Deron delivered strike after strike to the chain holding Milla. Finally one of the links gave out and he was able to separate it.

Quickly, Deron led the women through the sea of Venlordians, using his swings to clean their path. One by one the bastards went down, and it eased Amira's pain, yet it felt like it was too little too late.

She fell on her knees, trying to hold them for as long as she could, and failed. The Venlordians snapped out of their trance. Someone knocked Deron out.

Eliana screamed as she tried to reach her husband, but was dragged away by her hair and lifted back to her feet. Both Sofie and Eliana ended up in their clutches, daggers pressed to their throats.

Amira had no more power to use. None to borrow. She was helpless. She started to wane.

"His Majesty needs a lesson," one of the members of the Order spoke, looking from one woman to the other. "Which one?"

Amira held her breath as Regan shook his head, refusing to choose.

"Who is it going to be? Your wife, or your daughter?" the Venlordian prompted.

"Me!"

"Take me!" Pharell and Milla answered at the same time. "Leave my daughter, please. Take me," Milla begged.

"I believe I will," the man unsheathed his dagger and stepped closer.

"No—" it was Regan's voice that rang loudest in the maelstrom of shouts as he tried to protect his wife. Amira gathered her last reserves and aimed at the Venlordian, desperately trying to avoid the inevitable.

The dagger changed course.

It sank deep into Sofie's chest.

"No!" Amira shouted, waking up in her body.

The lightning struck the tree ten feet away from her, emphasizing both the rage and the impotence she felt. It struck again and again at the same spot, while all she could do was scream.

Even Jim and Willy hid, probably thinking her crazy, but she couldn't care less. Right now Sofie's scared eyes were all she could see.

Amira couldn't believe she was dead, or worse — dying on the cold, dirty ground in front of the sneering bastard. And she could do nothing to stop it.

Anger churned inside her, and the flames rose up into the sky.

"What's going on?" she heard a voice, and footsteps approaching. She couldn't care less. She'd just watched another being murdered. The same girl who had sung with her when they were little. The only person who was immune to her songs. Now she was dead. *Dead.*

She's dead, Amira yelled not realizing her voice was heard in only one person's mind.

"Who?" Raven asked, walking closer and sitting beside her. "Who is dead?"

"Sofie," Amira breathed out, unaware she was talking. "My sister. Sofie."

"I'm sorry," Raven whispered, his hand touching her cold cheek. "I am so sorry."

"Are you?" She brushed his hand away, not really knowing what she was doing. Not knowing how to cope with the sea of emotions swirling inside of her. She lashed out. "Are you really? Isn't the world better off without another witch in it?"

She stood tall and simply walked away, aware that even the gods wouldn't be able to help if someone crossed her right now.

Chapter 18

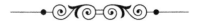

Amira scurried through the mansion as if her tail was on fire. She marched through the front door, sending it crashing open against the wall, and halted when the sound reached her ears. A dozen pairs of eyes landed on her.

She didn't know what she was doing, what was going on inside her. Her hands shook. The air sizzled with pent-up unleashed energy. She was losing control. She grabbed for the wall, fighting to stay upright. Another bolt of lightning cracked the sky.

Rampant emotions were her enemy. If she didn't manage to stifle this gnawing pain inside, she could become a danger to everyone. And yet, all she could think of was pain as she stood looking at people going about their everyday chores.

She looked with eyes blind to everything except visions of a girl who had been tortured within an inch of death. Of another, who had it relatively easy; and of all the others in the past and in the future.

She sensed, more than saw, someone approach. People were talking, but all she could hear was the slick glide of a blade plunging through the flesh, and the thud of the head meeting the ground. The sounds were deafening to Amira.

"Leave me alone," she hissed through gritted teeth, and watched as another lightning streaked across the sky. The pain in her chest was so strong, she almost screamed. She just wanted numbness. Wanted not to feel a thing. Not a single thing.

"Breathe." Strong hands wrapped around her as she fought against the urge to incinerate something. Her power was seeping through her clenched fists.

"How close are you?" Raven whispered against her ear.

She tried to concentrate on his voice, her body relaxing a degree, until she realized what he wished to know. At this, Amira tensed even more than before. Naturally, he wanted to know if she was in control. He was worried about the people she might endanger.

"I have it." Taking his advice she inhaled deeply. She turned around and freed herself from his embrace. "But I need a minute alone."

He watched her, eager to ascertain that she'd spoken the truth no doubt. Amira thought he would leave her. Instead, Raven cupped her jaw with his fingers. He lifted her head to meet his gaze and uttered, "There's nothing shameful in admitting you need help. And if you want to kill someone I would rather it be someone who deserves it."

Amira was floored by his words. How did he know what she craved? How had he seen inside her?

"Look behind you," Raven answered, to a question she wasn't aware she'd asked aloud, or even in his mind.

Amira pivoted and her blood turned ice-cold. Snakes were wriggling. People were running away. The sight—a true testament to how far gone she'd been.

She was so shaken, it took her a moment to notice a girl in the middle of the writhing sea of reptiles.

"Bright Eyes!" Nyssa called for her, determination evident on the girl's face, her feet quickly but carefully carrying her forward.

Amira watched silently as Nyssa fought her fear

and tried to avoid the hissing creatures by constantly jumping out of their way. Not once did she look back. Not once did she appear to be giving up. Not even when one of the reptiles came close to biting her.

Amira waved her arm and the snakes disappeared.

Nyssa ran the last few feet, her arms flying out and wrapping around Amira's body. Amira froze in the girl's embrace, only now feeling Raven retreating.

"Why did you do it?" She didn't know which amazed her more: Nyssa's determination to walk through the snakes, or this embrace.

"Because you looked like you needed it," Nyssa said, unwrapping her arms. "And I thought we could be friends," she said.

"I don't know how to be a friend," Amira admitted. She'd always been alone. Even when among people.

"But you do." The girl smiled, surprising Amira.

They walked together, somehow ending up in the sun-chamber, a place where she could come close to feeling calm. In the midst of plants and birds, in the midst of pure, untainted energy, Amira sensed her powers settling down.

"I need to be alone for a while."

"No you don't. But we don't have to talk." And they didn't. Amira just sat there for an extended moment in perfect peace, listening to the beautiful bird songs. She closed her eyes and didn't realize how easily she fell asleep.

Yet instead of the dreamless sleep she'd always begged for, instead of few moments of oblivion, she dreamed of death and blood and agony.

She dreamed of fear in huge brown eyes, of screams frozen in people's throats. And then she was back on the grass. Screaming. Being held by Raven. Only this time Amira didn't push him away. She embraced his warmth and buried her face in the crook of his neck. She actually sobbed in his arms. Honest-to-God tears were streaming down her cheeks, and he kissed the salty drops away.

Amira woke up, her body shaken to the core, her flesh heated up and her mind calling for him.

"What's wrong?" Nyssa jumped from the chair she was sitting in, immediately running to her side.

"Nothing." Amira shook her head. It was such a big lie she almost choked on it. She'd promised herself not to wish for things. She knew better than to hope, but the embrace she'd dreamed of was more powerful than any reason she could come up with.

Raven's insight into her soul when he'd held her today only bolstered Amira's foolish hope. Foolish, because she realized she wanted more than goddesses would ever allow her to have.

She had to forget, or it would tear her heart asunder when she was forced to leave. The problem was—she was afraid it could already be too late.

It used to be dreams of freedom she imagined when she let herself hope. Now, it was Raven's face she saw whenever she closed her eyes.

Stubborn as he was—full of secrets, sometimes even blind—she was beginning to know his heart. And it wasn't cruel or unkind. It wasn't selfish.

Amira may not have known all of his reasons for tying her up, but she understood why he might have thought it necessary. She wasn't even mad at him. She would have done the same in his shoes. More actually.

She was doomed; Amira struggled to contain a groan. It was so much easier when she could simplify her feelings into plain lust, when she could fool herself. She could no longer.

There was nothing plain about her feelings. Nothing simple. She was attracted to him in so many different ways; it got under her skin and consumed her.

The smile, which made her toes curl. Eyes, capable

of hypnotizing and taking her breath away. And the touch… She wouldn't even know where to begin, if she had to explain the feeling that overwhelmed her when she found herself in his arms. It was magical. She had only to remember his kisses, and her soul wept, thirsting for more. Much more.

As sensuous as it sounded, it was a fantasy. Her cravings aside, she knew very well they belonged to separate worlds.

"Thank you," she told Nyssa, taking her hand. "Go ahead and I'll be right behind." Amira had one more thing to do. She waited till Nyssa was out of the room and began singing. She had to return to the dungeon, to confirm her worst fears.

She saw Milla and Eliana chained to a wall, sobbing, while Regan and Deron rattled the cage they were in, just in front of the women, but out of reach. She didn't see Pharell anywhere, and Sofie's lifeless body lay on the ground between the four of them. Amira returned. She could not help them. Not yet.

She needed Raven's full trust now more than ever, and time was so short, Amira thought as she left the room and found him with a sword in his hands.

"Am I for beheading?" she asked, slowing down.

"Are you all right?" He lifted his head and their gazes met. His was full of worry.

"I always am," Amira assured him. She didn't have the luxury of being anything else. Never had.

"And I don't believe you," he stated as if he could see right through her mask.

"Ask me tomorrow then."

He stood up from the chair, and after coming closer to her said, "I'm sorry."

She blinked. She could see he was being honest, but she couldn't talk about it. Not yet.

"Why do you need the sword?" She changed the

subject.

"It's just a feeling I have," he tried to explain. "A pre-sentiment of something approaching."

Amira closed her eyes, opening her mind to her senses. She heard voices. A lot of voices. Laughter. She saw shadows. She felt danger.

The vision evaporated in seconds.

Amira groaned. When had she become so useless? How could she have missed such a thing in the first place? The man was a menace to her self-control. Moreover, he had proved to have senses sharper than hers.

If she didn't know any better, she would have thought him to be magical. Except, fairytales aside, their world was simple. It hadn't been thousands of years ago, but now only the witches possessed mystical abilities; and all of them were women.

"You better take few more of those," she suggested, lowering her eyes towards his sword. She might not have known what was coming, but the menace was unmistakable.

"Care to elaborate?"

"Not sure … yet," she frowned, rubbing her temples, but her legs were already carrying her. "Outside."

"Then outside is where we're headed."

She nodded, hastening her strides, ready for anything that might be thrown at her the moment she stepped through the front door. She wasn't ready for what she did notice. Nothing. Not a single hint of danger. Not the smallest thing out of the ordinary.

Outside, she said. Well, they were outside. And it was sunny, bright and full of laughter. People were scurrying to and fro at their chores. Children were playing. No danger there. Unless she counted the possibility of drowning in a bowl of water, or accidentally being stabbed with a pitchfork. Not that she saw any of those.

Amira inhaled, this time keeping her eyes wide open, forcing the vision to replay before her eyes. This time she noticed vials.

The image evaporated.

Potions? she wondered. Did it mean witches were already here? No, they couldn't be, could they? The Impenetrable Mountains were too far away for them to have come in the space of only a week.

At that thought, a scream assailed her ears. Her observant glare scanned through the crowd as more yells and shouts joined the initial frantic shriek. Raven stiffened beside her, his hand already on the sword. He was about to battle the horde of … wolves. No hesitation spared.

Amira placed her hand on his before he could unsheathe the weapon and received a puzzled glance in return. She waited. Raven nodded, surprising her again.

If she could, she would have smiled then. It was such a heady sensation to know that someone trusted her, even if just a little. It made her realize how important it was to her.

Suddenly, the image of Ciaran just popped into her mind. And not because right now, in her head, he represented everyone who thought her incapable; but because Amira sensed he was close by.

Later, she told herself. Right now wild animals and people who were a few seconds from creating a violent riot were her priorities.

She leapt to her feet, brushed her cheek against Raven's, and whispered, "Call me Amira."

Without waiting for his response, she stepped between the people and the pack of beasts.

Despite the danger, Raven smiled. He liked to watch her do magic, he realized. His dark enchanting angel glowed when miracles happened.

Amira. The name was beautiful and complex at the same time. Just like the owner herself.

"It's Shadow." Amira turned her crystal eyes to him, a moment before she was swept aside by the tide of grey fur.

"I can see that." He approached the pack, trying to ignore all the gasps and groans. "Why is he here? is what I'd like to know."

Raven found himself surrounded by beasts, for the love of gods. His sword was hidden; and the only emotion left for him was amazement. Well, maybe admiration too.

Controlling one wolf was a huge deal in itself, but the whole pack—that showed tremendous power and will. Raven knew how it worked, how a witch had to focus all her energy into one object to take control over another's will and suppress it. Normally, she would enter into some kind of trance, just to enable her to use that much power. It left her body almost lifeless. Amira, on the other hand, was very much alive, commanding not one, but dozen of beasts. Astounding.

"Shadow says he's come to help."

Raven watched as one of the wolves let itself be patted, smelled her, and licked her arm.

"Tell them they are too late. The damsel needs no saving."

Her eyes narrowed slightly, sending a jolt through his spine. He swallowed. Definitely no need for saving.

"He tells me he was never worried about you."

Raven had to return the narrowed glance.

"Well maybe a little," she shrugged.

"So where is the danger?"

"I don't know," she admitted, lowering her eyes.

"Are you supposed to know everything?" he wondered.

"They would never let me," she uttered, her voice soaked in pain.

He had no idea who "they" were, but he had a sudden urge to kill the bastards for transforming her beautiful face into such a heartbreaking expression.

"Adam!" Mode's hysterical scream woke him up, as the boy broke loose from his mother's clutches and ran straight to them.

Raven caught him, figuring he had better carry him back to his mother. The sound of weeping obviously annoyed the animals.

"But I want to see wolves," he cried aloud, "I never saw one alive and there's dozens…" Adam gestured with his hands, squirming and struggling against Raven's hold.

"Raven!" Amira's voice made him stop in his tracks.

"Don't tell me you want to introduce them to the boy?"

"No." Good, he breathed, returning Adam to Mode. "Another time maybe, but I want to hide them."

"Hide them?" he gaped. "Why can't they just run to the forest, or something?"

His gaze wandered to the gates and he noticed a girl running through the meadow. Alright, so maybe letting them go right now was not the wisest decision. Still … he sensed it wasn't about the girl either.

"Shadow says he needs to stay for a while, but doesn't want to scare her." Amira's gaze traveled to the same girl he was watching.

"Tell them to go to the old stables. But only if they're going to behave," he told her, gesturing towards the empty building at the end of the path.

"Mild as lambs," she promised. She motioned with

the sway of her hand, and the pack ran away into hiding.

Both of them returned their sights to the young girl.

At first Raven thought she was a child of maybe ten years, but as she ran closer, he could see it was her short height that made the first impression so deceptive. The girl was probably around fifteen years old, and she wasn't even that short. It was simply the way she held herself that made her look smaller than her skinny frame and below-average height.

With every step she took, Raven could see her features more clearly. Her dirty face, dress all torn apart. She kept clutching her arms around her chest, trying to pull the shredded fabric together, but it kept slipping through her fingers as she ran.

Another thing Raven noticed were her curls; they weren't simply short, they were cut, brutally chopped off, leaving her with only several tousled strands. She ran barefoot. Her legs were covered in cuts, her eyes were full of tears.

She ran so fast, she almost knocked Amira down. She wrapped her arms around Amira's waist and sank to the knees in front of his witch.

"Help me," she begged, her whole body shaking, "please, help me."

Finally Amira met his gaze, her hands holding the girl.

The enemy, he read loud and clear, *is coming.*

Well, if the girl was a witch as he presumed, a Venlordian must be hot on her heels. Raven exhaled and unbuttoned his shirt. He didn't need Shadow's help to deal with one lousy bastard.

"You know her?" he asked, taking the shirt off and covering the girl's trembling body.

She flinched at his touch, and after sinking deeper into Amira's skirt, gave in to sobs once again. Damn. He had a bad feeling about this.

"No," Amira told him, then looked down at the girl and brushed her tears away. "Don't be afraid Brea, he won't hurt you. No one will," she assured her, folding her into his shirt. "But witches recognize one another by sight." Amira raised her gaze at him. It was full of sadness and anger.

"Judy," Raven called, seeing that the maid, just like almost the whole household, had gathered around. "Take the child to Martha," he ordered, and waited a few moments till the girl was out of their sight.

"Was she—"

"Yes," Amira didn't let him finish the sentence. Damn it, he suspected as much.

"I'll kill the bastard," he gushed through his teeth. She was just a child, for the love of gods. Anyone who had dared to touch her was going to suffer. Painfully.

Sudden death was too easy. Raven decided he was going to kill him with his bare hands and feed in pieces to the wolves.

"Look at me," Amira said, cupping his clenched jaw.

Raven did so. And slowly, he felt the haze that had obscured his vision retreat. Crystal blue eyes mirrored his anger, yet her presence calmed him in a way he couldn't explain.

"It's not just the general brutality that you're against, is it?" The insightful question made him take an even closer look at her, but before he could say a word, a movement caught the corner of his eye.

He turned to the direction Brea had run from, and froze. It was not just one bastard coming. It was a freaking army of them.

Chapter 19

"Burt!" Amira heard Raven yell the moment he saw what she was looking at. "Women and children. Inside. Now!"

His hand unsheathed the sword.

"Jim! Willy! Take a few men and guard the door. Robin…" he continued issuing orders as the advancing Venlordians were practically at their doorstep.

"You—" he looked at her.

"Staying," she announced. Amira wanted a piece of those bastards too. For Brea, for Sofie, for all the nameless girls who had suffered at their hands. She wanted blood, and she wanted it now!

The rage she thought she'd buried came alive with a vengeance. It flared inside her, intertwined with hatred and anger. Her emotions churned, flooding her senses—with a force so powerful, a storm descended upon them all.

Dark clouds obliterated light, replacing the glorious summer weather with a brewing maelstrom swirling above their heads. The far horizons vanished. The winds rose and howled, catching her flimsy strapless gown, causing the purple, silky fabric to flutter in the air.

"Amira!" Raven's voice rang louder than the bellowing thunders, his expression all but promising to throw her over his shoulder and carry her inside if she didn't listen.

She shook her head. If he thought for one second

she would lock herself away like some coward...

The thread of her thoughts snapped when Raven's palm wrapped around the nape of her neck. He pulled her closer until their bodies met, and looking directly into her eyes, whispered, "Stay alive."

"Same goes for you," Amira breathed, conscious of their hearts beating with the same wild tempo. Conscious of the plea in his hoarse voice.

Theirs was a brief, stolen moment in the midst of a tempest. A fleeting touch that lasted a thousand lifetimes in Amira's heart, and yet ended way too quick. There was no more time. Her gaze was drawn away by a black sea of Venlordians streaming through the iron gates, in waves of raised swords.

Raven stepped in front of her, attempting to shield her with his body, but Amira jumped to his side immediately, refusing to be sheltered.

Reacting on pure instinct, she raised her hands, palms to the enemy and screamed from the bottom of her lungs for them to stop.

They did. The Venlordians smashed into her shield, just a few feet away.

"You can't hold them back forever like this," Raven said without turning to her, his eyes never leaving the enemy.

No she couldn't. Amira knew that only too well. The sheer number of them, of their amulets—it was overwhelming.

While normally an amulet wouldn't have caused her to blink twice, this many of them ... their collective force began penetrating, eroding her shield. To make things worse, Amira couldn't seem to curb her own power completely. The freakish storm was a true testament to how frail the grip on her control was.

"Release them. It's inevitable."

Still Amira hesitated. If she was to do anything at

all, it had to be now. Once the opposite armies merged together, it would be impossible to strike a blow that affected all of the members of the Order without harming the others.

Amira ransacked her brain, desperate for any solution, but the answer was not forthcoming. If she sang or tried anything massive, her power would not differentiate between those she wanted to die and those she didn't. Her emotions were still running amok, and she would be lying to herself if she said she could focus this kind of force.

What could she do? She'd never been in a battle. Had no knowledge of strategies. Her gaze ran across the army of Venlordians, and then the waiting men standing just beside her. The men on her side weren't vastly outnumbered, but the strain, even fear, in their faces was unmistakable.

She looked at Raven, whose face showed nothing but raw determination, his eyes sharp, hands steady. She understood that this was inescapable. She swallowed the lump in her throat and shattered the shield.

For the longest, tension-filled moment, both armies stood still, simply watching. Then a tall redheaded man pointed his sword straight at her.

"A nice morsel you have here. I believe it is my lucky day," he smiled. "Deliver the witch and we'll spare the others."

Of course — they were after her! Amira clenched her fists when she saw how recognition had lit up their faces. How did they always know she was the witch with a prophecy, when in her every reincarnation she looked different, was beyond her. She would have thought Ven herself was sending them, only what did she have to gain from it? The goddess had proven time and time again that she wanted her to fulfill it.

"What say you?" she heard the question and waited, telling herself she would not blame Raven if he delivered her to the Venlordians. There were just too many people to consider. Too many lives at risk. Though if truth be told, she feared her heart would break.

She had been in a similar situation once before. Only no people were in danger of being hurt then. Just one man who'd sworn he loved her, and had betrayed her to save his own hide.

"The only one who is going to be delivered is you. Straight to Zcuran!" Raven yelled, his words destroying the fragile, tense calm.

Hell itself broke loose all around her. Swords met and clanged. Amira watched for a dazed second how the men fought, her eyes wandering to the right, to Raven, as he engaged two men at once.

His body moved gracefully with such force and determination she bit her lip in admiration. She didn't notice a Venlordian breaching the line of men in front of her and advancing with his sword, ready to swing it.

One moment the male yelled his battle cry, going for her with full force; the next—he crumbled at her feet, his hand released the weapon.

Amira cursed under her breath. She was so helpful!

A hindrance, nothing more, she muttered, disgusted with herself. All the power in the world was no match for rank stupidity.

"What did I tell you?" Raven gnashed his teeth, pulling his sword out of the lifeless body. Blood splattered everywhere.

She stretched her fingers, energy flowed into her, and she swiped her hand through the air. The two enemy warriors, who went after Raven from behind, went flying.

"Stay alive!" Amira mouthed, her hands launching

energy bolts left and right.

"Nice to know I was heard." He was already in the fray of the action, his sword striking with lethal, but masterfully controlled blows. His movements were fluid like water—the strength behind the weapon brutal, but harnessed with perfect efficiency.

Amira threw another energy ball, then another, but all it did was faze the Venlordians slightly. It couldn't even hurt them enough to eliminate them from the fight—not unless she concentrated with everything in her. Her punch wasn't as strong as she would have liked. It couldn't kill.

She also had to aim very carefully. And whenever she incapacitated one of them, a few more took his place, it seemed. She groaned, watching how the men ducked, jumped and swung their swords. The storm intensified, thunders roared in the sky.

She swiped her hands right and left, throwing Venlordians around like rag dolls. But soon realized she could not continue this for long.

She was using magic quicker than she was gaining it. And her reach was very limited due to the many people around her—men she didn't want to injure.

Offence wasn't exactly working for her. She needed to find another approach. Needed to be smart about this.

She glared at the sword in the hands of a tall fair-haired Venlordian, about to descend and detach Robin's fallen body from his head, and tore it out from the hands of the enemy, plunging it deep into the other Venlordian's chest. The move cost her dear. The strength it took her to wrench the blade from the firm male grip got her panting.

"Thanks!" Robin jumped to his feet, prepared for another attack.

Amira took a calming breath and, instead of

fighting what she could not beat, began surveying the men more closely, looking for who needed help the most.

It took tremendous concentration to prevent the killing blows from hitting home; enormous strength to do it again and again without fail. And even if the army of the Order was falling, Amira had to wonder how long she would be able to keep this up.

* * *

A gust of breath oozed from Raven's lungs as a blade sliced through his side, leaving nothing but vicious pain in its wake. He changed hands in an attempt to sidestep the sneaky bastard who had attacked him from behind, but the slightest move caused the gaping wound to open up further.

A superficial cut, he winced, knowing full well he couldn't let it distract him. There were too many Venlordians left. Too much to lose.

Conserving his strength, Raven waited for the male to come to him instead of going after him, and plunged his sword the moment his opponent was within his reach. The sharp metal went through the ribs like a knife through butter, and the Venlordian collapsed, becoming yet another corpse.

That was when Amira brushed past him, her hands coming to rest on his torso. Her fingers moved outwards to his sides, sending a wave of sizzling energy through him.

"You are too pale for this." Raven grabbed her wrists in an attempt to stop her, but it was already too late. The flesh was knitting itself, his wound disappearing before their eyes. Only the thrilling sensation kept cursing through his veins.

"Have you looked in the mirror lately?" she shot back, and despite everything, Raven's lips curved.

"Stop exhausting yourself," he all but barked a moment later, instead of answering her.

He might have lost blood, might even be paler than her, but it didn't mean he hadn't noticed the vast amounts of energy she was burning up. Even the trees began to wither in her wake wherever she turned. Grass turned into a brown carpet around her feet.

Raven could see strain furrowing her lovely face. Even a droplet of sweat running down her temple. Or had it finally begun to rain?

The storm was a strange one, to say the least. With the sky brooding, clouds swirling, thunders bellowing; and yet, nothing happening.

"Stop worrying about me." Her fingers crept up to his cheek in a slow caress he felt to the marrow of his bones, the touch almost making him lose all rational thought. The battle went on, however. Forcing him to return to it. Forcing him to face the carnage under his feet, and a new wave of aggressors coming at them with full force.

He instantly pushed her aside, letting his sword intercept the strikes. The metal clanged loudly, producing sparks with each brutal hit. He kicked out, his foot connecting with a Venlordian's stomach; then as his opponent hunched slightly, his fingers losing their firm grip, Raven took advantage and swung his sword, getting rid of the obstacle.

He jumped over the body in front of him, his own skin beaded with sweat, heart raging. Breaths shallow. He didn't toy with enemy — plunged and pulled the sword back, sliced, and decapitated. Yet, he couldn't see an end to it. They were like worms crawling out of their holes. No matter how many you killed, they just kept coming.

As he engaged two or three at a time, his eyes lost track of Amira. When he did find her, his blood turned to ice. Four Venlordians were only feet away from her, while she was so absorbed in aiding someone, she didn't notice them approaching.

It was only a matter of time before the enemy picked on her weakness. They surrounded her from all sides, laying a trap. It became obvious to Raven that even if she snapped out of her stupor, she wouldn't be able to evade all four of them. Wouldn't even see some of them before it was too late.

Raven didn't hesitate. He grabbed a dagger from his belt and threw it straight into the heart of the first man. Grabbed another. Threw. Was out of daggers. He cursed, running to her side. His elbow smashed into somebody's face, and he plunged his sword deep into the third Venlordian.

He thought he was ready for the fourth, but the duel between them was an exhausting one. His every last muscle screamed in protest. Raven didn't know how much longer he could go on like this.

She turned when his blade swung through the air, separating the body from its head. Blood gushed out from the mortal wound and blinded him temporarily. Raven wiped it away in time to see another man ready to strike him.

In a flash of a second he realized that his sword wasn't going to be fast enough to block the blow.

Still, he tried to deflect the death-blow which … never came. It froze in mid-air as lighting struck the bastard directly. Skin ashen and smoking, the Venlordian went down.

What next? Their eyes met, both of them silently

asking the same question.

They had been fighting for ages, it seemed. Many of them were injured, some seriously, and the members of the Order kept advancing. With potions even, Amira realized, as she saw a few of Raven's men frozen in their tracks.

She immediately reacted, neutralizing the malign effect and broke all the vials she could see. It wasn't enough though. She knew it. What she needed was a miracle; otherwise they were going to fall. One by one.

Venlordians were all skilled, trained fighters. And only a handful of men on Raven's side possessed such skills. Others, despite their bravery, were deep in trouble. She could only keep them safe for so long. *She* could only be kept safe for so long.

Amira took a quick glance around her. At the carnage left after Raven had dispatched the ones intending her harm. She lifted her gaze up to the man in front of her — he was panting just the same as she was.

"Wolves! Summon your wolves," he rasped, and Amira covered her mouth, stunned she'd forgotten all about the beasts.

"Shadow!" she called. "Now!"

The animal appeared instantly. Ran straight at them. And behind him, the whole horde of wolves. They howled in unison, just before she yelled "Attack!" Her voice loud enough to startle everyone.

My pleasure, Shadow howled and lunged at the enemy.

The beasts terrified them, and most of them ran screaming like girls, forgetting their sacred cause along with the weapons. There were some of them whose zealotry prevailed — instead of retreating, they jumped into the fray more furiously, only to be ripped apart by wild animals.

It was a bloody massacre. She should have been

horrified by the image. Should have felt sorry for the pain they suffered before dying. Yet she felt none of those things. They deserved what they got. And would get even more in the afterlife for killing innocent women, raping children.

Now she was disgusted, but only by the vision she grudgingly painted in her own head.

She met Raven's eyes and the horrors vanished. A pure, untamable surge of energy swept her straight into his embrace, and she melted as he pulled her closer and kissed her.

"What are you doing?" her voice faltered, letting out a shuddering whisper.

"Isn't it obvious?" He took her face in his palms, smiled, and gently touched her nose with his lips, "I am kissing you."

She pulled back, placing her fingers on his lips to prevent them from finding hers again. "But—"

He didn't let her complete the protest; instead, he placed a gentle kiss on the tips of her fingers and uttered, "You wanted me to decide. I did."

Amira's heart skipped a beat.

He lowered his mouth again and nibbled her lower lip.

Amira was so tempted, but she found strength to take a full step back. "Here?"

Raven wrapped his arm around her waist and pulled her up against him, refusing to let her go. "You ask for it behind closed doors, but deny me in the open?" His brows furrowed.

"It's just blood talking. Emotions running high." She could feel every part of his body against hers, the heat of his consuming her senses. But... "You don't want people to see you with a witch."

"What makes you think I give a flying fig about what others think? The only opinion that would really matter to me—" he shook his head, and before she could ask whose opinion mattered, his lips descended on hers again.

This time Amira didn't fight it. She wrapped her arms around his neck and returned his kiss with a fiery passion.

"I told you he's under that thing's spell," Amira heard as if through the fog. She heard many voices she paid no attention to, but this one ... She turned her head to the woman.

"And he's happy about it. But since I don't find you attractive, think of how happy you'll be when I put you under."

Mode blanched and ran away.

"Don't fry her," Raven laughed, drawing her attention towards himself. Amira hardly even noticed that the skies were blue again. Not a single storm cloud on the horizon. "Mode, just like the other women, doesn't know what you did here."

"And yet, with all that blood and so many bodies around, all they see is me. Abusing others."

"Not all of them," he assured her and kissed her again. This time when their lips separated he kept looking at her as if expecting the earth to crack open under his feet and swallow him alive.

He did regret this, a thought crossed Amira's mind, and something inside her snapped.

"Say it," she demanded.

"Will you be mine tonight," he breathed, shocking her completely.

"Wha-at?" Amira could hardly believe her ears. It had to be a hallucination of some sort.

"Say you'll be mine," he repeated.

"What changed?" she needed to know, even if all she wanted was to feel his touch.

"I decided it's useless to fight the inevitable."

"That so?"

"It is so."

"And the other reason?" Amira pressed, not sure why she was doing it.

"I'll tell you later." He slowly kissed her neck and she moaned as her eyes drifted shut for a single, intoxicating second.

"Then I'll answer you later." Amira placed a kiss of her own on his lips. "Now come. We need to tend to the wounded."

He didn't let her go immediately. Instead, he took her hands in his, and without dragging his gaze away from her eyes, said, "No more channeling of any kind. I mean it."

Amira's eyebrows shot up at his order, but it was all she did before turning and sauntering away—aware of him watching her. Aware that this time it was he who had asked her.

If only she didn't hear a loud voice inside her head telling her it would be a grave mistake to accept.

Chapter 20

Raven watched Amira for an eternity, or so it seemed, only now noticing her dark, rich locks brushing against her back.

When did her hair become undone? he wondered, realizing his memories were shrouded by a mist. The scrambled visions of the battle were so surreal in his head, he could hardly remember the order of events.

Maybe in a few days, when his heart wasn't drumming in his ears. When he didn't see blood on the hem of her dress—a screaming reminder of this whole insanity. He sighed, finally letting her go. She would come to him when she was ready. If the wait didn't kill him first.

Raven looked around. The horror and joy on the people's faces brought him back to reality. It became painfully clear how lucky they had been to survive this. It was a miracle that the number of casualties was this low.

Half, if not more, of them would have been dead—Raven included—if not for the woman he still couldn't figure out.

Maybe it was the mystery holding him captive. Maybe her spirit. All he knew was that hour was chasing hour; the sun was setting, bringing them closer and closer to the night, and she remained in his mind despite all the blood he was drenched in.

One would think having time to cool off would

have brought him to his senses, but the intensity of his desires was simply undeniable. He couldn't even concentrate on the blazes around him. He was going crazy.

He was up to his ears in the piled-up bodies, trying to incinerate all the evidence of the fight, and it felt as if his insides were burning instead. His flesh felt too hot, his skin too tight around his bones.

It didn't leave him completely blind or deaf to the stolen glances and silent accusations of those grieving the loss of their loved ones. The malicious vibes he was picking up were few, but it didn't mean they didn't exist.

Raven was convinced no one would dare voice it — not after the very public display of their kiss, or of the powers she wielded. Even those who had been safely tucked inside the house had already heard many stories. Half of them exaggerations, but it helped to stem the murmuring.

Still, he wanted to spare her the pain. With her astute senses, he was convinced she knew everything, even if she didn't show it. That was the thing about Amira, he thought. She acted as if nothing fazed her — strong and unwavering on the outside, while inside, she felt things profoundly.

Even now, she was healing the wounded. Against his wishes. Not sparing herself even for a wolf. And never once she looked at him, while all he wanted to do was gather her into his arms and carry her to his bed.

If only she could answer the damned question, Raven almost groaned, starting yet another fire, his hands weary from it.

His body was demanding her. Or a cold bath, if this continued.

He had no idea what reasons she had for tormenting him so, but he'd spoken the truth. He didn't view her being a witch as something to be ashamed of anymore.

Raven didn't care what others thought of him. Only Dacian mattered. But once his brother awoke, he would hate Raven no matter what. That was the sad truth.

He had denied himself for so long, and maybe he would have succeeded, if it was simple lust he was possessed with. Adding another betrayal was inconceivable to him. Except, she was not responsible for who she was born—only for what she made of herself.

She was an angel.

A dark one, true, but still an angel, he smiled, wondering how a word he'd used as a mockery once had become a caress. *An angel with a body made for sin,* he added, as his gaze slid back to her.

With all of this horror and gore around, with fires burning in the dark, she was the most amazing and beautiful thing to behold. And her being so far away— was slowly killing him.

* * *

"You should use this." Nyssa caught Amira off-guard. The girl extended her hands to show what she was holding, and it took Amira a few seconds for her brain to digest the information. The white strips of material Nyssa held were bandages.

She should use bandages. Maybe then she wouldn't feel like the ground was going to come up swinging any minute and take a slap at her face.

"Shouldn't you be somewhere else?" she asked instead.

"Shouldn't you?"

Amira just stared her down until Nyssa raised her hands in surrender.

"You sound like my mother," the girl muttered. "It's not like they can hide all of this from me. And I thought you could use some help, but fine—I'm leaving. I just came to tell you that Brea was sleeping in Martha's room, but if you are so eager to get rid of me…"

Amira shook her head at the tirade. "There are plenty of things to do. If your mother doesn't object, that is." Amira didn't feel like she had patience enough for Mode right now.

"You can always turn her into a tadpole. Kidding, just kidding," she added on seeing Amira arch her eyebrows at the suggestion. "Was she right, though? Did you put a spell on master Raven?"

Amira sighed. How did she end up in this inquisition? Worse—she barely resisted the urge to rub her temples in frustration—the people around had suddenly become very quiet. Too quiet.

"Nah, he's too stubborn for that." She wrapped a bandage around a shallow wound after she'd cleaned it, only too aware of people listening in on their conversation.

"Why is he looking at you this way then?"

Amira groaned. That was a question she refused to answer. "And why are you asking questions instead of helping?"

"I'm not a child, you know. I've been kissed!" The scarlet color of poppies bloomed in Nyssa's cheeks when she realized what she'd said. She stood up with haste, and all but ran away.

The people around let out a laugh and Amira bit her lip. If only she could run like this. Instead, she moved around as if through a dream. Or a nightmare. She was tired. There was blood everywhere. The voice plaguing her didn't allow a single moment of reprieve. And then

… there was this other voice — the voice of a man whose gaze she felt burning into her back wherever she went.

Say you'll be mine.

Amira's pulse quickened, but she didn't turn. She was afraid there really was only one answer for her to give. The answer, if uttered — her inner voice advised — would set a different course in motion. Something would unravel irretrievably.

It was madness. She knew she wanted him. Craved him. But was it worth the risk? Was one night, maybe a few, worth dying for? She could enjoy this briefly, and then what? she had to ask herself. There would be no happily ever after for them. No matter how she spun this.

All she had was another week or so at this place. Then … who knew? She might be born again some hundred years later with new memories to haunt her forever.

Say you'll be mine.

Amira closed her eyes and took a deep breath.

Why did he have to ask? She could almost curse him for it. If he had carried her inside with his lips on hers, she would have welcomed him with open arms. Rational thoughts, consequences — nothing existed when she was being swept away by the tidal wave of desires.

Now, she had fears and doubts, and that damned voice telling her to wait.

Wait for what? Amira wanted to know. She could be dead tomorrow. Waiting had never been an option for her. Not when everything was changing so quickly. Either she seized what she wanted, or she was left with regrets.

She would be left with regrets either way — Amira realized the true reason behind her fear. She was scared of what could happen if she fell in love with him. She didn't want such memories, or feelings to live inside her when she wasn't Amira anymore. Except … except it was either memories of the few brief moments in time to haunt her, or regrets because she'd been too much of a coward to risk it.

Coward… she scowled at the word. When did she become one? When did she start whining? Finally, she turned her eyes to him—Raven's hair and body was dripping wet from him having washed the blood off. He turned, as if sensing her perusal, their eyes met, and his question rang again in her head.

Say you'll be mine.

"Yes," she mouthed, and witnessed as the bowl he held slipped from his fingers and hit the ground.

Water splashed all around, but the hot promise his eyes whispered refused to let her go. She shivered with anticipation, and found herself in his arms two seconds later.

There were no more words between them. None were needed. He swept her off her feet and carried her inside, almost running the whole way up the stairs.

The moment Raven kicked the door closed, his mouth was on hers, and Amira's blood sizzled. She sank her fingers into his wet, silky hair and moaned in his mouth, her nostrils filling with masculine scent. Her body felt like a powder keg, ready to explode any minute. All she needed was the few touches she craved.

She trembled at the thought of his hands on her, her nipples hardened and pressed against the material of her dress. She thought she would go crazy. But instead of carrying her to his bed, Raven released her.

"Leave me this time, and I swear I'll tie you to that damned pole," she breathed, her hands refusing to leave his heated skin.

"Kinky," he laughed. "Didn't know you were into that."

"And if I said I was?"

"I would have to persuade you to explore your desires here, not in front of a hundred people."

Amira felt the urge to laugh.

"Not big on sharing?" she asked.

"When it comes to this? No!" he stated firmly.

"Then come here." She stretched out her arms in welcome invitation, but the command in her voice was unmistakable.

"You sure you aren't too tired?"

"I'm sure I'll go mad if you keep looking at me like that and don't do anything about the fire I see in your eyes."

"Then kiss me." He issued an order of his own, pulling her so close she could feel every inch of his rock-hard body against hers.

She obeyed. Amira placed her lips on him, but not on his mouth. She kissed his neck, gently nibbling at the skin. She rained kiss after tender kiss down to his chest, and only then did she find her way back to his lips.

"Satisfied?" She uttered in a low-pitched, passion-laced tone.

"Not yet," —his fingers found the laces of her dress— "but I'm sure we'll figure something out." Raven lowered his lips to the hollow in her neck for a taste, but found himself unable to draw away.

He reveled in the feeling of her hands exploring his body. They slid up and down his chest, hands and abdomen, as if memorizing every rise and slope of his muscles. He took her earlobe into his mouth, sucked, and heard a delicious moan leave her lips. Her nails dug into his biceps.

"Oh, we will!" Her raw, husky voice reverberated inside him, just as her hand slipped inside his pants and her fingers wrapped around the length of him.

Raven thought he was going to explode when her hand began stroking. He wasn't even inside her yet, and the earth was already slipping from under his feet. And slipping. And slipping. Just like her dress—his fingers finally loosened it enough for it to fall down, pooling around her waist.

His mouth descended on her breast—his tongue relishing the feel of a hard, rosy nipple. His senses tottered so dangerously close to the edge, he didn't know how he managed to hold on as his hands moved lower, to the juncture of her thighs.

She was so wet for him, it took him one gentle stroke and she shuddered in his arms.

He had no recollection of how they ended up in his bed, but finally she was there. Where he had wanted her for so long. Under him.

Sweet heaven and perishing flames of Zcuran, but she was a perfect vision. Her long dark curls splayed like a fan on his pillows. Her eyes were misted by desire. Her lips parted into a seductive whisper he craved to taste. Her breaths came out strangled.

Her hands traveled higher, and for a second he mourned the loss of her heat burning through his flesh. But when she parted her legs enough to accommodate his lower body, he groaned and claimed her soft lips again. He was desperate in his need to devour her.

He shuddered when he felt her nails rake down his back, yet suddenly she ceased. Something changed in her.

"Show me your back," she whispered against his lips, her voice laced with horror. Horror?

"What?" His mind was so clouded by desire, the taste of honey still in his mouth, Raven struggled to fathom the meaning of this.

"Please," she uttered.

The stifled plea in her voice made him do the unthinkable—he lifted his protesting body from hers, and turned so she could take a look at his back.

He turned back to her, only to find himself staring at her eyes so misted, he couldn't see the crystal oceans he loved anymore. They were empty.

She pushed herself up to a sitting position, and turned her own back to him so he could see.

Desire forgotten, Raven stared at the marks, identical to his own. And at that moment the world really did slip from under his feet.

Chapter 21

"How?" Raven's voice came out hoarse, almost gruff. "How is this possible?"

"We were bound by destiny. I just … I had no idea it happened before we met." Her voice sounded strange to his ears. Her eyes—distant. It seemed like she was going through the motions, but she wasn't there. Raven was not convinced *he* was even there.

She cupped his face. The deep azure of her gaze bored into him, and she whispered in a barely audible voice, "Tell me."

Raven didn't know what kind of bizarre dream this was, but talking about it was the last thing he wanted. He'd never breathed a word to anyone about the day. He had never discussed it. Not even with Martha, who had lived the same nightmare. Well, parts of it. She'd been unconscious through almost all of it. She'd been lucky.

But now, seeing a plea in her hollow eyes … he found himself uttering the truth for the very first time: "We were attacked … my family slaughtered. And the scars…" His voice faltered.

Raven could feel his muscles tensing, his breathing deepening. Fifteen years had passed without a single day of peace. Without a single day of leaving the past behind. It was a bit easier when he was away from this place—a place where every corner was a reminder. A place that felt like a painted canvas, with images he could not escape even if he closed his eyes. They were imprinted on his soul.

"The Order." She got up on her knees, slowly approached him and straddled his legs.

She wrapped herself like ivy around him, every inch of her naked body touching him. And yet, there was nothing sexual about the way they held each other. In that moment she was his only lifeline as he dangled on the precipice of his memories.

"I hunted them down one by one," he confessed. It had taken him years and, sadly, when he was through, it didn't make him feel any better.

Her hands kept caressing his back, and every time her fingers touched a scar, he could swear he heard the swish of the whip as it came down.

"But the sound of the whip is not what haunts you, is it?" she spoke against the skin of his neck, and the breath of her words brought a punishing wave of heat.

Raven didn't know if he would have answered, but suddenly he found himself unable to breathe. It became unbearably hot. He was swept away by the waves of heat so familiar, the recognition of what they spelled turned his blood ice-cold.

"What did you do?" he demanded, grabbing her arms and placing them between their bodies. He didn't need the answer, though. The truth stared right back at him with the deep blue eyes he'd always found fascinating.

"If you'll let me—"

"Let you?" He shook his head in perplexity. "Did I miss something?" He unwrapped her legs, fastened his pants and stood up. Yet found himself unable to move. "You had no right," was all that escaped his tightly pressed lips.

Raven detested those marks with all of his might, but he could not imagine himself without them either.

In a sick and perverted way, they defined the man he had grown up to be.

Amira stood up on the bed, and the dress she had wrapped around her waist fell down to cover her long legs. She didn't even try to wrench the material up, leaving the top of the dress swiveled around her hips. Unabashed about her exposed flesh, she walked to the edge of the bed, and slowly, as if doubting herself, laid her palms on his shoulders.

The thought of refusing her touch didn't even cross his mind. But the strangeness of her behavior did surprise him—how could a person who was not ashamed of nudity have reservations about a simple touch?

"I'm sorry," she mouthed, and Raven had to strain his ears to hear the words.

He lifted his head to meet her gaze, not sure what he would find, but the emotions he came face to face with were something he was unable to name.

"I sometimes cross the line," she continued murmuring under her breath, as if talking with herself. "It's hard to know when desires are so … contradictory. It causes you pain, and yet, you want them back…"

"It also reminds me of something I can never let myself forget." He closed his eyes, only now realizing how stupid the words sounded. He didn't need the scars as a reminder. With or without it, it was not like he could ever forget.

"It sounds to me like you are punishing yourself, but if that is your wish…" Her hands slid down his back, her body leaned forward, and he had to steady her by placing his hands on her sides.

Raven knew what she was about to do. He knew he could have stopped her. He *should* have stopped her. But when her head came down and she kissed him, whatever he was about to say died before leaving his mouth.

Maybe it was because she kept kissing him, or maybe because causing a scar by using magic was different from gaining the welts after a beating — either way Raven felt no pain. No physical pain, that is.

With each mark she put in place, memories rose anew. The wails, the cries … it all returned. It seemed so real — the pleading sounds, the coppery smell of blood — he could swear it was happening again.

It took him a while to shove all of it away, but when he did, when he came to his senses, he noticed how stiff Amira's body had become. And it was not all he noticed.

Her lips were trembling. Her hands were shaking.

"Stop it!" he commanded.

Raven couldn't grab her arms, so he turned until she lost her balance and went down straight into his waiting embrace.

"Why didn't you tell me?" he all but yelled. He didn't want to hurt her. He didn't want her suffering.

"It does not hurt," she replied, closing her eyes for a deep breath.

Raven was not hearing her anymore. His attention went to his hands cradling her and — despite his mind refusing to believe in his senses — something dark grew inside his heart. He lifted his palm and his breath caught in his throat.

Blood. There was blood all over his skin.

He stared at his bloody hands disbelievingly for a moment. The meaning of what he was witnessing was yet to sink into his brain. His heart, however, didn't need time to digest the hot, red liquid he saw. It felt dread and horror, and even anger.

Anger at her — for not telling him about the consequences. At himself — for he, of all people, should have known better.

He laid her on her stomach and cursed when the image of her lacerated flesh greeted him. Her back was ridged with long, open wounds. Wounds that should have been his. Always his to bear and live with. Not hers.

His back should have been covered with those hideous slashes. *His* blood should have been flowing in rivers. Instead, he only felt a mild, tenuous throbbing in his healed scars, while she…

"It doesn't hurt," Amira repeated with a feeling he wasn't listening to her. "It only looks awful."

"No, of course it doesn't!" he laughed sarcastically. "Because open wounds never do!"

"Will you listen to—"

"Lie still," Raven ordered, pinning her down when she tried to push up. "I'll clean the wounds and—"

"Stop being stubborn!" she exclaimed, getting very frustrated. "I told you it does not hurt! It's only a physical manifestation."

"What do you mean by that?"

"When I was nine I got the scars, but it was you who bled." How did he survive?—it was a mystery to her. He shouldn't have been alive, not after this many strikes. "My nightmare was an onslaught of emotions so powerful, of screams so loud, I couldn't bear it."

Something died in her that day. And when she woke up, she was numb to everything. Until she met him.

"Now, you've got the scars…"

"And you've got the pain?" he said in an incredulous tone that told her he thought he had just caught her lying.

"That would have been true, if I'd beaten you with a

whip." This was different. "The wounds will close promptly."

"How promptly?"

"A few hours, maybe." Again, she tried to sit up, but he held her fast. His hands were firm, hold unbreakable, but she could feel how careful he was—keeping his palms as far as possible from the wounds.

"Are you even listening to yourself? *A few hours maybe.* You'll bleed to death by then." His voice was like sandpaper rubbing her senses.

"Stop growling at me!" Amira had had it with this lying on her front. Unable to turn, unable to see his face.

"Then start healing yourself," he whispered oh so calmly against her ear.

"You know I can't heal myself." She'd already told him this, days ago. Why would he ask her this?

"All I know is, if you can't figure this one out, it means you've already lost too much blood." Raven spoke to her slowly as if explaining the mysteries of the universe to a baby. It made Amira grit her teeth. "We are bound, you said. Then heal me and you'll heal yourself."

"You would let—"

"No, I'll let you to bleed to death," he retorted sarcastically. "What do you think?"

"I said I won't bleed—"

"And I said shut up and come here." Finally he helped her to get up so she could see his furious eyes, and all she wanted to do was trail her fingers along those stern lines of his face. And kiss him.

"Bossy," Amira almost laughed.

She put her hands on him and, inching closer, inhaled his scent. The world suddenly began swirling. She did have trouble with keeping her thoughts straight. They kept jumping from one thing to another so quickly, she found herself unable to keep up, and almost missed his next word.

"I think you need it. Considering the foolish things you keep doing." The moment Raven's scars were gone, he twisted her body so quickly, Amira didn't have time for even a surprised gasp. She found herself on her stomach once again, and a moment later felt wet cloth brushing over her back.

"I have too many bosses of me, already." She hated being bossed around. Except hate wasn't the emotion she felt now, was it? She shouldn't be telling him this — the thought crossed her mind a second before it was chased by another — when did he bring the water?

"Who?" his hands stilled.

Amira murmured something incomprehensible even to her own ears, but the answer must have satisfied him, because his hands resumed washing her back.

Amira must have fallen asleep, because the next thing she knew, he was taking off the blood-soaked bedding.

Everything still swirled as he lifted her from the bed and placed her in a chair. She felt drunk watching the way he changed the sheets, came back to her, and tore her dress off her body. And then, he took her back to the bed and wrapped her in a blanket.

"You finally manage to rip my clothes off and all you can do is look so grim?" She reached for his stubborn, thickset jaw, her fingers coming into contact only when he leaned forward, moving closer to her. "Remember what I told you about the pole?"

That did win her a small smile. He sat near her, but the slight curl in the corners of his lips was all too soon replaced by a stony expression.

"I hope you're not trying to tell me you feel great."

"I definitely don't feel as bad as you think I do." She braced herself, pushing her body up, but it turned out to be a feeble attempt.

"I see." Raven shook his head in bewilderment. "Hell will freeze over before you admit a weakness," he muttered under his breath and she heard the words only because he was an inch away.

Amira would have protested—she had revealed *too many* weaknesses to him—but she found herself limp in her bones, and lethargic in her brain. All she could do was to don a mask of false bravado and turn to him. It seemed he was mad at her, but he did help her sit up and lean her head against the bedstead.

"All right. So spill it," he said, his voice suddenly sounding as if it had grown teeth. "And don't think you are fooling anyone."

"You could curb your tone, you know," Amira suggested, but for some reason she found his growly commands thrilling.

"I don't think I have it in me right now," Raven admitted. "I'm still mad at you." But his hand went around her, pulling her closer until she was nestled against his body with his jaw on the top of her head.

"So what do you want to know?"

Was she really going to tell him everything he asked? Amira wondered. She was too tired to figure out the answer. All she knew was that trust, just like passion, worked both ways. If she wanted him to bare his soul, she had to be ready to bare hers.

"Many things. But let's start with why we are bound, and did you see what happened fifteen years ago?"

His hands kept rubbing at her arms as if she was freezing, when in truth she felt hot. Why was she shivering then?, she asked herself, listening to the steady beat of his heart. The sound captured her. Silence fell over them. Stretched.

Raven didn't press her. He let her lie in his arms,

mind wandering, and it became so natural for them to just drift away completely. But Amira refused to surrender.

"I don't know why," she uttered eventually. "Maybe because they wanted us to meet. It's not like they tell me their reasons. And no, I didn't see anything. I felt it." But at least now she knew whose horror she had survived, all those years ago.

They were destined to meet. She would have thought it a good thing, if only she didn't know Destiny as the heartless, cold-blooded bitch that she was.

"Who are they?" he inquired, his own voice sounding groggy now.

"Goddesses." Normally, Amira would have thought twice before answering this question, but she was half dreaming.

She remembered how heavy her lids had been, but the moment she had let them drift shut was already lost to her. Instead, her drowsy mind was focused on goddesses. On Ven—the goddess of hatred and vengeance—the cruelest one of them all. The most powerful one. Sidony—the goddess of all living creatures. And Destiny herself, with her cryptic ways and winding paths. The three strongest female gods.

The male gods had no interest in her, but those three...

"They yank my chain whenever they want to." Amira admitted something she shouldn't have under any circumstances.

"Are you telling me you have no free will?" The idea of someone playing with them as if they were mere chess pieces apparently worried him.

"Free will is a tricky thing." She yawned and shifted, sinking deeper into his arms.

"Let's say we reach a crossroads—it is up to us which path to choose, which way to go. But once the path is chosen, once … chosen," she yawned again. "…the next crossroads is inevitable, or the end of the road in some cases. No matter what we do … to keep this game fair, there are signs for every road, defining its straights and curves so to speak, but … people never notice the warnings until … until it is too late."

Amira had ignored a whole ton of them today. But right now, she could not find a single reason why she should be worried or afraid.

She was too tired to think of the consequences. Too tired to even remember that there would be any. She felt as if her mind was swimming through the clouds, and it brought a deceptive freedom.

"What you just told me—it doesn't apply to you, does it?"

"Not really," she admitted again.

How many times can a person jump off the cliff?—a question arose. She had already done that. There was no point in keeping silent.

"They make me jump through hoops whenever they want."

"Something tells me you are not that obedient."

She felt him smile, but before she could say anything, he got serious again.

"So let's get this straight. We *had* to meet. I've seen what you can do, so it's safe to say you could have avoided being captured. You didn't. Which leads me to believe they've yanked your chain, as you've put it. But then, there's Owen … Why didn't you kill him? Or was this another order?"

"Not exactly," Amira murmured. "That's what they do sometimes. They strip my powers and—"

"And leave you in the hands of an animal?" His voice sounded so angry. She shivered, feeling the rumble in his chest, but he must have repented, because his next words came in a soft whisper. "Sleep."

It was both a plea and a command, lulling her into succumbing. Amira might have hated being told what to do, but this time, she didn't need to be told twice. Her body was only too eager to obey.

She fell asleep.

Chapter 22

It was late morning when Amira rubbed the sleep from her eyes. Slowly, the hazy fog lifted from her mind, a familiar scent invaded her nostrils, warmth enveloped her—and she became extremely aware of the fact that she was not alone in the bed.

Her upper body was draped over Raven's chest, one of her hands wrapped around his shoulder, while the other lay by his side. Their legs were tangled, one of his legs pushed between hers. Or maybe it was her leg pushed between his—all she knew was that if it wasn't for the pants he hadn't removed last night, they would have been skin-to-skin.

Pants or not—this was the intimacy she'd never thought she would experience. There was something delicious about waking up in his arms.

She raised her head to discover him watching her— his dark gaze so calm and gentle, she had no idea why every nerve ending of hers tingled, as if he'd been devouring her with his eyes.

Their eyes met, and for a few endless seconds all she could feel was heat flooding her. Her heart gained speed. She lifted herself on one elbow. Her other hand moved up to his cheek, and her back arched when she felt his fingers travel leisurely down her spine.

Her breath caught.

"You are not wearing your amulet," she murmured, wondering how she had missed it. Was she so out if it yesterday?

"With you around, I figure it's just an accessory."

"If you had a hundred … "

Images came cascading through her mind— memories of a confession she should have never, ever breathed to any living being.

"You took advantage of me," Amira accused him. But she knew she had dug the hole all on her own. Now it was only a matter of time before the blade, constantly hanging above her head, would fall.

His hand stilled on her behind and she realized that time wasn't just running short—it had run out. "Now it's my turn."

There was no point in laying blame, or even thinking about it. What was done was done. She couldn't turn back the time, but she could enjoy what was left of it.

"What do you want to know?" he asked, erroneously thinking she would demand a secret for a secret. Not this time.

"Many things," she spoke with his own words. She still wanted to hear the story. She did. Even though she no longer thought whatever secret he carried could save her. The dice were already cast. But being in his arms … there was just one thing she wanted. "Let's start with how it will feel to have you inside me."

"You don't beat around the bush, do you?" His smile revealed a dimple on his right cheek she'd never seen before, but his hand didn't move an inch from the curve of her behind.

"I'll leave that to you. I prefer to act while I still have breath in my lungs."

"You'll leave what to me?" He flipped her to her back so quickly, whatever breath there was in her now left her lungs. "We'll talk about how you like to act without thinking later. Now—"

"You'll wake me up when you are through?" she couldn't help but tease. It was strange—Amira never thought she had it in her. But with him, it felt so right.

"When I'm through, I'll be sure to ask how your dreams were," he promised, his dark gaze capturing hers.

His hand ran over her skin in a beguiling caress she couldn't not respond to—she arched her back, her breaths deepened. His fingers trailed down her neck, to her aching breasts, and he cupped one the same time as his thigh came higher to press more intimately against her.

A strangled moan escaped her mouth. Her body shuddered when he rubbed gently at her swollen flesh. Her leg came higher, to wrap around his hip, and the next time he moved, she met him.

"Off with your pants!" It should have been a command, but it came out more like a husky plea.

"Are you talking in your sleep already?" His fingers played with her nipple, the light touches maddening her.

Her skin felt hyper-sensitized. Every stroke, every caress was like another log into a fire. Inside her, blazes roared.

"You are killing me," she confessed, her voice breaking when he finally lowered his mouth to hers. It was the hottest kiss she had ever received. "Kill me some more..."

His laughter was rich and sexy. The sound traveled down her body in a seductive wave. But when his lips began to follow the way, she knew she was a goner.

His lips on her neck, on her breasts, continuing their journey to her navel—her stomach muscles contracted—the sensual onslaught was maddening. Anticipation—a living, breathing entity inside of her.

I need you...

She didn't know whose voice it was—his or hers, but it mirrored her every single desire. Her heart was banging like a fist on a door. Her breathing hitched, and it took her time to realize that the loud sound wasn't coming from inside her.

"Ignore it," he spoke against the skin of her lower stomach.

Amira wanted to. Dear gods, how she wanted to, but the banging persisted, and with it came an ugly foreboding—their time was up. It was time to face the music.

"I swear," Raven muttered lifting his body from hers, "if I don't find another army behind those doors, someone's head is going to roll."

"I think I'm flattered," she said, pushing herself on her elbows. Her voice came out breathless, laced with desire, but the shadow in her eyes, for all she tried to hide it, made him pause.

"It'll be just two seconds," Raven promised. "You just stay here," he commanded when it became apparent she would try to get up.

He marched to the door determined to boot away the intruder.

"What?" he demanded on opening it. And froze in utter shock.

Brea leapt with affright at the sound of his voice, that came out even harsher than he had intended, and ran hiding.

"I tried to give the two of you as much time as possible, but the girl is scared. She needed to see Bright Eyes." Martha cast him an angry look and added, "You should be ashamed of yourself."

Raven wanted to curse. He looked at himself,

standing in the doorway half naked. Glanced at the girl, curled in the farthest corner of the hallway, sobbing. And brushed an open palm down his face.

"She'll come in a minute," he spoke to Martha's back, as the woman hurried after the young witch.

Gently, he closed the door, his palms landing on the wood, and he all but banged his forehead into the surface. His body felt strained all over. He sighed.

Is there anything that can't go wrong?

"You are just frustrated," she answered a question he didn't think he'd voiced.

Raven didn't turn. He heard the swish of the sheets, her bare legs landing on the floor—his mind easily supplied the visual to the sounds. But to actually see her discard any bedding she could've used to wrap herself in and stand up ... now he couldn't turn. It was too much for him.

"Uh-huh..." he swallowed, "you are right. A perpetual hard-on can be very frustrating."

She padded around the bed, the sound growing nearer and nearer, until he could feel her behind him. "Poor baby." She placed a kiss where his neck met his back. She came even closer. So close, he could finally feel her breasts pressing against his body.

She wrapped her arms around his torso and whispered, "I have to go. If you can, remember me..."

Raven would have thought her last sentence a joke, or more of a sensuous plea, but there was something in her voice that chafed at his senses and made the hair on his nape prickle.

She let him go. And the muscles in his shoulders turned to stone.

"Explain." He pushed himself off the door, swiveling on his heels. His eyes landed on her as she made a beeline for the closet—even the view of her back was too tantalizing for him at the moment. But Raven refused to let her out of his sight for a single second. He had a strange feeling and he didn't know why.

"Pay no attention to me." She cracked the doors of his closet open, and without so much as a glance took out a few garments.

Raven didn't miss the fact that their clothes were mixed together, or that he never thought seeing a woman get dressed could be this arousing. She wasn't even trying to catch his attention, Raven was certain. Her moves were assured, but too hasty for any kind of play. And yet, she held him immobile.

"How am I supposed to not pay attention when you are dancing around in your birthday suit?"

He would have paid attention to her even if she was covered from head to toe. She had something far beyond physical beauty. She had courage and conviction. She had spirit and heart. Most importantly, they had a connection—they understood each other.

"I could play coy, I guess," she sashayed, exaggerating the sway of her hips. "But I find it rather tiresome and time-consuming." *Time is what I don't have,* he read loud and clear from the deep light-blue eyes.

Raven knew he should have followed that thread, but it was when she had halted in front of him, kissed his lips, and turned. It had scrambled his brain completely. It took time for him to understand why she stood with her back to him, her hair pushed aside.

"You don't have to play anything," he whispered into her ear, his fingers fumbling to button up her yellow dress.

He loved how tall and graceful she stood—how she didn't have to go on the tip of her toes to reach him. How he could reach her. "Unless you'll invite me to play with you..."

Amira waited for him to finish with his task and

only then answered, "If I survive today, I swear I'll invite you anywhere you want."

It was a sizzling pledge she'd given, but the dark possibility he sensed behind those words forced him to abandon his idea of letting her go with Brea. It took him all but ten seconds to get dressed and open the door for her. The girl might be traumatized, but the urgency inside him to protect Amira from the unknown foe was undeniable.

Amira moved past Raven. She approached the girl who was still curled in the corner, and kneeled in front of her.

Despite her tear-soaked cheeks, Brea appeared to be calmer. No longer was she trembling while wrapped in a small ball, nor was she sobbing with her forehead pressed against her raised knees. She breathed deeply so concentrated on taking air in and pushing it out of her lungs, she stared forward with eyes oblivious to the world.

Whatever Martha had told her helped in shooing the fear away. Temporarily as it may be. Amira didn't believe wounds this grave could be healed with mere words. Unfortunately, her ability lay in knitting flesh and removing bruises. Healing the cuts of the soul was a foreign concept to her.

She reached for Brea's hand, and the moment the contact was made, the girl's eyes widened. What looked back at her was something wild and feral, the gaze of a cornered animal who was all too aware it had no teeth to defend itself.

For a flash of a second, before she realized who it was touching her, her pixie-like features contorted with dread. Her alabaster skin turned ashen.

The dark blue eyes focused on Amira, and she relaxed a fraction. Until her gaze traveled higher and to the left—to where Raven stood leaning against the wall. She cringed, but she didn't let go of Amira. If anything, her fingers clutched onto her wrists even more fiercely.

For a man his size, it had to be some feat to appear as unobtrusive as he did. Though it wasn't his height or the width of his shoulders that announced his presence to Amira. She knew she would never mistake his energy, not even if she lived a thousand years.

"Tell me you have him bound," the silent tone of Brea's voice came out pleading, laced with desperation.

Amira glanced at Raven and realized it was a lie she would not utter. Not even to placate the girl.

She'd insinuated as much to Mode. But the lie had been a lie then. She hadn't even pretended to pass it off as the truth. This felt different. This wasn't a joke.

Amira refused to sully whatever it was growing between them. It didn't matter to her that they had no future. Raven had proved that he wasn't ashamed of what she was—she could only do the same.

"How old are you?" Amira inquired, thinking she had to go about this the other way around.

"Nineteen." Brea let herself be pulled to her feet, coming into her full height—which barely reached Amira's shoulder blades. No wonder she'd mistaken her for a child. With her slight build and a pixie-face that Amira was convinced hid behind swollen eyes and a red nose, she looked so young.

"Then you probably know that what is freely given is worth a thousand times more than anything a slave can offer." She led Brea down the stairs, to a place where she always found inner peace.

"You value betrayal so much?" the girl exclaimed, pulling them to a stop just outside the entrance to the sun-chamber. "Because it's all they can offer!"

"Who betrayed you?" Amira asked, opening the door. The wild, pure energy washed over her the moment they stepped inside, and she knew she had made the right decision in bringing Brea here. Even if the young witch didn't see or feel the vibrations in the air the same way Amira did, the girl's breathing evened out and her hold on Amira loosened.

"My mother used to tell me not to trust any man who had power over you. Why didn't I listen…?" she murmured under her breath as if talking with herself.

She took a seat. Sighed. "He used to call me Goldilocks…" Brea whispered again, not aware she was caressing her chopped-off strands of hair, and Amira had an ugly suspicion it was Brea herself who had hacked her locks.

Her expression changed suddenly into pure disgust and she spat out, "until he found out who I was — and then my hair became nothing but a way to hold me down."

She didn't sob anymore. It was rage that seeped through her pores — rage Amira didn't like one bit. While she was not against punishing the guilty, this was something else. Something Brea confirmed with her next words. "If I had any real power, I would annihilate all the monsters."

Except in Brea's head, monsters were not only the ones who had violated her, or the one who had betrayed her to the Venlordians. Monsters were … all men.

"None of us are pure as snow. Men. Witches. We all are monsters then," Amira reflected. "Some act like them. Some hide them. While some — only look like them."

"I would rather be among witches. In the Mountains."

"In a few days you'll have your opportunity." It was only a matter of days now before the witches would arrive. Amira still didn't know how everything was supposed to go down. Who would survive. If any would. It was out of her hands completely. But the ones who left could take Brea with them.

"I can't stay here this long. I can't..." her voice cracked again, and she trembled.

"Remember what I told you about monsters?" Amira glanced around, her eyes running through the vista behind the huge floor-to-ceiling windows, through the verdure she had inside. They went to the birds, to Martha silently standing near the farthest wall, to Raven, who was barely even in the room—giving them privacy; to a silver wolf, who padded through the opened door.

"Some—just look like them."

Brea gasped when she saw the animal, her eyes flaring wide—and yet, there was not a shred of fear darkening her face.

"This is Shadow," Amira introduced the wolf. "If you'll let him, he will guard—"

"He talks!" Brea stretched her arms to Shadow. "No one ever taught me that was possible."

A lot of knowledge was lost in time, Amira thought. Though this particular little gem was possible only because of who Shadow was. The witches had lost the ability to communicate with animals eons ago.

"Don't try to abuse him and he'll be your friend." Amira wanted to make sure Brea understood that Shadow was not a slave to command.

"I would never..." she breathed in amazement when the wolf let himself be petted. "He's magnificent and ... hungry, I think."

That too, Amira thought, and turned to Martha. "Do you think you can find something for the wolf?"

Martha's pale brown eyes flared wide—surprise, confusion and fear flashed through them. "You want a carnivore in my kitchen?" she asked when she finally found her voice.

"He won't harm anyone."

"Uh-huh!" The woman didn't seem convinced of the meat-eater's benevolence. But she swallowed her dread and followed the girl and the wolf.

The moment they left, Amira turned to face Raven, and his gaze burned straight through her flesh and into her soul.

"So," he approached slowly. "What is my monster?" So much for giving them privacy...

He closed on her and gently trailed his fingers down her neck, sending ribbons of pleasure down her body.

He didn't even have to kiss her, and she was thirsting for him. For his touch. Breathing was once again becoming a problem. It was as if someone had managed to suck out the air from the room.

She lifted her chin, "What?"

Their lips were so close, focusing on his words was beyond her abilities.

"Do I need to check for horns or claws?"

It was then that the meaning of his question penetrated her mind. She stepped even closer and placed her palm on his chest, right above his strongly-beating heart. "Your monster lies much deeper than you are looking for. And it's eating you alive."

She clenched a fist over his heart, "You continue to lock everything in, and one day, it will tear you apart."

Raven closed his fingers over her fist. When he was with her, it didn't feel like he had any control over what he did or didn't lock in. It had always felt like she could see right through him. And at first he had fought it, true; but then — things changed.

Right now, having her so close, he didn't want to think about monsters. There were too many of them, and sooner or later they would pounce.

"Don't," he whispered.

"Don't what?"

"Don't try to heal every wound you encounter. Some are better left alone."

"Do you even believe it yourself? Is that why you search for salvation?" she demanded.

Not salvation, Raven thought. Some things were impossible.

Redemption? she voiced his deepest hope. Only she didn't voice it. Her lips remained closed, her eyes focused on him.

Her voice was forever in his head. "How do you do that?"

"The same way you do." Her answer didn't explain much, but he did remember the times he thought he was going crazy from the strangeness of it all.

"I don't appreciate you driving me mad, by the way."

"It never was my goal," Amira confessed. But she was not going to make any excuses. "At first I needed to know what I was up against, so I tried to break through your shields. They proved impenetrable. Then, when I had a chance, I realized I couldn't do that to you." She just laid it out in the open.

Amira was running against time now — she decided to risk revealing everything. There wouldn't be a second chance, so she'd be damned if she didn't take advantage of this one. And even if whatever he guarded could not save her anymore, Amira believed that maybe it could save him.

For too long he had let nightmares haunt him, because he believed he deserved it. *She* didn't.

He'd been too young to be the culprit of his family's tragedy — Amira could stake her life on it. She had always trusted in her instincts and they told her that whatever he thought he'd done that was so awful only

appeared so to a boy. Regrets were normal, but guilt …
She was convinced it was because he had survived
when they hadn't.

"You also read minds." His eyes narrowed. Her
hand slipped from his hold. Amira's senses prickled.

"Passing thoughts," she corrected, trying to
concentrate on the strange vibes she felt in the air. The
pure energy around her was turning into tainted wisps
of smoke that wrapped around them.

"Digging into someone's mind can be dangerous—I
never do that." If a person fought her, she could damage
their brain. For Amira, hearing the unshielded thoughts
was usually more than enough. She didn't want more
voices in her head.

All of a sudden, Raven doubled over, grabbing for
his chest as if it pained him, and took a step back.

No, no, no, no! Everything inside her screamed.

"Fight it!" Amira yelled out loud.

She watched as the smoke tightened its hold around
Raven's throat, and couldn't help but grab for her own.
"Whatever it is you see or feel—ignore it," she pleaded.
But it was no use. She knew what was happening and
no one, not even her, could fight and win against it.

"Go," she told him with her heart heavy. The putrid
spell wouldn't follow him. As for her… Amira almost
broke down when she saw him hesitate.

Goodbye, she mouthed, and all but shoved him out
of the room. She didn't want him to see this. She didn't
want to die in his arms. She didn't want to turn into
another nightmare for him.

Amira slumped into the chair moments before a
cold grasp squeezed her heart. Time was slowing down.
A feminine form was appearing in front of her.

She was on the verge of asking Hope to be quick,
but the words stuck in her throat. She refused to beg.
Instead, she lifted her eyes, slowly stood up, and

demanded, "What did you do to Raven?"

"As always, no respect," Hope's soft but accusing voice echoed in the room. "But I do like what you did here." With those words every single plant withered. The birds fell off the branches—dead. Her green sanctuary turned into a soulless wasteland.

"You bitch!" Amira couldn't contain her anger. Seeing this place turn to dust was just like feeling a dagger twist inside her chest.

She tensed her fingers, gathering every last drop of energy she could muster. She figured that if she was to die anyway, fighting was the best way to go. But this power—to transform energy into an actual energy ball—was too new to Amira. The process too slow. She didn't even have enough to do more than mess up Hope's hair, as she found herself pinned against the wall.

The goddess approached her in all of her glorious radiance and *tsk*ed under her breath, "You wanted to know what I did to Raven?" She stopped in front of Amira. "Not much. Or maybe I should say *a lot*. I should probably congratulate you. A few more days and he would have resisted."

Congratulate her? Amira gaped. This was like a bad dream. That's why they didn't give her those few more days, wasn't it? "So what now? You kill me?"

"There's a huge commotion up there because of you," Hope said, brushing off her hair. "And some are very displeased."

"I'm so-o sorry." Amira was still unable to move a single inch. "Next time I'll try to roll out the carpet when you arrive."

"That's just it. There isn't going to be a next time." Hope smiled, and Amira was forced to stifle a shiver. "We understood that while you may hate dying, you do not fear it. Not really. And that we went the wrong way about it."

Amira's breath caught.

Don't react, don't react, don't react, she chanted inwardly, convinced that the decision the goddess had brought her would affect her in a way she'd better not show.

"It is not you we need to kill, but him." Hope traced the line of a small, taunting smile with her index finger, which was at odds with the icy gaze, but all Amira could see ... was blood.

She forgot her determination to stay calm. She paled. Her hands started shaking. Fear was crawling under her skin, while she could do nothing to stop from gasping as she saw the vision of Raven taking his last breath in front of her eyes.

Begging was useless — she knew from experience of other women before her. Fear was only a hindrance. So when a scarlet pall of rage descended over her eyes, Amira snapped, "You do this and I swear I'll find a way to annihilate you all. I vow it!"

Hope laughed. The goddess had actually laughed and vanished, leaving Amira free from the shackles pinning her to the wall, and with pending doom looming over her head.

Chapter 23

For about an hour Raven rode, letting Lightning set the pace and course. He didn't feel the need to run away so much as he needed to sort things out in his head. Without the voices being there. Without the images—the ones he had believed to be memories—plaguing him.

He tried to go step by step through events to discover how he ended up on Lightning, miles away from Amira; but all he could see was her pushing him away. Her eyes had been filled with so much pain, he still felt it to the marrow of his bones.

He shouldn't have left her. He had a strong suspicion she was in danger. Her strange moods, even stranger words … him being so far … fear built in the pit of his stomach. He halted, turned around and kicked Lightning into a gallop, sending him tearing across the fields.

He had to reach her. Now. Yet no matter how fast he rode, the look in her eyes stayed in front of him. Could he have said something? Raven wondered. His memories were so fragmented and full of holes, it only reinforced his urgency to find her. Nothing human could have done this. And after what she'd admitted a day before … he was drawing some pretty ugly conclusions.

How had his world changed so fast? It seemed like only yesterday everything was so simple. He knew who he was and what he wanted. He knew his thoughts were his own. He knew what was possible and what was not. And then ... he had looked into the piercing crystal eyes, and his world had turned upside down.

You also read minds.

The wind brought back words he must have uttered. Memories were still shrouded in fog, but he knew the echo of the conversation he heard was true. After all, Raven had suspected as much, hadn't he? The feeling had been there from the first time she had looked at him with her searching gaze, as if she could see right into him, straight into the darkest corners of his soul.

To have her voice inside his head had become so natural, he'd never really thought about it in these terms. If he'd known she was a mind-reader from the start, he would have succeeded in keeping his distance. Maybe. Now, it was too late. Now, he knew the feel of her burning touch, and it was no longer an option.

Raven prompted Lightning to go faster, leaving a cloud of dust behind him. And, two riders.

At first he didn't think anything of it. There was a town nearby and it wasn't uncommon to meet travelers on this stretch of the road. But when he glanced over his shoulder and noticed them exchange a look and urge their horses with lashes and spurs, every instinct he possessed rose to the fore.

For a moment he debated whether to halt the horse and deal with whatever problem they thought they had with him, then they made his decision for him. By drawing a gun.

A bullet whistled an inch from his ear.

Instantly, he nudged Lightning toward the forest, making sure to appear as small a target as possible, his mind already going through his options. He never ran from fights, but sometimes you had to step back to be able to take a better swing.

With the skill of an expert rider familiar with his horse's capabilities, Raven navigated along a narrow, winding path. Lightning conquered each obstacle with confidence, not once hesitating in his steps, not once slowing down. When a gorge opened up before them, they jumped. Lightning crossed it with ease, and continued the run along the edge of the scarp.

Raven slowed down the pace and finally halted when they neared another bend. He jumped down from the horse, reached for his sword—his hand came up empty.

For the first time in fifteen years he was unarmed!

Fool! He shook his head, petted Lightning and let him go.

He climbed the hill around which the path curved, lowered himself to the ground, and waited.

The riders, when they appeared, seemed conscious of the difficult trail, but in Raven's opinion, the jogtrot was still too fast for the bend ahead of them—at least for strangers to the area.

Their horses saw the sharp curve before the riders did. They tossed their heads in protest, inadvertently coming to a stop. Ten more feet and…

Raven's body was crouched low, his every muscle at the ready.

"He can't be far," Raven heard one of them whisper.

"He would have been less far, if you haven't pulled the trigger." The answer was abrupt and angry. "You think I don't want him dead? But for now, we need him alive."

"I wasn't aiming to kill," came an excuse in a voice that seemed familiar, though he couldn't place it.

"You weren't aiming at all!" The words sounded as if pushed through gritted teeth, but that wasn't what interested Raven the most—they were within his reach. "Next time—"

"There won't be a next time," Raven announced, leaping down on them.

They all tumbled, hitting the ground hard. Quickly, he snatched a dagger from under the belt of the man he found himself on top of, and ground the blade into his throat. A second later, the other man put a gun to Raven's head.

"Leave my brother alone!

Oh, this one is going to be fun, he thought sarcastically, and tightened his grip on the dark-haired man beneath him. If there was a chance to get out of this alive...

Raven tilted his head so he could see both of them, and gaped. "You?"

Suddenly, he knew what both of them wanted from him. Or who, to be more precise.

"Are you going to shoot me with an empty gun?" he asked calmly and watched Logan's eyes fill with panic.

Oh, the pistol was loaded alright! But given the commotion and the fact that Logan had two under his belt, only one of them loaded, when Raven jumped on them, he hoped he could manage to confuse the boy.

Taking advantage of the few seconds the gun wasn't pointing at him, Raven rolled sideways and quickly stood up, dragging the dark-haired man onto his feet to use him as a shield.

Logan glared at him, his finger on the trigger. The other one stood still, not a word escaping his mouth.

Probably disoriented, Raven decided at first, when he noticed a gnash near the man's left ear. Blood was streaming down his neck, but on closer look it appeared too focused. His body too still. Add the power behind those frozen muscles to the mix, and it was a disaster waiting to happen.

What was his name? Raven tried to remember the other name Amira had used the day they met.

217

"Ciaran, right?" He finally asked. "How about we discuss this calmly without bullets flying around?"

"Oh you'll talk," Ciaran said, without moving so much as an inch. "Sing long and loud before we finish with you."

Arrogance—just what they needed! Was he suicidal?

"Amira is alive." Raven tried a different approach. He was really not in the mood for any of it. At least not for more blood on his hands than he already had. He sensed Ciaran relaxing a notch, then tensing only a moment later.

"If you've touched even a hair on her head, I'll have yours," he gnashed a warning, despite the fact that he didn't have the upper hand in this. Only this time Raven had a distinct feeling the threat was real. No wavering, no arrogance or empty bravado as before. He was deadly serious.

Ciaran had never killed anyone, Raven realized. He never had to rinse blood from his hands. And yet, he was willing to kill and die for her.

Wasn't he? Raven wondered, already knowing the answer. It brought such jealousy roaring inside him, his fingers tightened around the handle, and he barely managed to restrain himself from using the blade. It was a new experience for him, though lately he had had many of those. All thanks to her.

"Logan, throw the pistol to me and no one dies," he commanded, deciding not to dwell on details right now.

"If I do it," Logan stepped closer, "there's nothing stopping you from killing both of us. But if you release Ciaran and take us to Amira, maybe I'll spare you."

That actually made him laugh. Yeah, he was surely going to raise his hands in surrender before a teenage boy.

"You shoot, you shoot your brother. Think with

your head. Is a witch worth dying for?"

"Any witch—no," Logan said.

"But a sister—yes," Ciaran concluded.

The news took Raven by surprise. He froze, and Ciaran seized the opportunity. He grabbed the dagger and delivered a searing blow to Raven's gut with his elbow.

The air rushed out of his lungs, and before Raven could recover, he got punched again.

If he had time to think, Raven would have realized that fighting would only escalate everything. They were her brothers. If he harmed them, Amira would never forgive him. But in the heat of the moment, his reflexes roared to life and he didn't just block the next attack— he retaliated.

Raven swung his own fist—it connected with Ciaran's nose. Blood gushed down his face, but the man didn't surrender the weapon. They fought—wrestled for supremacy, their bodies constantly moving, their hands tightly wrapped around the handle.

"No!" he heard Logan's voice as if in slow motion.

Both he and Ciaran turned to see the pistol lifted high and a true foreboding washed over Raven. Without realizing what he was doing, Raven looked down, only now registering the sound of a gun being fired, the smell of powder, and a piercing pain.

Forgetting the dagger, Raven grabbed for his side in an attempt to staunch the bleeding, knowing that whatever he did, he couldn't lose consciousness.

He saw Ciaran snatch the pistol from his brother's hands and slide it under his belt.

"Thanks for the help." The tone of Ciaran's voice wasn't thankful at all. "It's a miracle the bullet missed me!" he yelled, his fingers tightening around the handle of the dagger till his knuckles turned white.

"I didn't—" Logan's hands started shaking. "I … I

wasn't—" his voice faltered. Or maybe Raven simply couldn't distinguish the words through the buzzing sound in his ears. It was deafening.

The world around him swayed. His vision seemed to be coming and going. The ground beneath his legs became less solid and he couldn't help but sway with the rhythm of the earth. Despite his determination to stay upright—Raven felt himself falling.

Pain transformed into agony when he pressed his fingers against the wound as firmly as he could in an effort to stem the bleeding. He blacked out.

When he finally cracked his eyes open, it was to see Ciaran's face up and close. And the look in his eyes confirmed Raven's worst fears—he was dying.

"Where is she?" The other man grabbed the lapels of his shirt and barely managed to restrain himself from shaking him like a rag-doll.

It was hard focusing on words; and when the meaning of the question penetrated his clouded mind, Raven found himself unable to answer. The dizziness from losing too much blood, weariness, pain—they all combined forces against him.

"Shit! He's drifting…" the words traveled as if he had his head under the water. "Logan! Stop your crying and come here!"

Suddenly a wave of pain assaulted his senses—pierced his insides like a sharp blade, and temporarily it woke him up like nothing else would.

Raven gritted his teeth, the bone of his jaw so tightly locked, it was close to cracking. It was almost ironic how life managed to surprise him with something he bloody well knew might come along. He had enemies aplenty. Armies of Venlordians only too eager to leave him for dead in some ditch. Moreover, he never had a reason to live other than saving his brother, and he always managed to walk out of dangerous situations unharmed. Well, alive, at least.

For the first time in his life he'd found something for himself. And he wasn't even going to get a chance to say goodbye.

Another wave passed through him. He coughed blood and for a moment there, the world got dark again. As if a black veil was cast over his eyes.

"Tell me how to find Amira, dammit!" The veil lifted and this time Raven uttered something. He didn't know what. He didn't feel in control of his body anymore. But whatever he said probably satisfied Ciaran, because the young man nodded.

"Did you harm her?" The next question was laced with fear.

Harm her? He bloody loved her. But he also knew he had done more than he could ever forgive himself for.

Standing on the threshold of death, everything became crystal clear—he'd been hesitant in revealing Dacian to her and the goddesses had used it—building upon it until he could not breathe.

He would have told her, had she asked. After everything she had shared … he couldn't have done anything less. It didn't mean he'd been eager, though.

Now, he finally knew the reason for his hesitancy. It had nothing to do with her being a witch, and everything with his own fear. Fear of witnessing her beautiful eyes fill with hatred or condemnation when she realized what he'd done to his own brother, his whole family. What part he had played in their inevitable demise.

Hatred was the last thing he wanted to see filling her eyes; and yet, he would have given everything just to see them one last time. Even if they were drowning with disgust.

It was a stupid desire—just as impossible as his salvation. Getting more so with every second.

His breaths were growing harder and harder — each one of them a challenge. His body was numb and finally painless. Indicating he had only seconds on this earth. Seconds full of regrets and unfulfilled desires.

He didn't want to go leaving so much unsaid and undone. But death waited for no one. It seemed he was destined to fail. To leave his brother before he'd righted the wrong done to him. To never win a single smile from the woman he loved more than he thought he ever could.

Now he would never have a chance to say to Amira how much he loved her — would always love her.

One moment he was feeling so much, and the next all his thoughts vanished. His body slumped as the world darkened and disappeared altogether.

Chapter 24

Amira was pacing Raven's room, more nervous than she'd ever been. Daggers were slicing her heart as the link to his essence melted away.

Please, please, please, she begged, well aware how out of character it was for her. *Come back to me…*

She had run after him. Mounted a horse and tried to look for him—all in vain. They had blocked her senses and left her blind, to wander aimlessly for three hours, until it dawned on her that maybe he'd returned.

Whatever it was that had affected him so couldn't have lasted this long, she'd reasoned. Otherwise Hope wouldn't have said what she did. Otherwise, she wouldn't have congratulated her. The fear the goddess had latched on to had to be vincible.

Right now, Amira didn't care about anything. So what if he had something he wasn't comfortable in sharing with her? She wasn't an immature brat to demand everything at once. Heaven knew, she never really had much. Secrets, or not, she simply wanted him alive.

Be safe, she whispered, clenching trembling fingers near her heart where their connection used to be. She hadn't asked for it to form or grow, but now she felt bereft.

Amira felt cold where blazes used to burn. She felt hollow instead of embraced. She felt lost. And she hated the feeling. But most of all, she hated knowing she could

223

not do a thing.

She approached the window, brushed the curtain aside, and looked out. The sun was still in the sky, but the red glow spreading over the horizon barely reached the hills. Amira sighed, pivoted, and walked to the bed. She curled up on it, wrapped her arms around her legs and laid her head on her knees. She felt so empty. Alone.

She tried to conjure up things, just to feel magic seeping through her fingers, to calm herself. It always did. Not now. It refused to obey her. She couldn't even steady the rhythm of her heart or her breathing enough to separate herself from her body. It was futile when every pore of hers was seething with fear for him.

She was so out of control, she couldn't spirit-walk. But even if she could, there was no connection, no guiding star for her to follow. Amira hoped against all hope they were simply punishing her—still blocking her senses. But she knew ... deep down she knew the truth. She just refused to believe it. Didn't want to believe it.

If he was to pay for her mistakes, she was sure as hell those coldhearted bitches were going to get what they deserved. Even if it killed her.

Dangerous thoughts! Shadow gazed at her as he entered the room.

"They have pushed me over the edge one time too many," she breathed, thankful for the company.

She was going crazy sitting there alone. Didn't trust herself around people. Shadow could at least take care of himself if her powers slipped their leash.

They don't see you as a threat. But that's their mistake.

"Shouldn't you be on *their* side?" Amira raised her brow at Shadow's words. He was the messenger of the gods. By the very definition, he was theirs.

That's just it—I'm not theirs. You are not the only one who has been pushed over every rational limit.

"Don't tell me you are planning a mutiny?" Amira asked with a new respect for the wolf. She definitely wanted to be part of it.

Not yet. But you are already playing a large role, worry not. Right now, I came to tell you what they don't want you to know, before it's too late.

"What?" Her back straightened instantly. For one fleeting second hope flared in her heart. Raw, desperate hope — it got extinguished as quickly as it blazed to life.

Lift the spell preventing your family from finding you here.

"Why?"

Do it! Shadow growled low in his throat.

Amira closed her eyes, took a deep, calming breath in, and began untangling the threads of energy she'd woven about a week ago. It seemed like a lifetime. And it took her a lifetime to finish, but finally when she was done, she opened her eyes. Her gaze landed on the silver wolf. "What now?"

Now, have the courage to do what you swore you would not. And then, pay the price, Shadow told her cryptically.

"I hope it's not what you teach Brea?" Amira sighed, trying to keep it light, because she felt like screaming. The wait was killing her.

It's too soon to be teaching her anything, he said, and left her alone with her thoughts instantly drifting away. To Raven.

Amira lifted her head up and glanced at the last sunbeams playing on the wall. It was almost dark. Soon it would be night and she would have done nothing but paced holes in his rugs. She jumped from the bed full of futile hope when she heard horses neighing; ran to the window and gasped.

Below her, two riders were trying to defend themselves from an angry mob.

Amira flattened herself to the glass. Her eyes

widened when she recognized Ciaran and Logan. Disappointment washed over her. But then, she noticed bloodstains on Ciaran's shirt. And the cadence of her heartbeat gained speed again.

She clenched her fingers, but the tingling in her fingertips could not be assuaged. The ugly presentiment, blooming in her chest, could not be rubbed away.

Time seemed to stretch out for eternity and contract all at the same time. With a fervent urgency she rushed through the door and down the stairs, ran headlong all the way up to the front door—and stopped dead in her tracks. The last step—too hard for her to conquer.

Deep in the marrow of her bones she felt that if she turned the knob now, there would be no going back. There would be no escape. But then she knew, there never had been.

Amira turned the knob and stepped outside, her heart pounding like a drum as every last pair of eyes turned on her.

"They are family, Burt," she addressed the angry man, who was at the front of few dozen others.

"They have done something to the lord. The young one all but admitted it!" He waved his dagger, the horses squirmed, people tensed.

"I'll bring him home. Safe," Amira promised, knowing exactly what those words entailed. "But I need a minute."

Burt took another glance at her cousin, obviously not convinced, but finally he nodded. "And not a minute more or we'll find out everything our own way."

"What are you now? The mistress of the castle?" Ciaran sneered at her when the men retreated, giving them space.

"Shut up! Shut up! Shut up!" She could not contain

it anymore. All the emotions she'd tried to suppress escaped their prison cell, blowing out the four walls with a loud bang. Splinters flew. Thunders bellowed with fury in response. The winds rose.

Ciaran and Logan's heads whipped round in confusion, but she didn't let them utter a single syllable. "What have you done?"

"He didn't—"

"I came to save you," Ciaran interrupted his brother, his attention now focused on her. "Now come. We are leaving."

"Stop bossing me around and answer the bloody question!"

"Someone needs to," he shot back, and Amira choked. Hadn't Raven said something similar to her just the other day?

"Take me to him." This time her command was too close to a plea.

"He's dead," her cousin said calmly, "and good riddance to bad rubbish, I say."

The callous words were like a punch to her solar plexus. Amira's world tipped sideways and forced her to face the cold black void those words left in her.

"Mira!" She heard her name like a background noise. "Mira."

Ciaran jumped down his horse, but strangely, it was hard for her to follow the movements.

"Don't cry." His voice came from so close, she blinked, unable to understand how he had appeared right in front of her so quickly.

"I never do." She heard a whimpering breath she didn't recognize as her own. And when her fingers went up to her cheek, she touched a wet trail.

A single tear had run down her face. Amira caught it before it could drop off her chin, and brought it to her lips. But even the salty proof was not enough for her to comprehend what was happening—she never, ever cried, after all.

"What did he do?" Ciaran asked, gently this time. Misinterpreting her distress.

"He … he made me realize I could be liked just the way I am." *He made me fall for him*—she kept the bigger truth to herself.

"Well of course you can be," he assured her. "I always did."

"We are blood," she whispered, no longer dangling off the precipice of her emotions. She was left numb. "You think I'm your responsibility."

"That too, but…" His fingers wrapped around something on his neck and his lips twisted into a small, but sad smile. "Do you remember when my parents died and we came to live with you? I was so mad at everything. Natalie could not stop crying and Logan … Logan was only an infant. And there were you, a little sprout of barely five years…"

"You were barely eight yourself."

"You came to me one day with this locket," he said as he revealed what he was holding, and Amira blanched.

"You told me it would guard me, and then you continued to plague me with jokes until I stopped growling at everything—your words. I still remember the bed full of frogs, you know. And yes, I took it upon myself to keep you safe, but it doesn't mean I don't like you. To me you will always be that girl who helped me deal with pain." *To me, you'll always be a sister.*

"If that's how you feel, you will take me to Raven. Please." She reached for his locket, and pulled her hand back immediately, not being able to touch it. It was another blow to her heart. Another punch. She didn't know how much more she could take.

The locket was an amulet of protection. Several

times more powerful than Arushna's. But where Arushna's protected only from dark magic, this one protected from all types of harm. And it made her realize just how much more guilty she was. Not only had the goddesses gone after Raven because of her, but now it appeared the one they had placed in his path had more than their blessing. He had extra protection. Her protection.

"You don't need to see it," Ciaran said as if she was some fragile flower. If only she could laugh.

"I need to see it."

"We can bury him properly if that's your wish, but—"

"My wish is to see him!" she yelled, and a lightning bolt struck a few feet away. The horses reared and Logan barely managed to control his.

"What the hell!"

"What do you think?"

"You are doing this?"

"No, the fairies are!" She struggled for control. "I've told you I'm not Natalie, many times."

"Alright," Ciaran finally agreed, but when they tried to leave, they encountered another problem—Burt was waiting near the gates, refusing to let them pass unless they took him and a few men.

It was the last thing she needed—a fight, once they saw how things were. So, after a talk, they decided on letting her go with Ciaran, if Logan stayed behind. No one was overly happy about the arrangement, especially not Ciaran, but Amira was adamant.

The moment they rode off, he tried to question her, but when it became crystal clear that she was deaf to everything except her own troubling thoughts, silence settled between them.

All the way to the woods, she fought with the gnawing feeling inside her. She struggled with the knot tightly wedged inside her throat she couldn't seem to swallow. She wrestled with the shakiness in her hands. Amira was afraid she would crumble when she saw him lifeless. Yet when she did, an utter calm washed over her.

There was something so eerie about death, but at the same time so natural, she found herself somewhere between worlds. Somewhere where the earth was frozen and yet, everything breathed—death. It was everywhere. In the shadow of the fallen tree, in the hollow of the knap, in the grain of sand. Everything reeked of it.

Slowly, she approached his cold body, kneeled, and took his face in her palms. Shadow's words were playing in her head but she didn't need to ask herself if she had the courage to pay the price. She didn't think she had the courage not to.

"I need a minute alone." She lifted her head and this time she didn't encounter resistance. Ciaran simply nodded and stepped aside, leaving her free to make a deal with the devil himself.

"Took you long enough," Dazlog's towering figure appeared without much drama. Without her even uttering his name.

He simply walked out of thin air, clad in black pants and shirt—he seemed so normal. But then, his pale green amethyst eyes flared, and the effect was stronger than if he'd emerged from a storm of cracking lightning, in a robe, or if the earth had split open and he'd appeared riding a pair of hell-hounds.

"An hour more and I wouldn't have been able to help you."

Amira closed her eyes briefly, digesting yet another of her crimes. If she had lifted her spell earlier, or if she hadn't put it in the first place, Ciaran would have found her quicker. Maybe ... just maybe she would have been in time to —

"You wouldn't have made it in time, so stop eating at yourself." The demon approached as if he didn't have a care in the world. "But I can only hold his soul for so long, you know. I need your decision."

"What do you want of me?" She focused her eyes on the face she held in her arms, refusing to let him go for a single second.

"A binding oath and nothing less."

"Binding me to what?"

"Three simple things." He leaned against the tree so casually, every hair on Amira's nape stood up. His nonchalance didn't bode well for her.

"Name them," she said, determined as ever.

"First, the prophecy. Second, the essence of the power. Third, he's not to know of any of this." As if this made any sense, Amira thought.

"Since you are so distraught right now, and apparently your brains are fried, I'll try to simplify this for you. First…" Dazlog repeated, pushing himself off the tree and crouching near her, "…I need you to fulfill the prophecy, and since I would rather it be this century, I'll help you again — when he's awake, find out what he keeps hidden, and through that, you'll know what to do next. Second — once the prophecy is fulfilled, whatever power you gain, I want the essence of it. And third — he cannot know what happened, otherwise, he'll die. And this is not my rule, in case you were wondering, so don't blame me for the difficulties it raises."

And it did raise difficulties, Amira realized. How was she to explain this? How was she to hide the fact that he had died — she was sure he would know it deep in his soul. These things were not that easily forgettable.

What idiot made that rule? she all but swore, lifting her eyes to the demon.

"Don't curse me. I only break the rules." He flashed

his pearly-whites so innocently, she clenched her jaws. "I don't make them. But I have the utmost belief in your craftiness. Once you are through with him—"

"Once I'm through with him, he'll know I was lying."

"Ah yes, there is that pesky little bond you two share, isn't there? But worry not, I'll even help you again. And this time, free of charge."

"What are you up to?" quizzed Amira, not liking the sound of it. It was better to know what she was getting herself into; but honestly, what more could he want?

"All the while you question me, the time is running short," Dazlog said instead of answering. "So what is it going to be? Do I have your oath, or do I not?" he asked as he conjured up a glowing sphere in his palm. Amira gasped—it was Raven's very soul he held.

Everything vanished. She no longer cared what the demon might do with the essence of her power. Her decision was made.

"You have it," she uttered. "But I want your oath that no harm will come to him. No harm caused by supernatural powers," she corrected her desire, knowing that no one could evade natural death if it was their time. "Directly, or indirectly."

"You strike a mean bargain," Dazlog laughed. "But I'll keep to my end of the deal if you'll keep to yours," he promised, and with those words Raven took a shuddering breath. Overjoyed, she hugged him, almost missing the last words of the demon.

You'll experience one small side effect though—but worry not, my sweet, it's all in the plan.

Chapter 25

Raven was dreaming. He was floating in the air. Only there was no air. No ground. Nothing. He couldn't even feel his own body. He simply knew he was. And at the same time he wasn't.

He saw Amira. He saw her brothers. He saw how he was shot, and how he went down — each and every scene repeating over and over again, faster and faster until there was only a blur.

"Took you long enough!" he heard a whisper echoing all around. He turned. But there was nothing. No person, no creature. Only a void, and the echo of a deep rumble.

Raven couldn't hear the answer, but he was certain the voice was not addressing him. He couldn't even hear his own voice as he shouted. Where the hell was he?

"A binding oath and nothing less." The same voice rang out again. And again Raven couldn't hear the answer. Why was he here? Who was speaking? And whose was the voice he couldn't hear? For a long, long time there was only silence, screaming so loudly in his ears, it hurt. He had a feeling, though, that the conversation was continuing.

"Once I'm through with him," finally came an answer. "You have it…" he heard the haunted voice of … Amira.

Raven jerked awake at the sound of a roaring thunder, then collapsed on the bed with a groan. The pain that shot through him had been so sudden and sharp, he could have sworn he was seeing stars right then.

The lights faded one by one, abandoning him in a room steeped in darkness. A few seconds later it was illuminated by a flash of lightning. The storm bellowed outside the window—the cadence of nature's fury in sync with the rhythm of his heart.

It resonated in his ears, making it impossible for him to remember anything at first. No matter how much he struggled. But then, fragments of the strangest dream he'd ever had assailed his mind—each of them emphasized by the wild, tameless beat of nature's music.

Could it be a memory? he wondered. Maybe he'd been semi-conscious when Amira had conversed with that being. Except, it didn't add up. His last real recollection, before darkness had swallowed him whole, was of a crystal clear conviction that he'd reached the end.

Frowning, Raven made an effort to push himself up. His second attempt went more smoothly and he managed to sit up.

Slowly, he pulled the covers away and looked down. His abdomen was bandaged—a single blood spot was showing on his right side.

Raven touched the spot, gritting his teeth, and pulled his hand away. He didn't have to examine further to know the wound was still there. Which meant Amira wasn't.

In the core of his being he knew she wouldn't have left him injured if she'd seen it. Had she left him altogether? The mere possibility tore his heart out.

Raven shifted in his bed, trying to settle more comfortably, and by turning his head, noticed a small piece of metal lying on the wooden surface. He stretched his hand towards it and grabbed. He rolled it between his fingers, remembering the incident—this small piece of metal could have ended everything. But, he was still alive, and before he left this world he had a few things to take care of.

All of them involved first moving and getting up.

He shifted again, trying to rearrange his body and reach for the clothes, but that proved to be too much of a challenge. His muscles felt numb. His wound throbbed.

For now, he had to be satisfied with the progress he'd made—though satisfied was hardly the word he would've used. Raven was sore, thirsty, a bit dizzy, confused, frustrated; yet everything else paled against the need to see her face. He had to…

The door swung open to reveal Martha and Amira standing side by side. His heart almost leaped out of his chest with joy. He waited for her to enter, say a word, anything, but she just kept standing. Looking at him.

Something inside him twisted as the happiness he experienced in seeing her melted into worry. Then, he remembered her pain-filled eyes, and an idea struck his mind—she needed to know he was done with keeping secrets. And there was only one way he knew she would understand. For the first time in his life, Raven opened all the locked doors.

He never imagined he would do such a thing. Never considered or thought what would happen if he did, but the possibility, that she might refuse to cross the virtual threshold the way she refused to cross the actual one, would have never permeated his mind.

Raven reached out, determined to dig down to the truth, no matter how unpleasant it could be, and smashed straight into a wall. The connection they had always seemed to share was no more. He couldn't feel her as he used to. He couldn't…

Their eyes met and he gasped. Amira's gaze was cold as the winter's night. Distant as the moon itself. Whoever the woman standing in front of him was, she was not his angel. She was not the woman he'd held in his arms.

Raven had an overwhelming urge to shake her. He wanted to demand an explanation, but instead he just watched, afraid to look away. Afraid to accept what was right in front of him.

He had to be hallucinating, he decided. No one changed that much in the space of a day. Raven refused to believe the hollowness inside him was the real answer. He refused! Yet, when he sank deeper in his bed, the pain stabbed strangely not at his wounded side, but at his heart.

"…once I'm through with him…"

He had a sudden flash of panic—the possibility of everything he had come to love about her being a lie—Raven rejected it instantly. There had to be another explanation.

"…once I'm through with him…"

He was torn asunder by the force of his own emotions, while she was standing there as if nothing had ever happened. Looking at his wound.

"…once I'm through with him…"

He would never have asked her to heal him, but for a woman who saved every stray dog and wolf…

"…once I'm through with him…"

Raven could barely breathe as the same words rang over and over in his head. The silence in the room became too loud. The beat of his heart—too fast.

"…once I'm through with him…"

No! There had to be an explanation, he insisted. It didn't matter how illogical it sounded—Raven was convinced the woman in front of him was not Amira. He refused to listen to all the doubts strangling him from inside.

"Who the hell are you?" he demanded.

"You don't remember us?" It was Martha who answered. Amira kept silent.

"Oh I remember," Raven assured her. "Your

brothers attempting to murder me is one of my fonder memories," he sneered as he focused on Amira, waiting for any kind of reaction; and witnessed her go pale as a sheet of paper.

"Now listen, you dolt — I won't have you blathering such preposterous things to the girl. Why, you should —"

"Don't," Amira interrupted, silencing Martha. Even her voice sounded strange to him. "He can think whatever he wishes." She cast him a narrow-eyed glance, turned, and marched down the hallway.

Raven could not believe his ears, or his eyes for that matter. It was just not in her to run.

She had always gone headlong against everything. For her, avoiding a confrontation was like stopping a stream from flowing.

Raven knew he had to uncover the truth. He had too few memories, too many contradictory sensations. He didn't know how he had ended up here, in his room. Who had brought him. He didn't know where his dark angel had gone. Who this distant creature with the icy stare was.

He could not bear chilling emptiness where he'd always felt the warmth of her presence. Silence, where he'd always heard her soft voice.

"What do you think you are — " Martha's question froze in her throat. The swish of sheets falling on the floor — the only sound in the room.

Raven groaned as his stiff body protested at being dragged out of the bed. It took all of his strength, and some extra, acquired from he knew not where, to get up, fasten the pants, and slowly walk to the door.

It was probably sheer willpower that kept him going; but he managed to reach the stairs, despite his trembling muscles, and Martha's insistence that he went back to bed.

He couldn't understand why it was so hard to walk. It wasn't as if his legs were broken. Only his abdomen hurt like hell. He paid no heed to it. His body seemed to be awakening from some kind of slumber. Or learning how to walk all over again. As if he'd been born anew.

Raven shook those thoughts away and returned his attention to the steps. His legs felt stronger and steadier with every step — managing each of them with more efficiency than the last. Soon, his hands no longer needed to grab every solid ledge for balance. By the time he conquered the whole flight, he was walking on his own.

* * *

Amira ran. Worse, she had not the tiniest inkling why she was running. All she knew was her trembling fingers, pounding heart, and heavy breathing. It didn't feel real to her.

She could've sworn she'd been dumped in some strange dream. Right in the middle of it. With no understanding of what was going on. Except she hadn't fallen asleep — she'd woken up.

She stopped, realizing she'd ended up in the sun-chamber somehow. She closed the door, leaned against it, and took a deep breath in. Out. Repeated it three more times.

The devastation in the room prevented her from finding the calm she sought.

By now, she was used to leaving her body behind, but this … this felt different. Wrong. It felt like an intrusion by an unfamiliar entity. A possession, maybe.

From the moment she'd taken the bullet out of Raven's body she'd felt a foreign power churning inside of her, suppressing her own essence — the small side effect Dazlog had mentioned without any explanation. Some small side effect indeed! And how many more of them had he forgotten to mention?

Make a deal with a demon, and you would end up paying twice—that was the rule. Her bill was already in the post.

He had tricked her—hadn't let her heal Raven completely. And by doing so, he'd taken away her only chance of convincing him that he'd never died. Worse still, now it appeared as if she'd left him for dead. And she couldn't even tell the truth.

Dazlog had laughed when she'd accused him, and asked if her knowing would've changed the outcome. He was right—it wouldn't have. Raven's life was more important than that. But the damned demon had the nerve to tell her that it was for her own good. As if any good could come of it now.

The only thing that was clear was the presentiment she had yesterday, when she'd woken up in Raven's arms and remembered how deep a hole she'd dug for herself.

Their time was up.

He might be alive. She might not die. But right now, she didn't see a way out of this mess.

The only good thing was that no one else knew the truth, except Ciaran and Logan. And it had taken her hours to persuade them to leave her. Hours filled with fighting, and quite a few lightning bolts.

Amira had tried to convince them she could take care of herself, that she didn't need guards to follow her around. That she was not a child, but a grown woman. That part of the conversation had definitely gone well.

She still didn't know how she achieved it, but they had left. With a promise to drag her home kicking and screaming if she didn't return in a week.

One step at a time, she told herself as she opened the

door.

One step at a time… and found herself face to face with the man who made her legs buckle.

He looked pale, his face strained with tension. His left hand was clenching the wound, eyes searching for something.

If she had ever thought such a predicament would turn him into a powerless human, she was wrong. She couldn't see weakness—only strength and determination. All focused on her.

"Did you think you could run away that easily?" He closed on her, eliminating the possibility of her slipping through the door.

Easily? she almost snorted. Whatever it was, easily didn't come near.

"Answer me?" he demanded.

"What do you want me to say?"

"The truth," he whispered, even now searching for it in her eyes. Just like she always did with him.

If he saw it … She closed her eyes for a moment. She had made many mistakes, broken many rules. She was not going to break this one. A lie was all she could give him.

"I don't know what you are talking about," she finally uttered, her voice never faltering. At least she could lie without blinking. She could have congratulated herself, if only she didn't feel like such a fake.

"Sure you don't," he said, closing in even more on her; leaving her no space, no air to breathe, only the warmth of his delectably muscular body to entice her senses.

Visions of them entangled in the heat of passion simmered before her.

Damn! Why was this happening to her? She couldn't let her feelings rule her. But as his hand reached for her, her eyes shot to his against her will, and Amira was forced to grab on to something for support.

How that something ended up being his neck, she would never know. One moment time seemed to freeze, and the next it flashed forward. One moment she was looking into his searing midnight gaze, and the next they were kissing.

This was insane. This was … magical. She moaned. For a second she let herself be swept away. She was lost in his embrace, and she never wanted to be found.

If only he could forget…

"Tell me again," he asked, shattering her illusion.

"Hmm?" Amira murmured, unable to summon up any rational thought so quickly. They had flown out of the window, and were refusing to come back.

"What happened, Angel?"

She loved it when he called her his angel. But if he knew how much she cared for him, he would know it was impossible for her to leave him for dead. She took a deep breath, mulling over how to throw him off the scent. She came up with a total blank.

"I am no angel," she uttered. "Never was. I'm not obliged to heal you just because I can't seem to stop wanting you. So let's just leave it at that."

"Let's not," his voice sounded harsher, sharper; but one of his arms was still wrapped around her. "Something isn't right. All I'm saying…"

"All you want to believe, you mean? Doesn't make it true, though."

"Uh-huh." He made it sound so skeptical, Amira had to take a deep breath.

"I had a choice. I chose. Simple."

"Lies," Raven rebutted, shaking his head.

Doubts plagued him. Suspicions had him worried. His wound pained him—as if in mockery of everything happening inside him. And yet, in all of this turmoil, it was impossible not to feel their bond pulsing anew.

The moment he touched her, it snapped into place so suddenly, he was still having trouble breathing. The wave that rippled through him could drive any sane man crazy. But it clarified a few things.

"You are lying." He leaned forward until their foreheads touched. "Worse, you are doing it with the truth." Which was more damning. And more revealing at the same time. "What are you hiding?"

"Didn't you get that the wrong way round?" She put effort into escaping his embrace. Raven pulled her closer, refusing to let her out of his arms. The strain it caused in his body made him wince from pain.

"Sorry…" she immediately came back to him, her hands gently landing on both sides of his bandaged wound.

Raven could swear he felt her desire to heal him, but for the longest moment her fingers simply caressed him. Her gaze was glued to the small red dot on the white material. Then suddenly, she curled her fingers tightly, as if in frustration, and lifted her face to his. Gasped.

"See, you can't hide it from me," he told her, seeing the unschooled expression in her face. Pure panic had flashed through her eyes. Panic he would never have noticed if he didn't know her so well.

She sighed, and her body shuddered. But before he could say a word, she laid her head on his shoulder and buried her face in the crook of his neck.

"Do you trust me?"

Strange question. They had gone through so much in the last few weeks—they pushed each other, they saved one another, each bled for the other. Even now, she was leaning on him, her hands wrapped around his back, but she didn't put any weight on him.

"I trust you."

"Two things I need to ask of you then," she murmured against his skin. "Don't ever ask me what happened. Don't push."

"Alright." He decided it was not worth fighting over. Besides, he knew she would only dig her heels in. He wouldn't ask. Didn't mean he wouldn't find out, of course. "And the second thing?"

"I need to know what you are hiding."

"With one condition..." Raven put his fingers behind her jaw and lifted her face in order to see her eyes. "Tell me why you never smile."

"What?" Amira twisted in his arms so she could face him properly. There was genuine curiosity etched in the lines of his face. Her brows furrowed in bewilderment. Of all the questions he could have asked her...

"You never smile. Why?"

"I never really thought about it..."

"But if you had to guess?"

"I better show you," she decided, and placed her fingers on his temples. Her touch felt cool on his feverish skin and he welcomed the sensation.

"This might not work," she confessed in a husky voice. "Never tried this before, but with you ... who knows? If you feel any discomfort, push away," she instructed him, and closed her eyes.

At first nothing happened. Then the tendrils of her energy began flowing in waves through him, and images formed in his mind. It took time for the fog to clear, but when it did, Raven almost wished it hadn't.

One vision followed another, then another, until it became impossible to track them. One thing remained the same—in all of them she was dying.

"I didn't think a person could die that many times.

Are these nightmares? Visions? Is that the reason I don't see any faces?"

"My prior lives," was all she said. "Now it's your turn."

Raven nodded, but instead of telling her anything, he took her hand and led her out of the room.

"Where are you taking me?" she asked, following him all the way to the grand stairs and up to the second floor. They turned a few more times before coming to a stop — in front of a very unremarkable door.

"Showing is better, right?" he uttered, reaching for the knob. Amira didn't have time to ponder over what could be hidden in the room in front of her, before Raven twisted the knob and pushed the door open.

The moment Amira stepped inside, darkness caught her unexpectedly — not the darkness of the room though. The darkness of another's mind. She waited for her eyes to adjust to the night that apparently reigned here, and approached the figure sitting on the bed.

His clothes were rumpled, and behind the unbuttoned shirt, she identified old scars marking his pale skin. A part of his torso and chest was damaged by fire, and, she would wager, his right arm also.

Amira gasped at the sheer number of other, more telling scars, not even daring to imagine what shadows were hiding from her. What other atrocities had been done to the man in front of her.

Hesitantly, she stretched out her hand, and brushed the long ebony strands from his face to reveal a resemblance that was uncanny.

He had the same midnight eyes. The same jaw. The same lips. This man's eyes, however, were completely unfocused. The face had none of the stern lines Raven possessed, but owned a long scar slicing his right cheek in half straight from his temple to the corner of his mouth. His body was slender, leaner than the muscular frame of Raven's. But most importantly, the person who sat several inches away from her was utterly lost.

"He is your brother." She lifted her eyes to Raven, who stood motionless from the moment she began her exploration. He simply nodded.

"But it's not the handiwork of the Order," she said again, not even pretending that it was a question. He'd been tortured by a witch for a very long time, and now she understood so much ... "but even if you'll manage to cleave the witch's head off, that won't return him to you."

"Why the hell not?" Raven finally found his voice.

"First of all, it's not you who needs to behead anyone. It's him." And Amira was not convinced it was feasible. "But the bigger reason is that the cause of his condition is not as simple as spell, potion, or curse. Were they used on him? Definitely. I believe they played a huge role in pushing him to this, but in the end, it was his decision to retreat into himself. No beheading can reverse this kind of damage."

Amira could still feel the residue of dark magic sticking to him like a wet cloth. The amount of it had to have been smothering years ago—no wonder it had succeeded in driving him mad. But it was not the worst part.

Amira had a nasty suspicion he was more like his brother than just in looks. Raven had fought against her spell once, so she knew he would have beaten any other witch's in a second. If his brother had the same immunity... It would explain the reason he'd been forced to endure so many spells and tortures.

If he hadn't fought against the slave-bond—if the witch had been successful in leashing him to her will—this wouldn't have happened.

"So it's doomed." The look on Raven's face was heartbreaking. And she knew she had done the right thing keeping the cruelest part from him. At least for the time being.

"Not necessarily," Amira said, not wanting to raise hopes. She was not sure it could work. Even if it did, what came out of the darkness might not be entirely whole; but she knew she had to try. "He is still there. I could try to reach him."

"How?" Raven crossed the distance he'd kept between them and crouched before her. "Is mind-healing another of your abilities?"

"No," she shook her head. She could heal a laceration, but not insanity. "But I won't be healing. Think of it as walking the labyrinth. He's stuck in the middle and needs help to get out. I can lead him out."

"So you see the way?"

"If I concentrate enough, I think I'll be able to. But for this to work, I need him to communicate with me the way you can." Hopefully, it was in the blood.

"If you'd do this..." she didn't let him finish. Amira took his lips with hers, and after a long and thorough kiss, murmured, "you'd teach me how to smile?"

"Anything, Angel." If she brought Dacian back, there was nothing he wouldn't do for her.

He watched how she placed her fingers on his brother's temples and closed her eyes. For the longest time nothing happened. He sat beside her in silence, waiting for the miracle as each minute was chased by another minute, then another. And then many, many more. Until he lost track of time, and almost of all hope.

But then, a miracle did happen—his brother blinked, and focused his gaze on Raven. His brow furrowed and his lips curled into a sneer.

"Your bitch just got sucked in." With those words, Amira's body swayed and slumped.

Fury roared inside Raven, and he did what he'd never thought he would, or could, do—not in a million years—he decked his own brother.

Chapter 26

A day passed, filled with worry and emptiness. Hours of attempt after fruitless attempt to wake her up. She didn't seem to hear him — she kept looking straight ahead, her too-familiar glassy eyes staring through him, rather than at him.

Raven was afraid to shake her, afraid to move her at all, but his hands refused to release her. As if afraid she would fade away if he let go of her. So he stayed in his room, with Amira, from the moment he carried her there.

The only time he'd left her was to find Dacian and demand explanations. His brother knew something, Raven was certain of it. But to his utter frustration, he refused to lift a finger to help a witch. He'd been close to leveling Dacian to the ground when he'd snorted, "What could you do that hasn't been done to me already? Or has your new bi … sorry, your woman taught you a thing or two, brother?"

There had been so much scorn in his words, Raven still felt the ugly emotions sticking to him like tar. Maybe he shouldn't have asked — Dacian wasn't exactly reasonable where witches were concerned, and with good reason too. But doing nothing wasn't an option. Raven couldn't just sit and watch her skin turn paler and paler with every second.

If only he knew how to bring her back. But he had not the slightest idea how to lead her out of whatever labyrinth she was trapped in. All he could do was hold her and pray.

She was a fighter, he reassured himself. There was no hurdle big enough for her not to overcome.

In this, you are wrong. Raven heard a voice. The same voice from his dream. *Of course, give her a decade and I think she'll make it. But are you prepared to wait that long?*

"Let me guess, you can help me?" He didn't like the voice when it was in his dream, and he sure as hell didn't like it now, but he *was* desperate… Worse, he sensed the truth in the creature's words.

I'm the only one who can help you.

"I'm listening."

Don't even think about it, Dazy; another being swirled like a tornado into his room. It suddenly got too crowded.

"Who are you?" he asked, addressing both of them. The second one was a female—a goddess? While the first one—he had a nasty suspicion it could be Dazlog.

The creatures remained cloaked, but it was not hard to sense dark power when you had it right there in front of you. The air around them seemed to crack with energy. This didn't bode well for any of them, Raven decided, and scooped Amira in his arms.

You want her well, or you want us to get to know each other better? the voice of an otherworldly female spread like a chill over his skin. Raven gritted his teeth, but kept his silence. *Just as I thought.*

Make no deals with that —

Dazlog's voice was interrupted by a cold wave that passed through Raven. Like a dozen lightning bolts, energy flashed in the middle of the room. Flared out. It spread outwards until the walls themselves seemed to respond to the surge. Everything shook. The sword he kept above the mantel fell. So did the mirror.

The frame crashed loudly to the floor. Shards of

glass flew everywhere. Then the dust settled, the room became so silent — Raven was convinced one, if not both of the beings, had left.

Are we ready to bargain? the female asked, and no male voice followed hers this time. It became apparent that Raven's options had just got sliced in half.

"What is it that you want?"

I want you to leave for Leonon, first thing in the morning. There are trials scheduled and I need you to save one particular person.

It seemed simple. Too simple. A nagging thread of doubt started to squirm its way into Raven's mind. "And Amira will wake up with no harm done to her mind, or body?"

She will wake up the moment you leave, with no harm done to her, I give you my word, she said.

"It's not enough." Raven wasn't stupid. Since he didn't know who exactly he was talking to, he had no idea if the word of honor in itself was binding to the creature. For some it was, but not for all. "I need a binding oath on your part."

Clever, she laughed. *But there is no need for such distrust.*

"A precaution," Raven assured her, and after she swore the oath, he gave his own word.

He wasn't thrilled about leaving Amira for four days — three if he pushed it, but a bargain was a bargain.

"I'll be back, Angel," he whispered, and kissed her lips. *Be safe.*

Saying goodbye to a person who had become his every breath was the last thing on earth he wanted. But he couldn't allow this to continue. What if she suffered? Dacian had, when he'd been stuck in his own prison.

It was so strange to have his brother back, and in a way worse than not having him at all. They'd been inseparable. Now, his brother treated him like an enemy. Raven hated what Dacian had become, what they had become. But most of all, he hated himself for the ugly feeling that seemed to rear its head every time they crossed words. It was a vicious cycle.

As he walked to the door, another thought came to him—for the first time in his life, he would be riding off without the same goal he had had for many years. For the first time, he didn't have a life-long purpose. And it left a bittersweet taste in his mouth.

He had dedicated everything to finding a salvation for Dacian, but he'd never thought about what would happen next. Now he knew that forgiveness wasn't for everyone. He also knew that he had no idea what he wanted to do in his life. Except for one thing...

Raven took one last look at Amira, so peacefully sitting on his bed, and closed the door. He knew he wanted her in it.

Fool, he heard Dazlog's voice once again. *Why did you bargain with that witch?*

"I don't remember hearing any offer from you," Raven's voice echoed as he marched down the corridor. He was afraid he wouldn't be able to leave if he stopped now.

Did you know it was a trap? You reach Leonon, she'll detain you. Amira ends up at her mercy because you were away. And I can assure you, Nially has no mercy.

The words struck him cold and forced him to stop dead in his tracks. "What? Are you saying she won't hold to her side of the deal?"

Oh, she will. She needs her in her full strength for what's to come.

"What is to come?" Raven demanded, tired of all this cryptic nonsense.

That, you'll need to find out for yourself. Right now the question is—can you avert it?

"Avert what?"

I'm afraid you have nothing of value to me to bargain for answers with, much less for help.

"Really?" Raven tilted his head, almost certain he knew where the demon stood.

"Is that why you came here? Because I have nothing you want? You know what I think?" He wrapped his arms on his chest trying to remain calm. It was the only way to find a solution. He willed his heart to slow down and pushed his worry aside for the moment. "You would help me no matter what, especially now that this Nially's got involved. I wager your plans don't exactly mesh well together."

My, my, aren't you the perceptive one, Dazlog laughed. *But you are right. I'll help you get back in time. For a price.*

"I'll be helping you to thwart Nially's plans. Isn't that enough?"

That got the demon laughing even harder. *But it's not exactly a price, since you have a stake in this.*

"And because *you* have a stake in this, you won't ask anything else."

I like the way you are thinking, human. Bloody inconvenient, but I like it. The demon laughed one more time and disappeared.

* * *

Amira was lost. For days. Maybe minutes. She had no way of measuring time when time didn't exist where she was. Only darkness.

It felt like being locked in a dark room with no windows and no doors. The walls were moving, shifting all the time, closing in on her; and the floor kept slipping from under her feet, preventing her from gaining any semblance of balance.

Dreadful screams pierced her ears, and if only it would cease for a second, Amira knew she would find the way out—but it kept growing and growing.

She had already walked through some of her prior lives, each time gaining a new bit of knowledge, but there was still so much left, she was afraid she would never get out of this predicament.

Suddenly she found herself transported back hundreds of years to a time when her powers were less than those of an ordinary witch. Her name—Shyra.

Shyra was innocent, and despite having lived six times, she'd never lain with a man. Was afraid to. She'd once witnessed a witch being taken by some knave and the girl had screamed her throat out. Till he'd gagged her mouth.

Shyra had been horrified. She'd wanted to help, but fear had kept her immobile, hidden in the corner of the barn. Curled into a small ball, she'd kept herself silent so not to alert anyone to her presence. She was ashamed to admit that all she'd done was pray.

Shyra didn't know why she was remembering it now, when she needed a spell that would work against an amulet-wearing Venlordian — be it only for a few moments. But she was scared, trembling like a leaf as the man's hands worked their way through her skirts.

She pushed and she slapped and she squirmed, all in vain. He was larger, stronger. He was shoving her skirt up, revealing her thighs and touching. Touching. Touching.

Shyra shivered, her hands searching for any kind of weapon on the table she was laid upon. She grabbed something, hopefully sharp, and stabbed the Venlordian with all her might once. Twice. Three times. Shyra screamed and stabbed, not even seeing what she held in her hand.

The Venlordian stopped touching, but before Shyra could manage to escape, he fell on her, his bodyweight pinning her down. Her grip tightened on the knife. Her blouse suddenly got wet. And red.

Shyra looked straight into the lifeless eyes in front of her and screamed.

Amira remembered the horror of the first life she'd taken. She remembered the fear and panic, but no more. Now she felt strangely safe and protected by a presence who guarded even her dreams. Amira felt herself moving forward until she stumbled into another lifetime, another place.

Loanne cuddled after making love, and sighed contently. Life was good. Finally.

She was through with following orders – she'd tried that already and it had brought her only pain and death. Now she wanted to live. To love. And to be loved. Tyrell was the first man she'd let into her bed, and she couldn't be happier. He loved her. He would protect her from the Order.

Just then a knock sounded on the front door. He shifted beneath her, kissed her lips and whispered, "I'll be back soon."

Tyrell opened the door and let two men in.

Loanne gasped, grabbed a sheet to cover herself, trying to understand what was happening.

"You can take the witch now," the man who had sworn his love minutes ago told the Venlordians.

Loanne knew she would not escape – she wasn't strong enough. She knew death was already breathing down her neck, but the pain in her heart was present and so powerful she couldn't contain her tears.

Amira jumped through time again. Another few hundred years. And found herself in the middle of the town square with another man.

She was careful this time. Didn't trust as easily. Hadn't slept with anyone yet, though the man in front of her had sworn many times he would lay down his life for her. He was bent on seducing her, and Hannah didn't discourage his advances, though she was not sure if she would reward his efforts.

"Tell me what you want, my sweet Hannah, and it's yours," he used to say, though she'd never asked anything of him. Now, when she spied a couple of Venlordians

approaching, she whispered, "do not let any harm befall me."

Hannah's magic, though stronger than that of her prior selves, was still too weak to fight the members of the Order. Men, yes; but not amulet-wearing monsters.

"You are safe, my sweet," he told her, but when the Venlordians demanded her in exchange for letting him go, her protector turned, whispered a pathetic sorry, and ran.

Again the setting changed, and the woman Amira found herself to be lived by gaining power.

Fiona was strong enough to rely on herself. But all the prior lives had left her jaded. She viewed men as cowards and traitors with only one purpose – to be used.

She slept with many. But not for the pleasure of it. She drained them of energy and grew so powerful she was convinced no one would be able to stop her. Until the goddesses stripped her of her powers.

Amira jumped again, finding Evet standing in front of a man whom she suspected knew the Prophecy she was supposed to fulfill. Thankfully she had already learned how to read minds.

Evet concentrated and entered his mind, breaking down one barrier at a time. But she lost control and suddenly, the man gasped and fell, too weak to withstand her intrusion.

Evet was forced to watch him scream and scream, his pain attracting passers-by. Until there was only silence, and she was standing near the body of the man she had just killed.

Amira jumped again, and again she saw a man dying in front of her; only this time because she had told him to, after he called her an abomination.

She stood near the body, not understanding what had happened. She'd never had such a power, such a voice to affect others. It seemed it sufficed for her to scream the punishment, and a life was lost.

What was she turning into? Her lack of control and knowledge took lives. Her inability to understand her own destiny made her suffer. She couldn't accept such a defeat, but the truth was inevitable. It ripped her apart. Kept lacerating.

And finally it was she who screamed. And screamed. And screamed as everything changed one more time.

Amira opened her eyes. The world came to her slowly, each detail crawling out of the shadows at its own pace. Shade and light finally coloring her view.

There were moments, maybe hours even, when she thought she would never escape the darkness. When no matter where she ran, it followed indefatigably. Without remorse.

Her magic didn't work in the darkness she had been locked up in, and every time she made the wrong turn she was forced to live through her own memories—nightmares, mostly.

But every time she felt powerless and scared, about to meet her execution, she sensed a calming presence. Her prior selves did not know the source, but Amira knew. Raven was there standing by her side, protecting her, defending her. The dream of him was so entangled in her brain, it seemed real his being with her, even hundreds of years ago; giving her strength and hope.

Even now she could hear him whispering, his hands gently touching her. She dreamed of him kissing her.

She shook her head, still unable to fathom dreams or distinguish them from reality, wishes from actual events. Suddenly, she realized she was laughing. Almost hysterically. As if she was truly crazed.

Amira swallowed, quelling her mirthless laughter, her eyes desperately blinking until she registered a person in front of her. So familiar, and yet a stranger. His midnight gaze was full of distrust. Dacian, she remembered. Not Raven. His mere name causing her heart to leap and fall painfully, knowing he wasn't here.

"Where is he?" she asked as soon as she recovered her voice.

"Some place far away, I hope." Dacian's eyes never left her, and she noticed uncertainty hidden behind layers of disgust. A lot of his hatred was directed toward his own brother, and Amira had a hard time believing what she felt.

"After everything, you still care for him?" he asked her, interrupting her long, silent stare.

"And you hate him," she simply stated.

"How could I not?" his anger rose with every word uttered. "He destroys everything he touches."

"Then why haven't you tried to harm me? You know you could hurt him that way." Amira rose to her full height and stood in front of him. Eye to eye.

"I've looked into the eyes of the monster—I don't want to become one," he whispered, and in that moment, she noticed a scared child hidden deep in his eyes. He blinked, and quickly it disappeared.

"I've seen glimpses of you, you know. When you came into my consciousness I got fragments from yours. Maybe that's the reason I can't seem to hate you." *I have no idea where half of the things in my head come from.* The last sentence he said to himself, his voice frustrated and almost desperate, but she heard it nevertheless.

"If you've seen me, then you've seen your brother." *Don't be hard on him,* she wanted to ask, but was afraid of what his reaction would be if she were to project her thoughts straight into his mind. He might be capable, like Raven; but Dacian wasn't ready.

"Ah, yes, let's see … the pole. You, almost being raped. Should I continue?"

Amira sighed. It was fruitless to argue with him. Not when everything was still too raw. Too new. About fifteen years of his life taken away. It could not be healed in one night. It was impossible to make him understand that to her, those fragments were irrelevant. She tried not to get distracted by the past.

The whole walking down memory lane thing was also not the most exhilarating experience she'd ever had, but it was necessary in order to put the pieces together.

Every life she had lived had brought her a new power—she had known that; yet she had never considered the importance in their progression. Now she did. Different powers became like ingredients to put into the pot, and the potion that resulted was a conjuring ritual.

She didn't know the details yet, true, but she suspected the witches would tell her when they came. And after she played her part, she would be free.

So many possibilities were suddenly available for her, she actually wanted to smile.

"Unbelievable," Dacian raised his hands as if giving up. "I am talking about what he did to you and you … smile?"

Was she? Yes, yes she was, Amira thought, and her smile broadened.

She supposed one had to go through everything to know how she felt. But from the look on Dacian's face and the way he was shaking his head, he probably thought she'd lost her mind. Or hadn't recovered it.

"I can't explain it to you," she said, "I don't think you would understand, but maybe one day." One day, if he was lucky enough to find the meaning in his life. There was nothing else she could do for him. It was up to him now.

"Let's just leave it," he suggested. "I have a feeling we are never going to agree on this subject."

"For your own sake, I hope it isn't true," Amira told him. She was ready to face the world. Ready for anything.

Chapter 27

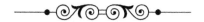

After conversing with Martha, Amira knew where Raven had gone to, but when she mounted a horse and rode off, it was not Leonon she headed for. She went in the opposite direction, urging her horse as much as she dared to, stopping only when absolutely necessary.

She encountered no difficulties, no Venlordians lurking behind trees. The journey was smooth and gave her time to mull over the memories she'd walked through. It let her discover how time had changed her from those girls she'd once been.

Shyra had been so fearful and weak. Loanne so desperate for love. Hannah—wary, Fiona—vindictive. Unsure, scared, furious, disgusted by herself—she had been all of those things. Finally, Amira was the culmination of them all.

Sometimes she was scared, sometimes vindictive. There were moments when she felt weak, and times when she was stronger than ever. Nothing held her back, no matter how much fear gripped her heart. Amira was determined, and she was a fighter. Most importantly, she was in love with a man she believed would never betray her. Not after everything they had gone through.

Her lips curled in a smile that was still so new and strange to her, Amira had to touch it to know she was not imagining it. The happiness she felt, the lightness in her heart, however, was impossible to miss. Something inside sang. Freedom at last. The only thing she lacked was a strong and protective embrace, a searing kiss, and the dark gaze she vowed she would have again.

For just once in her life, Amira wanted to stop and dream, but as always, she had no time for it. She had to accumulate as much energy as possible. After a day and a half of riding, she was finally a few short miles from her destination, where she would need every last drop of magic. Especially since the cold stone walls of the dungeon she was heading to would offer none.

Amira jumped down from the horse and with confidence walked to the same entrance she'd seen her family use days ago. As expected there were guards, who unsheathed their swords the moment they spotted her. But before they could reach her, she sent them flying straight into the wall.

There was a thump, a yelp, and then silence. She didn't stop to check on them. Didn't have time, and honestly didn't even care. Amira took one last breath of fresh air, unlocked the door and stepped through.

Her first thought was that the stench of blood and suffering was even stronger and more poignant than when she was spirit-walking. Her second, that she was going to level this place. And her third—she hoped someone would attack her. It was almost impossible not to desire blood when all of her senses were reeling from the magnitude of torture, pain and death this place held.

She took a moment to silence the screams in her head of souls abandoned and trapped, and slowly descended the stairs.

Careful not to make a target of herself, and ready should anyone jump with a sword from around the corner, Amira encountered only damp walls and an occasional torch.

She felt as if she had entered a grave. Except graveyards felt more peaceful. This place had such a strong energy about it, it enveloped her with its darkness.

Amira shivered. She wanted to turn and run as fast as she could. She wanted to rip her clothes from her body and burn them.

A place where only the stench of death lived was the last place a witch like her should venture, let alone risk being locked up in. These catacombs were deceptive—hidden underground, where Amira should have been able to tap into the pulse of the earth, but the cold, dead walls were impregnated with so many putrid shadows of lingering pain, it prevented her from accessing what she needed. Not unless she took all the stifling rot inside her first.

Quickly, Amira retraced the same path she'd once walked in her spirit form, scanning her surroundings and looking for any sign of witches being tortured or kept prisoner. She found none. Every holding cell was vacant. If one didn't count the rats, blood and urine. Even the corridors were no longer illuminated. Torches were either burned out or the sconces empty. It was evident the place was not being used anymore. Still, the stench of pain followed her.

Amira hoped she was not too late. She hoped her family had not been relocated—or worse—no longer alive.

She quickened her paces, wondering where the Venlordians were. A lot of them died in the battle, true. Some were probably in Leonon right now, but there should have been more than just those two on the surface. Besides, they were guarding something, weren't they?

She turned another corner, finally hearing chains being rattled, words whispered, though it was hard to decipher their meaning. She breathed a sigh of relief when she spotted the people she had come to get, and lowered the hood of her cloak around her face. Being recognized was not in her plans; not when she couldn't return home with them.

She saw her father pacing in his prison cell, her mother praying with her eyes closed. She saw Regan clenching his fists around the bars that held him captive, begging his wife to look at him, but Milla's eyes kept moving down to the lifeless body left to rot on the cold, damp ground.

Amira swallowed the bile rising in her throat as she realized the bastards had left Sofie's body in the middle on purpose. Forcing them to witness their brutally-slain daughter and niece decomposing in front of them. Forcing them to smell the stench of her remains.

Amira knew the picture she witnessed would be etched in her mind for years to come. Milla's sorrow, Regan's rage so live and sharp—she could practically touch it. Amira didn't stop to pray; she approached Sofie, making a vow to avenge her death, and maybe...

Dazlog! she yelled, kneeling near her dead cousin, drawing all the gazes onto herself.

"Who are you?"

"Let us out of here!"

"Please, please help us!"

She heard demands and desperate pleas—for the moment she ignored everything.

"It's getting tiresome." Dazlog appeared on the other side of the body, irritated as hell.

His eyes flashed green fire, the flames promising doom. His fierce gaze fell on her, and Amira heard someone gasp—the demon could appear menacing when he chose to.

"Bring her back," Amira whispered, afraid she would be recognized.

Everyone stilled. It seemed time itself ceased to exist as they waited for the answer.

"Sorry, no can do," he simply said, wrapping his

arms in front of his broad chest.

"Can't do, or won't do?" Amira had to tighten the reins on her emotions. She tried to breathe in and out. Slowly, very slowly. She could not lose control. "What is your price?"

"There's nothing you could offer to interest me. Besides, it is kind of a once in lifetime—or lifetimes in your case—deal. My answer is no." Dazlog leaned against the wall as if scenes like this were common to him. And they probably were, considering where he lived. "Now can I go?" he asked sarcastically, lifting his brows.

Amira wanted to tell him no, but before she even got the chance to open her mouth, Milla sobbed, "My life! I'll give my life for my daughter's!"

Amira's head whipped round towards her aunt. She released her from the chains, released everyone, but the moment Milla could move, she ran straight to Dazlog and fell at his feet, begging.

"Milla!" Regan breathed, trying in vain to gather his wife in his arms, just as Deron did with Eliana. Milla struggled against his attempts, wrapping even tighter around Dazlog's legs.

Amira was afraid Dazlog would shove her unceremoniously away, make her pay for the outburst, or take her up on the offer. She didn't know which of the outcomes she feared the most. The demon's response, when it came, left her bewildered.

"Your life is not mine to take, Milla. Don't ever offer it." Dazlog lifted her aunt up, handling her strangely more gently than Amira would have expected. He even wiped her tears, which perplexed her completely. "But know that she is in Azariel."

He brushed his hand through the air, conjuring up the image of a beautiful girl with brown curls—Sofie—sitting on the swings and laughing. "She is happy."

Amira could hear the intakes of breath and watched as Milla carefully, as if unsure, lifted her right hand and tried to touch the image of her daughter. Of course, her fingers went straight through it, and a second later it disintegrated. Milla retracted her hand, took a few seconds to look at her fingers, and succumbed to another wave of sobs, this time letting Regan embrace her.

"Thank you," she finally whispered, and judging from the look on Dazlog's face, Amira could swear he only now registered what he'd done. He was obviously uncomfortable with the gratitude. Who would have thought?

"Finally some flavor." He winked at her and turned his head to the entrance. As if conjured up, the distant sound of footsteps reached them, and Dazlog smiled.

"Are you going to help?" she inquired.

"Why would I want to end everything before it's even started?"

Amira didn't have time for conversations anymore. The first pair of Venlordians entered—she sent them flying across the hall. They didn't lose consciousness by her hand, but Regan and Deron made sure they wouldn't stand up again, and borrowed their swords.

"Do I know you?" someone had asked her, but Amira ignored the question again. She had other worries to think about, enemies to face.

In the end, there were eight warriors they dealt with. Except for the last one—the one who had killed Sofie. He stayed safe through the entire skirmish as if an invisible hand had been protecting him. And it didn't take her long to realize whose hand it was.

"What are you still doing here?" she yelled at Dazlog, who had kept his composure throughout the whole thing.

"Trying to enjoy the show," he told her with a sigh,

"but you sure know how to kill the fun." He glanced at the bodies lying around and lifted his eyes to her again. "Did you really have to interfere?"

"Yes," Amira almost groaned. "I believe you wanted to leave," she said.

"Now I want to do this." Dazlog pushed himself off the wall, took Milla's hand, and led her to the last surviving Venlordian.

Milla followed without a word, against all her husband's protests. She took a dagger from the demon's hands and without a moment's hesitation, plunged it deep into the cold heart of the killer.

His body slumped to the ground. Lifeless.

"Again, I thank you." Milla turned to Dazlog and presented him the dagger so regally, one could have thought she was holding a court.

"An eye for an eye," the demon bowed his head slightly. "My work here is complete." He vanished.

"Out. Now." Amira had no time to waste.

"I am not going to leave my son," Regan said, making no attempt to obey her.

"I'll take care of it," she assured him, and without giving them the opportunity to argue, disappeared around the corner.

She didn't have to look far. Pharell was being held in the hall at the end of the corridor, his arms shackled to the ceiling—his body suspended a few feet above the ground.

He kept his head down, and for a second Amira thought he was unconscious. He was so still, she couldn't even see his bruised chest moving.

She stepped forward and he lifted his head, eyes full of hatred. His face was beaten and swollen, his nose—broken. Amira could barely recognize him.

Pharell's gaze locked on her, and his blue eyes gentled. He knew she was a woman, Amira realized, and immediately witnessed a shadow cross his face. Fear in his eyes. For her.

"W-what—" he breathed, his voice hoarse and abrasive like sandpaper. "Run!" he managed, "Save yourself."

Amira didn't respond. She approached and placed her hands on him, ignoring his attempts to shove her away. Her fingers slowly moved around his chest, gently examining the damage done while trying not to hurt him further. He hissed as she touched his side. She let go.

His ribs were broken, his abdomen strangely swollen as if he had internal bleeding. He was hurting, but she had to touch him, to support his weight, for once she unlocked his chains, Amira was afraid he would fall, causing even more damage to himself.

If only she could heal him, but she dared not. Not in this place, not while there was still a chance of being attacked. Amira's powers were waning as it was; healing would weaken her immensely.

"Hold on," she told him, as she embraced his masculine body and released the cuffs from his wrists.

Pharell went down groaning with pain, but with Amira's help managed to stay upright. Still, it was a struggle—his weight a whole ton on her shoulders, pressing her to the ground. They had to reach the surface, and soon. Otherwise, she was not sure how long Pharell would be alive.

"You'll have to—"

"Mira?" he uttered, "what are you doing here?"

Amira should have been shocked he recognized her; then again, Pharell and Sofie always had more perception of her than her own parents.

"No questions, please," she asked, brushing his sweaty hair from his eyes. His hip-length black tresses were plastered to his skin. Matted and dirty. "I'll explain, but not now."

"Just promise to run if we come across those bastards. I can't lose you too." His haunted look told her that something else, something awful had happened to him down here. Though strangely, Amira could not read him at all. He was wrapped into himself so tightly, it reminded her of how Raven was when they'd first met.

"Try not to talk," she said instead of promising anything.

Amira was worried they would not make it. No matter how hard Pharell pushed himself. He was severely wounded and she didn't have the strength needed to carry him by herself.

Deron and Regan took over just as she thought they would collapse. For once in her life she was glad her father and uncle hadn't listened to her.

It took little effort for the men to steady Pharell and help him reach the surface, taking along their wives and Sofie's body.

Don't tell the others, Amira asked Pharell. His eyes widened, but he nodded ever so slightly, taking it all in his stride.

She emerged from the dark and briefly closed her eyes against the setting sun. The warm sunrays played on her skin, and Amira could finally take a breath in. She felt restored in nature's embrace. Alive.

She instructed them to lay Pharell down, but the moment he was free, he crawled near to his sister and took her hand in his.

For a fleeting moment, Amira saw deeper. She heard his scream of pain, and she sensed his sadness and rage at the loss. She placed her hands on his shoulders and healed him — or at least the wounds in his body. The ones in his soul she had no idea how to approach, once again realizing how useless she was in the face of heartache.

There was one last thing she could do — she dug her fingers deep in the soil, letting the magic flow through her, and the earth trembled under their feet. The damned place was no more.

"Who are you?" they asked her one more time.

Amira was tempted to lower her hood and witness their reaction. She wanted to be around for the burying of Sofie's body. She even wanted to make sure they reached home safely. But revealing herself would only complicate things. So without another word, she mounted her horse and rode off.

Her path curved in a different direction right now. A direction she was only too eager to explore.

Chapter 28

Raven left Leonon behind, pushing Lightning to fly the last few miles. He kept his eyes forward, refusing to think about the insanity he'd witnessed. There was no purpose for it. At least none he could see. It was one thing to hunt down witches for sacred, misguided, noble, vengeful—whatever the cause, but this—this defied all rational explanation. It served no purpose.

He didn't even want to think about the damned errand Nially had sent him on. Dazlog had been right—it had been a trap. And if not for the demon, he might have died along with a third of the town's population.

Dazlog had also told Raven to prevent Amira from heeding the call. He would be lying if he said he knew what it meant, but forewarned was forearmed.

With that in mind, Raven rode through the main gates, thinking that fate had a nasty sense of humor. He'd always thought he would never place a foot on this piece of land, if it weren't for his brother. His brother didn't need him anymore, and yet, he was still crossing the yard.

Raven rode on. He led Lightning into the stables, unsaddled the horse, and leaned his forehead into the creature's. It was a thank you to a friend for giving his all.

As he stood there in utter silence, a familiar honeyed aroma rolled inside, enveloping him in its warm embrace. He sensed her approach, and everything inside him reeled into infinity.

"You left me," she whispered, stopping by the entrance to the horse's paddock.

"Guilty." Raven turned, desperate to know how mad she was.

"Don't you know that denial is the key to weaseling out of accusations? That, and groveling. Or was it flattery?" Her gaze bored into him. Deep, clear and ethereal, her eyes were a whirlpool of emotions swirling, pulling him in. He was a drowned man, but when she looked at him he felt alive.

How did she manage to chase away the bloody scenes from his mind with just a few choice words?

"I'll keep it in mind," Raven promised, wrapping his arms around her waist and pulling her into him. His clothes were dusty from the road, covered in soot, but she didn't seem to mind as her hands moved around his neck.

"Is that all you are going to say to me?"

"I need to wash off?"

"Now you are just asking for it!" She thumped on his chest with an open palm, but her lips curled into a wicked smile. It was like watching the sun come out from under the clouds. The day brightened. And Raven couldn't resist—he kissed her.

"Aren't you assuming too much?" she murmured against his mouth.

"Stop me any time you want." But she didn't. Amira responded with a moan he caught between his lips. She tilted her head to allow—no, demand—a deeper contact, her fingers clutching at his shoulders.

"Interesting." A single, silently-uttered word flooded over Raven like a bucket of ice-cold water. He lifted his eyes and met the mocking gaze of his brother's.

Dacian's hair was down, covering the scar on his

cheek. His shirt was buttoned up all the way to his neck. He was standing in the doorway — one shoulder leaning against the door-frame, hands wrapped over his chest.

"An interesting way to make certain you never run out of the need to wash your dirty conscience. Then again, to each his own poison, is it not, brother?" Dacian's forcedly-cheerful voice made him clench his teeth. He closed his eyes for a second and counted to ten. But when he opened them, everything remained the same.

Raven's jaw grated — he refused to apologize for his feelings. For his past mistakes — yes — but not for this. "One more insult, even remotely regarding Amira, and I'm..."

"Let's go," she interrupted him, taking him by the hand.

"You better listen to her. Run," Dacian laughed a mirthless laugh. "Or I might tell her the truth."

Raven went, but he wasn't running. If anyone was going to tell her the whole truth, it would be coming from his mouth. And then ... only time could show.

He wanted to find some place quiet, but the moment they stepped over the threshold of his house, Martha ambushed him with questions in her eyes. The woman didn't even have to voice it. He knew what she wanted to know. And with that knowledge, memories rose in his mind — tortured pleas, the smell of burning flesh.

"I was too late," was all he said. By the time he'd ridden through the gates of Leonon, the fires were already blazing.

Martha covered a gasp with her palms, and every last question vanished from her face. Horror and sadness were all that remained in her eyes.

Amira waited it out until they were alone, letting him marshal his thoughts. She didn't push. Nor did she press. She watched as he loosened the few buttons around his neck, rubbed at it and moved toward the window.

He turned from her, his palms landed on the windowsill, and for the longest, silence-filled moment, he simply observed the setting sun. The vista was almost serene, so unlike the tempest raging inside him…

"If you are willing the sun to stay in the sky, it's futile." As always, her voice permeated through his memories and senses, giving him a strength she alone could.

"No," he shook his head, but didn't turn yet. "I was just wondering why I keep torturing myself. I used to find such scenes whether I wanted to or not. It's inevitable when going from town to town."

"But now you don't have to."

"But now I realize I know no other way of living."

"It's an admirable trait—the desire to help others."

"I don't have the necessary resources, and I sure as hell wouldn't mind living without memories of charred flesh peeling," he whispered as Amira approached him. "One lone man is not a warrior to make a stand against an army."

"You are not alone," she assured him as her nails trailed up his back, all the way to his nape. They traveled even higher, until her fingers sank in his hair. Without even meaning to, he closed his eyes and the most wonderful thing happened—he saw no fires, heard no screams.

"I see you," she said against his ear.

"Do you?" Raven turned and her palm landed on his chest, over his strongly-beating heart. Her own heart was lodged in her throat, and all Amira could do was nod.

"Did you know it was me who invited the evil into this home?" The words that left his mouth were emotionless. Dead. He looked at her, but Amira had a feeling Raven was seeing his past in front of his eyes.

"Is this about what Dacian hinted at?" she asked as she touched her hand fleetingly over his cheek.

"I think I should start from the beginning..." A part of her wanted to stop him and spare the wound from being opened again, but Amira knew better than anyone that in order to heal a festering wound, one needed to reopen and clean it.

"Fifteen years ago a witch knocked on our door. She seemed so scared, running from the Venlordians. Ethely ..." Raven paused. Amira saw how his fists clenched, jaw tightened. "...she begged for help, for one night to hide. We let her in..." his voice almost fractured, "she repaid our kindness. In spades."

Raven closed his eyes and opened them with a frown, as if he didn't like what he saw lurking in the darkness. Considering the story he was telling her, Amira knew he hated the images playing on his mind.

"By the time we discovered what she was up to, it was too late. She placed some kind of spell which ensured that it was my mother whom the members of the Order mistook for a witch. My father died fighting— protecting us, and..." He swallowed hard, punched the bridge of his nose and shook his head. It was obvious he was miles away, even if they stood but a few inches apart.

For a young boy it must have been horrific to lose his family this way. Amira wanted to hug him. Better yet, to go back in time and change everything. If only she had the power. All she could really do was let him finish. Raven had to let out everything that had been lying in his heart for so long.

"I remember thinking I could lift the spell, so I snuck out and ran to the nearest forest. A complete idiot I was." Raven sighed and raked his fingers through his hair. "First, I should have ridden. And second, I shouldn't have bothered at all. The witch who lived in the forest refused to help me no matter how much I begged. Do you know what she told me?"

His eyes finally focused on her, and her throat tightened in response to what she saw in his face.

"She told me my mother was not one of them. Not one of them!" His voice rose with fury, but he couldn't hide the tremor in his hands. Not from her.

It was an ugly truth, but witches rarely helped others—now she could see Raven's confusion when she'd healed Nyssa in an entirely different light.

"When I finally got home, I found the front door smashed in and Martha unconscious," he whispered absently. "Dacian was already gone. And my mother..." Raven's voice trailed off and Amira thought he would remain silent, but his voice rose once again and the words began pouring out more rapidly as if every damning syllable was burning his tongue, and he couldn't spit it out fast enough.

"I ran into the hallway only to see my mother being dragged down the stairs by her hair. Screaming and kicking. The bodies of our trusted servants were lying butchered all around. Evolyn was crying in her cradle. I snatched the dagger from the wall and tried to thrust it into someone's chest, but barely managed to nick an arm."

Suddenly Amira wanted him to stop. To desist. The nightmare he was drawing was gaining a hold on her, sucking her in deeper and deeper. For the first time in their lives he had let her in completely with no walls or boundaries to keep his inner feelings from her. She was caught breathless by the intensity of it.

She saw everything through his eyes. She experienced the pain of witnessing how everything he had held dear was being destroyed. It was something more than physical. And Amira realized that dying was easy, no matter the manner of it—losing the ones you loved had a tendency to stay with you forever.

"They tied my hands to the banister, ripped the clothes off, and made me pay…" His voice was laced with so much anger, she almost missed the agony underneath it. "Maybe they would have killed me, maybe they should have … but my mother had pleaded with them to spare me…" Now his voice did fracture.

Amira wrapped her arms around him and felt him shaking. Again, she wanted to beg him to cease, but all she did was embrace him tighter.

Raven responded to her—he buried his face in her hair and whispered, his voice barely audible, "she told me to close my eyes and I did … like a coward I did as she begged me to … but I knew what was going on … I knew … no matter how hard she tried to protect me…" His throat locked and he raised his head. Dark, glassy eyes bored into her, and Amira felt her nails cutting into her palms. It tore her apart to see his anguish.

"How old were you?" She cupped his face in her palms, refusing to let this preposterous self-beating continue any longer.

"Almost fifteen"

Almost fifteen! "You were fourteen years old and you think yourself a coward?"

"I think myself worse."

"Why?" she wanted to know.

Instead of answering outright, he continued with the story, never once trying to shake off her hold.

"Do you know how it feels to see your mother being burned alive? To hear her scream as you never before knew any human could?" His breaths came out ragged,

275

his fingers laced with hers, and Amira was afraid she would crumble.

Seeing his hollow eyes made hers fill with tears.

"You would probably not believe it, but Dacian and I, we were inseparable once. Wherever there was one, there was the other—drove our parents crazy. I think it was one of the reasons my mother was so happy when after more than ten years she had another baby. A girl." The memory was like a small island of tranquility in the ocean of pain, but all too soon the earth disappeared, and Raven's memories took an ugly turn.

"They killed little Evie. They laughed as I desperately tried to free myself, though I could barely hold my head. And Dacian... We found him wandering in the woods. Six years later. Six years... Sick and wild like a rabid animal."

Finally Raven took a deep, shuddering breath in. He didn't know if he'd breathed throughout the entire story. He didn't remember. But now came the last part—the one he dreaded telling her all along.

"You asked me why I consider myself worse than a coward, and the answer is—because I not only invited evil into our home; I armed it against my own family." The words were like stones in his heart.

Amira's eyes blinked in confusion, and it caused a tear to fall down her cheek. A tear for him. Raven felt undeserving. But as long as she held him, he almost felt whole.

"I realize that you might have opened the door, or convinced your parents," she said. "You have a heart of gold—but armed her...?"

He snorted at the ridiculous notion she had in her head. "I always thought you were smart, but this perception of yours..."

"You didn't send Brea away when you could have. And she *is* a witch," she stated, her face serious with determination. "So don't you dare tell me what I should or shouldn't think of you!" Her passionately-uttered words were both a warning and a threat. And despite everything, it made him smile.

"I love you." It just came out, and time itself seemed to stop. She froze. Her eyes widened. And Raven had one of those "Oh shit, what have I done?" moments. It ended in about a tenth of a second, when she kissed his lips.

When they were together the past didn't matter. When she was caressing him he didn't feel the pain. He had no idea what demon possessed him, but Raven broke the kiss. "You need to know the rest."

Amira simply nodded.

"I tend to remember her as a monster, but the truth is, she was very beautiful. And I was too young and too stupid to understand the real reason why she came into my room that night."

If it was possible, Amira's eyes widened even more. "Oh!" Her lips locked in that precise form. It was all she said.

"Dacian saw her leaving and he knows that she would never have succeeded if not for me."

"Dacian knows many things. Half of them lies." She didn't release him. If anything, she embraced him even tighter. "Your brother's mind is poisoned. Give him time."

"Did you not hear what I said?" he asked in frustration. He had finally admitted to what had always been like a black hole in his soul, eating him alive — and she simply chased it away with reassurances.

"Oh, I heard you, alright," she laughed, and it floored him. He was so not used to that sound. "You were telling me how you lost your virginity. Just what every woman wants to hear after a love declaration, I'm sure!"

All Raven could do was gape at her.

"I swear, sometimes I don't understand you," he admitted. But he would be lying if he said he wasn't happy about it right now.

"No one is stopping you from amending the situation." Amira knew he wouldn't appreciate the truth. Raven had lived with this betrayal, as he viewed it, for so long, he was blind to reality. So she kept it light. Though deep inside, she was livid.

He'd been used from the start—Amira had not a shadow of a doubt. But instead of seeing himself as another victim, he grew up thinking himself the culprit. She just wondered how much of it was due to his personality. Some people knew how to be victims just too well, while others ... rejected outright even the slightest possibility.

"Something is always stopping, if you haven't noticed."

She had, but... "I've never pegged you for a quitter."

"Now that's a loaded challenge if I ever heard one." Raven smiled, gazing at a pure wickedness in her eyes. And there was only one thing he could do—he took her lips with his.

Chapter 29

"So, I'm to understand you are willing to give this another try?" Amira uttered, then they finally closed the door of the bedroom with the weight of their bodies. The loud bang didn't even register in her senses. She was too preoccupied to notice anything but him.

Raven brought his face to hers and nibbled at her lower lip. "Am I supposed to answer that?"

He braced his hands on the surface behind her, on either side of her shoulders, caging her in.

"You are supposed to take this off." She kissed him back as her hands went to the buttons of his shirt, working their way through the obstacles. When she was finished, he simply shrugged it off without ever releasing her mouth.

He kissed her deep and long—the way it made desire build up in the pit of her stomach. Made her toes curl. She trailed her nails down his torso, loving the feel of hard muscles underneath her fingers—and moved to work on his pants.

With fingers not too steady, Amira unbuckled his belt and felt his hands come to her aid. Breathing heavily, he broke apart from her to kick out of his boots and pants. The sight of his raw masculinity got her licking her lips. She saw his cock twitch under her scrutiny and her nipples puckered, begging for attention. Her thighs pressed together.

The look of a predator gleamed in his eyes—a

predator who had just found the prey he craved to devour. He moved so quickly, it caught her off guard, even though she'd expected to end up in his arms again. His mouth took her prisoner.

Her hands wrapped around his body, caressing every inch she could reach, and his kiss increased in intensity and passion.

She moaned as she felt the erotic sensation of his erection pressed against her. She found it with her hand, touching it lightly at first, but when his shaft throbbed against her palm in response, she stroked it.

"You'll push me over the edge too soon." His words came out in a grunt against her lips and she shuddered. She was so hungry for him—not ready for the kiss to end, but he refused to relent. "Turn around."

"So bossy." Amira smiled, but turned without protest. She trusted him.

He brushed her hair to the side and traced the line from her collarbone to her jaw with the tip of his tongue. She moaned and threw her head back, giving him an easier access.

"Admit it, you like me bossy." Raven kissed her hot skin as his hands searched for the tiniest clasps holding her dress up.

"The only thing I'm going to admit…" she panted as he slowly peeled her out of her strapless gown, "…is that turnabout is going to be…" he cupped her breasts, squeezed them gently and she whimpered. The thread of her thoughts melted away.

Amira leaned back against Raven, but when she tried to use her hands on him, he grabbed her wrists in a tight hold.

"Hands here." His tone was uncompromising. He placed her palms on the wood and Amira found out that she did like him bossy. On some occasions.

"Am I not to touch you?"

"Not unless you want this to end before it got started," he warned as his hands traced the line of her arms, down her front, all the way to her tiny waist.

He pulled her gown over her hips, letting it fall around her feet. Her panties followed shortly, and she could do nothing but close her eyes at the onslaught of sensations.

She was finally naked—his erection pressed against her buttocks, his hands went to her aching breasts and her blood turned into a flowing lava. He cupped them, fondled, his fingers played with her nipples until the buds went taut with need. The tension in the apex of her thighs coiled tight, and she couldn't help but rub herself against him.

Raven groaned when their bodies created friction. His lips landed on her neck, tasting the raging pulse beneath. One of his hands travelled lower down her taut, flat belly and she thought she would fall apart into thousands of tiny pieces without him even reaching her wet, swollen flesh.

His hand moved lower so slowly, she wanted to beg for his touch. The pressure was maddening. And when his fingers did slip into the wet crease, she shuddered and made a mewling sound she was not aware she was capable of making.

"Raven!" she swallowed, arching her body. "I'm … I'm going to come…"

"That's the plan," he whispered against her ear as his fingers continued circling around her sensitive bud. "For you to come."

With those words he pinched at her clit and pure ecstasy shot through her body. A scream left her throat and her legs bucked.

Raven held her against his body, savoring the hot intoxicating moans that tantalized his ears. Her breaths were coming in brief, shallow pants. His own breathing was just as ragged and he knew he should have carried her to the bed, but turning her around was the best he could manage in the heat of the moment.

Instantly, her hands wrapped around his neck, and the full skin-to-skin contact had him groaning. But when she lifted her huge eyes to him and uttered, "I need you," it slew him.

Raven had her backed against the wall, with her thighs around his waist in two seconds. With one powerful thrust he filled her to the hilt and his whole body quaked with pleasure.

"I knew I would feel every inch of you," she moaned as her head rolled back.

"You are too tight." She felt like a glove around him and he stilled, trying to give her body time to get used to his size. Raven didn't want to hurt her, but refusing this primal instinct cost him—his muscles shook from the strain of holding back.

"And you are not moving." The hungry expression in her eyes bored into him.

Amira tightened her grip on his shoulders and lifted herself up his shaft. It was all that was needed to snap the twig of his control. He took over.

He pushed inside her again, at first trying to go slow, but when she made a sound of frustration, he squeezed her lush curves and gave her all she demanded.

Raven moved fast and hard inside her, his body pounding her against the wall. She met his every stroke with her own, and soon the heat rose. Her fingernails dug into his skin and he welcomed every new sensation.

The pressure built. Her moans grew louder. Soon, he felt her walls spasm around his shaft, and the sensation of her muscles contracting around him pushed him over the edge.

One last thrust and Raven spilled inside her with a

guttural groan muffled against the skin of her neck.

He wanted her wrapped around his body forever, but all too soon her legs came down.

"I don't think I can walk," she admitted.

He wasn't sure he could either, but somehow, they managed to find the bed, and that's when Raven felt a wave of icy water wash over him. "Why didn't you tell me?"

"What?" she pushed herself onto her elbows. "That you were amazing?"

"That you were a virgin!" he growled. The proof of her innocence was staring at him accusingly, and Raven felt bewildered at her reaction.

"Oh, that?" Amira laughed, and laid her head on the bed again. "I didn't think it mattered."

"Well of course it did!" he exclaimed, pulling her into his lap. He had a hard time understanding her attitude. "I felt how tight you were, but I didn't think ... I should have taken greater care with you."

"What? More foreplay?" She straddled his hips and cupped his jaw between her palms. "I had weeks' worth of foreplay. All I wanted was you."

"But for your first time..." he persisted.

"Hold your horses!" she kissed him fast and quick. "It wasn't my first time."

That got him beyond confused. "What?"

"Remember when I mentioned my prior lives?" Amira asked, and her hands slid around his neck and down his back.

"Of course."

"Well, not all of those women died virgins. Some of them, had been pretty ... how to put this ... adventurous," she added the last word after a long pause. "Amira is only the latest facet of me."

"Those other women aren't you," he stated with conviction, as if finally understanding something she didn't.

"No, they aren't me," Amira agreed. "But I was once them. Their memories live inside me. They shaped me." Those memories weren't just a blurry dream. They were clear and vivid and sometimes it felt like it happened to Amira herself. A day before.

"It sounds inconvenient."

"You have no idea." The corners of her lips curved, and she placed a kiss on his neck. Raven's breaths grew heavier, but instead of kissing her back, he stood up from the bed with her in his arms.

"Are you contemplating pounding me against the wall again?" She relished the thought. He'd drowned her in sensations until her mind had turned to mush and her body had liquefied underneath his caress as if it had been made of molten metal. The pleasure had been annihilating.

He groaned as if in pain, "No. I'm contemplating us having a bath."

"That too has possibilities." She smiled as he carried her to the bathroom, and right into the bear-claw tub he proceeded to fill with the warm water.

Amira settled in between his legs. She leaned her back against his chest, his arms came around her, and her eyes fluttered shut. She felt so relaxed, at peace.

"You got it wrong," Raven whispered into her ear. "Amira is not the latest facet of you. Amira *is* you."

His hands began caressing her skin and she had a hard time focusing on his words.

"You have to commit to her. Otherwise, you are simply waiting for another one to come along."

It was probably true. For the longest time she hadn't even tried to connect with people. She had kept everyone at an arm's length, figuring there was no point in seeking relationships that wouldn't last. Unconsciously, she'd been waiting for the next lifetime, no matter how much she'd tried to avoid it.

And those other women hadn't even been emotionally dead like Amira had.

"I don't think there is going to be another try," she confessed what Hope had hinted at, the last time she came.

Amira still didn't have time to digest the information, but when Raven's hands cupped her breasts, all she could do was moan. Thinking was beyond her.

"All the more reason to embrace who you are." He kept his touches light, his lips landed on her neck and she felt his erection throb against her backside.

"And who am I?" She wriggled in his lap until she managed to turn. The sudden and sharp pull of breath he took, as she straddled him and rubbed herself at the length of his shaft, got her smiling.

"Mine." The single word that came out of his mouth was hoarse with desire. She shivered against the power of his conviction and realized that she was still caught by the wave of his need as it rolled through her.

Raven pulled her even closer from the small of her back. Her smooth, slick breasts crushed against his chest and a moan escaped her lips. The heat of the contact was maddening. Her sensitive nipples throbbed, and when she arched her back, his mouth landed on her breast as if he knew what she craved.

Amira's fingers sank in his hair as she tried to hold on—find some shred of control—but it proved impossible. The way his tongue played with the peaks of her breast … the way he grazed lightly with his teeth … Her breathing hitched in her throat.

His skin was so hot against her, the water felt cool as it lapped around their bodies.

"Um … Angel?" his breath traveled over her sensitized flesh and she shivered again. "I don't think this should be happening…"

"Happening?" she tried to gather coherent thoughts—she was failing miserably. "What happening?"

"The water is getting hotter."

"That could be a problem," Amira realized.

Sex generated energy. But this? Considering her lack of control she didn't see another option but to… "I suggest we get out of it."

"Hate to admit it, but I agree." He quickly made use of the soap before letting her go. And even though his moves were hasty, he got her panting by the time he was through. They stepped out of the water just in time to see it boiling.

"Is this because you didn't take anything from me?" he asked as she secured a towel around her breasts.

"I took plenty from you." Amira winked and witnessed his eyes narrowing on her. She sighed. When he got serious, he got serious.

His insight still amazed her, but it got her thinking. This had never happened to her. The energy had always stayed where it was if she didn't draw it out. Here, it seemed they had a surplus of it, accumulating all around them. She was afraid something would literally explode if she found herself in his arms again.

"I think I have a solution," she said, banking everything on her suspicion why this had happened.

"I'm not getting out of this alive, am I?"

"What makes you say that?"

"The sparks dancing in your eyes…" Raven wrapped his arms around her waist, but this time she resisted. She couldn't become a prisoner to his passion again. Not if she wanted to achieve her goal.

"You'll enjoy it, I swear." She conjured up three silk scarfs in her palm. He raised his eyebrows—but it was all he did.

"Trust me?" Amira asked.

"With my heart." His answer made hers leap with joy, but she didn't let herself get distracted. Not now. Amira pushed him back, until his legs touched the edge of the bed, keenly aware that she was able to do this only because he'd let her.

One last push and Raven tumbled on the bed. "I want to test my theory first… and for that, you can't see anything."

"Why do I have a feeling you'll say no touching as well?" Raven folded his arms under his head.

"Because you are perceptive?" She came onto the bed next to him, bent down to kiss him lightly on his lips, and wrapped the delicate fabric around his eyes.

"It feels like a turnabout," he admitted.

"If you say so." She straddled his waist and Raven regretted leaving a towel wrapped around his hips.

She didn't speak at first. She simply trailed her fingers up and down his chest.

It was a sheer torture to lie still not knowing what was going to happen. What she planned, what she thought. And yet, his body responded to the unknown.

"Now I want you to tell me what you think I'm doing?" She ceased her caress and the only thing he was aware of was their breathing.

"Leaving me?" he asked as he felt her leg going over him to the other side, and soon she placed distance between them.

"I'm still here," the voice tinted with lust reached him. "It's better if we don't touch right now."

Better for whom? He wanted to ask, but suddenly, the air he took into his lungs heated up. "What *are* you doing?"

"You tell me." No longer was her breathing even, and when he concentrated, he could swear he heard her thoughts. "Your palms are cupping your breasts and …

and you want to ease the pressure building between your thighs."

Raven heard her make a squeaking sound at his words that told him he'd been right. Which in turn made him harden further. He had no trouble seeing her pleasuring herself. Her fingers would travel down and sink inside her wet heat. She would gasp and her eyes would flutter shut.

"Sweet heaven," she whispered in a husky voice as she leaned over him, and he understood that this had been about the connection they shared—she had just heard his thoughts.

Amira kissed him then. She placed kiss after kiss on his neck. Moved to his chest. Raven found out he could no longer withstand this sensory deprivation. He needed to touch her. Needed to see her. But the moment he tried to lift his hands, hers locked around his wrists. He felt scarves on his skin, and she uttered a warning. "You break it, I stop. That's the only rule."

She didn't wait for his answer but resumed her ministrations. She kissed him and caressed him until his body shook from pent-up tension. And not once did she touch his throbbing cock. He was close to begging.

His skin felt too tight, his blood too hot, and everything was reeling around him. He was not sure he could take any more, and at the same time all he wanted was more.

He craved her hands and her mouth on him. Without any conscious attempt on his part, erotic images of her formed in his mind—Raven desperately wanted Amira to see.

Her breath hitched, her hands stilled, and he immediately regretted the loss of her caresses. Then, he felt the tip of her tongue swirl around the ridge of his shaft and he lost his ability to think completely. He was ruled by the sensation of her wet, soft and hot touch.

"Oh ... my..." his breathing intensified. One more flick and he was going to step over the edge and fall into oblivion. Just one more touch...

She ceased. "Not yet."

Raven sucked a deep breath in as his body went taut—a denied release threatening to overpower him.

Amira waited until the wave passed, to return to him again. She climbed on top of him and slowly, taking him inch by excruciating inch inside her drenched body, sunk down onto him.

For the longest time she sat with his cock sheathed inside her completely, and then just as slowly as she'd lowered herself onto him, she lifted herself up. Her breath came out in heavy gasp, and the thought that she was close made him even hotter. He couldn't suppress his urges—his hips went up, her palms landed on his chest and he knew she wanted him to move.

The sweet abrasion between their bodies was addictive. Raven didn't know if it was the loss of sight and touch that highlighted his sensations, but one thing he knew with certainty—he had never felt anything like this in his whole life.

The pressure built quickly and this time, there was no prolonging it. He knew he was sure to come. Withholding touch would not work. He was so close, so sensitive, that even her merest breath sent shivers down his spine. His control was shattered. He couldn't hold back any longer.

"I won't take from you. But we can share." The sentence ended with a delicious moan. Her inner walls contracted, palming his shaft in its delicate embrace. Pleasure spread like wildfire through his nerve endings. Pure, white-hot energy flooded his senses and he felt her magic swirling inside him.

That was when the laces around his wrists loosened and he rose up, tearing the delicate fabric in two.

In a second, his hands wrapped around her, their lips found each other, and he knew he was never going to let her go. She was his. Forever.

Chapter 30

Amira woke up in his arms warm, blissfully sore in places she'd long ago forgotten about. She breathed in his earthy smell and a smile stretched her lips.

"I love it when you smile," she heard a sleepy whisper. His hands tightened around her and he placed a gentle kiss on her shoulder.

"How do you know I'm smiling?" Amira asked. He was spooning her against his chest—he couldn't have seen her face.

"I just do." Raven nuzzled at her neck with his lips, his breathing tickled her skin, and he ran his tongue along her pulsing vein. Desire sparkled in her blood.

"What are you doing to me…" she murmured as his tongue traced the shell of her ear. His lips drew her earlap inside his mouth.

"Nothing you aren't doing to me," he spoke against her ear.

Hot breath danced on her flesh, causing goosebumps to spread over her skin. Amira shivered. Her arm came up to his head, fingers sank into his silky dark hair, and her eyes fluttered shut.

Her body was pliant in his arms. A slave to his passion. Sensations built as his mouth and hands caressed her and once again Amira found out she cared not what he would do to her—all she cared was that he wouldn't stop.

It would have been so simple for him to thrust inside her, pulsing against her entrance as he was, but he didn't. Raven pushed up onto his elbow, leaving Amira no other option but to turn until she was lying on her back. She looked at him.

"Any requests?" The gaze that greeted her sent a jolt of energy down her body, right through to the tips of her toes. Pure, unadulterated hunger glittered in his eyes. The fever of his need reached out to her, and Amira gave in to the raw power of it.

"Kiss me..." her voice was husky, the plea—a response to the stark, blatant yearning she witnessed in the dark depths of his eyes. She'd never known she could beg and feel this powerful at the same time.

For as long as Amira could remember, she might have searched for passion—some of her prior selves might have craved love—but she'd never wanted, nor had she tried surrendering to it. It had always seemed too dangerous. In Raven's arms she found out just how heady a sensation it could be. Most important of all, she wasn't afraid.

"I hoped you would say that." His lips came down on her breast and her back arched, forcing her nipples to jut forward.

"I think you have mistaken my breasts for my lips," the words escaped in a moan as pleasure rippled through her.

"You never specified where I should kiss you." He grinned a wicked smile, followed by a very deliberate flick of his tongue. By the time he was through playing with her nipples, Amira was one big ball of tingling nerves.

Leaving her breasts, he left a trail of kisses down her abdomen, and the heat rose with every one he gently placed. His tongue swirled around her belly button before it dipped inside, forcing Amira to dig her nails into the sheets.

Seconds later, strong hands spread her thighs. For one long moment, impregnated with nothing but shallow, rabid breaths, he simply looked at her. She thought she would go mad. But then he grabbed her hips, pulled her closer and placed the most carnal of kisses on her damp, throbbing flesh — his lips robbed her of any coherent thought she might have had.

He tasted her like she was some delicacy — his clever tongue circling and flicking over her sensitive bud. She dug one of her heels into his back. As if in response, his finger slid inside her inner folds and her body went taut. Her breathing hitched.

He added another finger and the pleasure intensified still. She didn't think she could take it anymore. It was obliterating. The edge beckoned her, and she was so ready for the plunge, she couldn't help but cry out in disappointment when Raven withdrew his fingers.

"Patience is a virtue," he chuckled as his body moved over hers. He positioned the tip of his erection at the entrance to her starved core and slowly, holding her hips, pushed himself in.

Amira had an urge to close her eyes and simply ride the waves, but she forced herself to keep them open. Their gazes locked together, and what she saw in Raven's expression made her gasp. Pure ecstasy in his burning eyes raised her sensations to impossible heights.

He was so sexy, she could hardly believe he was hers, even though she felt every inch of his thick length moving inside her, his hands caressing her.

His thrusts intensified. Air came and left her in wracking, shuddering blasts of breath and she came crying out in rapture.

Spears of sheer pleasure lanced her body, but it was

the force of their mixed energies that had her in throes. With the power of a lightning bolt, it cracked her open until she felt herself splinter into thousands of pieces. And come back stronger than she'd ever felt.

"I don't think I'm ever going to get used to this." Raven said when he finally rolled from her. She missed his delicious weight already.

"I don't think I could prevent the walls from crumbling if you won't take half of it," she admitted.

Control was the last thing she had on her mind when he made love to her. "Whatever blood flows in your veins, it only ensures the necessity of sharing the generated energy. Otherwise, it could be lethal."

"It just seals the deal." He kissed her mouth in such a possessive way, Amira sighed.

"Deal? Have you forgotten to show me the fine print?" she couldn't help but tease him.

His brows rose, but as he was about to answer her, a familiar wave of frost assaulted Amira's senses. Raven stilled, as if experiencing the same. He wrapped his arms around her, but to her amazement, he didn't freeze.

"Who is that?" he whispered into her ear.

"Trouble," was all she managed to say before Hope appeared in the room.

"Now this is insulting!" The goddess wrinkled her nose at them. A moment later they were clothed.

"You are the one barging into the bedrooms of others like some pervert," Amira shot back.

She attempted to get up, but Raven held her fast. He stood first, trying to keep her behind him. It warmed Amira's heart, but she knew it to be useless. If Hope wanted to reach her, she would.

"It's an interesting development. Let's see if it changes anything," the goddess uttered as if to herself, though Amira knew that Hope was referring to the fact that Raven stood unaffected by her powers. It was only logical — if it wasn't meant to affect Amira, it held no power against him either. They shared the same energy, after all.

The goddess approached. She lifted her hand, her palm landed flat on Amira's forehead, and she pushed. Amira stumbled. She shook her head, and if not for Raven, she wouldn't have been able to hold her footing.

"Amira?" his voice implored her, but she couldn't answer.

She fought against the dizziness assailing her, and found out she may as well have tried holding back a flood wave. She was engulfed. Darkness enfolded her in its steely grasp, shackling her resistance, blocking her magic. Amira took one last breath and submerged even deeper, searching for her inner strength. No one was going to control her like that. Not any more. Not even a goddess.

Her eyes flared wide as she felt it soul-deep, piercing through her — strength she'd never known existed.

You found it, Hope simply stated, unconcerned about the fact she could be dead in a second. *Fast, I might add. Only proves that this time you are ready.*

Ready? Amira stopped in her tracks, the hidden meaning of words suddenly alarming her senses.

For the Prophecy, of course, the goddess answered.

The witches have come, Amira whispered, trying to separate her reeling senses. They had come for her. To take her away from…

I am not going, she almost yelled, horror transfixing her heart.

She was stronger than a legion of witches, she reminded herself. They could not take her freedom so easily.

The only thing that had kept her going through the

years, through the deaths, was … suddenly she could not remember.

You already feel the pull, Hope circled them slowly, whispering something under her breath… *feel the power. Invited it yourself, I might add.*

I did no such thing! This time, she did yell. Though she couldn't deny she didn't feel something happening.

When you made a bargain with Dazlog, you made yourself vulnerable, if only for a second, and she was able to breach the walls.

What? This was the same entity who'd enslaved her body before?

So you are working with a demon now? she asked, completely lost. How can this be?

Not in a million years, Hope assured her, *but unfortunately it had to happen. It'll take you to your destiny. Don't resist.*

Amira did. She resisted. It was compelling her to surrender, to accept and follow. She tried to shake it off.

I'll fight it, she promised, already up to her ears in a battle against an unknown and stronger foe.

It will only grow stronger, while you weaken. It will scream inside your head while you forget everything that ever mattered to you.

It already was. Her body felt no longer hers alone. Her mind—confused and unfocused. And the power pulling her strings was intensifying. With every breath she took.

Amira could swear all of her emotions were numbing, leaving an empty void inside her. Soon she would not feel anything, she realized. Soon she would be her old self. Except that wasn't right either. Soon, she would be a background voice in the head of another, and half of her didn't even care.

Fight, damn it! she ordered herself, but the new presence in her body was so much stronger.

Resistance waning, only her belief in Raven sustained her. A ludicrous hope probably, but she believed deep in the heart that still belonged to her, that she would forget this numbing feeling, this siren call she could no longer quench, if only he would...

Amira lost the trail of her thoughts. More than that, she felt like she'd lost herself.

* * *

Raven was going crazy. Amira didn't feel hurt or suffering in his arms, but the nagging feeling that something was wrong persisted.

He glanced at the icy redhead, convinced she was responsible, and her lips curled into a chilling smile. Every hair on Raven's body stood, and in two seconds he had her pinned to the wall.

She shrieked and tried to push him away—the strength behind her seemingly delicate hands only proving she was no human.

"What did you do to Amira?" he panted, but held on.

She tried to zap him with her powers, but strangely, it had no effect on him.

"I'll kill that demon," she thrashed even harder.

"Tell me what you have done!"

"The Prophecy must be fulfilled" was all she said before managing to free herself and disappear.

Raven swore under his breath. He turned to where he'd left Amira, but there was no sight of her. He swore again—this time loudly, and listening to his every instinct, ran after her.

The moment he stepped outside and his eyes landed on Amira, a shiver coursed through his body. Her gaze was cold as ice, and devoid of any human emotion. Yet he could swear he felt her fear and frustration.

He took a step and found himself chained to the stake as she lifted her hand toward him.

"What the—"

She approached and cupped his face.

"You…" Amira's voice sounded dead to his ears, then she blinked and regret shone from her beautiful eyes. Regret and sorrow.

"I can't…" she shook her head. "No, I won't!"

Raven had no idea who she was yelling at. It didn't seem she was talking to him. All he knew was this feeling inside screaming at him to hold her. Except he was in chains and no matter how hard he pulled, they didn't give under pressure.

He was enfettered. She was possessed or something, judging by the way her expression changed every two seconds—it was like watching a mask being put on and taken off of her face. And while she clearly struggled, a dozen witches watched them.

"Angel," he breathed.

"Please forgive me," she cried, this time talking to him, "please…" but before he could convince her there was nothing for him to forgive, a black curtain fell over her gaze and her eyes turned empty, soulless.

"Forget," she told him, and that voice compelled him to obey.

Raven shook his head, struggling against the power of the dark spell, knowing he couldn't give in. And by the look in her eyes he realized she was convinced she had succeeded. So he decided to play along for the time being.

"What is happening?" he blinked, and attempted to pull at the chains.

"It is your turn to taste the shackles," a malign voice he instinctively knew was not Amira's told him.

"Neither force nor help will do you any good. You tied me once—now we'll get even."

"You want revenge?" he asked, trying to sound enraged.

He hadn't succumbed to her spell, but that didn't mean he understood what was happening. Who was this creature? He was convinced he'd seen her once, but that didn't explain much to him.

"Revenge is already mine," she laughed, and he could swear he heard Amira screaming in his head.

Her voice was frantic with horror and pain. Her scream rose, the force of it making her lose her balance. She blinked, and when she looked back at him, the ice melting in her eyes gave him hope. But all too soon the ice froze. Chill spread.

Her fingers landed on his temples.

"Watch," she said, and an image appeared in his head of Amira in bed with his brother.

Now that was just sick, he thought, not buying it for a moment. But despite it, he had a sudden urge to kill Dacian.

Raven shook off her touch and roared his anger aloud. He figured if he kept up the charade, maybe Amira would win against the entity he knew she was fighting. Maybe she just needed time.

He tried to imagine how he would feel if it was true—instantly knowing it would rip his heart out of his chest while it was still beating, if she ever decided to leave him for another. It wasn't hard to imagine the pain of his love being thrown away like trash.

He gave in to the feeling and found himself struggling to breathe. Red was all he saw while his body heaved in an attempt to inhale air. Every muscle of his went taut. His fists clenched. He tried to break free, but all he could do was rattle the chains. He didn't give up. He couldn't.

"Bloody hell..." she narrowed her eyes at him, "I should just kill you now." But instead of fulfilling her threat, she vanished. Into thin air.

For a moment Raven's only reaction was his jaw hanging down. And then, he realized all his efforts had been in vain. Amira was gone.

Chapter 31

"Burt! Jim!" Raven roared at the men, "Get me an axe, find the key, something! Just get me out of these damned chains!"

The urgency to find Amira was overwhelming. That was the call Dazlog had warned him about, wasn't it?

He was supposed to stop her from heeding it. He failed. Now, he had not the slightest inkling where to search for her—she could be anywhere. If he ever got out of those damned chains, that is…

The men rushed to his aid immediately—little good that it did him. The key got stuck in the lock. The axe shattered into pieces. And by the time Burt and Willy managed to separate the two connecting rings of the rusted chain, it had actually joined itself together again.

After three hours of one futile attempt after another to get free, hope threatened to abandon him. Raven realized that that woman had spoken the truth—neither force nor help could free him. But what did it leave him with?

Was he supposed to grow old and die here? He refused to contemplate that possibility. He leaned his head against the wooden pole, closed his eyes and the image of Amira appeared in front of him. She leaned forward and whispered into his ear. It felt so real. The fleeting touch so … hers, the cadence of his heart gained momentum.

He opened his eyes with impossible hope in his

heart—even though his mind kept telling him it was just a fantasy—and found nothing but air where she was supposed to be. Yet even the dream of her was strength in itself. One thing she'd taught him: *no one can shackle you, but yourself.*

He glanced at the iron chains fettering his wrists, trying to imagine them gone—just the way she'd told him to—and a moment later, the chains fell off.

Raven's eyes widened in awe. This was just too weird, but he didn't stop to think about how it was possible. He glanced at the wooden pole, thinking it was time to bury the past; time to live in the now, with all the tomorrows ahead of him.

The stake went up in flames.

It was then it dawned on him. *I won't take from you. But we can share.* Amira's words from last night drifted into his mind. He had felt it churning inside him, had he not? He just didn't think he would be able to do this...

For a moment, he was scared he could hurt someone. The power he felt seemed to have a mind of its own. It demanded release.

Was this how Amira felt? he wondered. She had to be waging a constant battle for control.

Pure instinct was what guided him back into the mansion. He followed it, having no real alternative. He walked the corridors, opened the door of his own bedroom, and the first thing he saw was the bed—rumpled sheets and a pillow on the floor.

He picked up the pillow and was just about to place it down when he noticed a scarf on the covers. He lifted it and rubbed his fingers over the delicate silk.

The urgency inside him was like a beating pulse by now, but he tried to stay calm and figure out a way to reach her. Running like crazy would do no one any good. He sat down on the edge of the bed and looked down, finally noticing the chains he held in his other hand.

He let go of the rusty manacles only capable of tethering by force, and concentrated on the delicate lace that could bind with nothing but care and passion. If they shared the energy their love-making had produced, it only stood to reason he should be able to do what she'd done. Maybe he didn't need to know where she had gone, Raven reasoned, trying to remember how she'd explained the use of her powers to him.

She'd talked about willpower and concentration. About wishing and channeling. As much as he wished it, however, going to where she was didn't seem to happen.

He stood up and closed his eyes, trying his best to curb the unruly power churning inside him. He took a deep, calming breath in, and a second later his senses perceived a change in the sounds and smells around him. The wind was blowing in his hair. The sun caressed his skin.

He opened his eyes, barely managing to maintain his equilibrium. The world he stepped into was spinning so wildly, he could do nothing but stand still and wait for it to stop. When it did, Raven noticed he was in a middle of nowhere, miles away from his home, with a group of witches staring at him as if he were Dazlog himself with an army of demons come to slaughter them all.

Those were the same witches who had come to take Amira, yet his Angel wasn't among them. He didn't even see Brea or the wolf.

They shrieked. Grabbed for the vials of potions…

"Could we not do this right now?!" He didn't have time to play these stupid games. He felt too raw to have any type of consideration right now. But apparently it was too much to expect. The potions were already in the air.

Instinctively, he stretched his hands out to protect himself and the vials exploded in the air, frightening the witches. They jumped, squealing like banshees, as glass shards flew at them. This, he did not expect at all.

"Would you listen to me now?" He rubbed at his temples where a headache was threatening to explode. No one heard his words. Raven was afraid he would not be able to hear himself soon, if their hysterical screams continued.

Oh, for the love of gods! He gnashed his teeth, praying for patience. It was hanging by a mere thread. "Stop the racket!"

Finally, one of them stepped forward. "Spare them," she implored. "Take me instead."

Raven rolled his eyes. His frustration was running high, the need to find Amira an incessant hammering inside his skull. He clenched his fists and managed to close his throat around the blue streak of curses he wanted to let out.

At the rate this was going, he was afraid he would grow old before he found out what he needed. The wide-eyed, trembling slip of a girl was dragging her feet as if on the path to the gallows. Or worse.

By the time she managed three small steps, he'd already grown weary of it. He marched over to her, intending to get to the truth. She jumped from affright. The other witches ran.

His gaze flickered to the women scurrying away — their sudden retreat raising his suspicion — but when it snapped back to the young witch in front of him, Raven did let out a curse.

She lifted her trembling hand to her shoulder and unstrapped the only string holding her ankle-length tunic. The material slid down her body and pooled around her feet. She fisted her hands till her knuckles turned white and closed her eyes, unable to stop tears from rolling down her cheeks.

"Oh for goodness' sake," he pinched the bridge of his nose with his fingers. He lifted the tunic and covered her shivering body. "What the hell is wrong with you?"

His impatient, angry tone only made it worse. She wrapped her arms around herself and gave in to sobbing. He almost groaned.

"Look at me." He lifted her chin, but the words came too close to an order. Damn. Her eyes only squeezed more fiercely at his command.

"Open your eyes," he repeated more gently this time. He needed her rational-minded and cooperative to get to the answers he sought. "I won't hurt you," he added.

Slowly, very slowly, she complied. She looked up and relaxed a degree. It was a start—a small one, but still a start.

"Tell me, why did they leave you?" He meant to ask about Amira, but somehow he couldn't shake the nagging sensation that there was more to it than self-preservation.

"Better to sacrifice one … in order … in order to save others, than for all to die," she said in a small voice.

"Since when?"

"Since every single one of us are needed for the ritual to succeed."

"What kind of ritual?"

With every second the worry inside of him intensified. Raven sensed a strange feeling of coldness every time he thought of Amira. What was even stranger—when he concentrated on it he could swear the coldness was melting. He could feel her.

She wasn't well. The things she felt made his heart bleed. She felt lonely and scared and… There were so many emotions; the force almost brought him to his knees. His angel needed him. And he was coming.

"To welcome Nially." The answer woke him up, bringing him back from the coldness. Only he was not sure it was a good thing. Then, at least he felt her. Now, she was a mist once again. Always around, but never there to touch. The name the girl uttered, however, made his insides twist.

"Who is she?" He'd talked to her, but he had no idea who she was.

"She's—"

"What does she have to do with Amira?" he interrupted her, "And what kind of ritual are we talking about here exactly?"

There were so many things he needed to know, and so little time—standing there was getting harder by the second.

The girl opened her mouth and shut it again, apparently at a loss for words; not knowing where to begin.

"Just start from the beginning," he prompted. "And once you've answered all my questions, you're free."

She nodded again. "Thousands of years ago magic ruled the world and witches were the only habitants of this earth. Immortals—that's what they were called."

Raven listened silently. He had said to start from the beginning, he just didn't think she would take it literally and begin from the dawn of humankind—not to mention give him an unofficial version that mostly only witches believed in.

"They were strong, powerful, never-aging. It was almost impossible to kill them. See, their powers were different from ours. We are just…" she lowered her eyes, "…just a shadow of the magic that once existed. They were more like…"

"Amira," he offered.

"Yes, but greater."

Alright, so she was one of a kind. He didn't have to

be told that to know it. But it still didn't explain what the extinct witches had to do with her. Even if their powers were related.

"Nially was the most powerful of them all—a princess, who bore a mortal male child. The one she protected with her life when the council of elders tried to kill him for fear of the future they foresaw he would bring. Nially hid him, despite the knowledge that it would cost her her life. By the time he was found, it was too late."

Too late? Raven arched a brow. How could it be too late for the ones who were immortal? Then again, not a single one of them had survived till now.

"No one knows how it happened, but immortals vanished, giving way to humans. Some say they died, others—that they retreated someplace, but the only thing we know for certain is what the Prophecy tells us."

She took a step back, lifted her chin, and proudly recited a few lines.

Brought forth with vengeance a soul shall rise,
The vessel waiting for the time.
And once is filled the path shall clear,
The enemies shall know the fear.

The witch then continued with a tale of how Nially was destined to come and save them from slaughter, heralding the new age with their enemies vanquished from the face of the earth.

Raven barely managed to suppress a snort. What kind of delusional fantasy did they live in? He'd had this Nially in front of him, and benevolent was the last thing he would call her. What's more, there was nothing remotely close between what he heard in the lines the witch had recited and her suppositions.

Nially might be coming to wage a war, but Raven could bet his life it was with her own enemies and not with the Order.

"And Amira?"

"She is the vessel. She was born to become her."

"What?"

"The ritual brings Nially into Amira's body. It alone can sustain the princess."

"And Amira?" he asked again with dread.

"Ceases to be."

"That's murder!" he growled.

"The Prophecy must be fulfilled." He heard the same damned words the goddess had spoken, having difficulty in understanding how they were capable of saying it so casually. For the longest moment he couldn't talk. He felt as if someone or something was choking him.

"Where and when does the ritual take place?"

"Two days from now, in the Mountains," she answered, obviously not afraid he would try to stop it. No man could venture into the Impenetrable Mountains, and he hoped he would find Amira before then.

Raven tried to sum up what he knew. She was not there right now and the witches were still traveling, which meant they would meet someplace in between, since the witches couldn't make the journey in such a short time. If he followed this girl... No, it was too risky. He had to find her now.

"Do you know where she is at the moment?"

"Home, I suppose. Saying her goodbyes."

Goodbyes... his insides twisted again. No way, if he had anything to say about it. And he most definitely had.

"That's all I wanted from you," he said curtly.

She immediately created distance between them as if expecting him to stop her. No, she was afraid he would not keep his word, Raven realized, reading her without even trying.

He could always feel things about others, but it was usually so undefined, so misted he could barely name it. But now, it was ten times stronger. If not more. It was overwhelming.

Raven definitely didn't want to know, or worse, feel her fears and worries, but he could not seem to find a way to turn it off. Time to go, he decided, before he got another headache.

"About Ethely..."

Raven glanced at the girl without the slightest hint of interest.

"I thought you would want to know..." she explained.

"I really don't," he told her, and walked back into the mist to search for the only witch he cared about.

* * *

After three wrong turns, a pond and a cliff, Raven finally emerged dripping wet in front of his home. Appearing someplace within the blink of an eye was a nice way of traveling, if you got the hang of it—his soaked clothes proved he hadn't quite. Not to mention it was not his home he was trying to reach, but hers.

He'd never imagined how much concentration it required. That any passing thought could throw him hundreds of miles from his destination point. Maybe riding Lightning was a better way. A safer one, for sure.

He remembered the moment he had reappeared on the edge of the cliff, only to fall down into the abyss. Needless to say, trying to concentrate while falling was an experience he didn't relish repeating ever again.

He ran to the stables, determined to saddle

Lightning, when he realized he didn't know where he should go. He had no idea where her family lived. The forest where he'd found her was the only clue he had.

He ran into the building and almost smashed into his brother who was leading a horse from his paddock.

"The truth," he demanded, remembering that Dacian knew something.

"This new look suits you," he laughed, and continued on as if Raven hadn't even been there.

Raven grabbed his brother by his shirt and slammed him into the wall, hard.

"The truth!" he repeated. He was done tiptoeing around him.

"Or what?" Dacian's defiant eyes met him. His brother struggled against Raven's hold, but soon realized it was futile.

"Don't make me forget we are brothers," he all but pleaded.

"I forgot it years ago. When you left me with that monster."

"I did no such thing!" Raven's hold loosened and he raked his damp hair with his fingers. "What the hell are you talking about?"

"You put me in the cage yourself! That memory is crystal clear." Dacian's accusation left him speechless as he stared back at the angry face of his brother.

"You truly believe that?"

"I..." Dacian grabbed for his head as if it pained him. His fingers dug into his hair so tightly that Raven thought he would try to tear his hair out.

"Breathe," he ordered, steadying his brother. "In and out."

After several minutes Dacian blinked at him and frowned. "I don't know what to believe anymore," he finally uttered. "Half of the things in my head don't make any sense. There are holes upon holes. And what I do remember... I wish I wouldn't."

"I didn't sell you out," Raven told him, willing him to see the truth in his eyes. "I searched for you, for years."

"Now I need to do some searching of my own," was all Dacian said, and Raven noticed that his horse was saddled for a long journey.

"Before you go, tell me what you know of Amira..."

Dacian halted, sighed. They stood in silence for so long, Raven thought he was not going to answer, but finally he did. "I remember Ethely talking about a witch it was obvious she was green with envy of. She liked to hear her own voice, you know. Mostly I didn't listen, but from what I can gather, I can tell you that if it's Amira — and I believe it is — she is not for you. Never was. Only for the purposes of gods. The sooner you understand that, the better."

"We'll see about that," Raven pledged. He would sooner die than let her be sacrificed for some ten thousand year old princess, who couldn't just stay dead like she was supposed to.

"That serious, huh?" Dacian's eyebrows lifted.

"Just tell me where I can find her."

"You know Deron St. Clair?" his brother asked.

Raven nodded. He'd heard of him. And frankly, who hadn't? The man was a saint, according to the people of Trinton.

He used all his influence and money to keep the Order outside the fortified walls of the town. There were no burnings. No executions. No stakes in the town's square.

"Good, so I guess you'll have no problem in finding his mansion, or his daughter." His lips curved into a smile, "If they don't shoot you on the doorstep for kidnapping her, of course."

"Is that why you are sending me there?" he couldn't

help but ask.

"No you dolt," Dacian rolled his eyes. "I'm sending you to save the woman who brought me back to life."

"Thank you."

Dacian didn't utter a word more. He simply turned, took his horse by the bridle and led him out of the stables. It was the first civil conversation they had had in fifteen years, and it finally gave Raven a glimmer of hope that one day they could be brothers again. But right now, he had his own journey to undertake.

Chapter 32

Amira placed a pendant between her breasts, smiling bitterly. The sacrificial lamb was prepared. Or as prepared as she would ever be.

She glanced at her dark purple gown, knowing this ancient ceremonial garment was the last thing she would ever wear. Knowing she probably had hours to live, minutes to feel, and not even a second more to be happy. Still, her eyes were as dry as a wasted desert in the heat of the scorching sun. Not a single raindrop fell from the sky. Not a single teardrop ran down her face.

Not that she wanted to cry. Maybe deep down, where she still felt herself—locked in a cage she couldn't get out of. Inside, she was screaming—her emotions too raw to bear. Inside, she was Amira, and she was heartbroken.

Looking at herself in the mirror was like looking at a different person—a creature who possessed her body, her voice, even her magic, but was only a shell, a vessel for the transformation to take place in.

She felt everything the other one did, but she almost didn't feel herself anymore. The cell of her prison she'd been shoved into was getting smaller and smaller by the second and she knew, soon—she would have no air to breathe.

The being inside her was dormant most of the time, waiting for the ritual she needed to permanently silence Amira. But it never failed to wake up the moment she attempted to return to Raven. If she concentrated enough, she could still take over—for mere moments, no more. Moments that were not enough for her to accomplish anything.

She felt powerless. Desperate. She felt sick thinking of what Nially had tried to make him believe. It mattered little that Amira was confident he would see right through the lie. It was a knowledge she guarded close to her heart, but that same knowledge was like a double-edged sword.

If he conquered the spell, he would only be coming to witness her death. Or worse, die himself. But at the same time, she hated the possibility of him not coming. The sword cut her on both sides.

"Oh stop it!" the creature frowned, tracing her thoughts, "he's only a man. You had them before."

True. Some of the women she'd once been had known men. None had the heart, the touch and the magic that sang to her soul. None was her Raven.

"You should be grateful I left him alive," Nially's voice hardened as if irritated.

I wouldn't have let you kill him, Amira yelled inside the head she no longer felt was hers alone. *Ever!*

"And, I let you come and say your goodbyes to your family. What more do you want?"

For you to die! She gnashed her teeth.

She did say her goodbyes, even confessed to what she was, but did they listen? Her father thought her crazy, or suffering from anxiety and stress after her ordeal. Her mother tried to console her, but she didn't believe her. She didn't even know there was such a thing as a prophecy—but that was the way of witches who had never lived in the Mountains. All her parents wanted to do was interrogate her. Ciaran was the only one who listened. He appeared somewhat doubtful, but for the first time she could see he was listening. Which was a feat in itself.

Suddenly, an eerie calmness settled over her. It was a lull, nothing more. She felt so detached, she almost welcomed the sensation. At least until a serene presence wrapped around her. The heat of his embrace was so unexpected and so encompassing, Amira gasped. It was strength and it was life. It was him, so near, she could practically taste it.

"Enough!" the creature's voice cut her off. She felt her shoulders straighten, her chin go up. Nially marched out of the chamber, for Amira to greet darkness, but when they approached the stairs, Amira heard arguing.

The hall was packed with people. Everyone so absorbed, they didn't notice her at the top of the grand stairs. She froze at the sound of her father yelling—for all the years she had known him, he'd never once raised his voice. Then, the meaning of his words sank in and her heart leapt with joy, all but bursting through her ribcage.

"You dare come here after kidnapping my only child?"

"I didn't come to fight."

She easily found Raven in the crowd and realized how much she'd missed him. But when she opened her mouth, it was not Amira's voice that flew out.

"Why did you come here?" Every single pair of eyes landed on her. "I thought I made everything clear."

"Crystal," Raven said as he focused his gaze on the woman descending the stairs. "Except you are not Amira, are you?"

"More than just looks ... hmm ... who would have thought," she laughed. Her long skirt swished as she walked, revealing shapely legs with every step she took.

Amira or not, but the woman was a vision in a purple silk gown, the likes of which he'd never seen before. Raven wasn't even certain it could be called a gown. It looked more like she'd wrapped a silk scarf around her breasts, leaving her abdomen bare. And even though the skirt was long, the material was see-through with so many slits, she would have been more covered up if she wore a fishing net.

She had golden snake-bracelets wriggling around her arms from the pointing finger all the way to her neck, and braids in her loose hair enlaced with some kind of golden thread.

Yes, she was a vision. Wrong on so many levels.

"What for the love of all that is holy are you wearing?" someone inquired.

"Can someone just shoot him?" she asked at the same time as her father ordered her to cover herself. Raven would've been amused seeing all those stupefied faces, if not for the fact he'd sensed she was ready to disappear.

"You bargain with the demon to bring him back, and now you want him dead?" The conviction in Ciaran's voice shut everyone up. "Call me crazy, but this just doesn't add up."

Well, at least one of them wasn't stupid, Raven thought.

"I knew I sensed something strange about him," one of the women whispered.

Raven was convinced she was a witch. She had been ogling him from the moment he'd stepped foot in this house. Yet despite everything, his eyes never left the woman who approached with confidence. Until Ciaran's words had left his mouth.

She blanched. Huge eyes met his, and Raven witnessed dread shadowing her face—the face of Amira. She stared at him as if expecting the earth to part and swallow him whole. As if she feared something awful was about to happen.

Seeing her reaction, knowing it was so strong that she was able to take control of her body, Raven set the last piece of the jigsaw into its place.

"I already knew I was dead." And now he knew why she hadn't told him.

Amira's hands shook when she took his face in her palms. "Nothing is happening," she murmured.

"What did you expect? Me to die?" He wrapped his arms around her waist, ignoring the racket in the room.

"If you ever found out..." her voice trailed off. A second later her eyes widened and Amira realized why he hadn't died. Dazlog himself was protecting him because of the condition she'd placed.

"I don't want to talk about me right now," he said. "Better tell me how to get rid of Nially."

Amira shook her head in despair, her eyes welling up. "It's not possible," her voice was laced with parts of both of them. It was as if that creature inside her wanted to show that she was the commanding force.

"You'll never get rid of me!" Nially's voice echoed and bounced around the massive room, despite Amira's struggles to stay in control.

"I don't believe that," Raven insisted, as his fingers brushed the hair out of her face. He seemed so determined to fight her monsters, it was overwhelming. "I am not giving you to some vindictive old witch so she can relive her glory days. You can fight her. Together we can win."

It was too much. The way his midnight eyes were looking at her, asking her to stay, she ... Amira's tears spilled.

She would have loved nothing more than to stay with him, in his arms. Forever. To have his touch melt her bones and quicken the beat of her heart. It was killing it now. The thought of him coming for her, of still believing she could win — was killing her. She could barely suppress the princess as it was. Moments were all she had.

Hot tears were running down her cheeks in earnest now. She was ruled by a pull to follow her destiny. A pull so strong, her body quaked. It hurt fighting it, but fight it she did. Amira was not ready to let go. Not ready to lose him.

She needed more time. Wanted a few more moments in his arms. She held him as a drowning man would his last straw, no matter that it was destined to break in half. And when Raven wiped her tears and kissed her, a wracking sob broke out of her chest.

As through the mist she felt her father's anger, her mother stopping him, saying something sounding a lot like "at least she cries." She sensed worry from all around. Concern and confusion. She pretended it didn't exist.

"Angel..."

For one fleeting second Amira pretended life was good.

"Could you say something?" Ciaran's voice woke her up. "It's annoying to see a man make a total fool of himself. If I shot him now, it would surely be a mercy kill."

"Thanks," Raven snorted, his eyes never leaving hers.

"You are welcome," Ciaran returned with the same tone.

Amira managed a weak smile. "I never told you I—"

"No," he interrupted her confession, shaking his head fiercely.

"I love you," Amira said despite his objections.

"Don't say goodbye to me. Not now!" he whispered, words barely audible, but the emotion behind it shook her to the core.

"You saved me how many times?" Amira wondered, not knowing why she was even bringing this up.

"After I put you in danger in the first place, you mean?"

"No one is perfect." She laughed now, but there was no mirth and her laughter died instantly. "You can't save me this time." She didn't want this impossible quest to cost him his life.

Amira was aware of Raven saying something to her, but her eyes drifted shut and for a moment everything stilled. She heard no whispers, no commands. Felt no pain, no love, no fear. Deep inside she knew she was leaving behind something important, something amazing and priceless, only she could not hold on to it anymore. She was no match for Nially's power. She was being pulled away.

"No, no, no!" Raven yelled, trying to grab a tighter hold on her as she began disappearing into a mist in front of his very eyes.

"Fight her, Angel," he pleaded. *I know you can.* But she only glanced at him one more time and vanished.

Raven was left standing in utter shock in the midst of women crying, men gaping at him. He would have welcomed a bullet right about now. Without her, or his brother, Raven had no one. Her father had threatened to shoot him when they had met. Except now, he seemed to have lost interest.

You lost her! The reality was yet to sink in.

Raven had a hard time believing this was it—the last time he would see or hold her. He'd believed with all his heart that if he found her, talked to her, took her in his arms, she would stay. She hadn't. And now, what was he to do?

"Think," he pinched the bridge of his nose with his fingers desperate for a miracle. Instead, he was forced to face reality—no one knew what to do. And seeing her mother's tears as she kept gripping her husband's shirt was not helping. Her heartbreak was invading his mind, making any attempt at concentration impossible.

How did Amira do it? Raven couldn't help but wonder. Standing so close to barely-controlled emotions was wreaking havoc with his senses. He had to get out of there if he wished to hear his own thoughts. But before he could take two steps, Eliana blocked his way out.

"What was the bargain?" Her question stupefied him.

"What does it matter now?" her husband echoed Raven's thoughts.

"It does," she insisted, "Besides, what else should I think about? About my baby I won't ever see again?" she said, wiping her tears furiously.

"I was dead at the time, so how should I know the details?" Raven prayed for patience. "You should ask them." He pointed at Ciaran and Logan with a slight tilt of his head. "Now, if you are not going to shoot me, step aside. 'Cause I'm going after her."

"I don't remember shooting you in your head," Ciaran also stepped forward, and Raven had a distinct feeling he was hiding what really happened from his family that day. It wasn't a coincidence that he all but admitted pulling the trigger.

"I don't remember you shooting me at all," Raven couldn't help but utter. He realized Eliana was right. Thinking about losing Amira every second didn't help.

"Maybe you remember a small detail, like *why* the mountains are called Impenetrable?" Ciaran rolled his eyes disbelievingly, only confirming Raven's suspicions.

But despite lying through his teeth, Ciaran was right. No mortal man could enter the sacred domain of the witches.

"And no horse is fast enough to carry aunt Eliana in time," he seemed to follow Raven's thoughts.

"True," Raven nodded, ready to end this conversation. He needed silence, space to concentrate, distance himself from all the emotions swirling in the room.

"What were you not telling?" Ciaran caught up with him again when he stepped outside, leaving the crowd behind.

"I think I could still reach her in time," Raven said, hoping he could.

"You are not joking, are you?" Amira's brother suddenly got very serious.

"Do I appear to be?" His patience was holding on by a very tenuous thread he imagined would snap at any second. He needed to go, to find her, to save her. He needed to be with her. And these questions were not helping.

"You bring her back," Ciaran whispered, approaching him quickly, "and I'll owe you bigtime."

"You already do." Raven shook his head, took a deep, calming breath in and, thinking about his angel, followed her path.

Chapter 33

A deceitful hope grew wings the second Raven appeared in front of the Impenetrable Mountains, with a narrow passage beckoning him right before his very eyes. It's wings stretched, just as his hand did when he stepped forward, but it never learned how to take flight.

The resistance he encountered was not solid like the barrier Amira could create. It was a thick fog wrapping itself around the mountains—but it was a barrier nevertheless. When he tried to cross the obstacle, the fog enveloped his body like quick sand restraining his movements. It swallowed him whole, refusing to let him through.

If he could just take one bloody step forward…

"Let me in, God dammit!" he yelled with anger and frustration. His every muscle was so tense, something threatened to snap inside him. He grasped those vehement emotions as one would an anchor to sanity. Otherwise, he was afraid he would drown in fear. His and hers.

She was so close yet so unreachable, it seemed like an awful nightmare. He couldn't believe he'd succeeded in making it all this way, just to fail at the last few steps. There were probably feet between them, but it could've just as easily been hundreds of miles, because he couldn't reduce the distance by a single inch.

When he looked closer at the fog, he saw skeletons of men dead long ago. There was no meat on their bones, and still they stayed upright. The fog was like a web, he realized, and he was caught in it.

Raven tried not to succumb to despair of having to sense her fade away without being able to do anything. Her powers had been his last hope, the key to opening the doors of the forbidden domain. It had failed. And now he needed a miracle.

Raven could feel her fear growing, her weakening voice screaming in his head. He could feel time unmercifully running out, while the only thing he could do was stand there and die along with her.

I've been waiting for you, he heard a voice in his head.

"Who is there?" Raven was unable to turn. He couldn't see anyone.

An answer came in a form of a feral howl.

Either he was hallucinating, or there was a wolf behind his back. And the animal was talking to him.

Why not, he all but snorted. Next thing he knew, he would be talking with trees.

You want to get to her, or not?

"What do I do?" Raven asked immediately.

You'll need blood.

Easier said than done, Raven gritted his teeth as he tried to reach his dagger.

He had around ten inches to overcome, but it had taken him an hour to get his fingers wrapped around the handle. About three more to slice his palm. And all this time he fought against the dread of feeling Amira slowly fading away.

Good. Now touch the shyvaar beith with your bloodied palm and repeat after me: Shakor entar obive mot loaveru su shyvaar kattar.

"The what?" he asked, not understanding a word the being said, though his palm was already turning, as if instinctively knowing what to do.

The substance around you. Also called the Mist of the

Dead.

When Raven finally managed to do what he was told, his blood soaked into the fog, painting it red near his hand. The substance began solidifying and then turning into dust before his eyes. It wasn't long before a huge hole was eroded away around him, and he could move again.

The gap increased in its size and Raven wondered if it would stop the moment he had his path clear. He turned to take a quick glance at the one who had helped him and came face to face with a wolf.

"Shadow?"

The one and only, the wolf said. *And yes, the corrosion will spread until it has consumed every last inch of the Mist. Now go!*

Raven didn't linger. He ran.

Through the mountain passages he was led by Amira's raging heart, her strong and rapid beat pounding in his head. The closer he got, the fiercer it reverberated inside him until it became all he knew as his legs devoured the distance between them.

Hold on, he begged, feeling her sorrow and fear as if it were his own. *Hold on, Angel.*

He ran the narrow paths taking turn after turn until he was forced to a sudden halt by a wall. He reached for it, his fingers searching every nook and cranny for some kind of lever to open up a door, window, a portal … anything.

Raven knew she was behind the stone formation. He simply needed to discover the way in.

Like a blind man feeling the world around him, he explored the rocks, his movements becoming more frantic with every second. His hands shook and beads of perspiration formed on his forehead when his diligent search turned up nothing.

"Not possible," he forced out through gritted teeth,

hitting the damned barrier with his fist in frustration. He almost fell flat on his face as his body slid through the solid stone wall. Raven righted himself, suddenly well aware he was facing a sea of witches.

They were in a carved round hall, probably a crater with smoothened walls full of sacred symbols on it. The space was devoid of anything except for a flat rock in the middle, where Amira lay dying.

For a moment he couldn't breathe, seeing the woman he loved laid on an altar while hundreds of witches chanted, forming circles upon circles around her.

Raven barged through the crowd, encountering no resistance. Every single one of them seemed to be immersed in a trance not even his pushing managed to break. And he wasn't gentle about it. As far as he was concerned, a few bruises were a small price to pay for participating in a murder.

He approached Amira, took her hand and kneeled beside her.

"Don't want you to be here," *to watch me die.*

She looked at him with eyes hardly human anymore. The crystal ocean he'd always found himself drowning in was clouding. She was fading before his very eyes. "She may not let you live."

"So don't leave me," he begged, barely able to hold back the tears. He couldn't lose her. He couldn't stand to see the sacrifice she was forced to endure in order to fulfill some silly old prophecy.

"Fight it," he pleaded, but at the same time was afraid it would do nothing. Her numb body didn't even react to his touch.

"Trying to ... but..." Her weak voice scared him. Her face was so pale, skin cold, eyes almost completely empty. He was too close to losing her forever.

Raven took her in his arms and lifted her from the

altar. He couldn't stand to watch her lying helpless waiting to be butchered. It contradicted everything he knew about her, everything she was. And yet, she was fading.

But if she couldn't fight, maybe he could. For her, he was prepared to kill every single witch around him, to end their cruel chant, stop them from turning her into a bloody sacrificial lamb.

"Don't...," she whispered, "it is not ... not who you are ... not who I fell in love with." She sank in his embrace, her eyes not even blinking anymore.

"Then fight! Damn it!" Raven yelled. His heart stuck in his throat. He was losing his mind. The love of his life was unmercifully vanishing from his life and he had no say in it. He could not accept it.

"Not ... strong enough," she mouthed, the sound no longer coming out of her mouth.

"Then take from me." Raven shook her, refusing to let her drift away. "Whatever you need. Just fight!"

"No ... too ... weak."

A painful grimace etched her face. It hurt. It hurt so much to leave him, to lose the last part of herself she'd managed to preserve for so long. She could no longer. The magic of Nially was invincible. Too strong for her.

Even if she was still able to use his life force, she wouldn't do it. She wouldn't suck him dry to save herself. But she was moved beyond words that he was willing.

Amira wished she could touch Raven's face one more time, wipe those tears away, but her body no longer obeyed her. Not even for a moment. No matter how she willed it.

She was dying. And Nially was coming. Just like it

was written in the stars.

The ancient magic was something she could never have imagined—she felt powerless against it. Moreover, she was in pain from a futile battle she knew she'd already lost. In pain from leaving him and witnessing his agony. In pain from imagining what his lips uttered, but not hearing it. In pain from knowing the sweetest kiss was touching her skin, and not feeling it.

She was in so much pain she thought her body should be shaking, not lying lifelessly in his embrace. And yet, for a few more moments she was still here. Entrapped by his sheer will. His …. now … and … forever.

Yours, she whispered, the echo of her thoughts fading away. Just like her soul.

Raven closed his eyes, his fists tightening. All went still. Even his own heart stopped. The only sound disrupting the silence was a strangled, agonized roar flying out of his throat. A sound he did not recognize as his own.

The pain of holding her limp body in his arms was not bearable. He could feel himself trembling, unable to control the anguish as the whole world darkened in front of his eyes.

She was lost. All was lost.

Chapter 34

Kneeling on the hard ground in the midst of the unconscious witches, Raven could do nothing but clutch Amira's lifeless body in his arms. He closed his eyes. It was easier this way—easier to imagine she was simply sleeping, because a part of him refused to accept anything else.

He was afraid that if he let go of her, he would have to admit the truth. If he did, he would end up sobbing like a child, and a vision of her eyes opening would vanish into the thin air.

"How touching." Her eyes did open, and yet there was no mistaking them for Amira's. The azure he'd always found captivating was no more. Instead, he saw dark sapphires encrusted with ice.

She pushed at him in an attempt to break free of his embrace, and the force of her thrust sent him flying into the nearest rock.

Raven landed on his back, hissing from pain, and it took him three attempts to stand up.

He hadn't been raised to hurt women, but life had taught him that monsters didn't have gender. Male, female—it had never mattered what face they hid behind. Until now.

He knew that the woman in front of him was not Amira. He could see it clearly in her eyes, in the curl of her lips. There were so many small details betraying her as Nially, Raven had not the shadow of a doubt that

Amira was no more. Still, he couldn't harm her.

He righted himself and his hesitation to retaliate cost him—he felt another hit. This time it was from his head connecting with a hard surface. The bang resonated inside him, making him see stars.

"You'll pay for trying to interfere with my plans," she promised, stretching her hand and curling her fingers into a fist.

Raven felt a pain in his neck as if someone was strangling him.

"Rot in Zcuran!" he breathed harshly and felt his body become weightless—then by the force of her will, it hovered above ground.

The beautiful face that once belonged to Amira turned pink from anger.

"Stupid mortal!" she snapped, and he went down again. Hard.

At this point he didn't care if she killed him. It was not worth fighting for anyway. He'd died the moment Amira had.

"All this defiance, and for what? For some stupid emotion?" she asked, slowly approaching.

She trailed her fingers down his jaw and captured his face. "You must be very good in bed, since she screamed your name till the very end. Maybe..." she smiled then, and he couldn't help but feel bile rising in his throat at seeing her expression, "maybe I'll just try you out. See how quickly you'll forget her."

Before this, Raven hadn't fought back because he didn't feel he had anything to live for; but now he began to struggle in earnest.

"Don't make me vomit!" He shook off her touch. Betraying Amira was the last thing he would do.

Nially didn't seem to hear him. She tried to pin him to the ground using her magic, but Raven resisted—though if he said he didn't feel like a whole herd of mustangs had trampled him, he would be lying. The power the witch possessed was enormous.

"What are you, a bitch in a rut?" he grunted as he rolled to the side. "Get it through your thick skull— Amira is the only one I want!"

I'll never leave you. An invisible hand touched his face lightly. The feel of it wasn't repugnant. On the contrary, the sensation was so familiar and so desirable, he craved to close his eyes and imagine those hands against his flesh were solid.

"You dare breathe her name!" Nially slapped him hard. "You should be honored, and yet your every thought reeks of her," her voice grew stronger, harsher with every word. "I'm ten times her superior!"

Raven couldn't stifle a laugh. "More powerful maybe, but you are not worthy of breathing the same air!"

Suddenly, thunder crashed all around him as Nially stood up, swearing under her breath. Murder in her eyes. At least she was no longer trying to touch him, Raven sighed with relief. Dying he didn't mind.

Don't give up…

The presence around him gave him strength to stand tall against Nially's chilling gaze. Even in death, it appeared, his angel held him. And it was all that mattered to him when the witch's eyes narrowed and he felt an iron grip clenching his heart.

A trace of a smile played on her lips as she squeezed it slowly with her powers, and soon his vision clouded. No longer did he see Nially. Amira stood in front of him.

The apparition of her seemed eerie and ethereal at the same time. She was so beautiful in her anger he wanted to smile, but her transparent form didn't let him forget that she wasn't real. Nevertheless, his eyes caught her, refusing to let her out of his sight even for a second.

She glowed in front of the recently risen full moon, and it reminded him of the time he'd walked in on her, reciting the first verse of that silly old poem. Those words hadn't been for him, Raven knew. But if she truly was there, lingering, waiting for him, he wanted her to know that the other lines his mind was producing right now were, and always would be, for her.

I am nothing, but a lonely sailor
Lost in the tangles of your flames,
Your bewitching smile would be my savior,
Your effulgent eyes would be my fate.

His body was refusing to cooperate. His head swayed. Strange how the world around him appeared blurry, yet the words in his head were crystal clear.

My world lies in your hands

He was barely able to take in the air he so desperately needed.

My soul completely given.

He collapsed on the ground, his knees no longer supporting his weight. Every muscle in his body seemed to have been pierced with a sharp knife, slicing each piece apart straight from his bones.

He had a sensation that someone was chopping him into thousands of pieces while he still lived. The pain was excruciating, but at the same time he was glad he would hold Amira soon.

Her lovely transparent face appeared an inch from him, as if summoned. Yet instead of a vision to soothe him, her trembling lips and the dread in her crystal eyes were like another dagger to his heart. Raven was imagining, hallucinating probably. And yet... He struggled for breath, begging her not to suffer. Never to suffer.

I only ask of you to glance...

His throat tightened. His fingers clenched around his neck and his body convulsed. The world plunged into the dark, depriving him of the last few words.

As if you treasure the heart I'm giving.

His eyes cracked open a sliver. He peered into the darkness, convinced he'd died. The perception was shattered by a strong pain that followed the soft whisper. It had him groaning through his teeth.

"Don't you dare die on me now," the voice he never thought he would hear again washed over him like a balm. He could hardly see the face, but he knew in his heart that the woman kneeling beside him was Amira. It was his angel's gentle touch he felt.

Not in a million years, he wanted to assure her, but all that came out was a cough of blood.

* * *

Amira didn't smile, not yet. She concentrated all her energy into healing Raven, bringing him back from the edge he was already slipping off.

Her hands not too steady, she willed the magic she possessed to weave his torn flesh together, and was stunned when the blast of power tore her away from him. Like a rag doll she was thrown to the other side of the hall, landing with a loud thump.

She blinked, at first confused at what had transpired. Immediately, she scrambled to her feet and ran to him, afraid she would be too late as she kept tripping over the unconscious bodies lying all around. She kneeled once again, and this time, let the energy coursing inside her flow more slowly, almost killing her from worry in the process.

He was injured too severely—his insides all but a mush—for her to play safe, but the raw essence of what lived in her was too hard to control. It wasn't even a power left by Nially, but a living entity. There were no other words to describe it. And thankfully it wanted to help.

Given the strength of this unknown entity, Amira had not the slightest of idea how she had managed to come back. The moment she'd sensed his soul being torn out of his body, she went into her own with a fury, hoping against hope, and here she was—able to heal him in seconds.

The moment she was about to remove her hands, she felt his unyielding grip. She lifted her gaze to meet his eyes and gasped at the intensity searing right through to her soul.

It was the most profound moment in all of her lifetimes. His every fear, every desire was her own. There was no need for words and yet, she shivered on hearing his promise.

Their fingers entwined together, breaths grew heavier, as for one endless second they did nothing but stare into each other's eyes, hearing something snap inside. There was no sound for her ears to catch, yet she heard it deep in her soul. A bond strong as the finest metal and light as a feather itself. It solidified…

"… for eternity," he whispered, his gaze heating up.

Amira nodded, starved for contact, desperate to feel his touch. She didn't care about the witches surrounding them. She didn't think about the possibility of them waking up soon. All she knew was an insatiable desire to feel him against her.

She wrapped her arms around his neck, and when he lifted her and placed her on the only surface possible, she trembled with anticipation. They were on the same page. She was wet, panting. He was hard. And neither of them wanted foreplay. They simply needed one another.

Raven covered her mouth with his and stepping between her parted legs, filled her with one powerful push. He moved fast, demanding everything she had, yet giving so much more. Amira screamed — for the first time in days doing so from pleasure.

He watched her misted eyes, finally able to slow down a bit. There was no need to rush anymore. No need to seize the moment because he felt there might not be a tomorrow. And yet, he dared not close his eyes. He was afraid to witness her gone the second he opened them.

If it was a dream, he didn't want to wake up. If he was dead, he didn't want to know. If she was a figment of his imagination...

I am real, she promised, as if knowing his deepest fear; and wrapping her legs tighter around him, drew him even closer.

Just as she knew his fears, he knew her desires — Raven angled his hips, pushing his shaft all the way to the hilt. Pulled out. Repeated the same move a few more times until her eyes drifted shut, her back arched, and she dug her nails into his ass, riding each wave with the smallest hitch in her breathing.

"Oh, yes!" she gasped, sinking her nails even deeper and driving his hips forward. Hard. Between her heated folds.

Raven groaned, almost coming. He tasted her luscious skin, wringing moan after moan out of her until she was undulating beneath him. Until he felt the first tremors coursing through her.

He became mindless. The strain in his body no longer bearable. He was so close ... especially listening to her breathless cries.

He increased his tempo under her encouragement, knowing two seconds were all he had. The moment Amira's body spasmed with release, it was a done deal. He could do nothing but bury his head in the crook of her neck and hold her as the wave of pure ecstasy rushed through them both.

Raven didn't trust himself to move for the longest moment afterwards. He would've been content simply to stay this way. For an eternity. Unfortunately, reality couldn't be denied—he heard a weak moan, turned his head and cursed his stupidity for succumbing to this craving to have her. In the middle of a witches' convention, of all places.

What the hell was he thinking? He would've kicked himself if he wasn't in such a hurry to fasten his pants.

Amira couldn't contain a laugh. "If my memory serves me right, someone had assured me he wasn't into kinky stuff." She flicked her skirt down and jumped off the stone formation. "Just look at you now."

"Funny," he glowered.

That only made her laugh harder. "Raven, relax." Her hands landed on his and she took over the task of buckling his belt. "It'll be a good half an hour more till they become lucid. I thought I'd lost you," she whispered the last sentence so very solemnly.

In response, his arms came around her and he placed a kiss on her lips. He didn't remind her that it was he who had lost her. He simply held her. "I am here."

"How? How did you pass through the Mist of the Dead? No mortal can."

"A mortal cannot. But an immortal can." The words were dripping with cold arrogance as Hope appeared out of nowhere, freezing time immediately, and along with it the hundreds of witches around them. Only Amira and Raven were left unaffected.

"What?" Raven tightened his hold on Amira, all but pushing her behind him.

"Did you never wonder why you were able to channel her power? Why you could contain it in the first place?" Hope raised her brows mockingly. "Your bloodline is diluted, true. Just enough that you couldn't access your powers alone. But now that you have, it's who you are." The last words were said in such a way, Amira had a feeling Hope was not happy about the latest development.

"Immortal?" Raven's voice sounded bewildered to Amira's ears, though she was convinced Hope wouldn't notice the difference.

"Precisely," the goddess confirmed. "We didn't just need someone who was willing to die for her. We needed someone powerful in his own right to reach her in time. Someone she would cross over from the beyond to protect."

"You've orchestrated everything," Amira said absent-mindedly.

Her brain was still digesting the latest revelation. No wonder Raven was able to contain and use her magic. No wonder she gained an ability to travel between places with just a thought after one night with him. His bloodline had to be a very strong one.

"Of course we did," the goddess stated so proudly, it rubbed Amira the wrong way. "That wolf thinks he's so clever. He thinks he outsmarted us when in truth, he did exactly what we wanted him to do."

Her bargain with Dazlog was what set the wheels spinning, Amira deduced, going over the events one by one. She had been played. Like some piece on a chessboard, she'd been manipulated into moving exactly where they needed her to by placing other pieces in strategic places. She'd always thought she had at least a modicum of freedom, but now she understood that it had been all an illusion. She'd been cornered, courtesy of every single step she'd made.

"You never wanted Nially to rise, did you?" It was the conclusion everything pointed to.

"Only a fool would want her alive," Hope snorted.

"We had to prevent it whatever the cost," she explained, her words causing Amira to wonder what they had done to the princess to fear her so much? "Unfortunately, she made sure her resurrection couldn't be thwarted. But," the goddess paused and Amira knew it was where her nightmare began, "there is always a way around."

"So I kept dying and dying just because you needed time to figure out the way around Nially's prophecy?" Amira almost yelled, barely containing her rage. The callously uttered words made her blood boil.

"Calm down, Angel," Raven said, wrapping his arms around her. It helped to quell her fury a bit.

"Better listen to him," Hope retorted, threat shining from her emerald eyes. "And no, at first you kept dying because you weren't strong enough to survive transformation. We had nothing to do with it. Nially made certain the vessel would be able to contain her spirit." Hope kept talking as if she was a thing and it enraged her even more. "And then, once you were, we had to be certain you fought and actually won. Who would have thought it would take this long. And don't look at me as if it is my fault you are so unlovable."

"Now listen here!" Raven stepped forward, his voice nothing but a threat. "One more insult and you'll find out just how unlovable you are."

"Maybe it's not your fault," — it was a moot point right now — "but you are responsible for the fate of Raven's family. You made sure they all suffered. Or am I mistaken?" Amira shouted, her anger flaring bright red. How could they? Well, it was a silly question, was it not?

"Oh, stop your sputtering. You sound as if a tragedy has struck." Hope had the nerve to roll her eyes, "It had to be done. Without it, he wouldn't have been ready to sacrifice everything for what he loved. Not to mention it's necessary — we have to kill off all the descendants at some point so they won't notice they aren't aging."

Amira felt Raven stiffen. Enough was enough. It was one thing to play with her, but quite another with the man she loved. Not to mention, apparently, with many other people whose only crime was the blood flowing in their veins.

Many times she had dreamed of possessing the power to take on the gods. Many times she'd threatened to avenge them. Finally, the hour had arrived, and before Amira could take the time to weigh up all the pros and cons, she dived headlong, as she usually did, and opened up her mouth.

"Too many souls have screamed in pain – because you treated life as a game." The entity inside her swirled as if agreeing. Encouraging her, even. *"Well from now on it all shall cease – what you've sown you soon shall reap."*

The remaining energy broke from within, forcing Amira to stagger back while it weaved itself through her words, like climbing vines would through an iron trellis. She could feel anger transforming into promise. Her desire for justice – into law. It was all taking shape, being molded, until her words were etched in stone. Inescapable. Eternal. A prophecy bound to pass.

The moment she recognized it as inevitable, the same energy exploded, touching Amira with a final verdict she was compelled to voice, *"...the one who screams with mortal's bane might yet save his wretched tail..."*

"Take it back," Hope paled before her very eyes. "How can you do this to us?"

Amira gaped. "Do what?" she asked slowly and calmly. "Torture you simply because I can? Set traps with no way out? Strip you of your powers just as you are about to be raped or murdered? What I did is justice, what you did..."

"But you never got raped, now did you? You may

have suffered, but not in the same way the girls do in those dungeons." Hope got more and more flustered with every word. "You may have died hundreds of times, but it was always bearable and quick. You didn't feel the whole brunt of it."

"And if I was a naïve chit, I might even believe you," Amira shot back, "But I do know that the only reason you softened those experiences was because you didn't need a headcase incapable of doing anything except drooling over her shoes."

When Hope didn't deny it, Amira sighed and leaned into Raven, "I really shouldn't have uttered the last part."

"Of course you should have," he kissed her neck. "You believe you deserve to survive, so prove it," he told the goddess.

"The mortal's bane..." Hope whispered as if to herself, "but what is it?"

"I suggest you find out..." and she was gone before Raven finished the sentence.

Time began ticking again. The witches finally stood up, looking around with expressions Amira could only describe as wishful. Yet, upon seeing how little the world had changed, their faces fell. And then their gazes landed on her.

Here we go again, Raven's voice permeated Amira's thoughts.

Be nice.

Says the one spelling doom for the gods, she could almost hear his laughter.

They both watched as a smaller group of elderly witches separated from the others and approached. One, who Amira assumed was a leader among them, stepped forward, dividing the distance between them in half.

"I am called Tanisha," the woman curtsied, her eyes traveling from one to another. Tanisha hid it well, but

Amira could still feel wave after wave of rolling fear. Confusion, as to why Amira was caged by a man's embrace.

"I am not your princess," Amira answered before the others made their reverences, "and I would rather you didn't." She gestured toward the bowed heads.

They slowly lifted them, but the fear in their eyes was a living flame.

I don't understand, Amira admitted, *they should be angry. Irritated.*

Oh they are, he assured her, *but I believe they fear you and tomorrow more.* Still he pulled her closer, enveloping her body with his until her back was pressed to his chest, the strong beat of his heart calming her senses.

For the first time in her life, she was not about to meet uncertainty alone. She knew he would protect her, even though she was more than capable of meeting it herself. And it felt damn good!

"We are doomed!" After the longest pause a silent resignation echoed between the stone walls.

"You are delusional if you think Nially would've helped anyone but herself." Raven found it impossible to keep silent.

So don't you dare feel guilty, he told Amira.

No one would have noticed how she flinched at Tanisha's words, but he felt it in the marrow of his bones.

"The shield..." someone gasped, and he cursed, feeling another flinch.

We have to help them!

I don't really feel magnanimous toward those who tried to rip your soul from your body, Raven replied. Scratch tried — they succeeded.

Not every witch is evil, she countered.

They'll have to prove it before I'll lift a finger.

"Thank you," she whispered for his ears alone and,

pivoting in his arms, placed a kiss on his lips.

"Those of you who'll brave the world and find yourselves in mortal danger, all you need to do is call us. That's the best I can offer."

"When exactly did I agree to this?" Raven wondered, still confused.

"When you said you'd help the innocent."

"I said that?"

"Not in those precise words, but yes," she assured him.

From hunting witches, to saving them—Raven mulled over the concept. *At least one thing won't ever change.*

Which is?

"Life won't ever get boring." He cupped her face and kissed her mouth, trailing his tongue over her bottom lip. "Let's go."

There was nothing they could do here. Those witches needed to make some very important decisions and he'd gathered they were only interrupting. Not to mention scaring half of them. Who knew whether a nervous, frightened witch could be trusted not to make rash moves? Another fight would definitely be counterproductive today.

"Where?" she finally smiled. Raven intended to keep it on her face.

"Don't know. Don't care. As long as we're together."

* * *

Deep in the Underworld, Dazlog was laughing as he never had before. He couldn't believe his luck. Sure, he'd hoped everything would fall into place as he needed, but this… it was even better than anything he could have imagined.

He'd gambled bigtime not going to Amira the moment she came back, but it had paid off. Tenfold.

It may take him a hundred or so years longer, but … he smiled dreamily, listening to the words the wind brought him.

Too many souls have screamed in pain
Because you treated life as a game.
Well from now on it all shall cease
What you've sown you soon shall reap.

Amira's prophecy pulsed with a life of its own. She truly didn't know what she had set into motion by the words so carelessly uttered. But he would be the one to make it come true.

Finally, after fourteen thousand years, he could see hope. He could see a path taking him to his goal. And when he reached it, the whole earth would tremble.

"Damn you!" he heard a fleeting sound of Nially's voice. Cursing him as always.

"You already did, more than once," he replied, knowing that nothing, not even the princess, could spoil his mood. And luckily, in a short moment she would be contained in her own prison once again. Somewhere he wouldn't be able to reach her. Not that he wanted to.

"Why?" she asked, "after everything you've done to me…"

Dazlog almost snorted. What was done was done—and besides, it wasn't as if she hadn't repaid him in spades.

"You should never have touched the boy," Dazlog told her, glad that she had. He gave a bound oath no harm should befall Raven after Amira pleaded for his life. And Dazlog kept his word. Always. So he gave the little push she needed to return to her own body.

"Hate you!" the faint sound of her voice lingered

long after she'd vanished completely.

"Never would have guessed," Dazlog spoke to the empty space, making himself more comfortable. Oh, she would try to come after him, of that Dazlog was certain, but right now he had other problems.

A shadow of a smile played on his face — *but not for long, not for long…*

Epilogue

Raven was fighting for his life. His opponent — a good swordsman he should still be able to defeat on any day of the week — was actually deflecting each and every thrust with graceful ease. Worse still, the man was coming at Raven with blows he was struggling to block. Strike followed strike. Metal was scraping metal, as the force of the man's assault drove Raven back ... back...

Fool, you'll lose your head if this continues, he chastised himself, but his heart simply wasn't in it today. He could barely concentrate. The ominous shadow following him since the morning couldn't be ignored much longer.

Blows continued to rain on him. Sparks were flying as their swords clanged loudly. Yet every time their blades met, instead of the metallic noise created by his own sword, Raven heard hundreds of weapons clashing against each other. The sound was ringing in his ears with a vengeance. Disoriented and partially deaf, he tried to shake the weakness, yet the haze descending over his eyes refused to dissipate.

One moment his opponent was wearing a dark-blue shirt and black pants, and the next he appeared in nothing but torn, ugly-brown, barely hanging by the rope, trousers — the kind Raven had seen even beggars shun. Barefoot, a bit paler, with chest almost twice as large as a second ago and hair twice as long, he disengaged with a twist and came at Raven again.

"And the student becomes the teacher," Ciaran announced proudly a few seconds before going into the motion. His voice scattered the mist. Or was this a premonition? Sometimes, Raven still had trouble with his powers.

"Not just quite yet," Raven smiled, finally able to think clearly. He sidestepped and slammed his blade across Ciaran's, forcing it to the side, low.

The unexpected move made the man lose balance and without a moment's hesitation Raven spun to the right. His body came so close, his elbow collided with Ciaran's jaw and before he could recover, the steel of Raven's blade was pressed length-wise against the skin of his throat.

"That," Ciaran rubbed his jaw, "actually hurt."

Raven merely shrugged, easing his hold and finally sheathing the sword. "You are still projecting. Especially when you think you are winning." He doubted it would last much longer.

Ciaran was a natural with a sword. Seven months ago he'd taken one into his hands for the first time in his life, and now each and every encounter they had was a challenge. Practice was just a word they used, because they both knew it was more than that.

He needed these practices, needed someone against whom he could wield a sword without getting his hands bloody in the process. Especially when his fighting days were nowhere near over. And Ciaran just needed to be the strongest. It seemed arrogance was his constant companion. Although Raven made it his mission not to let it blow out of proportion, it wasn't an easy task — strange visions in the middle of fighting or not.

"I will so enjoy beating you the next time," he promised. As he did after their every match.

"I don't believe you learned how to lose yet."

"You shouldn't tease him so," Natalie said.

Finally, after a few months of observing him from afar, whenever he and Amira visited, she was not afraid to approach him.

"Sometimes I fear this attitude will be his undoing. Thank the goddesses at least Logan came to his senses."

Ciaran just rolled his eyes heavenwards.

"And I think he's about to challenge you again," she added.

"Looking forward to it," Raven bowed his head slightly, "Oh, and speaking of Logan, where is he?"

"Guess," Natalie gestured, which could only mean one thing. Nyssa.

Lately those two were always together. Either it was here, in Trinton, or his own place, where Raven rarely set foot. So it was Logan who oversaw things down there, quickly growing into his responsibilities, especially now that Ciaran was not breathing down his shoulder. And that, Raven thought, made a difference.

"Love," Ciaran snorted, "makes time pass by, I guess."

Raven and Natalie turned to him, their brows raised in question.

"And time makes love pass by," he uttered, returning the look.

"Rather poetic," scoffed Raven. He avoided the challenging eyes and lifted his shirt from the grass. For Ciaran, everything was a challenge. Every word, every move. Sometimes it was easier to keep one's mouth shut than try and convince him of something. Sometimes.

"If not pathetic," Natalie added.

"Look who's talking," Ciaran shot back. "Galen looks at you with stray-puppy-dog eyes and you automatically profess to be the expert on the subject?"

Natalie smiled, "I am sure he will be thrilled to learn how his friend refers to him." She straightened the line on her skirt, took the hem in her hands and turned, prepared to march back home. "Oh, and in case you were wondering," she bit her grin, "looking was not all he did."

Ciaran froze for a second. Then after a moment, he launched himself from the spot like a mad man. "What—"

"She was teasing you!" Raven stepped in front of Ciaran, blocking his way. "Just teasing," he repeated the word, giving more weight to it, and finally saw comprehension light up Ciaran's eyes.

"You think I am stupid?" It wasn't exactly a question, but it wasn't a statement either.

"Not stupid. Rash maybe."

"What aren't you telling me?"

"I was just wondering how I would have reacted if it was Evolyn." It no longer hurt to talk about his family as it used to, but sometimes he couldn't help but wonder how it might have been.

It was strange the way life could change. The way a person could become someone he'd never imagined was possible. But, if he had learned anything, it was that anything was possible. Even the man who once tried to kill him could become his friend—a brother in the war they were waging. And while his true brother was off to see the world, searching for himself, Raven had found himself in the eyes of a witch. And he couldn't be happier about it.

In his heart he believed there would come a day when Dacian would accept him again. When he was ready. As for now, he was exploiting every moment life gave him, every opportunity, every second.

If you are done playing... her soft voice reached him, filled him, warmed him.

I could play some more.

My thoughts exactly. He could feel her smiling.

How are you feeling? He headed toward the front door, taking two steps at a time, trying to reduce the distance between them as quickly as possible.

He may have been able to use magic, but he preferred to use his legs, just as he did his sword instead of energy balls.

Raven resorted to using his powers only when it was necessary. Amusingly enough, the dozens of steps to the bedroom they shared when visiting her family, the few doors and the vast number of protective males, were not obstacles he deemed huge enough to warrant it. Though he had to admit, her father was somewhat of a pain in the ass. Almost qualifying as one. Especially in the beginning.

If not for Eliana diffusing volatile situations, they would've come to blows. Luckily, the fact that Amira was happy had finally registered in her father's head. And once Deron realized Raven would walk through fire for her, married or not, the fact that they were not and could never be didn't bother him anymore. Much.

Sometimes, it bothered Raven though—not being able to claim her as a wife. He would have loved to ask for her hand in marriage, except with Venlordians on the throne, they would sooner see them dead than married.

Amira always reminded him that they were bonded for eternity. No words spoken by some murderous knave could ever be as powerful. And she was right. They were soulmates. Still, he lived in hope that one day the situation would change—he was working on it.

The journey ahead was a long one, but he was on the right path. Even if it was paved with frustration and worry at seeing Amira rush into the fray of the battle in her delicate condition.

You worry too much, she reminded him. *I am more than capable, even in my seventh month.*

She *was* more powerful than ever, not to mention more pigheaded. It didn't mean he'd leave her side for a single moment. No matter how much she glowered at him—he was not about to let danger come close to her, or the little hoyden he imagined would be born in just a few months. He couldn't wait to become a father.

Raven reached for the doorknob, suddenly feeling sick. A sharp pain sliced through him, causing the earth to sway under his feet. His hand tightened around the knob, but his legs failed to support him and he doubled over.

"What's wrong?" Ciaran ran to him, offering his hand.

"Amira," he uttered, finding strength to straighten up and disappear in front of Ciaran's eyes. To reach her in a split second.

* * *

Eighteen hours had passed since he'd found Amira lying on the floor with her hands on her abdomen, wincing from pain. Now, she was in labor. Two months early.

Everything was wrong, just wrong. And he couldn't do a thing. Moreover, he was forced to wait outside along with all the other males, while she was suffering.

Raven was going crazy. The pain his angel suffered was inside him—a living being tearing him apart every few minutes. He felt like he was the one giving birth. Only he wasn't. He was wearing out the carpet in the adjacent room while he longed to be with her. The unknown was killing him.

What was taking so bloody long?

Raven ... only the dim semblance of her once adorably determined and strong voice echoed in his head. Was it fear he sensed? Hers? He couldn't stand the thought.

I am coming, Angel. He tried to comfort her, his legs already eating away the distance.

Her father tried to stop him though, "I know how you feel, but—"

Raven pushed him aside, not listening to what Deron had to say. Not caring. He only knew she needed him. And he was coming.

The moment he entered the room, Raven realized the reason she was calling. There was something—someone—else in there.

Ignoring the women, he closed his eyes, concentrated the way she'd taught him, and slowly swiveled around, searching. Finding. He stopped and looked directly at the wall opposite the bed Amira was lying in, still moaning from pain. He almost let out a groan of his own.

"Reveal yourself," Raven commanded the intruder who was threatening his woman and child with his mere presence.

A moment later, a man appeared leaning against the said wall. Grinning. His arms were wrapped across his broad chest, body relaxed—but the green eyes watching them were too intense, the gaze too sharp, belying the ease in his pose. Raven's lips tightened into a frown.

Someone gasped behind him. He paid no heed, but strode toward the unbidden guest, pinning him to the wall.

"Leave," he barked, blocking the view of Amira and … his child. His heart leaped with joy at the sound of a cry.

"It's a boy," Milla announced. His gaze remained on the intruder, though it tore him to pieces to hear the baby cry and not be able to look at him, to take him into his arms. He had to get rid of this creature, and soon, because despite his appearance, there was no way he could be a human being. That much Raven knew.

"Others won't take that long," the creature informed them.

Every nerve in Raven's body prickled at the sound of that voice. He knew who this male was. And a sick feeling settled in his gut. Someone wasn't going to leave this room alive...

"Others?" A curious question broke his line of thought.

"Well of course—three Immortals to change the world. For better or worse," Dazlog smirked. Raven narrowed his eyes. He didn't give a damn if there were three or thirty of them, as long as they were safe.

Raven seized him by his throat with every intention of throwing him out. He merely laughed back, "My, my, such a temper."

There came another cry. Another baby was born. Raven resisted the urge to turn around—barely. His eyes remained on the intruder, refusing to let him out of his sight as if he knew something horrible would happen the moment he did.

He grabbed Dazlog's arm and after twisting it behind his back, kicked him out of the room. "Get the hell out of here!"

Dazlog jumped straight at Raven's face, his emerald eyes exuding violence. Flames rose, surrounded them— their fiery tongues licked his flesh. Just as quickly as the fire ignited, it simmered down.

"You don't want to anger me, human," the demon threatened as he straightened his crinkled black shirt, his moves calm and precise, as if moments before the surroundings hadn't been set on fire by his fury. Just then another cry echoed.

"Ah, finally. The full set." The male disappeared.

Raven swore. He knew the room was full of people

now. Deron, Regan, Pharell, even old Giles, all prepared to fight. Ciaran with the sword already unsheathed. None of it gave him comfort, though. The being was more powerful than … he swallowed the last thought and instantly followed after him.

"How nice of you to show up," the demon teased, evidently undisturbed by all the protective males surrounding the bed.

Raven glanced at Amira, who seemed exhausted. Her breaths were shallow, her damp hair clinging around her dismayed expression. But what bothered him most was the trembling hands in which she held one of their babies, and the panic in her eyes.

"My payment," the intruder demanded, suddenly serious. All smiles and teasing forgotten. "We made a deal. His life for the magic. And don't make me wait."

"I can give you everything I have," Amira whispered under her breath, raising her head from the pillow. "But you never wanted my power, did you?"

She paused, rocking their son in her arms and gathering her own strength, added, "Nially's power was never mine to hold and you knew it. Should have come sooner…" The essence would have left her no matter what she did.

"Oh, but I beg to differ." Dazlog approached the bed, ignoring the unsheathed weapons being pointed at him. He brushed his hand through the air, and the human wall separated, letting him pass through.

He sat on the bed near Amira, and Raven gnashed his teeth. Every cell of his being wanted to attack, to drag Dazlog away from his angel. He clenched his fists, reminding himself he had to stay smart. Brute strength won't be enough to defeat the demon.

"The power I want is still here. Divided among three, but here," the demon said as he trailed his eyes from one baby to the next, and the sick feeling Raven had felt before turned into true horror.

"Such imbalance," Dazlog *tsk*ed.

"You are not taking our babies—"

"You know it's impossible to separate essences at such a young age without killing!" Raven and Amira spoke at the same time.

"And whose fault is it?" The demon arched his dark brows in question. "Did I force you to compose poems? Good thing you two can't keep your hands off each other, otherwise..." He stood up from the bed and moved closer to Mila. "Not to mention the missing soul I snatched from under everyone's noses."

"You didn't mind the risks earlier." Amira sat up straighter with their son resting in her protective arms. She hated being so weak as to not even be able to stand, while Dazlog's mere presence threatened her babies.

Just keep him talking, Raven told her, needing time to liberate at least a few of the males from their stupor. He had an idea. Or a vague semblance of an idea. Either way, help was necessary.

"If everything went according to my plan, I wouldn't have given a damn even if thousands of souls went missing—but no," Dazlog raised his hands dramatically, "you had to open your mouth."

He approached the queen, who was shielding one of the babies with her body. And just as he was about to place his hand over the small forehead, Amira raised her voice, "Why do you need it?" She was close to scrambling out of the bed.

"It is a tidbit I'd like to keep to myself," he answered without elaborating further this time.

"Pretty, isn't she?" Dazlog put his palm over the newborn girl. His girl. And began murmuring something under his breath.

He said he needed to be smart? Well, fuck smart— Raven's control snapped at the sight of a mist forming

around Dazlog and his baby. His blood boiled. Raven
lunged. He knocked the demon down, dissipating the
mysterious fog in one second, and getting thrown to the
other side of the room the next.

Raven jumped to his feet, shaking off the pain, but
instead of charging again, he composed himself. He
watched as Dazlog moved closer to him, slowly, like a
panther stalking his prey. Danger and fury radiated
from every cell of the being—all focused on Raven.

Raven waited ... waited ... The moment the demon
was almost on him, as far away from his family as
possible, Raven opened fire.

White searing bolts of energy shot from Raven's
palms, targeting the enemy. Blast after blast, the
demon's chest was hit with power he rarely used. A
power he hoped would be enough to kill a demon. After
all, they weren't indestructible.

Dazlog staggered back, grabbing at his heart. His
breathing became fast and shallow. Raven doubled his
efforts, his own breaths coming in quick, strangled
huffs. His skin covered by a thin sheen of sweat. The
strain of the power he was channeling was catching up
with him.

He had to finish it! He sent one last jolt through the
demon and lifted the spell lingering in the air. The men
rushed to his aid immediately—Pharell and Deron
grabbed Dazlog by his elbows from behind and turned
half a circle, for the vicious kick Ciaran delivered. The
demon sank into the chair and a moment later, was
staked to it as Ciaran's sword drove all the way through
Dazlog's chest.

"Feisty, aren't we?" Dazlog slowly pulled the sword
out, not once displaying a single frown or wince to
indicate he felt pain. He wiped the blade clean with a
cloth he manifested, and threw the sword to Ciaran,
who clumsily caught it, eyes wide with shock.

Very calmly, Dazlog disposed of the bloodied cloth, parted his torn shirt to reveal a massive hole decorating his chest, and an eerie silence enveloped the room. Those who had the sense not to openly gape till now, hung their jaws loosely at the sight of flesh knitting before their eyes. The wound disappeared in seconds, leaving nothing, not a single scar, not even a reddened spot to mar the demon's smooth bronzed skin.

"Give me one good reason not to kill you all." He lifted his steady gaze, buttoning what was left of his shirt.

"I won't let you!" Amira staggered to her feet after handing her child to Natalie. She could no longer lay in bed. But the moment her hand brushed her sweat-soaked hair out of her eyes, her legs wobbled, and if not for Raven catching her, she would have stumbled.

Dazlog laughed, "Yes, I see it clearly." He made himself comfortable in the chair he was in, as if he was an honored guest rather than an unwelcome intruder. "You'll faint me to death."

Amira inhaled, knowing he was right. She was too weak. And she hated it!

"Look at you in that damp, bloody robe," Dazlog continued, "barely standing on your feet. Pale and shivering … while the gods think you possess Nially's power. Otherwise they would be storming your castle for the stunt you've pulled."

Amira gulped, hearing his words for what they were. A threat. But deep down she registered another thing…

He can't take it, she told Raven. For whatever the reason he'd failed to capitalize on her promise when the power was in her, was the very reason Dazlog was now sitting and talking, instead of seizing what he wanted.

Amira's promise still bound her, but all she could give was her own power — something he had no use for, evidently. And her children, the ones who possessed it, had never bargained with him.

They are safe?

"Not even close," Dazlog smiled, apparently able to listen in on their private conversation. "The gods weren't happy to allow Raven to come into his powers, but it was considered a lesser evil than allowing Nially to wreak havoc. Do you honestly believe they would allow these three to live after everything they have gone through just to rid themselves of Immortals, especially of Nially? Twice." His eyebrows lifted slightly.

"One word from me and you know what happens," he said evenly, without an ounce of threat in his voice. Only promise.

Amira felt panic mounting, overwhelming her senses. If the life of her children depended upon the mercy of the demon — they were doomed.

"And, if that is not enough for you," he said as he finally rose from the chair, "then think about the Underworld. When they find out a soul is missing, they'll come to collect." He approached. "Since both of you are already dead, technically speaking, it could be anyone or everyone. And you know I am not lying."

She did. Demons didn't care which soul they took. As long as they took.

"I'll defend my family, whatever it takes. From whoever threatens it."

"I believe you," he simply nodded, "but in the end you will lose. Are you ready to watch your little Kiara perish into the flames?"

"Her name is Evolyn," Amira shot back, hoping Raven wouldn't mind.

"Maybe so, but she is a Kiara. The dark one." Dazlog added, "or she would be if she had a chance."

Amira hoped there was a chance. But how could there be? It was either gods, or demons, or this particular demon. She didn't know which choice was the worst, but there was no best, that was for sure.

Dazlog smiled as if he took a fiendish delight in torturing her, leaving her without options, without hope. But then again, he was a demon. What else could she expect from him?

"But you can prevent it," Raven finally spoke, after considering all possibilities.

"And I would do this because of my noble heart?" Dazlog laughed.

"Because we both know you can't get the magic you need, and you won't ever be able to if my children are killed," Raven rationalized. "Besides, after the others find out about the missing soul I don't imagine they will pat you on the back."

Dazlog narrowed his eyes. "So what are you proposing? To cover my deceit before someone notices, in exchange for leaving these three parcels at peace?"

"And never to come after them," Amira added.

"Not if you keep your end of the bargain," Dazlog promised. "Now agree, or I am taking the triplets."

"Agreed," Amira said. Anything to save her children. Even her life.

"Next time I won't be so charitable." Dazlog turned his gaze from Amira to Ciaran. "Let's go."

"No," Eliana shouted, her voice full of dread. It woke up the infant sleeping peacefully in her arms. He began to cry. All three began to cry.

"Take me instead," Pharell spoke for the first time. He was always calm, but after his sister's death and what happened to him in the dungeon, he had distanced himself from everyone completely.

"I made my choice," Dazlog told him. "It's either him or the little ones."

"I'll go," Ciaran finally spoke, sheathing the sword. "You won't get what you want."

"Typical human." The demon laughed. "Must you all be this narrow-minded?" He put his hand on Ciaran's shoulder. "I just did," he grinned and a second later, they both disappeared.

Sobs broke from Natalie, tears rolled down Eliana's cheeks. Deron crumbled on the ground, shaken by the sudden loss of their son, while Amira stood stiff as a ramrod, her trembling fingers clutching Raven's shirt. She couldn't move. And even if she could, what was the use? She was bound by her own words.

* * *

Amira stood near the crib where three little angels slept. She was so deeply sunken in her thoughts, she didn't notice the door creaking, or two strong hands wrapping around her.

"You are thinking about it again," Raven whispered, placing a kiss on the crook of her neck.

Amira closed her eyes and leaned back, welcoming his heat. She'd been too cold these past few days. Her joy of having healthy and strong babies overshadowed with worry over Ciaran's fate.

She felt so guilty. Thoughts of him being tortured invaded her mind day and night.

"If only I could..." her words faltered. How was it possible to be this happy, and at the same time ... Amira was afraid to show her face to others, knowing full well the nightmares it caused them.

"It's going to be alright," Raven assured her.

"How do you know?"

"I just do."

"Did you see something?" she asked, hoping against hope Ciaran wasn't suffering.

He did see something, Raven thought. But explaining it was beyond him.

"Did you?" she persisted. "Sometimes I can see the future, but this time all I see is the unknown."

"Maybe because the future is for him to determine." Martha stepped inside, and tears spilled down her cheeks.

Finally, Raven expelled a sigh of relief. The way she locked everything inside had him worried. She needed to let go of her emotions. He didn't like her distant. With no smile on her lips. No tears in her eyes. It wasn't healthy. And even though she did show emotions around him or their children, they were the only people who saw anything except the shell she hid in.

He watched Martha, who was freed from her curse for quite some time now, approach them slowly. Not with the same impatience and ardor as Adam and Nyssa did, but steadily, taking one step at a time. She spread her arms into a welcoming gesture. His angel lifted her head, eyes glistening, and walked straight into Martha's embrace. She put her head on the woman's shoulder and closed her eyes.

"There are three miracles who I think need you more than your cousin. And here's an old woman waiting to see her grandchildren," Martha smiled.

"Don't forget us," Nyssa interrupted.

Amira didn't know how Martha did that, but she managed to comfort her. The words penetrated her, and for the first time in the past couple of days she had faith.

Thank you, her gaze touched Raven. *I love you.*

He smiled. *I love you too. And you'll see, we will find a way to get him back.*

Amira nodded and took the hand he offered. Even tragedies weren't so awful, when she had friends to rely on and the man she adored to love and stand beside her. No matter what.

LYN C. JOHANSON

Lyn C. Johanson

Turn the page for the preview of Forged in Fire …

Prologue

As the old rusty gates creaked in an attempt to crawl up and let Ciaran in, a realization hit him like a ton of bricks — this was it, the last second he would be allowed to breathe.

With each inch his life rushed towards an end, and skidded to a sudden halt at the sight of an open entrance. He knew he had to go in. He had traded his soul for the lives of three innocent babies, yet now his legs turned wooden, as if rooted into the ground, unable to move. Worse still, his hands shook, and fear gripped his heart.

Ciaran swallowed hard, and took the scariest step he'd ever taken. He stopped just behind the boundary line, and without glancing back waited for the iron monstrosity to seal him in.

He didn't have to wait long. Almost instantaneously he heard a deep rumble, the rattle of chains, and finally the explosive sound of the impact, which reverberated through his bones. And then, silence. An utter darkness.

No way back now, the verdict echoed in his head, and it felt like something had died inside. Everything went still. A second later, the creature he had come here with clapped his hands twice, and torch after torch lit, illuminating a huge cave.

Ciaran's breathing quickened, and the desire to jump out of his skin consumed his senses. He couldn't help but glance back. He didn't know why he needed to see the gates he'd passed through, but he did. Desperately.

He squinted his eyes, then blinked, but no matter how hard he tried, it was simply gone. The wall of solid, unyielding rock stood in its place, mocking his attempts to calm himself down. The longer he stared at the wall, half convinced he was hallucinating, the faster his heart raced; and before Ciaran knew what was happening, rocks began to move, closing in on him.

His lungs froze, refusing to accept the air he so desperately needed; yet the beat of his heart only accelerated, until his pulse thudded like a sledgehammer in his ears.

"Breathe, just breathe," he uttered from under his nose, ordering himself to snap out of this.

"It's too late for second thoughts." The demon all but laughed at Ciaran's childish reaction. The mocking tone fueled Ciaran's anger. His emotions clashed, and finally the choking grip the fear had on him loosened.

"Well, if you stopped quaking in your boots, I would rather we proceed." The words only added insult to the injury.

Ciaran gritted his teeth, cursing the need to draw the reins on his temper when every cell of his being demanded retribution. Usually, if he had an urge to punch someone, he just did it. But it wasn't the knowledge that Dazlog would wipe the floor with him that stopped Ciaran. Nothing but pain awaited him anyway, and at least he would have had the satisfaction of swinging a punch.

No. What made him swallow his pride were the consequences for his nephews if he was to fight. So for the first time in his life, Ciaran clenched his fists and let the words slide.

It felt like sandpaper going down his throat, and he had to force himself to count to ten to keep his calm.

"Good boy," the demon said, picking up the pace. "A piece of advice, and this one's for free" — Dazlog stopped abruptly — "if you want to keep your skin on your bones, count to a thousand."

Ciaran's eyes flared wide, but before he could form a single thought, the ground under his feet disappeared, and he went down so fast he forgot how to breathe altogether.

Once again he was in an utter darkness, falling from a cliff he would have known didn't exist if his mind had only stopped for a second, but all it could think about was what awaited him below; and how long till his brains got splattered on the rocks.

Moments stretched into minutes, minutes into hours; and still his body remained in the air. Ciaran relaxed a bit. His eyes adjusted to the darkness and finally he noticed a figure by his side — stretched on his back, hands folded to support his head. He seemed to be floating. And maybe he was, Ciaran thought, as pale amethyst-green eyes flashed at him. After all, only one of them was falling into a pit of Hell to be tortured.

The torture might not have been mentioned in their deal, but Ciaran wasn't naïve. It wasn't him Dazlog really wanted, and the only way the demon would get it was if Ciaran ran. Deluding himself about the method to achieve that was pointless. Probably as pointless as entertaining an idea of sprouting wings to make the same way back.

The only hope he had was to survive till Amira's children grew up to defend themselves, but until then ...

he took a fortifying breath and focused on the landscape below.

Soon, shadows transformed into shapes, and before his eyes a city appeared and grew to an enormous size. The buildings resembled temples built by the humans above, except the tall walls, domes and pillars seemed somehow grander. Rivers of fire flowed, bathing the structures in an orange-red glow. The view was mesmerizing, and it almost made him forget his destination. Then his fall changed course, and a foul stench invaded his nostrils.

"You didn't think you would be living in a castle, now did you?" Dazlog asked, the moment they began slowing down.

Ciaran didn't bother answering. His eyes remained fixed on the vista, as the city gave way to a rocky, cracked terrain which seemed to sputter and growl. With each explosion he witnessed, dirt and liquid burst out of the ground, washing over a line of meat prepared for cooking on a spit. Only when screams tore from the bleeding throats did Ciaran realize it was a line of humans tied up, impaled and hoisted like pork, not animals. Suddenly, he wanted to throw up at the sight of convulsions and the acrid smell of blistering flesh.

"Welcome to the Underworld." Dazlog chose the moment to interrupt the piercing sound of some poor soul screaming its guts out. And Ciaran realized that somehow, while he was distracted by the gruesome sight, he hadn't noticed how they had both landed on their feet.

"These mines are going to be your new home," Dazlog continued, as Ciaran trailed his gaze across the plains, trying not to contemplate his fate. The options seemed bleak at best.

He turned and froze.

Two huge dogs, each the size of an elephant, were guarding the entrance to the cave. Big and black, and strangely leathery looking, they bared their canines — impressively scary, dagger-sharp fangs — and zeroed in on him. Ciaran didn't know how he was holding it together. Those canines were five feet long, and only three feet away. Saliva dripped from their mouths, forming puddles, and their eyes — obsidian, without an inch of white — looked soulless. One wrong move and he would be shredded.

"Oren, you lazy bag of fleas," Dazlog suddenly yelled, "lift your bony ass and let us through."

One of the dogs growled low in his throat, approached the demon, and all but ground his huge wet nose into Dazlog's.

"Stop your slobbering, you big baby." Dazlog reached behind the dog's ear and scratched.

Ciaran couldn't help but raise his eyebrows at the exchange.

"Bribery won't help," the other dog said in distorted human voice. "No one steps inside without the council's decree."

"No one?" Dazlog folded his hands on the chest and stared the dog down. The beast actually flinched.

"Alright, but just this once. And I mean it." The dog howled, lifted his head and closed his eyes. Oren yapped, and before following the other one, licked Dazlog's face.

Ciaran could barely contain his laughter at the sight of Dazlog cleaning his drooling face with the hem of his sleeve. Probably a good thing, as otherwise he would be nicely roasting — like the unfortunates behind his back.

They stepped into what appeared to be a diamond mine. Gemstones the size of his fist sparkled all around — walls, ceiling, floor — wherever he looked.

"It is not the stones that give this mine such value," Dazlog said as a matter-of-fact without elaborating further. He would probably find out, Ciaran thought, especially if he was to stay here.

"A few simple rules," the demon spoke again. "Listen to the wardens, do your work, and the whip won't sting. Much. Oh, and not a word about how you got here. To no one." Dazlog emphasized the last words, and swiped his hand through the air in front of Ciaran.

Cold settled in his bones, the chill resulting in a puff of breath each time he exhaled.

"And one more thing..." Dazlog stretched his hand to the wall where a trickle of burning river ran, brushed his fingers through it, and before Ciaran could move, pressed the dripping lava-coated fingers into his chest.

The cold suddenly disappeared.

Ciaran jumped back, ripping the front of his shirt in two and saw a spider's web being drawn on his exposed chest. Inch after inch the miniature lava rivers spread through his skin to his arms, his neck, behind his belt. The sight of it made him want to peel his skin off. And then, after covering him with millions of red interconnected branches, it began seeping into his skin, flowing under it.

The stinging sensation intensified. It sharpened, until pain more excruciating than he had ever known before assaulted him. A scream bubbled in his throat as his insides began melting—yet no sound came from out of his mouth.

"You'll thank me one day." He didn't know how he heard Dazlog's voice through the noise ringing in his head, didn't know how he managed to lift said splitting head; but Dazlog was no longer there. Ciaran was alone, in the land of the dead. He was in Hell. And he was burning.

Want more?

Before you go, please consider writing a review, and posting it somewhere online so other readers can enjoy my book. Your review will help me see what is and isn't working so I can make my future stories even better.

Thank you.

About the Author

A computer science major, Lyn C. Johanson discovered her passion for writing romance stories during the long and stressful months spent finishing her master's thesis. It encouraged Lyn to open a new blank page and let her imagination take flight. Several years later, her first romance novel was born.

Her stories transport the reader into the darkly sensual world where the magic of romance meets fantasy. When she's not writing, she enjoys spending time with her husband and sons.

To learn more about Lyn, visit her website at http://lyncjohanson.com.

Printed in Great Britain
by Amazon

22848846R00212